Praise for the nove... ...heila Roberts

"With this neatly wrapped, sweetly charming treat, Roberts once again proves her mastery of uplifting, heartwarming love stories."
—*Booklist* on *A Little Christmas Spirit*

"Christmas wouldn't be Christmas without a Sheila Roberts story. This can't-miss author has a singular talent for touching the heart *and* the funnybone."
—Susan Wiggs on *A Little Christmas Spirit*

"A tender story guaranteed to warm your heart this holiday season. When I read anything from Sheila Roberts, I know I will laugh, cry and close the book with a happy sigh."
—RaeAnne Thayne on *A Little Christmas Spirit*

"Family, friendship, love, and loss all play their part in the perfectly executed plot of this stellar standalone from Roberts, whose gift for distinctively bringing to life each character in her diverse cast is truly commendable."
—*Booklist* on *One Charmed Christmas*

"[Roberts] creates characters with flaws and challenges, characters like us, human and imperfect. But also, characters who grow, evolve, and learn from life's lessons."
—*The Romance Dish* on *One Charmed Christmas*

"No one is better at expertly fusing small-town charm and holiday cheer than Roberts, and her latest sweetly satisfying holiday romance so perfectly captures the warmth and good will of Christmas, it is the literary equivalent of watching *It's a Wonderful Life* with a mug of hot chocolate and a plate of cookies."
—*The Booklist Reader* on *Christmas from the Heart*

The
Merry
Matchmaker

SHEILA ROBERTS

/llMIRA

/I|MIRA

ISBN-13: 978-0-7783-6960-8

The Merry Matchmaker

Recycling programs
for this product may
not exist in your area.

For questions and comments about the quality of this book, please contact us
at CustomerService@Harlequin.com.

TM is a trademark of Harlequin Enterprises ULC.

Mira
22 Adelaide St. West, 41st Floor
Toronto, Ontario M5H 4E3, Canada
MIRABooks.com

Printed in U.S.A.

To Jamie

1

WHO KNEW THAT THE WORD *HELP* COULD TURN INTO A whole other four-letter word? Not Frankie Lane, that was for sure.

Although it wasn't *help* that her friend Viola muttered when the two women stood looking at the pile of wallpaper that had slid down the wall and onto the floor in the dining room of Viola's fixer-upper Victorian. The section Frankie had put up, not Viola's.

"I don't understand what happened," Frankie said, gaping at it.

Viola heaved a sigh.

Everything had looked fine before they'd stepped into the kitchen in search of wine to celebrate the completed job. By the time they were back in the dining room to toast to their success, the wallpaper was toast. Soggy toast. Frankie had to get back to her shop, and here was...this. Obviously, she couldn't leave her friend with such a mess.

"I'll just put this back up again," Frankie said, hurrying over to the sodden pile.

Viola rushed after her. "No! Don't touch anything. I know you want to help."

"I do!"

"But please don't."

Ouch. That hurt.

This had all been Frankie's great idea. "You have to have wallpaper in an old Victorian," she'd said. "It will look so cute with the wainscoting," she'd said as she showed her friend what she'd found online.

"I don't think wallpapering is your forte," Viola said in an attempt to remove the sting. "Anyway, you should get back to the shop. We can drink our wine this evening. Terrill won't be home until late."

"Are you sure? I can get it right this time, and I hate to leave you with this mess. It won't work for your blog."

"Sure, it will. Every home improvement project has setbacks. This will make my finished project look more impressive. Anyway, your mom's probably ready to throttle you by now for leaving her in charge for so long."

"Are you kidding? Mom loves being in charge, and I haven't been gone that long. But you're right. I should get back. How about I make this up to you by picking up a pizza for us?"

"Excellent idea," Viola approved. "And ask Adele not to hate me for stealing you on Small Business Saturday. I forgot about that when Terrill deserted me to go to work."

"It's okay. We weren't that busy. Yesterday was our big day." But Viola was right. Frankie had a business to run, and she needed to get back to it.

She got into her Prius and headed off to beautiful downtown Carol, where she had her shop, Holiday Happiness. Thanksgiving was over, and the shop, which featured all manner of Christmas decor, had done a whopping business the day before with customers crowding in to take advantage of the Black Friday sale, check out the latest Christopher Radko ornament or pick up an Advent calendar. Or simply chat.

Downtown was now decorated for Christmas, thanks to all the shop owners and the chamber of commerce getting busy early Friday morning. The lampposts were ringed with red plastic ribbon tied in bows. Swags of greenery and fat old-fashioned lights hung over shop windows, and the big banner strung across Main Street announced A Carol Christmas— Santa Walk December 21.

The Santa Walk had been Frankie's brainchild, and this would be its third year. All the downtown shops would be offering coupons and special discounts and passing out treats. Santa would come to town and set up in the town square gazebo. Mrs. Claus would be on hand to accompany him during the Santa parade and to help greet the children who were excited to see him as well as their parents.

Frankie had been Mrs. Claus both previous years and was looking forward to a repeat performance. After all, she was Mrs. Holiday Happiness.

She didn't go right into her shop. Instead, she walked next door to Handy's Hardware, which would be the perfect place to get an apology prezzie for Viola. With all the work she and her policeman husband, Terrill, were doing on their house, the hardware store had become their home away from home.

Terrill happened to be cruising by in his patrol car. He stopped and let down his window and called, "How'd it go? Am I still Mr. DooDoo?"

Frankie snickered. "Maybe. She wound up calling me to help her finish."

"Did you?"

"Sort of but not really. I'm on pizza patrol."

"All the works?" he asked.

"Of course," she replied. "If you're lucky, we'll save you some."

He gave her a thumbs-up and cruised on down the street.

Pizza would go a long way toward making up for the wallpaper mess she'd left her friend with. Hopefully a Handy's Hardware gift card would do the rest.

The hardware store was ready for Christmas. Someone had made fresh popcorn in the circus popcorn cart, and the aroma made her mouth water. No popcorn for her today, though. She was on a mission.

She moved past the display of artificial trees and the shelves of Christmas lights and garlands and went straight to the checkout, where she selected a card with a hammer on it and Handy Holidays written above it in red. She spotted her pal Mitch Howard in the paint section and, after purchasing the card, went over to say a quick hi.

A hefty fiftysomething man in Carhartts ogled her as she walked past. She wasn't dressed to inspire ogles in her jeans and boots and the old letterman jacket that had belonged to her husband, Ike, but she was still good-looking enough to attract attention. And she appreciated an occasional ogle (as long as it didn't turn into a leer).

Fifty had been a hard birthday. Even though she was fit and her hair was still a rich auburn thanks to her hairdresser, she felt the passing of time like an insult with those tiny wrinkles digging into her face and the gray hairs that were constantly multiplying and kept her going to the salon. When it came to aging, Mother Nature was not very nice to her daughters.

But oh well. What did it matter, really? Frankie wasn't in the market for anyone to replace Ike. He was irreplaceable, and it had broken her heart and shredded her world when she lost him four years earlier. The kid who'd taken him out had been texting and driving and had felt terrible, but feeling terrible after you've killed someone wasn't enough to bring the person back.

The community had come alongside her, offering sympathy, hugs, meals and cards, and her family and friends had checked in on her often. She'd felt their love, but nothing could replace the love she'd lost. She soldiered on, keeping the shop going, keeping her life going, reminding herself to be thankful for the people she still had left—her mother, her sister, her daughter, Natalie, and Natalie's little family.

And Mitch Howard, who owned Handy's. He had been there for her both when she first started her business and again during that awful time after Ike died.

"You've got this," he'd said seven years earlier after she'd signed the lease for her shop and then instantly experienced a confidence crisis. He'd said it again when he stopped by Holiday Happiness a month after Ike's memorial and she'd confessed that she didn't think she could go on.

"Yes, you can," he'd assured her. "You're a strong woman." He kept stopping in, often with a latte from The Coffee Stop just a couple doors down from their businesses. Next thing she knew, she was returning the favor.

It was only natural they would become close. They already were friends. She and Ike had known Mitch before she'd opened her shop and become business neighbors with him. Of course, everyone with a house knew Mitch.

He'd taken over the hardware store after his father retired and his parents moved to Arizona. Mitch himself had moved away for a while, but he had returned and settled right back in, working again in the same store that had employed him as a teenager. Eventually he'd become the owner.

He was Frankie's favorite pal, always up for helping her test out a new cop show or watching a Seahawks game together. Like her, he was single; unlike her, he was divorced with an ex-wife who was ancient history. He was a great guy—fun-loving and kind and easygoing. And handsome—slim but broad-shouldered, with a perfect square jaw and dark hair turning to salt and pepper at the temples. Then there was that lopsided smile that her mother once said made her think of Harrison Ford. *When he was young…oh, baby!*

(Mom had been in touch with her inner cougar for years.)

Mitch was probably the fittest fifty-eight-year-old man in town. Him being single was a waste of man, if you asked Frankie. Not that he had.

"Leave the poor man alone," Ike had said whenever she'd talked about finding someone for Mitch. "He's smart enough to figure out what he wants and go for it."

Still, she'd persisted in trying to set Mitch up because Frankie was convinced that, when it came to love, very few men were smart.

"You're a fine one to talk," her mother had said. This was after Frankie had shared her profound observation a few months earlier, after her latest attempt to help Mitch had failed.

"It's different for me," Frankie said.

Unlike Mitch and his ex, there had been no parting by mutual consent. Frankie didn't need to try again and do better. She'd had a great marriage only to have her man snatched violently from her. One minute Ike had been off to go for a run and the next he was gone. His death had left a hole in her heart that refused to completely close. She doubted it ever would, and even if it did, she had no desire to put herself in a position of facing such a loss again.

"Hey there," Mitch greeted her as she joined him. "How's the wallpapering going?"

"Hers or mine?"

He cocked his head, studied her. "Let me guess. Something went wrong."

"Only on my side of the wall. Doing penance." She held up the gift card, and he chuckled. "And I'm taking pizza over after I close up."

"Can't screw that up," he said.

She frowned. "I hope not. I suck."

"Nah, you don't. It's not easy to hang wallpaper. Anyway, you have other talents."

"Like?"

"Helping people."

The way she'd helped Viola. Frankie gave a snort.

"You're good at making things happen." He pointed out the window to where the banner hung. "The Santa Walk's been a big success. People love you, Frankie. Not everyone can say that."

"It's nice of you to say it."

"Just speakin' the truth."

"Thanks for making me feel better."

"Call it an early Christmas present. We still on for *Cop Stop* tomorrow night?"

"Absolutely," she said. "I've already got the chips and salsa."

"Good," he said with a nod. "I'll bring the beer."

A blonde in black leggings, thigh-high boots and a pink wool coat strolled over. "Hi, Mitch," she purred. "Can you help me pick out some paint for my bedroom?"

Gack, thought Frankie in disgust.

"Be right with you," Mitch said with a smile.

"You can do better than that," Frankie said as the woman sashayed away.

"Yeah? How?"

She could tell by that lopsided grin that he was teasing her. She pointed a finger at him. "You need help."

"There's a lot of things I need, Frankie, but you helping my love life isn't one of them. Now, if you'll excuse me, I'd better go help my customer," he added with a wink. "Try not to be jealous."

"You should be so lucky," she said to his retreating back. "Stubborn man," she muttered, and left to go next door to her shop.

Honestly, Mitch could have his pick of women. He shouldn't be living alone, eating takeout and tuna fish sandwiches. Getting hounded by predators in pink coats. What if one of them succeeded? Mitch needed someone special, someone with some depth to her, someone who would see him as more than a big slice of beefcake. He really needed a guiding hand. Hers.

Of course, whoever he wound up with would have to share because Frankie had no intention of giving up her best buddy. All the more reason to help him find his perfect Mrs. Claus.

Walking into her shop always lifted Frankie's spirits. Always dressed for the holidays, Holiday Happiness was a treasure house of artificial trees of varying species, both green and flocked, decked out in different styles and colors with glowing lights and every imaginable kind of ornament to tempt lookers into becoming buyers. Then there were the ceramic village displays, nativity sets, Santas and nutcrackers in varying sizes, Advent calendars and stuffed bears wearing Santa hats. Come January, those bears would make way for ones bearing satin hearts with I Love You stamped on them. Holiday Happiness celebrated every holiday.

Except for Halloween. Frankie put out very few decorations for that one, opting instead to focus on fall and Thanksgiving items. After losing Ike, she'd lost her taste for skeletons and fake grave markers.

Her twenty-nine-year-old daughter, Natalie, who worked part-time in the shop, was ringing up a customer's purchase as Frankie walked in. In addition to being pretty with her father's green eyes and light brown hair, Natalie was also sweet and impressively creative. She was her mother's pride and joy.

At the second cash register next to her, Frankie's full-time employee, Elinor Ingles, was also ringing up a sale for someone. Barbara Fielding.

Theoretically, Frankie and Barbara should have been friends. They were close in age, with Barbara only a couple of years older than Frankie, and both owned businesses.

But Frankie wasn't a fan of Barbara, and Barbara didn't like Frankie. She'd never said so or done anything overtly hostile, but Frankie could tell by the frosty smile the woman reserved only for her. Barbara's long nose had been out of joint ever since Frankie had beaten her to the punch and taken the space for Holiday Happiness that Barbara had wanted for her yarn shop. She also hadn't been happy the year Frankie had been elected president of the chamber of commerce instead of her. She'd been especially irritated when she learned that her on-and-off boyfriend Ned Boreman, who had turned the old Roxy Theater back into a movie house, had voted for Frankie instead of her.

Frankie was no longer president, but the old rivalry continued, and Barbara and Frankie remained frenemies.

Barbara had raised objections when Frankie first proposed the Santa Walk. The downtown shops already gave out candy for Halloween, merchants were always being hit up to donate merchandise to various events for door prizes, the holidays were a busy time and shop owners would be stressed. Et cetera, et cetera, et cetera. She'd been voted down, and Frankie had been given free rein.

This year Barbara was the head of the Santa Walk committee, thanks to a coup d'état where she ousted Frankie from the chair position that she'd held for the last two years.

Barbara didn't deserve to get anything from Santa.

"I'm surprised you could leave today," Barbara greeted Frankie, as if Frankie had abandoned her shop. "Business must not have been that good."

You wish, Barbara. The Holiday Happiness ship had sailed along just fine for a short while without its captain. "Business has been fine," Frankie said. "And I have a great staff to handle things if I have to step away. I'm surprised you're out and about. Nobody at your shop today?" she fired back.

"We've been busy," Barbara said with a lift of her chin.

Probably not as busy as Frankie's shop. Location, location, location. He-he.

"I just stopped in to tell you that we now have Dickens Carolers lined up to stroll the sidewalks and sing during the Santa Walk."

And gloat over her latest accomplishment as chairman of the committee.

"That's a great idea," Frankie said, and meant it. Why hadn't she thought of that?

Barbara gave her a superior smile. "I thought so. The committee has some other ideas…for a few changes. But I won't bore you with that now. You're probably ready to get back to work." She took in Frankie's outfit. "Or maybe not."

Frankie was not a match with her daughter and Elinor, who were wearing their red Holiday Happiness aprons and Santa hats.

"Oh, I am. Just had to step away. But not for long. We're

always busy here. It's such a good location," Frankie couldn't resist adding.

Barbara frowned, deepening the lines on both sides of her mouth. She ran a hand along the side of her sleek black hair, smoothing it out. As if so much as one strand would dare get out of line.

"I need to get back to work, myself. We're always busy, too." Barbara changed gears, shifting to a smile for Natalie. "Natalie, my salesclerk tells me you're contributing your fabulous Christmas bonbons to the teacher appreciation lunch. That is so nice of you."

"Just doing my part," Natalie said humbly.

"I know it's appreciated."

"Thank you. And I hope your granddaughter enjoys the Advent calendar," Natalie said.

"It's important to support our local businesses," said Barbara.

This was said for Frankie's benefit, of course. "Someday I'm going to learn to knit," she promised.

Now, why had she said that? The crafting gene had skipped a generation in her family, and she wasn't any better at creating confections like her daughter or crocheting like her mother than she was at wallpapering. Anyway, Mom spent a small fortune at Some Kind of Yarn, and that should be enough business to give the entire family brownie points.

Barbara merely rolled her eyes and made for the door.

The other customer, who had been following the exchange, took her bagged ornament and asked, "What's the Santa Walk? We're new in town."

"It's our yearly holiday festival," said Natalie. "All the stores participate and offer bargains and door prize drawings, and there's a parade with Santa. Then, later at night, there's a Santa pub crawl where the men dress up like Santa and the women like elves or Mrs. Claus."

"Or Santa," put in Frankie, thinking of what a fun Santa Cindy Carlson had turned herself into, wearing long red underwear and a long shirt that said Off Duty, Buy Me a Drink.

"We'll have to check it out," said the woman. "And your candy sounds wonderful," she told Natalie.

"It is," said Frankie. "She'll be making another batch soon, so be sure to check back."

"Maybe," added Natalie.

"I will," said the woman.

Frankie turned to Natalie as the woman went out the door. "See? We could sell twice as much of your candy."

"If I had twice as much time," Natalie said. "But I don't. Gotta go, Mom." And she took off her apron, ending a discussion that they'd had on more than one occasion. "Jonathan and Warner are back from his mom's, and I need to get home."

"Okay, fine," Frankie said, sounding mildly grumpy. "Thanks for putting in the extra hours," she added, opting to lose the grumpy mom tone once Natalie had donned her coat and was headed for the door. "Kiss my boy for me."

"Will do. See you tomorrow at Gram Gram's," Natalie said, then left.

Frankie sighed. Another business pep talk aborted. Why on earth her daughter balked at taking Frankie's advice and turning her candy-making hobby into something lucrative was a mystery to Frankie. Natalie's bonbons were wonderful, with fillings ranging from nutmeg to peppermint mocha, and always decorated with tiny royal icing fir trees or candy canes. Come Easter, they would turn into eggs.

"Why are some people so blind to what's good for them?" Frankie muttered. She walked around to the other side of the counter to dig out a small red gift bag for Viola's Handy's Hardware card. "I swear, nobody listens to me."

"Natalie?" Elinor interpreted.

"Yes. I know she's got a six-year-old, and she's working here. But still, this isn't really where her heart lies. She should be developing her gift. People can be so stubborn."

"People?"

Frankie couldn't help but think of Mitch, who never took her advice and was at that very moment flirting with a predator in a pink coat. Frankie had been able to tell instantly that woman was wrong for him.

"Take Mitch for example. He should be dating. He's such a gem."

"And so handsome. I'll be forever grateful to him for coming over on Thanksgiving and helping me when that pipe broke and flooded my kitchen."

"Have Shop-Vac, will travel," joked Frankie. "Seriously, a man like Mitch single? It's wrong."

"Maybe some people are meant to be single," Elinor said wistfully.

Elinor had moved to Carol a year earlier and was still finding her feet. They hadn't talked a lot about her past. All Frankie knew was that she was single, that she loved to read and that the local library and the bookstore were her favorite haunts. She tended to be on the shy side, and she didn't dress to impress. With her fair skin and quiet demeanor, she was the human equivalent of…white paint. Present but not noticed. Frankie had assumed she wasn't really looking for anyone. Maybe she'd assumed wrong.

"I bet there's a perfect man for you somewhere right here in Carol," Frankie said.

"Do you think so?" Elinor didn't sound convinced.

"I'll keep my eyes peeled," Frankie promised.

"Keep your eyes peeled for what?" asked her mother, Adele, who'd just come up from the back of the shop.

Adele worked in the shop, partly to be supportive of her daughter and partly because she liked being at the center of things. Which, thanks to their steady flow of customers, was exactly where Holiday Happiness put her. With her white hair and soft-pillow figure, Adele looked like the quintessential grandmother, all sweet and cozy...until she opened her mouth.

"For a perfect man for Elinor," Frankie replied.

Adele gave a bark. "There is no such thing as a perfect man. Not even your father, God rest his irritating soul."

"Mine was close," Frankie said, and Adele lost her cheeky smile and came over to hug her.

"Yes, he was." Happily, for Frankie, Adele didn't add, *And he'd be the first one to tell you not to get stuck in the past.*

They'd had this conversation more than once. "I'm not stuck, and I don't mind being alone," Frankie always said. Only at night when she went to bed. Or when she and Viola watched a great rom-com. Or when she was scrolling on her phone and saw a recipe Ike would have loved.

"You don't need to be meddling in other people's lives," Adele said. "Let Elinor handle her own love life. I'm sure she's perfectly capable. Aren't you, Elinor?"

Elinor looked dubious, but she said, "Yes."

"There you have it," said Adele. "And now, I'm going home to watch the end of *Blue Bloods*. Wish that show had gone longer. Tom Selleck is hot." She began to fan her face. "Every time I see that man, I—"

Frankie held up a hand. "I don't want to hear. Come on, Elinor, let's get out of here. I have a pizza to pick up and a present to deliver."

As she followed her mother and Elinor out the door, she saw Miss Pink Coat leaving the hardware store. The woman carried a bunch of paint chips in her hand and was frowning.

It looked like Mitch would not be going over to help her pick out paint for her bedroom. Lucky escape for Mitch.

She couldn't resist texting him. No hot paint date?

Ha ha, came the reply.

Cheer up. Maybe Santa will bring you a cute elf for Christmas.

Elves are creepy.

What a thing to say!

I like Mrs. Claus better, he texted. Think she'll ever be interested?

Only if you leave her a plate of chocolate.

I'd buy her a sleighful.

She sent him a laughing emoji, but then got to thinking. Was that crack about Mrs. Claus a subtle cry for help in spite of his insistence that he didn't need any? Could she find a Mrs. Claus for Mitch? He hadn't done well finding someone on his own. Maybe she should give him a helping hand. Maybe she would.

2

"I DOUBT MITCH IS LOOKING FOR A MRS. CLAUS," VIOLA SAID as she helped herself to another slice of pizza. The wallpaper fail had been fixed, and *Happiness for Beginners*, one of their favorite rom-coms, was playing on Viola's TV in the background as they sat in the living room. At the moment, happiness for Mitch was taking top priority.

"You saw the text," Frankie said. "It's obvious he wants to be with someone. But he needs help. And protection. There are some skanky women out there."

"Men like skanky," Viola said, and took a bite of her pizza.

"Men like whiskey, also, but too much isn't good for them. Seriously, Vi, I think I can help him."

Viola laughed. "Just like you did when you introduced him to Laura Harding?"

Frankie waved away the Ghost of Mismatches Past. "That was last year."

"I bet it feels like yesterday to him. Then there was Delilah Norman."

"She was a mistake," Frankie admitted. "I had no idea she was so...needy."

"Needy? There's an understatement. The woman was practically a stalker."

"I introduced him to other women."

"Whom you then talked him out of dating," pointed out Viola. "Let's face it, you'll never find anyone for him who passes the Frankie test."

"I will," Frankie insisted. "But this needs to be done scientifically."

"Scientifically? You gonna use AI?"

"No, HI. Human intelligence, online dating."

"Oh, yeah, he won't find any skanks there," Viola said with an eye roll.

"Lots of people find their perfect match online."

"Not if you're involved," Viola teased.

Frankie ignored the crack. "This is a great time of year to get to know people. All that Christmas cheer, just waiting to be shared." She began thumbing the keys on her phone. "Hey, have you heard of this site?"

Viola leaned across the couch and looked over her shoulder. "Best for You," she read. "Hmm." She picked up her own phone and did some quick research. "Best for You is listed in the top ten dating sites. It's geared for people fifty and older."

"That's just what we want," said Frankie. "There's bound to be someone there who'll be a match."

"As long as you find someone who can keep up with Mr. Fitness," said Viola. "Call him and see what he thinks."

"I'm not going to call him. He'll balk. He's such a chicken."

"You're just going to sign him up?"

"Sure. I know everything I need to know to get him set up on here." Frankie scrolled through the pictures on her phone until she found one she'd taken at the chamber of commerce Fourth of July picnic. He was perched on the edge of a picnic table and wore a gray T-shirt that showed off his well-formed pecs along with Levi's encasing muscular thighs. Flip-flops on his feet. He had a beer bottle raised in a toast. *Here's looking at you, kid.* It was what he'd said to her right before she took the photo.

She showed it to Viola. "If you were single, would you date this man?"

"I don't do white," cracked Viola. "But yeah, that picture sells him. It oughta sell him to you."

Frankie gave a snort.

"Seriously, Frankie, why are you trying to give Mitch to someone else when you and he would be great together?"

"Because I don't need to be with someone." She didn't. She couldn't be.

"Ike wouldn't want you to give up on love," Viola said softly.

"I know. And I have plenty of love in my life. I've got Mom, I've got Stef…"

"Who will probably get married again and move away."

"She wouldn't leave her job at the paper. But if she did, I'd go visit her. And I have Natalie."

"Who has a life."

"Which I'm part of. And little Warner."

"Grandsons grow up and get girlfriends and ignore you."

"Who told you that?"

"Terrill's grandma."

"I'll still have you. You're not going anywhere, are you?"

"No."

"And we're still going to live in the same nursing home when we're old, right?"

"Probably. It's either that or end up on the ice floe my daughter's threatening to put me on."

"So, there you have it. Who needs a man?"

"You do."

"Not happening," Frankie said, and went back to the dating site. "Ha! Educated singles only. So, they're snobs."

"Looking for the cream of the crop."

"Mitch qualifies as that. He's got an MBA," Frankie said, and checked Man seeking woman, then got busy setting up his profile. It was easy to fill in interests—football, hiking, kayaking, nature. Likes to go glamping, she added.

"He does?" asked Viola.

"He does now," Frankie said, and Viola giggled.

I'm a small-town guy with big-city tastes and hometown values, Frankie typed.

"What the heck does that mean?" Viola demanded.

"It means he has good values, but he has sophisticated tastes."

"Unclear," Viola said.

"Fine. I'll add this. 'Love my country, serve my community. Like playing Santa every year,'" Frankie said as she typed.

"That's better. You should have him ask a question. It'll make him more approachable."

What's your favorite holiday? Frankie typed. "Bonus points if she says Christmas."

"Not bad," Viola approved.

Frankie added more pertinent information and Mitch's picture. Okay, that was it. He was good to go.

She hesitated. "Maybe I shouldn't do this. Maybe Mitch won't appreciate it."

"Do ya think?"

"But he will if I bring him the perfect woman." Frankie gnawed on her lip, considering. "I do want him to be happy, and he obviously needs help getting there."

Viola washed her last bite of pizza down with her cola. "Most of us do, I guess. Just keep in mind, if you find him someone, it's going to change your relationship."

"Don't be silly," Frankie scoffed, then thought of the maneater in the pink coat. Candidates needed to be screened.

So, online dating it was. She finished the process. "Okay, we're official. Let's see what kind of Mrs. Claus we find."

Frankie decided not to share about Operation Match Mitch when she joined her family at Adele's house for their usual late afternoon meal after the shop closed. It would only inspire her mother to give her a lecture about meddling. And this wasn't meddling. It was helping.

She also decided not to tell Mitch when they met up later that evening to watch their favorite reality TV police show. She'd checked earlier, and he'd already attracted plenty of interest. Hardly surprising, considering how good-looking he was.

Plus, she'd made him sound perfect. Saint Mitch. He could be stubborn. What man couldn't? Both his office at the store and his home tended toward clutter, but a good woman could help him organize that.

"My house next week," he offered after the show had ended.

"You going to have eggnog?"

"Of course."

"Then your house next week."

Although by the next week he could be out with someone. No, not on Sunday night. That was *Cop Stop* night.

★ ★ ★

The shop was closed on Mondays, so Viola came over to Frankie's cozy two-bedroom cottage for brunch and joined her at the kitchen table to check out Mitch's prospects.

Babe Number One looked ready for an ugly Christmas sweater contest, wearing a bright green sweater overpopulated with reindeer and felt baby Santas dangling from the bottom like fringe. She was wearing a tiara on her head that said Queen. I love glamping! she declared. Do you cook? Love me a man who cooks. Uh, no.

Babe Number Two did not look even remotely fit enough to keep up with Mitch. I hate football, she confessed. But I love Super Bowl parties. Wait till you taste my Hawaiian sliders and Coca Cola cake! I'm about to join the gym. I could use a coach, by the way.

"Coca Cola cake," said Viola with a grin.

"Mitch would not have the patience to coach someone into fitness," said Frankie.

She moved on. One woman had put up a picture of herself and her "three fur babies"—ironically, hairless Sphinx cats, one perched on each shoulder and one in her lap. Do you love cats? she wanted to know.

No. Mitch was a dog man. His German shepherd, Whizzer, had recently crossed the rainbow bridge, and he was already considering taking in a rescue come the new year. Knowing Mitch, it would be a big dog, the kind that would eat all three cats for breakfast.

Yet another woman was pushing eighty and claimed she needed a younger man who could keep up with her. It wouldn't be Mitch.

Two more applicants sounded...desperate.

Another had a smile that Frankie pronounced fake. "There's a beyotch hiding behind that mask."

Next came a blonde wearing a business suit. "How about this one?" suggested Viola.

"She's not a fit."

"Why?"

"She's too…polished."

Viola raised an eyebrow.

"What?" Frankie demanded.

"You are being way too picky. I think, when it comes right down to it, you're having second thoughts. Admit it. You're too attached to Mitch to share."

"I am not," Frankie insisted. "What about this one? She looks good."

Wilhelmina Fritz proclaimed herself fit and fifty. Her profile picture showed a slender woman with brown shoulder-length hair and a pretty round face. She was on a hiking trail, posing surrounded by fir and maple trees, with a golden Labrador by her side. Love to hike, she wrote.

"Looks like you found a Mrs. Claus for Mitch," said Viola. "Let's start chatting."

And so "Mitch" began a correspondence with Wilhelmina. By Wednesday, Wilhelmina was ready to drive on over from nearby Cedarwood and meet him for coffee at The Coffee Stop. They made a date for the following day.

"Now I just have to get him over there," said Frankie when she called to report to Viola.

"What if he balks? Then it will be you wearing a Santa hat and meeting Wilhelmina."

"I'll make it happen," Frankie said.

"Let me know how it goes."

Hopefully, it would go smoothly.

Of course it would. If there was one thing Frankie was good at, it was organizing things—events, parties…meetups.

"Mind the shop, Mom," she said to Adele when it was time for the big moment.

Adele looked up from the nativity set she was putting back into place after a young visitor had scattered the shepherds and wise men every which way. "Where are you going?"

Elinor was in another part of the shop, unpacking a shipment of ornaments, and Natalie was at the grade school, helping with the teacher appreciation luncheon. Adele hated being on her own at the cash register.

"Just a quick coffee with Mitch," said Frankie.

"Santa Walk business?"

"Santa business," Frankie replied vaguely.

"Make it quick and bring me back an eggnog latte, okay?" Adele requested.

"Sure." As soon as she'd gotten Mitch and Wilhelmina squared away. Having to get coffee for her mom would make a good excuse to vacate the table. Her excuse for being at the table in the first place would be... Well, Frankie wasn't sure what that would be.

"Coffee break time," she greeted him as she poked her head in his office.

"Rain check?" he replied. He held up a sheaf of invoices. "I'm up to my eyeballs here."

"All the more reason you should take a break," she insisted. "Your eyeballs will thank you." He was about to say no, she knew it. "Come on. Just a few minutes. I need your advice on something."

That hadn't been the wisest thing to say. What on earth did she need advice on?

"Okay, then, a quick break," he said, and grabbed his Handy's Hardware windbreaker from a hook on the wall. "Brock, can you hold down the fort?" he called as they started out.

"I'm on it," came a disembodied voice from the other end of the store.

"Who's Brock?" asked Frankie. She knew everyone who worked for Mitch. She'd drafted all of them to help build Santa's sleigh for the first year's Santa Walk parade. "Oh, wait. Your new manager?"

"Yep. Just got here last week from California."

"You never said. Did he bring a family with him?"

"Nope. He's single."

Single. Hmm. "How old is he?"

"What? Are you in the market all of a sudden?" Mitch asked.

"No. I'm just wondering if he might like to meet Stef." It was past time for her sister to find someone.

Mitch shrugged. "He's about the right age."

"Stef could help him find his feet, introduce him around." Small-town newspaper reporters knew everyone.

"How about giving the poor guy a chance to catch his breath before you go hitching him up with someone?"

"You want him to feel at home in his new town, right? And stay."

"He might already have a woman."

"You don't know if he does?"

"He barely got here. I've been too busy bringing him up to speed in the store to get all the details of his love life. Now, how about instead of talking about my new manager, we talk about what you need help with," he said as they arrived at the coffee shop.

He opened the door for her and the aroma of coffee danced out to greet them. Morning rush hour was over and only a couple of tables were occupied, one with a senior man reading a copy of the *Carol Clarion*, and another had two young women, one with a baby in a stroller, visiting over their drinks.

The place was ready for Christmas with gold tinsel strung along its windows. An instrumental arrangement of "I'll Be Home for Christmas" was playing.

"Let's get something to drink first," she said, stalling. "I'm buying. You want your usual Americano?"

"I can get my own drink," he said.

"This is on me," she insisted. "Consider it payment for your advice. How about you grab us a table?"

He gave in and settled at one of the small, scarred wood tables, stretching his long legs out in front of him. He was such a good man. He deserved a good woman. Wilhelmina fit the bill. Frankie hoped she was as nice as she'd sounded in their online conversations.

She picked up their orders, Americano for him and a peppermint blended drink for her, then made her way to the table.

"So, what do you need my advice on?" Mitch asked as she set his drink down in front of him.

She grabbed the first thing that came to mind. "How do I get Natalie to turn her candy-crafting hobby into a business?"

"Been on her about that again, huh?"

"Her bonbons are to die for. I know she could make a success of it."

"She's already selling them at the shop."

"Only small batches."

"She's not ready yet, so don't push her. Meanwhile, you've got a good worker."

"I do, but Holiday Happiness is my dream, not hers."

"She has time to work on her own dreams. Let her be, Frankie. You've got your hands full managing the shop and your own life. You don't have time to run everyone else's."

Frankie tried not to think what Mitch was going to say when he learned she was trying to run his. "Sometimes people need help," she argued. "I only want what's best for her. I want what's best for all the important people in my life."

He smiled. "I know you do. You've got a big heart."

And once she found the woman of his dreams he would be forever grateful for her big heart.

Speaking of the woman of his dreams, who was the woman marching into the coffee shop, stuffed into red leggings and a red coat, carrying a manila folder under her arms? The face looked vaguely familiar.

Oh no. It couldn't be.

3

"MITCH," THE WOMAN CALLED AS SHE APPROACHED THE table. "It's so good to finally get to meet you!"

Both of Mitch's eyebrows flew up to his hairline.

"It's me, Wilhelmina Fritz," said the woman, plunking down at the table and smiling at Mitch. "Ho, ho, ho," she said, and held out her wrist, jiggling the holiday charm bracelet on it.

Mitch stared at it, shook his head slowly. "Uh…"

"Christmas. Get it? It's my favorite holiday, too."

He nodded and shot a look at Frankie. *Help!*

"I know I look a little different than my Best for You profile," Wilhelmina said.

A little? She could have been her own mother. If Wilhelmina was in her fifties, Frankie would eat her Santa hat.

Where was the fit-looking outdoorsy woman Frankie had hoped would be a match for Mitch and become her new friend as well? The woman who bragged about the marathons she'd run? The only thing that looked the same about her was her hair color, and Frankie could see gray roots lurking under the brown. Not that she had a problem with a woman keeping the same hair color as long as she wanted. And she didn't have a problem with someone's weight. But she did have a problem with a woman passing herself off as completely different. She frowned.

Wilhelmina didn't see. She was too busy giving her sales pitch to Mitch. "I've gained a few pounds since that picture I posted was taken."

And a few years.

"But I'm in much better shape than I look. And my bones are perfect. My teeth are great, too. I brought my dental records to prove it." Wilhelmina smiled and gave the folder a tap.

Mitch was still a step behind. "Best for You?" he repeated.

"It's so hard to find a good man these days," Wilhelmina said. "There are so many losers and cheaters out there. When I read your profile, I could tell you were special, and so genuine."

"My profile." He looked at Frankie again, this time with narrowed eyes.

"I promised I'd get a latte for Mom, and I need to get back to the shop," Frankie said, and began to rise.

Mitch caught her arm and pulled her back down onto her seat. "Stay a little longer." It wasn't a request.

"Is this your sister?" Wilhelmina guessed. She almost smiled at Frankie.

"No, this is my wife," Mitch lied. "We're getting back together."

Wilhelmina pulled back as if he'd slapped her. Then she

glared at him. "Of all the rotten fakes," she snarled, picking up her folder. "You should have taken your profile down. And you sure shouldn't have been flirting online with me!" She stood and pushed away from the table, almost knocking over her chair. "Men like you are scum. Scum!"

"Want to explain what just happened?" Mitch said to Frankie as Wilhelmina marched out of the coffee shop. "You are behind this, aren't you?"

"Well, um, I just got to thinking."

"Is that what you call it?"

"After your text. It sounded like you wanted a Mrs. Claus."

He let out a frustrated breath and shook his head. "I was referring to you, you goof."

"Me!"

"Were you or were you not Mrs. Claus at the Santa Walk the last two years?"

Frankie's heart missed a beat and her face felt hot enough to roast chestnuts. Mitch and her—that wouldn't work. They were pals, that was all.

Her thoughts must have raced across her face because he veered away from the topic of them and returned to scolding her. "Is that the kind of woman you think I need?"

"She looked totally different in her profile picture," Frankie explained. "In fact, she looked great. And she likes to hike and camp. And she loves Christmas."

"Is my picture still up on that site?" he demanded.

"It won't be. I'll take it down right away."

"See that you do," he said shortly. He stood, raised his cup to her. No smile. "Thanks for the coffee." With that, he made for the door as fast as Wilhelmina had.

"Mitch, wait. I'll walk back with you," Frankie called, jumping up.

He didn't turn around, just held up a stay-away hand and

kept going, shoving the door open with enough force to al-most pull it off its hinges.

This was awful. She and Mitch never fought. They were besties, always there for each other.

She ordered her mother's latte, pretending she didn't see Suzie the barista's curious stare, and then walked back to her shop, feeling like she was carrying all of Marley's chains on her shoulders. Except unlike Scrooge's old business partner, she hadn't done anything bad.

She had done something stupid, though. She should have listened to that little poke from her better sense when she first created his profile. Deciding to surprise Mitch with the per-fect woman had been a bad idea.

But her motives had been good. Surely, he could see that.

Holiday Happiness had no customers at the moment, which was just as well, since Adele greeted her with, "What the heck happened with you and Mitch? He just walked past the win-dow looking ready to lynch Santa."

"I happened," Frankie confessed, handing over the drink. "I was only trying to help," she was quick to add.

"What have you done?"

There was no point hiding it. "I signed him up on a dat-ing site."

"Oh no. You didn't."

"I thought he was looking for someone," Frankie said in her own defense.

"And he can't do that without you?"

Frankie frowned and put her Holiday Happiness apron back on. "We've got it taken care of."

"I can tell. He certainly looked mollified," Adele said.

A little sarcasm, just what Frankie needed for Christmas. She frowned at her mother.

Adele shook her head. "You'd better go over there on your knees and beg for forgiveness."

"I will."

"I'd suggest now," Adele said. "Elinor's here, and all is quiet for the moment. Perfect time. Cry a little. That always helps."

"Manipulative," Frankie muttered.

"It always worked for me," said Adele, refusing to see anything wrong with her suggestion. "Let this be a lesson to you. Meddling in people's lives will only blow up in your face. Oh, and while you're there, pick up some light bulbs for me."

Frankie sighed, took her apron back off and left to beg forgiveness.

She was on her way when Stef texted to see if she wanted to grab an early lunch at The Salad Bowl. Anything to stall talking with Mitch.

The popular restaurant was housed in a low brick building one street over from Main Street. It followed its theme with planters overflowing with plants and herbs perched behind booths. Many of those plants had grown out of control and liked to reach out and tickle necks of unsuspecting diners. The place always smelled like curry and roasting chicken, thanks to one of its popular menu items, the Curried Clucker, a curry chicken salad loaded with celery, onions and sprouts.

Stefanie Ludlow, ace reporter for the paper's lifestyle section, had already staked out a table. She was twelve years younger than Frankie, with the same hazel eyes and even features, but her hair was a different color, a light brown with golden highlights. She was a little slimmer, too, something Frankie was fond of advising her to enjoy while it lasted. "Just wait till menopause," Frankie liked to tell her. It had sure taken its toll on her the year before. She'd had so many hot flashes the previous Christmas she could have powered half the houses on her block. At least that had simmered down.

"Hey there. You look stressed," Stef said as Frankie slid into the booth.

"Mildly. Mitch is mad at me, and Mom is in full lecture mode."

"Uh-oh." Stef leaned both elbows on the table, ready for the gory details. "What have you done, sissy?"

Frankie looked over her shoulder.

"Don't worry. Angie's out sick today," said Stef.

"Okay, good," said Frankie.

Not that she didn't appreciate their favorite server, but Angie fell on juicy tidbits the way most women fell on chocolate. She had the largest Christmas village in town and was one of the shop's best customers every Black Friday. Her own village complete, she was now starting one for her newly married daughter. Angie came into Holiday Happiness so often, she considered herself a good family friend and, as such, entitled to knowing everything that was going on with the family. And sometimes she also felt entitled to share with others what was going on.

"So spill," said Stef.

Frankie was filling her in on the whole fiasco in between bites of salad when Viola texted to see how the meetup went. Don't ask, Frankie texted. Which, of course, prompted Viola to call her instantly.

"I'm at The Salad Bowl with Stef," Frankie answered.

"Enjoying a Toss Your Tacos?"

"Of course." They made a better taco salad than the Mexican restaurant.

"Was Mitch mad?"

"Yes. Wilhelmina was a faker."

"Oh boy. Sorry. I'll let you get back to your lunch. Say hi to Stef for me."

"If you're going to be looking for perfect matches, you could at least look for one for me," said Stef after Frankie ended the call. "Oh wait. Never mind. I've seen how that turns out, and the last thing I need is another Dick."

Richard Swineburn, Stef's ex of two years, had never liked it when people used the outdated nickname, for obvious reasons. Although he lived up to it. The man had been a narcissist. Sadly, Stef hadn't seen it until it was too late. She'd been too impressed with his good looks and his good job as a CEO of a seafood distributer in Seattle.

Adele had had one of her famous prophetic dreams when Stef first started dating him. Stef had only laughed when Adele had reported she'd dreamed that Stef was caught in a net with a school of tuna and Richard was on the tuna boat pulling in the net, dressed in a Dracula cloak and cackling, "Gotcha now."

Frankie hadn't been a fan of Richard, either, and had tried to persuade Stef to slow down. She hadn't. Until after she married. The marriage dragged on for seven years before Stef got free of him.

She deserved better. It had been two years since her divorce, and so far she hadn't found it. Not that she'd been looking until the past few months, and that search had been hampered by cynicism thanks to how badly she'd been hurt.

"Every online match isn't a fail," said Frankie.

"You gonna tell that to Mitch?" Stef teased.

"Uh, no, and I'm removing him from the site."

She did that while they waited for their desserts—lavender cupcakes, the restaurant's specialty.

"Too bad Mitch is too old for me," said Stef as she watched his profile disappear. "I'd take him in a heartbeat."

"You're right. He's not the one for you. But I know there is someone. He might even be here in Carol."

"I doubt it. I think I've dated every single man within a

twenty-mile radius. Love shouldn't be so hard," Stef said with a sigh. "Trying to find the right person is like looking for a needle in a haystack."

"Or finding a needle in a Christmas tree," quipped Frankie.

Although it really wasn't funny. There were a lot of good people out there looking for someone with whom they could share a life. It didn't seem right that it was so hard to do.

"Maybe I'll write a feature about dating for the *Clarion*," mused Stef. "I'll title it 'Looking for a Needle in a Christmas Tree.'"

"Or 'Where's Santa When You Need Him?'" Frankie suggested.

"'Cupid Takes a Holiday'?"

The sisters snickered until Stef turned serious. "I swear, I've met every loser in Carol and Pine Valley in the last few months." The server brought their cupcakes. "Consolation cupcakes," she cracked with a frown, and took a big bite of hers.

"Maybe Santa thinks you need more time to heal," Frankie suggested.

"Maybe I'll be healing for the rest of my life," Stef said. She shook her head. "I should never have stayed so long."

"At least you left."

Stef picked up the rest of her cupcake and crumbled it onto her plate. "Love is a crapshoot. At least you got lucky."

Yes, Frankie had. Ike had been a good man with a big heart. They'd both been big on family—she because she had one, he because his had been fractured and he'd always wanted a solid one. They'd enjoyed sports and entertaining, especially during the holidays. Super Bowl parties had always been a highlight of the new year. So much in common, so much in love. How she missed him!

"Oh, well, no point resurrecting the past. All you get is

zombies," said Stef, bringing Frankie back to the present. "This time around, I'm looking for a man who will give me credit for having some brains and who won't spend every dime we have as well as ones we don't on himself."

"If at first you don't succeed, date, date again," said Frankie.

Eventually Stef was sure to find someone who deserved her. And Frankie was going to be watching carefully to make sure she got exactly that.

They finished their dessert, and Stef announced she had to get back to work. "Got to get the first batch of letters to Santa up online before end of day."

That meant Frankie had to quit stalling and go to Handy's Hardware and apologize to Mitch. She picked up the tab, then followed her sister out of the restaurant and dawdled her way to the hardware store.

She found Mitch at the help island, showing a customer a YouTube video on his phone about replacing a garbage disposal.

"This sounds like a pain," said the man, who was dressed in designer jeans and an expensive-looking suede jacket.

"You can do it," Mitch assured him. "You've got everything you need." He pointed to the pile of tools and parts assembled on the countertop. "But if you get stuck, give me a call."

"Will do. Thanks, Mitch," said the man as he gathered up his purchases to take to the checkout register.

"No problem," said Mitch with a smile. The smile fell away as Frankie approached. "Need something?" he asked politely.

"Yes, as a matter of fact, I do. I need you to not be mad at me."

He made a face, sighed. "Shit, Frankie."

"I know, I know. I should have asked you first."

"It would have been nice."

"I'm sorry I didn't. I won't do it again, I promise. Let me

make it up to you. Come on over for dinner tomorrow night. I'll invite Stef, and we'll make it a party. And Elinor. She needs to get out more. You can have a regular harem."

"Just what I don't need." He leaned on the counter. "What are you planning on serving?"

"How about pasties? Your fav." If those little meat and potato pies didn't do the trick, nothing would.

He shrugged. "What else?"

"Sidecars?" she added to seal the deal.

"I like that drink. What's for dessert?"

"What would you like?"

"Humble pie."

"I thought I just ate a big helping of that now," she said, and ventured a smile. "How about peppermint pie?"

He nodded and gave the counter a tap. "Okay, deal."

"Good. And now I need to get some light bulbs for Adele."

She forgot about the light bulbs at the sight of the man who came around the corner of the plumbing supplies aisle.

Mitch summoned him. "Brock, come on over and meet Frankie."

He was taller than Mitch and had Jack Reacher–size shoulders and pecs that filled out his brown Handy's Hardware polo shirt beautifully. Brown hair, gorgeous brown eyes, and bonus, he looked about Stef's age. Was this a gift from Santa or what?

"Hi, Frankie. Brock Adams," he said with a high wattage smile, and shook her hand with his big one. Big hands, big... heart. Stef would love this man.

"Hi," she said. "I hear you're new to Carol."

He nodded. "Yep."

"Lucky us. You look like a great addition. I hope you're liking it here."

"I am now," he said. "Mitch, you didn't tell me you knew a model."

The man had a gift for making a woman feel good. Was he as nice as he seemed? She smiled at him. "Flattery, what everyone wants for Christmas."

"Just speaking the truth."

"Oh, you are good," she said. "Say, I'm having Mitch and a couple other people over for dinner tomorrow. How'd you like to join us? I make amazing pasties."

"I'd like that. Whatever they are."

"Trust me, you'll like them," Frankie assured him.

"I'm sure I will," Brock said, and his smile got bigger.

"You sure you don't have plans?" asked Mitch.

"Nope. Don't know anybody to make plans with. Yet," Brock added, still smiling at Frankie.

"Well, after tomorrow you will," she said. "We'll make sure of that. Mitch can tell you where I live. Both of you come over at seven."

"Seven," Brock confirmed. "Thanks for the invite."

"Glad to have you," she said.

She texted Stef as she headed for the door. Don't make plans for tomorrow. Dinner at my house with a new hunk. You will love him.

New hunk????

Mitch's manager. Perfect for you.

You've seen him in person?

Just talked to him. Trust me.

Not after your mess with Mitch. Stef added a laughing emoticon.

Ha ha, Frankie texted back, then put her phone in her jacket pocket.

When Frankie walked back in the store, Elinor was handing a customer her purchase in a bright red Holiday Happiness bag. Adele was on the other side of the shop, demonstrating a mechanical musical bear in a Santa hat to a little girl who looked to be around five.

The little girl clapped and jumped up and down as the bear played "We Wish You a Merry Christmas."

"Maybe Santa will bring that to you for Christmas," said the child's mother. "Can I come back?" she asked Adele.

"They're going fast, but I'll save this one for you," Adele promised.

They weren't going all that fast, but Adele never let details get in the way of merchandizing hype.

"How'd it go?" she asked Frankie as their shoppers left the store.

"We're good. He's coming over for dinner and bringing his new manager, who happens to be single. Stef's coming, too."

Adele gave Frankie a suspicious look. "Meddling again?"

"No, helping," Frankie corrected her. "Want to join us?"

"And witness the train wreck? No, thanks."

"There will be no train wreck," Frankie said irritably.

"So you say. Anyway, I can't. My bunco girls are having their Christmas party."

"Oh, that's right. I forgot. Elinor, join us," Frankie said to Elinor. "It will be fun."

Elinor's cheeks turned pink. "That's really nice of you, but I don't want to intrude."

"Who said you'd be intruding? It's a party. Anyway, I already told Mitch I was inviting you."

Elinor smiled. "What can I bring?"

"Nothing but your smile," said Frankie.

"I could bring something to drink," Elinor ventured.

"Whatever makes you happy."

"Did you remember to get my light bulbs?" Adele asked.

"Snotballs! I forgot."

Adele shook her head. "I know. You had more important things on your mind than your poor old mother's needs. Never mind. I'll pick them up later."

"Daughter guilting does not become you," Frankie said, and turned back around.

Brock was nowhere in sight when she reentered the hardware store. Mitch was in the lighting section, helping an older man select the proper switch box.

"I forgot to get Mom's light bulbs," she said, and grabbed a box.

"Distracted by my manager?" It sounded like teasing, but it was accompanied by a rather stingy smile.

She frowned at Mitch. "Oh, you are funny."

As if she was interested in someone who was probably ten years younger than her. As if she was interested in anyone.

Come Friday evening, Frankie's house smelled like balsam fir and good food and looked ready for a magazine shoot. Her tree was up, all done in pink and silver this year. Greens ran along her mantel, with mercury glass candle holders in between, the lit candles inside them glowing softly. Pillar candles decorated her coffee table and the ceramic nativity set Adele had made for her years ago was proudly displayed on the dining room buffet. Her table was set with her favorite Christmas plates, Holiday Gatherings by Lenox. Red cloth napkins matched the centerpiece: red ribbon and, nestled in the greens, three candles in small hurricane lamps.

She'd made her pasties the night before and had them heating in the oven. The peppermint pie, also made ahead of time, was ready and waiting in the refrigerator, and the makings for the drinks were set out on the counter. Stef had promised to put together a spinach salad with pomegranate and feta cheese. It would be a stellar meal.

Stef showed up with her salad, looking adorable in jeans and a soft red sweater and faux fur–trimmed green suede boots on her feet in honor of the light snow starting to dust the sidewalk outside. Her hair hung in a perfect cascade almost to her shoulders, and her makeup was perfect. Like Frankie, she wore red lipstick because, well, why not? It was a good choice. Who didn't love red lipstick? Brock would go crazy for her.

Five minutes after Stef, the doorbell rang again. Mitch had arrived. He wore boots, jeans and his favorite old peacoat that had been his grandfather's. He looked rugged and handsome.

Looking at him, Frankie wished she could cut part of their coffee shop conversation from the day before out of her mind—it seemed to be stuck in there like a thorn, taunting her with possibilities she had no intention of exploring.

She wasn't going to give her heart to another man and then lose half of it to the grave. With the age difference between Mitch and her, it was a given that would happen.

"Hi, ladies," Mitch said as he stepped into the entry, brushing snow off his shoulders. "It's starting to come down out there."

Stef was doing door patrol. "Give me your coat," she commanded, and he shrugged out of his. He wore a plain blue shirt that matched his eyes. How on earth had he stayed single for the last fifteen years?

"Once burned," he'd answered when Frankie had asked him several years ago. It must have been a bad burn.

He never elaborated. Mitch wasn't one to talk about his past. "No point in it," he liked to say. "You move on and make the most of now."

Which he was doing. Everyone in town liked him, and he seemed to have a good relationship with his two sons, young men in their early thirties, both married, who checked in with him regularly from different parts of the country and came out to visit him at his lake house on their summer vacations. Frankie had met the sons, and they seemed nice. One had a boy who was the apple of Mitch's eye and video-chatted regularly with him. As for the ex-wife...who knew where she was? Or what she was? Undeserving, if you asked Frankie.

Even though dinner was her way of apologizing, Mitch had brought wine and flowers. He joined her in the kitchen, where she had a cinnamon-scented candle burning, handing over an arrangement of red carnations and white roses in a miniature sleigh. She'd seen it in the window of Flora's Flower Shoppe and commented on it when they were passing by one day.

"You didn't have to do that," she said, setting it on the counter.

He shrugged. "I know. I knew you liked it."

She smiled at him. "I do. Thanks. Does this mean I'm truly forgiven?"

He smiled back. "Depends on how good the pasties are."

"You know they'll be good." She couldn't hang wallpaper, and she couldn't crochet like her mom or create candies that were works of art like her daughter, and she couldn't pull words together like Stef, but she could cook. And make cocktails.

She had just made Mitch his promised sidecar and handed it to him when the doorbell rang, announcing her next guest. Again, Stef did door patrol, letting in Brock.

There stood Holiday Hunk Number Two, wearing jeans and boots and a black parka. Stef was looking up at him as if he was one giant candy cane. Yep, it could end up being a very Merry Christmas for Stef.

"Hi there," she chirped. "I'm Stefanie Ludlow, Frankie's sister. May I take your coat?"

"Sure, thanks," he said with a polite smile. He looked to where Frankie stood in the kitchen with Mitch, and the smile grew wider. "Hi, Frankie!" he called, and Stef's shoulders stiffened.

A little premonition that things weren't going to go as planned wriggled into Frankie's mind as Brock strode toward the kitchen, a red-and-white floral arrangement like the one Mitch had brought in his hand.

She pushed the uneasy feeling out. This dinner was going to be a success.

MITCH FROWNED AT THE SIGHT OF THE FLOWERS BROCK had brought. Brock didn't notice.

Frankie did. "Great minds think alike," she said, and set it on the counter next to Mitch's offering. "You two are the perfect guests."

"Never show up empty-handed, my mom always said," Brock told her.

Stef joined them. "Your mom sounds like a smart woman," she said.

He nodded. "She was."

Was. One short word that said so much. "Your mom's no longer alive?" guessed Frankie.

Brock shook his head. "She was only fifty."

Frankie's age. Yikes!

"Didn't even live to see me graduate from college."

"That's rough," said Frankie. "It's hard to lose a parent."

He nodded. "I miss her every day."

Frankie handed him a drink. "I bet you do. Is your dad still alive?"

"Oh yeah. Still working his butt off at the factory. Waiting for my little bro or me to grow up, get married and give him a grandson who'll make it to the NFL."

"You look pretty grown up to me," said Stef in her silkiest voice.

"Forty come February," he said.

Stef was thirty-eight. Perfect.

"But Dad says we're still kids in big bodies."

This particular kid had a very nice body. If he and Stef got together, they would have gorgeous children.

"There comes a time," said Mitch. "Even though my marriage didn't last, I got two great sons out of the deal."

Brock shrugged. "I don't know if I want kids."

Stef did. She'd change his mind.

"Kids are the best," said Mitch.

"Yes, they are," Frankie agreed.

"Something sure smells good," said Brock, changing the subject.

"Pasties. Miners in England used to take them to work for their lunch," Frankie explained.

"You'll love 'em," said Mitch. "Nobody's better in the kitchen than Frankie."

"My mom was a good cook," said Brock, "but she only got as far as teaching me how to make an omelet and French toast. And grilled cheese sandwiches."

"That's all you can make?" Stef asked in surprise.

"I can grill meat," he said, looking mildly offended. "I

wouldn't mind learning how to make some more stuff in the kitchen."

"Stef's good in the kitchen," Frankie said, and Stef tried to look modest.

The doorbell rang, and Frankie went to let in Elinor so Stef could have the opportunity to brag about her culinary skills. She wasn't as much of a foodie as Frankie, but she made an awesome Crock-Pot stew.

Elinor stepped in bearing two bottles of sparkling cider. "I hope this is enough," she said as she handed them to Frankie.

"This is perfect," Frankie assured her, and Elinor's cheeks turned rosy.

The pink got deeper once she had her coat off and joined the others in the kitchen. "Hello, Mitch."

"Hi, Elinor. You're looking nice tonight," he said.

Nice was such a bland word, the kind of compliment you paid when you had to say something. It fit Elinor perfectly. She was hiding under a bulky cream-colored sweater worn over tan pants, and she had on brown boots that said, *Yes, we are part of the whole boring vibe.* With her light blond hair and fair complexion and pale pink lipstick, she could have been a ghost. A slightly darker shade of lipstick and brow liner would have made a big difference. She wasn't bad-looking, but she definitely hid her assets. She needed someone to take her in hand.

Elinor smiled at Mitch's compliment and dropped her gaze. "Thank you."

"Elinor, I don't think you've met Brock," said Frankie.

He gave her a nod and a friendly hello and she said a soft hello back.

Elinor needed to look men in the eye. No wonder she was

single. She had to get in the game and quit sitting on the sidelines. The woman obviously needed a life coach.

"So, Brock, where did you move here from?" asked Stef.

"California," he said.

"That's where my ex was from," Stef said. "I sure got Californicated."

Seriously? thought Frankie, and frowned at her. "Everyone moves here from California. I just wish you all would bring us more of that sun in the winter."

"I wouldn't mind that myself," Brock said.

"Anyway, we're glad you're here. I'm sure Mitch is, too," Frankie said.

"I hope he's not ready to fire me yet," joked Brock.

"You're too good to fire," said Mitch. Then he'd clearly had enough of talking about Brock. "How are those pasties coming?"

Oh yes, them. Frankie took the sheet of little meat pies out of the oven. Piping hot and golden brown. Perfect.

"I guess we're ready to eat," she said.

"Those look amazing," said Brock.

"They are," said Frankie. "They're a lot of work, but they're worth it. Just make sure you save room for dessert. We have peppermint pie. Have you got a sweet tooth, Brock?"

"Oh yeah, I like sweet things," he said, and grinned at Frankie, raising his glass to her.

Stef frowned.

So did Mitch.

This was becoming…awkward. Frankie put the meat pies on a platter and handed it to Stef. "Let's get these pasties on the table before they get cold. Brock, sit down and make yourself at home," she said to him as Stef took their main course to the table. "And, Elinor, how about you take out our drinks?"

Frankie suggested, and Elinor followed the others to the table with her sparkling cider.

That left Mitch. She handed him the bowl of salad. "Let's eat."

"What's he doing bringing you flowers?" Mitch demanded in a low voice.

"Being a good guest. Like you."

"I guess," said Mitch.

Dinner did not go as planned. Elinor's sparkling cider was ignored in favor of another round of sidecars, followed by the wine Mitch had brought, and she gave up asking if anyone would like some. Stef threw a couple of flirty compliments to Brock, which he acknowledged politely without throwing anything back. He raved over Frankie's pasties but merely pronounced Stef's salad good. After being prompted by Frankie.

Mitch, at least, was more enthusiastic. "I'll have some more of that salad," he said, and helped himself to a second serving. "What are these red seeds, Stef?"

"Pomegranate," she said.

"Well, they give it a nice kick," he told her, which brought out a smile.

"More salad, Brock?" Frankie prompted.

"No, that's okay," he said.

Mitch forked up a bite. "You know what Popeye said. 'Strong to the finish 'cause I eats me spinach.'"

"I'm already strong. I bet I could take down Popeye," joked Brock.

"I bet you could," Frankie said. The man looked like he could push over a brick wall with his pinky finger.

She'd said it unthinkingly but realized the minute the words were out of her mouth that it sounded like flattery. Brock appeared pleased. Mitch didn't.

Time for dessert!

Frankie brought out the pie, along with coffee, and both men vacuumed theirs up.

"I could eat that entire pie," said Mitch.

"Me, too," said Brock. "Frankie, you could have your own cooking show."

The way he grinned at her, it was…nothing. No more than a sugar-induced sappy grin.

"Cougars in the Kitchen," quipped Stef.

She'd said it lightly, but it came off snotty, and no one so much as chuckled. *Way to put your best foot forward*, Frankie thought, irritated.

"Nothing wrong with those big cats," said Brock. "Cougars are sexy."

Brock was definitely under the influence of sugar.

The way Mitch's eyebrows were dipping into a V, Frankie could tell he was under the influence of something else. He was obviously not enjoying the company of his new manager.

"More pie, Mitch?" she offered.

His expression fell back into polite lines. "Absolutely," he said.

"I'll take some more, too," Brock said. "This is the best thing I've had in a long time."

Frankie set out more pie for the men. Everyone stayed at the table, drinking coffee and talking.

Actually, mostly Brock was talking…about everything from his college football days to his new truck. Stef threw out compliments where she could. Mitch turned into a clam about his own life although he certainly could have bragged about his own accomplishments. Frankie knew that, like Brock, he'd played football in college—had gotten a full-ride scholarship. Earlier in the year, he'd picked up his third Ironman medal. Instead of chiming in, he simply sat, eyeballing Brock.

Elinor wasn't eyeballing anyone. She was simply looking at her coffee cup.

Frankie switched topics, hoping to pull in all her guests by polling them for their favorite movies. Sports and action movies topped the list for the men. Stef mentioned a favorite rom-com, and Frankie threw in a couple of serious movies that had stuck with her.

"Although I love all those classic sports movies, like *The Blind Side*," she finished.

"Can't go wrong with football," said Brock.

Frankie turned to Elinor. "How about you, Elinor?"

"I'm not much into movies," Elinor said apologetically. Then added, "The books are always better."

Conversation faltered as the others all nodded politely.

"It's always better to be out living life than watching it," Frankie tried.

"Yeah, but it's hard to pass up *Die Hard* at Christmas," Brock joked.

"True," Frankie agreed. She and Mitch had watched it the year before with one of his sons who'd come up for the holidays.

"My ex loved to watch that movie," Stef muttered. "I always thought it was too far-fetched." Then she frowned and took a gulp of what was left of her coffee.

"I guess everyone's got an ex," Brock said. "But I learn from my past mistakes and move on."

"Oh, I've moved on," Stef insisted. Her scowl and tone of voice implied that in the process she'd trampled Richard with the highest spike heels she could find.

"Good. 'Cause you never know what you might find right around the corner. Or in a new town," Brock said, and grinned at Frankie. Which didn't have Stef looking happy.

"I should be going," Elinor said.

"Already?" protested Frankie. Not that Elinor was adding much sparkle to the evening, but Frankie hated to see her give up and run off.

"We do have work tomorrow," Elinor said.

It was only nine. How much sleep did the woman need?

But Elinor hadn't exactly been having fun. Frankie needed to let the poor woman escape.

"Okay," she said, and walked Elinor to the door where she fetched Elinor's coat from the coat closet.

"I'm glad you came," Frankie said.

"Thank you for having me." No mention of having had a good time. No surprise.

Poor Elinor. It couldn't be fun being a human shadow. Frankie was going to have to find a way to help her get out there and get a life.

She returned to find the two men at the table, talking about the Seahawks while Stef was in the kitchen, shoving dishes into the dishwasher.

"There, you're good to go," she said curtly to Frankie as she inserted the last dinner plate. "And now I'm going."

"What? You, too?" Frankie demanded.

"I'm not wanted here," Stef hissed. "Good of you to invite me over to meet someone you've already latched on to," she finished in disgust.

Good grief. Weren't they a little old for sibling rivalry?

"I haven't latched on to anyone," Frankie protested in a whisper. "You're being ridiculous."

"Whatever." Stef left the kitchen, gave both men a smile and announced, "The dishes are done. It's time for the help to leave."

Mitch looked surprised. "Already? Thought you'd want to stay and play some cards."

"I've got another stop to make tonight," Stef said brightly.

You do not, Frankie thought, irritated.

Stef gave Mitch a hug, then turned to Brock. "Welcome to Carol."

"Thanks," he said. "I think I'm gonna like it here." He looked at Frankie.

"I bet you are," Stef said sourly.

Frankie followed her to the door. Stef already had the coat closet door open and was pulling out her down coat.

"You are being difficult," Frankie whispered, exasperated.

Stef ignored her, concentrating instead on holding her empty bowl while shrugging into her coat. "Good night," she said.

Then she was gone, and Frankie came back to the table to join her two remaining supper guests. "I imagine you guys need to get going, too," she said.

"I'm in no hurry," said Brock.

Mitch leaned his arms on the table and looked across at him. "Me, either."

So, what to do now?

"Ever played To Hell and Back?" asked Brock.

"Sure. Bring it on," said Mitch. "Get the cards, Frankie."

Oh, why didn't they both go home?

"What a waste of a Friday night," Stef grumbled as she drove back to her condo. "Come on over, sister. I've got the perfect man for you. Only he's not interested in you. He's interested in me. Ha ha."

And why? Stef wasn't bad-looking. She knew she had nice eyes. Even Richard the narcissist had told her so. She had great hair—thick with the smallest amount of wave to give it body. A symmetrical face, which, she'd read somewhere online, was supposed to be the ultimate in beauty. She was also in great shape—Richard had constantly goaded her into that. Plus, she was younger than her sister by twelve years, for crying out loud. What did Frankie have that Stef didn't?

Wrinkles.

Okay, they were laugh lines around her eyes. And Frankie did have a great laugh. She had great eyes, too. Bigger boobs. Maybe that was the lure. What else could it be? Unless Brock was into older women. Maybe he was looking for a mommy replacement. If he was… Eeew, Frankie could have him.

But he was hot, and he was nice, and Stef had expected him to, if not fall for her, at least show some passing interest. Getting shown up by your older sister—how humiliating. Especially when your older sister was trying to match you up with the guy, for crying out loud. And honestly, all that raving over the peppermint pie.

You should have brought dessert instead of spinach salad. What man wants salad when he can have pie?

It was as if Richard the Dick was standing at her shoulder, whispering in her ear. It sounded like the kind of thing he'd have said.

In fact, it was exactly what he'd have said. He always had a put-down handy to dole out.

Not at first, though. He'd had to win her before he could stomp on her. He'd pulled out all the stops when they were dating, living the high life like he could afford it—nice restaurants, flowers, a surprise trip to Vegas, where he'd proposed.

Boy, had she bet on the wrong man.

He'd said a lot of snide things over the course of their seven-year marriage, and when he wasn't disrespecting her, getting on her for whatever latest thing she'd done wrong, he was ignoring her.

That actually hurt the worst, but in retrospect, it was hardly surprising. Once you'd dangled the bait and caught the fish and mounted it, why bother to spend time with it? It was just a dead fish on the wall.

He'd done so much to rattle her and make her doubt her worth that it still surprised her she'd been able to walk away and rediscover her self-confidence. She didn't have to go groveling for any man to pay attention to her.

So Frankie could have her boy toy. It was fine with Stef.

Three games of cards later, Frankie's two remaining guests looked ready to stay for three more, but Frankie had had enough of cards. And of the men. Between Brock's flirting and Mitch's scowling, she was on man overload.

"Well, that was fun," she said. "And now, I'm going to quit while I'm ahead."

"You won the last two games. You're not going to give us a chance to get even?" Brock protested.

"Afraid not. I have to be in the shop bright and early tomorrow, and I need my beauty sleep."

"That's something you definitely don't need," Brock told her.

"You're right, she doesn't," said Mitch, not to be outdone. "But she does need to recharge. Saturdays are always busy downtown this time of year, especially in Frankie's shop."

"Then I guess we'd better go," Brock said.

Once at the door with coats on, both men stood there, each one trying to outwait the other.

No, no, we are not going to stand here all night.

"Okay, you two. I'll see you both tomorrow," Frankie said, and swung the door wide.

There was nothing for them to do but walk out.

As soon as they were gone, she called Stef. It was half past eleven, but Frankie knew her sister would still be awake. Stef was a night owl. Plus, her feathers were ruffled. She'd be too stirred up to go to bed.

Sure enough, she answered on the second ring. "What?"

"What, indeed?" Frankie said irritably. "What is wrong with you? Here I go to all the trouble to plan a dinner..." which had not gone according to plan, but that was beside the point "...and you turn into a lemon, say obnoxious things and then leave early. And that 'cougars in the kitchen' crack. Really? That showed you in a good light."

"There was no light left thanks to you, and there was no point in staying. Brock wasn't interested in me."

"He might have been if you'd gotten in touch with your inner Sugar Plum Fairy instead of acting like the Grinch in drag," snapped Frankie.

"Okay, so I got a little sour."

"A little?"

"But really, watching you two flirting was enough to sour anyone."

"I was not flirting!"

Stef talked right over her. "It was obvious he wasn't into me, and I refuse to grovel for a man's attention. I'm through bending over backward for men. You can have him."

"I don't want him," Frankie protested.

"Well, he wants you."

"Oh please. He does not. He's way too young. I could have been his babysitter, for crying out loud."

"He's no baby now. Honestly, Frankie, if you were trying to set us up, you could at least stay out of the way. You and your peppermint pie," Stef grumbled.

"You love my peppermint pie!" Frankie protested.

This was met with an exasperated exhale. "I do. And I love you. But right now, I'm pissed at you, and I need to get some work done on the Letters to Santa page. So good night and ho, ho, ho." With that, Stef ended the call.

The Letters to Santa page on the newspaper's website had been Frankie's idea. She'd suggested it to Stef's editor the year before, putting in a good word for Stef (just a little nepotism). Camille had liked the idea and offered Stef the chance to run the page. It had been a big hit, and Frankie had been delighted. There wasn't anything she wouldn't do for her sister.

Including making sure Stef found a truly good man this second time around. Brock and Stef could be good together. He just needed a nudge in the right direction, and if there was one thing Frankie was good at, it was nudging.

"Thank you again for last night," Elinor said to Frankie the next morning as they got to work in the shop.

"I'm glad you could come," Frankie said. She opened a box of blown-glass ornaments to add to their blue-and-silver artificial tree and got to work. People loved the blue-and-silver combination, and the decorations on that tree went as fast as she could put them up. "I hope you had fun." Frankie seriously doubted Elinor had, so that was a silly thing to say. Still, she wanted Elinor to understand that she'd had her best interests at heart when she'd invited her.

"It was nice. I guess I'm not much of a party person," Elinor added.

"Everyone's a party person," said Frankie. "Although we all have a different definition of what that looks like."

"It's not that I don't like people," Elinor said. "I love working here. It's just that I seem to…disappear in groups."

"I think you need to advertise more," said Frankie.

"Advertise?"

"You know, add a little window dressing."

"Window dressing." Elinor frowned. She obviously wasn't getting the message.

"These days, whether it's a product or a person, we have to do things to stand out," Frankie explained. "You really have a nice face, but with the right makeup you could be…" not stunning. She wasn't that pretty, but "…really lovely. Eye-catching. I bet there's someone whose eye you'd like to catch, someone you've taken an interest in."

"Well, there is someone," Elinor admitted.

So Brock had made an impression on her. She hadn't made one on him, though. At the rate she was going, Elinor was never going to make an impression on anyone. Still, she had potential.

"Why not let me treat you with a makeover? We could go shopping, check out the makeup counter at Macy's in the mall. Have lunch."

"That's really kind of you. Thanks." Frankie was about to suggest a day when Elinor added, "I'll think about it."

"Thinking and doing are not the same," Frankie cautioned.

At that moment William Sharp, who owned Carol Reads, the bookstore around the corner, came in, ending the conversation. He'd become a regular visitor over the last several weeks, popping in to buy presents for his mother or his sister or his little niece. So far, he'd bought a glass pumpkin, two Fitz and Floyd candlesticks shaped like turkeys, an illuminated hand-painted cornucopia and three blown-glass tree ornaments shaped like pilgrims. One purchase at a time, which added up to quite a few visits.

William was probably somewhere in his forties and still single. He was tall and long-faced, with stilt-like legs that made Frankie think of the famous character Ichabod Crane.

But his lack of looks was offset by a kind smile and a kind heart. He was one of the biggest contributors to the chamber of commerce's Help Santa fund, which offered financial aid to parents who were struggling to pay their bills and provide presents for their children. Any organization looking for donations for their fundraiser could always count on William to donate books.

"Good morning, William," Frankie called. "How are things at the bookstore?"

"A little slow," he said, "but we'll get busier this afternoon."

"Are the streets still icy? They were when I got here, and I'm half thinking of calling Mom and telling her not to come in until later," Frankie said.

"It's starting to thaw," he said. "She should be fine as long as she drives carefully." He joined Elinor at the nearby tree she was restocking. "It looks like you got in some new ornaments."

She held up a Christopher Radko. "I love this one."

"That is nice. May I see it?" he asked.

Of course, he'd end up buying it.

Frankie's mom blew in, bundled up in her favorite puffy black coat, a red scarf around her neck, a stocking cap on her head and red mittens on her hands.

"It's freezing out there," she announced. "I feel like I've been groped by Frosty the Snowman."

"Eww, Mom," Frankie said, shaking her head at her mother.

"That was kind of funny," said William as Adele made her way to the office to shed her coat.

"Don't say that to her. You'll only encourage her," said Frankie.

She followed her mother to the back room. It housed a desk complete with a computer and a chair to go under it, a cart with a microwave and a stack of cups—which no one used as they all frequented the coffee shop—along with a couple of ancient straight-backed chairs. It also held a filing cabinet with supplier invoices and three stacked boxes of merchandise that had recently arrived and hadn't yet made it up to their storage space on the second floor.

"Okay, let's hear the excuse," Frankie teased as Adele hung her coat on one of the many hooks on the wall. "Besides icy streets. I was about to call and tell you to wait to come in."

"The streets were fine. It took me a while to get going this morning. I had a terrible night's sleep."

Adele always had an excuse for sailing in late. Which she did frequently. Considering how much she did for so little, Frankie would never complain. Frankie was more than willing to pay her more, in fact, but every time she tried to give her mother a raise, Adele turned it down, saying, "I don't need to be robbing you of your retirement money."

So she pretty much came and went as she pleased, joked with the customers, sold people things they hadn't realized they wanted and made outlandish statements. Everyone loved her.

No one more than Frankie. Adele had always been her best friend, her biggest fan, the rock she'd leaned on when she lost Ike.

"Did your terrible night have anything to do with drinking too much wine with the Bunco Babes?" Frankie teased.

Adele ignored her teasing. "I had this awful dream and then I couldn't get back to sleep. I dreamed Fuzzy was alive, and he was all emaciated and trying to eat my arm."

"Our long-departed cat was chewing on your arm?"

Adele was famous for her crazy dreams, and she was always sure they had meaning. "Yes, I think it's a message."

"From Fuzzy?"

"No," Adele said in disgust. "From on high. I need to make a hefty donation to PAWS."

"I think that's an excellent idea," Frankie approved.

"I think you and Stef are supposed to make donations, too."

"Even though Fuzzy wasn't chewing on my arm."

"He might if you don't heed my warning."

"I can do that."

"Speaking of Stef. What happened at dinner last night? I called her before I came here to see how it went, and she said I should ask you."

"Things didn't go according to plan," said Frankie.

"They rarely do, and you should know that by now."

"Well, Stef didn't do anything to help. I had the perfect man there."

"Perfect, like beauty, is in the eye of the beholder. Anyway, I'm not sure she's ready for another relationship yet, even if she is dating."

"Well, then she should quit looking and quit whining."

Adele pointed a finger at Frankie. "And you should quit trying to meddle."

"I wasn't meddling. I was helping. She wanted me to, and then when it didn't work out, she blamed me."

"Darling, I know you've always been a caring big sister, sometimes even second mother, and there have been times when Stef really needed help."

"Yeah, like rescuing her from Richard." Getting Stef deprogramed and away from that garbage can with legs had been a team effort involving not only Frankie, but Adele and Stef's editor, Camille, as well.

"But she's a grown woman, and she can sort out her own love life."

"So far she's not doing a very good job of it."

"When the time is right, and she's ready, she will," Adele said, and left the back room, ending the conversation.

Frankie followed her out to see that Natalie had arrived. She'd ditched her coat behind the counter and was ringing up a sale. Natalie sometimes came in a little late, also, but

Frankie cut her lots of slack. Getting a child ready for school while getting ready for work was no easy feat, especially when part of that involved carefully boxing and loading specially made candy.

Two new customers were browsing the shelves, and Elinor was handing over the ornament she'd shown William, now nestled safely in a cute little red box inside a small Holiday Happiness shopping bag.

"It will look great on your tree," Elinor said to him.

"It will look great on someone's," he said as he took the bag from her.

"William, I think we're going to have to come up with some kind of loyalty rewards program just for you," Frankie said to him, and his cheeks turned russet.

"No need. I'm happy to be loyal. Anyway, your mother gives me plenty of business. By the way, I'm saving a copy of the new holiday rom-com by Melissa Ferguson for you, Natalie."

"How about my book?" asked Adele.

He nodded, and Frankie could have sworn that russet turned a little darker. "Got that, too."

"What book is that, Gram Gram?" Natalie asked as William hurried out the door.

"*Santa's Naughty List.* It got four hot peppers on the Red Hot Reads site."

"Sorry I asked," said Natalie.

"Romance is good at any age, and the young don't have a corner on love," Adele informed her. "Or hunks," she said as the bell over the door jingled and Brock walked in.

"Looking for something?" Adele called.

"More like someone," he replied, and came over.

Frankie made the introductions, then, hoping to prime the pump (but not meddling), said, "I bet I know why you're here." He'd obviously decided he wanted to get to know Stef better. Good.

"Yeah?"

"Yeah. Got your phone ready? I'll give you my sister's number."

He looked puzzled. "Your sister?"

"I thought maybe…"

He nodded, getting where the conversation was going. "Yeah, Stef's great. She's probably got a ton of men after her."

"She can always use a ton and one," Frankie quipped.

"She's nice, but I'm not really interested in her. I didn't feel a connection."

Hard to connect when someone stomped around the kitchen and then left early. Darn her silly sister anyway. But all right, so he and Stef hadn't clicked. There was still Elinor. Once Frankie got her polished up she was going to be a real gem.

"Actually, I stopped in to see if you'd like to get something to eat after work," he said.

"Me?" she squeaked.

"Well, yeah."

"Sure, she'd love to," said Natalie, who had better hearing than most dogs.

"You don't have plans for tonight," Adele informed Frankie.

Frankie scowled at both of them, then took Brock's arm and led him a little ways away. "Look, that's really sweet of you, but you don't need to pay me back for last night."

"This isn't payback. Just hoping to keep a good thing going."

A good thing going. What did that mean?

"Do you like Italian? I hear La Bella Vita has great food."

"Um, Brock. You may not be aware of this…" how could he not? "…but I'm a bit older than you." A big bit.

"Not that much," he said. "Anyway, what does age matter

if two people like hanging out together? There's an age difference between you and Mitch."

"True, but we're just friends. We've known each other for
years."

"So, let's go out to dinner as friends," Brock said.

He wasn't giving off casual-friend vibes. That smile, that tilt
of the head, they both said, *Casual is the starting gate, then we're
off to the races.* She was not about to go racing off with a man
ten years younger than her.

"You don't have any objection to being friends, do you?"
he added.

"Well, no."

"Great. How does seven work? I can pick you up," he offered.

No, no picking up. Then this would feel like a date, and it
was not going to be a date.

"I'll meet you there," she said firmly. *And we will have a serious
discussion where I make it clear to you that friendship is as far as we go.*

"Okay, see you there," he said, and sauntered back out the
door.

Frankie marched over to where her mother, her daughter
and Elinor were all standing. Elinor looked at the expression
on Frankie's face and seemed to realize she needed to go stock
some shelves on the store's upper level.

"What did you think you were doing?" Frankie demanded
of Natalie.

Natalie looked back at her, wide-eyed. "What?"

"You know what."

"I'm just getting in touch with my inner mom and interfering in your life. You do it to me all the time."

"Don't feel special, dear, she does that to everyone," joked
Adele.

"And you, Mom," Frankie said in disgust.

"There's nothing wrong with getting out and having some fun," Adele said.

"And you need to," Natalie continued gently. "It's time."

"I already have plenty of fun," Frankie insisted.

"Not the kind of fun she's talking about," said Adele. "If you need inspiration, I'll loan you my book when I'm done with it."

"Very funny," Frankie said, frowning at her. "The man's way too young."

"Age is just a number," Adele said with a flick of her hand. "And since you don't go for the hunks with the high numbers like Mitch, maybe someone younger will do it for you."

No one was going to do it for Frankie, no matter what his age. She couldn't, wouldn't fall in love again. The risk was too great.

Tonight at La Bella Vita, it would be anchovies and arrivederci.

5

DONE BEING A PIB, STEF TEXTED FRANKIE.

PIB was right. She had, indeed, been a pain in the butt.

Want to go to Carol's Place for happy hour sliders and peppermint martinis?

No way was Frankie telling Stef she was going out with Brock. That would be salt in the wounded pride. Can't. Catch you at Mom's tomorrow?

KK, came the reply.

Thank heaven Stef hadn't gotten nosy and asked what Frankie was doing. Frankie was surprised she hadn't, but never look a gift reindeer in the mouth.

This was probably only a short reprieve anyway—the topic

of Frankie's dinner with Brock was bound to come up. Adele loved living vicariously through her daughters. And romance novels.

"Pretend men are always better than the real deal," she often joked, but Frankie knew that her father had been her mother's hero. Just like Ike had been Frankie's.

"Ike would want you to find someone," Adele had told Frankie on more than one occasion. When she did, an image of Mitch would always spring to mind. Mitch was her buddy. Maybe, in another life, another time, he would have been her man. She'd occasionally caught herself checking out his biceps. Or his pecs. Or enjoying the deep rumble of his voice. That was simply friendly admiration, though, and she didn't indulge those moments for long.

"Dad would have wanted you to find someone, too," Frankie liked to shoot back, turning the spotlight off herself.

"At this age, it's too hard to train a husband," was her mother's typical response. "But you're still young."

Frankie was hardly young. Although, she supposed age was a relative thing. To Adele and her friends, Frankie was a mere baby, with lots of time left for love. But one experience of love dissolving into loss was enough for her.

She kept on her work pants and black sweater for her dinner out with Brock and left the perfume on her dresser. She hadn't worn it since Ike died. Other than brushing her teeth—because who wanted anyone to have bad breath—she did nothing to fix herself up. Not even any makeup refreshing or messing with her hair. To look like she'd tried would send the wrong message.

"You look great," he said when she walked into the restaurant.

Who was he kidding? "Thanks," she said.

He looked great, too. He wore jeans, and she could see a

clean shirt underneath his jacket. She caught a whiff of cologne as she got closer.

She wasn't about to tell him how good he looked. And smelled. It would only make him think she was interested. And she had no intention of becoming interested. Instead, she pointed to his shirt. "You're brave, wearing a white shirt to an Italian restaurant. Or else you're an amazingly fastidious eater."

"I'm no slob," he joked.

You sure aren't, she thought. He and Stef should have hit it off. Why hadn't they?

The host seated them at a table with the requisite red-and-white checked cloth and a candle in a red globe holder. The Italian standard "Volare" was playing softly in the background.

"Nice ambience, huh?" said Brock.

"Yes, it is," she agreed.

"I'm glad you're here," he said.

She wasn't. She should have told him no.

Their waiter appeared, saving her from having to respond. "May I start you out with something to drink?"

A little wine would make a difficult conversation easier. She ordered a glass of the house red. Brock changed it to a bottle.

"We're in no hurry, right?" he said.

"Well." It was all she could think to say.

He began to peruse the menu. "How about we start with an appetizer?"

She'd never get out of there. "I think I'm fine with pizza," she said.

"Well, then, pizza it is," he said.

The waiter appeared with their wine. Once it was poured, Frankie took a healthy slug of hers.

"Are you ready to order?" the man asked.

"Not yet," Brock said.

"Let's go ahead and order," Frankie said. The less time she

spent at this cozy table with Jack Reacher the Second, the better.

Brock looked surprised but said, "Okay. Pizza with everything on it?"

"Sure," she said.

"Works for me," he said, and gave the waiter their order. "If there's any food better than pizza, I don't know what it is," he added as the man left.

Frankie didn't want to waste time rhapsodizing about pizza. They needed to get right down to business. "This was nice of you," she began.

"You're easy to be nice to," he said.

"Thank you, but I don't think we should make a habit of this."

"Of what, eating?"

"You know what I mean," she said. "You're going to want to get out there and start dating."

"I thought this was a date," he said.

"No, this is...pizza. A friendly dinner sharing pizza," she added, reminding him of the whole friends thing.

He studied her. "It's okay to admit you're interested."

"I'm not interested."

"You could have fooled me. All that flirting."

She gaped at him. "Flirting?"

"'Lucky us.' Remember saying that? And inviting me over for dinner."

"I was just being friendly. Brock, I invited you for dinner because I really wanted you to meet my sister," Frankie explained. "Stef's actually a lot of fun. And she's closer to your age."

He studied Frankie again. "Have you got some kind of age hang-up?"

"It's not a hang-up. It's just practical. I'm not looking to get into a romantic relationship, especially with someone who's so much younger."

"I can't be that much younger," he protested.

"You're forty, right? I'm ten years older than you. I could have been your babysitter."

"I liked my babysitter."

Was he leering? Yes, he was! "Oh, stop that," she said irritably, and he laughed.

"Come on, now, seriously, at this point in life what does it matter if two people aren't exactly the same age?" he argued. "Admit it, Frankie. You're attracted to me."

"Any woman with a speck of estrogen left in her would be attracted to you." Oh, good grief. Where had that come from? She grabbed a bread stick from the bowl on the table and chomped on it, but it was too late to plug her mouth. The words were already out.

He grinned. "You know, older women with younger men is becoming a trend. Lots of movie stars are hooking up with younger men."

Hooking up. That produced an image that had her reaching for her wineglass and taking a big gulp.

"And lots of younger men end up splitting with their older woman when it dawns on the guy that he wants children." She set down her glass and leaned forward. "Brock, I've got a grown daughter. I'm done having kids."

"Okay," he said slowly.

"Now, someone like my sister..."

"Sorry, Frankie, not interested."

"Or Elinor," she tried.

He made a face. "Too quiet."

"But a good listener," Frankie argued. Brock liked to talk about himself—what man didn't?—which made a woman who wasn't a big talker a good fit for him.

"You seem to listen pretty good. And I think you want to be with me."

She'd have to have been dead not to find this man attractive. Their pizza arrived. He took a piece and set it on her plate.

"You're a great guy, there's no denying that," she said. "But I'm not interested, and even if I was, I don't see this turning into anything lasting. Like Mitch said the other night, there will come a time when you'll want kids."

His eyebrows pulled together. "There's more to a relationship than kids."

"You'll want them at some point," she insisted.

She still remembered what had happened to her friend Char. Char was beautiful, fit and fun. She'd gotten together with a younger man, and their relationship had been perfect...until he wanted children. She'd tried to hide the fact that she was going through menopause from him, but in the end, he discovered the truth. And he left.

"I really don't want kids," Brock insisted.

She shook her head. "You don't know that."

"Yes, I do. Frankie, I'm really into you. We could have a lot of fun together."

"Yeah? Tell me your favorite band."

"The Strokes."

"That's one of Stef's favorite bands."

"How about you? Do you like them?"

"No. I like the Backstreet Boys. Ever hear anything by them?"

"I've heard of them."

"See? We don't have anything in common."

"We like different bands, and that means we don't have anything in common?" he protested. "Oh, come on, Frankie. That's ridiculous, especially since only last night we were having a pretty good time playing cards."

Okay, that had been a bad example. She tried again. "People are at different stages at different times in their life, and when they're years apart the stages don't match up, especially as you get older. I'll be ready for retirement long before you will."

I'll be a hag while you still look like a stud. It was a thought she didn't particularly want to acknowledge, but there it was. And it was true. A woman got wrinkles, and people said she was old. A man got wrinkles, and people said he was distinguished. Men aged beautifully. Mitch was proof of that.

"Maybe I'll retire early," Brock said. "Frankie, you're a beautiful woman. And full of life. I want to spend time with you. I think we could be great together."

No, great had been her and Ike.

Brock leaned forward and ran his fingers along her arm, giving her the shivers.

No, no! No shivers with this man.

"Let's give this a chance," he said softly. "Go out with me again."

"Oh, I don't think so," she began.

"Look, I'm not saying you have to jump in bed with me. But let's hang out and see where this goes. You know, there are advantages to being with younger men. They last longer."

She knew what he was alluding to, but she couldn't help thinking in broader terms. If she were looking for someone to spend her life with, someone who would make it clear to life's finish line with her, gambling on a younger man would be the safest bet.

And did she want to spend the rest of her life sleeping in that queen bed with only memories, eating breakfast at her kitchen table by herself?

Oh good grief, what a pathetic picture she was painting. It wasn't as if she had no life. She hung out with her mom and her sister and daughter. And Mitch. She had a business to run.

And when was the last time she'd sat down at her kitchen table to eat? Breakfast was always an English muffin with peanut butter that she ate at the bathroom counter while putting on her makeup. She wasn't some sad, lonely thing.

"Give me some time to convince you," Brock urged. "Dinners out."

The pizza was good.

"West Coast swing at the White Owl. I hear they have a club that meets there."

"You dance?"

Now there was temptation. Frankie had watched many a post on TikTok with dancers showing off their sexy moves. The dance that had started in the forties had come a long way.

"I do. Used to dance with my ex. I could teach you some great moves."

She just bet he could. She could feel her resolution weakening.

"You deserve to be happy," he said.

"I am happy," she said. What did she look like, some lonely loser?

"Okay, happier?"

She frowned. "I should get home. I have paperwork I have to catch up on." What that paperwork was she wasn't sure, but she'd think of something. And she'd definitely think of a reason to say no next time Brock suggested getting together. This wouldn't work. She didn't care if he could dance.

"Okay," he said, and called for the check. "But I'm not giving up."

Temperatures had dropped while they were in the restaurant, and once outside Frankie saw the light snow that had fallen earlier had turned into a crust of frozen lace that crackled when they walked on it. She slipped a little, and Brock took her arm. Then, someone new appeared, taking her other arm. Where had he come from?

"Mitch, what are you doing here?" she asked.

"Yeah, what are you doing here?" Brock demanded. "You said you had plans."

"Met someone in the bar for a drink," Mitch said, tugging Frankie a little closer to him.

Brock tugged back, making her feet slide.

"Hey, you two, this isn't tug-of-war," she protested.

"Sorry," Brock muttered. Then, to Mitch, "I've got her."

"You sure?" said Mitch.

"Yeah, we're good."

Mitch let go, and Brock escorted Frankie to her car, which wasn't parked far away. In fact, from where he was leaning in the restaurant's doorway, Mitch had a very good view of the two of them.

"I had a great time," Brock said. "I think you did, too, whether you want to admit it or not."

"Thank you," she said. "I enjoyed the pizza." The conversation, not so much. It had left her feeling unsettled.

"Give me a chance to show you some more good times." He caught both her arms and gave her a gentle pull toward him.

This was how the ocean felt when the moon called to it. Powerful as the sea was, the moon was stronger. Primal urges drowned common sense. Maybe she should give him a chance. Give herself a chance.

Brock almost had her lips.

She could feel Mitch's gaze as if he was standing right there between them. She glanced his direction. Yep, there he still stood, leaning against the building, one ankle crossed over the other, his hands shoved in the pockets of his peacoat, an eyebrow cocked as if to say, *What are you doing?*

She recentered herself and turned her head so that all Brock caught was her cheek, then smiled up at him. "Thanks again for dinner," she said, and slipped into her car.

She drove home, thinking of celebrity matches where the woman had been older, ignoring the success stories and dwelling on the ones that hadn't worked out. Demi Moore and Ashton Kutcher came to mind. So did Hugh Jackman and Deborra-Lee Furness. Infidelity, infertility, losing the zing— all were causes cited in media speculation. Zings could, of course, be lost at any age, any time, but why stack the odds against you?

She drove cautiously, slowly...like an old woman. No, like a woman who didn't want to skid into anything.

She passed Adele's house on the corner of her street. The Christmas lights winked at Frankie from the roof, and through the living room window, she could see images flickering on her mother's TV. Adele was probably watching *Elf*, her holiday favorite. If Frankie had been smart, she'd have turned down Brock's invitation and joined her mother.

The rest of the houses on her street all greeted her with glowing multicolored lights, inflatable snowmen and Santas waving at her from their yards as she drove past. Then came her house, with the wreath on her red front door and the icicle lights Mitch had strung for her dripping along the roofline. She smiled at the sight. She loved her house. She loved her life. She didn't need to be shaking it up with a man she'd never become serious over.

But dancing at the White Owl?

Bad idea, Frankie. He can't replace Ike.

Once inside, she turned on her electric teakettle and pulled out hot cocoa mix along with her bottle of peppermint schnapps. She and Ike had loved to drink jazzed-up cocoa on a cold winter's night.

The memory of them curled up, side by side on the couch,

drinking and listening to Christmas music made her sigh with yearning as she dumped the packet of cocoa mix in her mug.

She had just finished making her drink when the doorbell rang. She opened the door to find Mitch the guard dog standing on the porch.

Honestly, she wouldn't stalk him if he was out with someone. At the rate he was going, he was getting a dog collar for Christmas.

"This is a surprise," she said.

"I wanted to make sure you got home safe. You gonna invite me in?"

"I guess I am," she said, and moved aside to let him in.

He stepped inside, smelling like fresh air.

"I'm having hot chocolate. Want some?"

"Has it got schnapps in it?"

"Of course."

"Then I want some." He took off his coat, dropped it over the nearest chair, then followed her into the kitchen.

"I suppose it was just a coincidence that you happened to be at La Bella Vita tonight," she said.

"Like I said, I was meeting someone for a drink."

"Who?"

"Just someone."

He watched while she worked. "So, did you have a good time?" he asked casually.

"I did." She handed him a mug.

He nodded, took a sip of his drink. "What do you think of Brock?"

"I think he's nice."

"Kind of young for you, isn't he?"

Never mind the fact that she'd been thinking the same thing. Had said it to Brock. Hearing Mitch say it made her frown. "What's that supposed to mean?"

"Nothing, just that he's too young."

"Or more like I'm too old?"

Mitch mirrored her frown. "I didn't say that. I just meant that you should be with someone…" He faltered.

"Someone what?"

"More like you. Someone older."

"Older? As in I'm…old?"

He frowned. "Don't go putting words in my mouth."

"What would be the point? There's hardly any room with your foot already in there."

"Hey, I just meant you need someone more mature."

"I don't need anyone," she snapped. "And I don't need you telling me what I need."

He set down his mug. "Obviously, I hit a nerve."

"No woman likes to be reminded that she's getting old. We have mirrors for that," Frankie said shortly.

"Hey, you're beautiful. And you'll always be beautiful, no matter what your age."

Okay, that was better.

"All I was saying was that he'd be a better fit with Stef. Isn't that who you had in mind for him?"

"I did. He's not into her," Frankie said. "But he is into me." *So there.* She agreed with Mitch, so why was she being so perverse? Because he had just double-dog dared her to prove that she wasn't over the hill, that was why. She'd show him.

What she'd show him she wasn't sure.

He frowned. "I don't want to see you hurt. Brock's a nice guy, but he's just a big kid. He won't stick."

Now he was insinuating she couldn't hold a younger man's attention. "Thank you for your advice, oh wise one." She pointed to his mug. "Are you done with that?"

He frowned at its contents. It was still half full. "I guess I am?"

"I guess you are."

He heaved a sigh, got up and trudged to the front door. She followed him and handed him his coat.

"Well, good night," he said.

"Good night," she said, and opened the door.

He walked out, frowning, and she shut it after him. Firmly.

6

STEF REFUSED TO SIT HOME ON A SATURDAY NIGHT. SHE'D
rounded up a couple of friends and gone to Carol's Place for
those sliders and peppermint martinis. They'd stuck around
for part of Christmas karaoke and made fools of themselves,
singing Mariah Carey's "All I Want for Christmas Is You."
Two tipsy men took the song to heart and offered to buy the
women drinks, then wound up at their table. They were loud
and obnoxious boors. In fact, one of the boors Stef knew on
sight. He worked in the frozen food department at the grocery store.

"You're the hottie from the store," he'd declared. "You can
melt my frozen corn dogs anytime."

This was what came of putting yourself out there on a karaoke stage. The jests had gotten stupider and cruder, and she'd

remembered she had work to do at home. Those bozos confirmed it; every man in Carol was a loser.

So, now here she was, parked on her couch with a latte, a pile of handwritten letters and her laptop, pulling together the next edition of the *Carol Clarion*'s Letters to Santa page.

She loved doing this page, although it did make her a little wistful. She'd envisioned herself helping a child or two of her own write a letter to Santa by this point in her life.

Richard had stalled and stalled. She'd finally convinced him they needed to get moving. They didn't move far. She'd miscarried. Sometimes she told herself it was for the best. With her twenty-twenty hindsight, she could see Richard would have made an awful father.

But she would have made a good mother, she was sure of it. She was a good aunt, after all. A great aunt, no pun intended. Natalie's son, Warner, adored her. Or course, Warner adored anyone who would build LEGO creations with him.

She had a job she loved and a great family. Maybe it was time to forget the man quotient and start her family by adopting. There were plenty of kids in the world who needed a good parent.

Meanwhile, back to work.

She giggled as she went through the latest batch of letters. A couple of them were silly and obviously sent in by children who had passed the age of believing but weren't too old to enjoy a prank. *Yo, man, I want my two front teeth*, wrote one. *I been waiting for years. When are they coming?*

Snort. Some smart-ass's grandparent had inspired this letter with that old song. Front-tooth dude's letter probably wouldn't make the cut. For sure the letter that begged Santa to run over Grandma wouldn't. Tacky. Besides, there were too many earnest little kids out there, hoping to see their letter on the Santa page.

Pleez bring me a pink instant camera so I can take pictures on Christmas Day, wrote a little girl named Claire.

I want a Legos Avenger Tower!!!!! wrote another child. With all those exclamation points, Stef hoped little Tommy got it.

I want a bow and arrow, wrote another little boy. *I promise not to shoot my sister with it.*

Please bring me drums, begged ten-year-old Jordy. *I asked for my birthday, and Mom and Dad said no.* Poor Jordy. Stef suspected Santa wouldn't be able to come through on this request, either.

Dear Jordy, she typed, Santa loves to bring presents to children, but I will have to check with your mom and dad before bringing you drums. They know best. There. Put it right back on Mom and Dad so Santa didn't take the heat.

She had room to answer one more letter for Monday's page. What would be a good letter to end with? She thumbed through the stack, casually reading. Most of the kids wanted toys.

But then she came to a letter that broke her heart.

Der Santa, I wrot last year abot bringing me a new mommy but daddy furgot to mal it. Aunt Jenn is going to for me. Can you bring me a mommy for Christmas? Thank you.
Sincerly,
Corcoran Marks
P.S. I am in second grad. I am geting better at spelling.

She put a hand to her heart. How sad and sweet was this? Of course Corcoran would get to see his letter in the paper.

Dear Corcoran, she began.

And stopped. She tapped a Christmas red nail against her teeth, thinking. What on earth did you say to a child who wanted a mommy? Where was Mommy? Had she run away? Was she dead?

Stef suddenly thought of the old movie *Sleepless in Seattle*. It was one of Adele's favorites, and it had become one of Stef's, too. The little boy in that had wanted a mommy, and in the end, he found one as Daddy met his future love at the top of the Empire State Building. Stef loved the scene where they all walked happily back to the elevator to go down to a new and wonderful life.

Sigh.

But that was the movies. She frowned. What to do with this letter? It was certainly beyond Santa's powers to bring the child what he wanted. Corcoran's daddy needed to have a long, comforting talk with his son.

This was another case of taking Santa off the holiday hook. She began to type, her fingers flying over the keyboard faster than the old guy's sleigh.

Dear Corcoran, Santa would love to help you, but there is no room in my sleigh for a mommy. Why don't you ask Daddy to find you a mommy? I'm sure he'd like to help Santa out.

She reread her answer. Yes, that was the best possible reply. Maybe Corcoran's dad would read it and…take a trip to the Empire State Building. Or whatever. Her job was to respond in a way that let children know they'd been heard.

But she hoped someway, somehow, little Corcoran got what he wanted for Christmas.

Frankie's cocoa was long gone, and the Christmas movie she'd streamed but paid no attention to was over. And she was still as grumpy as she'd been when she started it.

What on earth was wrong with her? She didn't really want to date Brock, and yet now she was determined to. She didn't want to squabble with Mitch, and yet she had.

She didn't want to be alone, and yet she was.

What she really wanted was to turn back the clock to the days when her life was as close to perfect as a life could get, and she'd thought she had all the time in the world to enjoy it with a wonderful man.

She closed her eyes and envisioned Ike and herself in the living room, slow dancing to Boyz II Men, him singing "I'll Make Love to You." They had just bought the house and were so happy, their future laid out like the yellow brick road.

But then the flying monkeys had come.

Frankie grabbed a sofa pillow and hugged it, sobbing for what she couldn't have. Sometimes loneliness blew in like a biting cold wind, and no matter what fires you built from memory, they weren't enough to keep it away.

"All you have is today," she reminded herself with a sniff as she went in search of tissue. Wasn't that what Adele always said?

So Frankie's today wasn't the romantic, picture-perfect story that yesterday had been. It was still good. And really, yesterday hadn't always been perfect. Grief had encouraged her to paint it that way.

Like all couples, she and Ike had had their share of arguments over the years. He sure hadn't been supportive when she'd shared her dream of opening the shop, had predicted it would be a bad investment. He'd eventually come around, but not before a couple of big-time shouting matches.

He had been glad to be proved wrong, though, and she was glad he'd lived to see her succeed. She was also thankful he'd been around to walk his daughter down the aisle and meet his first grandchild. But sometimes she couldn't help it; she resented the fact that he'd been snatched from her so suddenly.

She wanted him back. She wanted *them* back. They'd never celebrate a fiftieth wedding anniversary, never take a fancy river cruise like they'd talked about, never sit together in the bleachers at their grandson's baseball games—all those experiences that she'd taken for granted would be there for them in the future had been aborted.

She found a tissue and blew her nose. Dried her tears. That was enough self-pity for one night. Time for bed.

Before turning out the living room lights, she gave her street one last admiring look. There was something so comforting, so all-is-right-with-the-world about the sight of snow-topped houses with colored lights. She could see TVs still glowing behind a couple of living room windows—neighbors finishing up holiday movies. The Martinsons down the street had several cars parked along their curb, a sure sign that they were entertaining their pickleball friends. Mrs. Fortunata's lights were out. At ninety-six, she was an early-to-bed kind of girl.

Adele's lights were still on, and an SUV was parked along her curb, almost in front of the house. Drop-in company? That was hardly surprising. Adele had plenty of friends and was happy.

She'd experienced her share of hard times, though. She'd struggled to cope with widowhood and finish raising her two daughters, impulsively picking a spot on the map and moving them to the town of Carol after Dad died from prostate cancer. With Stef coming along so late, he never lived to see most of the important moments in her life—first date, prom, wedding. Divorce. (Probably a good thing he'd missed that. Richard may have come to bodily harm.)

Adele had struggled but eventually pulled herself out of the deep well of grief and done her best to give Stef, if not a perfect childhood, at least a happy finish in her teen years.

She'd jumped into small-town life with a vengeance, finding a church that she attended when it suited her, taking up line dancing at the grange hall, starting a bunco group.

She loved working at the store, baking cookies for regular deliveries to the town's nursing home (and usually drafting Frankie's help) and hosting regular coffee klatches with the neighbors. Then there was the weekly family Sunday dinner gathering after the store closed. Adele always had something in the Crock-Pot, ready and waiting. Over the years, she had pulled busyness around her like Superman's cape, making it her superpower.

Frankie once asked Adele if she didn't have times when she still missed Dad. "Of course I do," she'd replied. "You never stop missing the love of your life. But I can't be like Lot's wife, just standing in place, looking back. There's no rewind in life, Frankie. All we have is forward."

Mom was right. All Frankie had was forward, so forward she would go. And maybe she would go forward enjoying some fun with a sexy younger man.

But she knew she'd never be able to totally commit. She never again wanted to experience the kind of grief she'd felt when Ike died.

Meanwhile, she had enough to keep her busy—Christmas festivities to plan and a shop to run, a daughter and grandchild to enjoy, friends to help.

And a busy day ahead of her.

She took a warm bath to relax herself, then climbed in between the sheets, where she slept well until around midnight, waking up for no good reason.

She wandered down to the kitchen for some warm milk. She needed to get going and bake some cookies soon. Milk without cookies was naked.

Milk heated, she wandered back into the living room to turn on her tree lights. Might as well enjoy them as much as she could. No TVs were glowing behind living room windows now, and the neighbors had all turned off their Christmas lights.

Except for one. Frankie pressed her face against the glass, trying to get a better look at her mother's house. What were Adele's Christmas lights doing on at this hour? Her friends were usually done partying by ten, eleven at the latest. A light was on in the living room, but the drapes were drawn. And whose SUV was that still parked at the curb? Most of Adele's friends drove smaller cars.

Frankie found her phone and called her mother.

"What's wrong?" Adele answered. "Are you okay?"

"Yes, I'm fine."

"Then why on earth are you calling me in the middle of the night?"

"I got up and saw your lights were on." That sounded… snoopy. "I just wanted to make sure you were all right."

"I'm fine, daughter dear."

"You still have company?"

"Yes, I do. It's a myth that all seniors go to bed with the birds."

Frankie had to chuckle. Adele always had a smart remark ready to dish out. "Okay, I get the message. Have fun."

"And go back to bed, or you'll never make it up in time for early service. At your age, you need your rest."

There was no point trying to come back with a clever quip. Adele would always have the last word. Maybe by the time Frankie reached her mother's age, she, too, would be partying at midnight.

But who the heck was Adele partying with?

"Your mom is a party animal," Viola joked when Frankie saw her at church the next morning. "How did things go with Brock?"

Frankie stared at the coffee in her disposable cup. "The

pizza was good." Beyond that, it was hard to put into words how the evening had gone.

"He seems nice."

"He is. But, really, the age gap. Mitch as much as said I wouldn't be able to hold him."

"He did? The stinker! And listen, girlfriend, you got what it takes to hold any man you want."

"I have half a mind to give him a chance," Frankie said. Of course, the other half was solidly against it.

Viola studied her. "Because you're into him or because you've got something to prove to Mitch?"

"I don't have anything to prove to Mitch," Frankie insisted.

"You know he's bound to be jealous."

"That's ridiculous. There's no need. Me seeing Brock wouldn't affect our friendship."

"Yes, it would. You start seriously dating Brock, and things will change between you and Mitch, mark my words."

Frankie didn't want things to change between her and Mitch. She liked what they had and valued his friendship. "Nothing's going to change between us, no matter what," she vowed.

"Okay," said Viola, but she didn't sound convinced.

Adele waltzed into the shop her usual ten minutes after their Sunday 11:00 a.m. opening time.

"Thought I'd see you at church this morning. Did you still have company?" Frankie teased.

Adele didn't take the bait. "I just took my time over break-fast." She pulled her apron out from under the counter and started tying it on. "How was your date last night?"

Frankie would much rather have talked about her mom's social life. "It was okay," she said, and started fiddling with the little display of Natalie's candies near the cash register. She wished she had something to unpack, but Elinor was already on it upstairs, unloading the last of the ornaments they'd gotten in. Maybe a customer would show up.

No customer entered, and Adele was far from finishing this conversation. "Just okay? He seems like a nice man."

"He is. But there's such an age gap. I don't know."

"So what? He's not that young, and you're not that old. Get out and have some fun."

Fun was one thing, but letting her emotions get all tangled up was another. "Speaking of fun, I'm going over to The Coffee Stop. Want a latte?" Frankie asked, putting an end to the conversation.

"Sure. Make sure they give me a double shot of caramel," said Adele, accepting defeat.

"Will do," Frankie promised, and made her escape.

When she returned, Adele was helping a customer, which meant Frankie was safe from motherly lectures. Elinor returned from upstairs a minute later, and Adele thankfully turned the spotlight on her as their shopper left the store with a bag full of goodies.

"Did you do anything fun last night, Elinor?" Adele asked.

"I started that book you loaned me," Elinor replied. "It's really good. I loved the scene where Jock first sees Amanda in the sexy red dress."

Adele nodded. "So true to life. Men often have to see us in a new light—or a new dress—before they really see us."

"I loved the makeover scene," Elinor said, nodding.

A hot dress and some equally hot lipstick, and Elinor would become a whole new woman. "My offer of a shopping spree still stands," said Frankie. "Have you ever had a makeover?"

Elinor's cheeks turned pink, and she shook her head. "I really appreciate the offer, but I don't think I'm the makeover type."

"Everyone's the makeover type," Frankie assured her. "Come

on. What do you say? I bet you'd look awfully cute in something Christmassy."

"Oh, I don't know," Elinor began.

"Look. The store's closed tomorrow. I think an employee bonus is in order. Come on. How about we go shopping?"

"An excellent idea," Adele approved. "Getting a new look can be such a confidence builder."

At that moment, Mitch entered the store on the heels of a new shopper. He was carrying a cardboard tray with lattes in it, a man bearing a peace offering.

He took one look at the cups in Frankie's and Adele's hands and said, "Looks like I'm too late. Except, Elinor, you still need a peppermint latte, right?"

Elinor blushed and beamed and took one from the tray he was holding out to her. "Thank you. That's so sweet."

"I can be sweet," he said, winking at her. Then he looked at Frankie.

"When you're asleep," she said.

He followed Frankie as she moved away to see if she could help the newcomer find anything.

"Just looking," said the woman.

As the customer moved farther down the artificial Christmas tree aisle, Mitch lowered his voice. "You done being pissed at me?"

"I don't know."

"Think you'll be done in time for *Cop Stop*, or do I need to watch it by myself?"

"That depends. You gonna take back what you said?"

"I said a lot."

"Yeah, you did."

He looked heavenward, probably searching for help from whomever the patron saint of men with foot-in-mouth disease was. "I'm sorry I pissed you off. Come over tonight and watch *Cop Stop*. I'll make Parmesan popcorn."

Parmesan popcorn was his specialty, and it was hard to resist. It was also hard to stay mad at Mitch. He hadn't meant to offend her.

"All right. I'll be over after I'm done at Mom's. As long as you promise not to interfere in my life."

He half chuckled. "Said the woman who only recently was interfering in mine."

She frowned at him.

"Okay, okay. Not gonna say another word."

"Good."

"See you later."

He turned to leave.

"Where are you going with that coffee?" she teased.

"What was I thinking? I'll leave it with Adele."

She trailed him back to where Adele and Elinor stood, filling in a moment of downtime by assembling more of the shop's gift boxes.

"See you later, ladies," he said.

"Thanks again for the drink," Elinor said.

"Anytime," he replied.

Elinor sighed as he went out the door. "He's such a nice man."

"Yes, he is," agreed Frankie. Even though she'd decided it was just as well she'd failed in her matchmaking, it did seem a shame that she had. Men like Mitch were few and far between.

"Do you think Mitch would ever be open to…someone?" asked Elinor.

"I think Mitch already is open to someone," said Adele. "He's not bringing over lattes for me, that's for sure."

Elinor looked toward the door. "Frankie, is the offer of a makeover still good?"

"Sure," said Frankie. If they got Elinor all fixed up like a sexy holiday present, who knew what man might decide to take her home?

"Giving Elinor a makeover is a great idea," Natalie said approvingly. The women cleaned up the last of the family's Sunday supper while Warner and his daddy played with the LEGOs Gram Gram kept on hand for him. "She's not bad-looking."

"A better wardrobe and some makeup, and she'll be great," Frankie predicted.

Adele started the dishwasher. "You ready to make those snacks with Warner now?" she asked Frankie.

"Yep." Frankie moved to the counter where she'd set the bag with the goodies she'd brought over. "Warner, it's time to make treats," she called.

The little boy came racing over, carrying something that resembled an airplane, his father following behind. "Look what I made, Nana," he cried, holding it up for Frankie to inspect.

"Did you make that all by yourself?" she asked, bending over to examine it.

"He sure did," said Jonathan as he moved to the counter to get more coffee.

"The boy's going to grow up to design rockets," Adele predicted.

"Or maybe he'll grow up to be a baker," said Frankie. "You ready to help me?"

Warner nodded eagerly.

"Okay, then, off to the bathroom to wash your hands," said Natalie, herding him out of the room.

"You never did say. How are things going at work?" Frankie asked Jonathan. "Any better?"

He kept his back turned to them. "They're still laying off. I hope I'll be okay."

"I hope so, too," said Frankie. Even if Natalie came to work at the shop full-time, it wouldn't be enough for them to live on. "You know what they say, a good salesman is worth his weight in gold, and you're the company's top salesman."

"Life's always full of challenges," said Adele.

"At least you have each other, and that's nothing to take for granted," said Frankie.

Jonathan nodded but said nothing.

Stef filled in the silence. "I had an interesting letter for Santa. A little boy wrote in, asking Santa to bring him a mommy for Christmas."

"What happened to his mom?" Jonathan asked.

Stef shrugged. "Don't know for sure, but I suspect she's dead."

"What did Santa say to him?" Frankie asked.

"That Santa can't fit mommies in his sleigh. I think Daddy needs to have a talk with his kid."

"You've got to give the boy credit for working every angle," said Adele. "Children are good at trying different ways of getting what they want."

"Poor little guy. I hope he gets what he wants," said Stef. "At least I've let Santa off the hook."

"Maybe you should have told the boy to come see Santa at the Santa Walk and bring his daddy and they could talk," suggested Frankie. Stef would be there, interviewing people and taking pictures for the paper. Who knew? Maybe she and Daddy would hit it off, just like in a Hallmark movie.

"I wouldn't want to put Mitch on the spot. After seeing Santa, the little boy would be convinced he'd be getting one, and I wouldn't want to disillusion him," Stef said. "Kids have to grow up too fast as it is."

Frankie knew she was talking about her own life; when she was five, Stef's daddy had disappeared from her life forever. She, too, had written to Santa, asking him to bring back her daddy. Adele had read the letter and sat Stef down at the kitchen table that very afternoon after school, explaining again about Daddy being in heaven with the angels. Frankie had pretended to be absorbed in her twentieth-century history book, but she'd felt herself tensing and listening.

"I don't want him to be in heaven," Stef had protested.

Adele had pulled her onto her lap and with tears in her own eyes said, "I don't, either, but that's where he is." She'd kissed the top of Stef's head, then set her back on her chair, given her a cookie and fled the kitchen, off to her bedroom to cry.

"Daddy can visit you in your dreams," Frankie had improvised.

Stef had looked at her with such hope. "He can?"

"Of course," she'd said.

Stef had nodded, her tears drying.

The next morning, she'd announced to Frankie that Daddy had visited her and said he loved her. Who knew whether she'd really dreamed about their father or imagined she had? Either way, it had helped. Their father visited Stef again in her dreams, a week later, the night Adele had called the real estate agent about putting their house up for sale.

The house had sold in January, and they'd moved in February, and it had felt like their father wasn't the only one whose life was over. Frankie had balked, and Stef had cried, but in the end, they'd found a new house in Carol, the one Adele still lived in, and life eventually turned onto a pleasant path. Paths never ran straight, though, and they never stayed smooth.

But you had to be grateful for the smooth parts.

Natalie returned Warner to the kitchen, all scrubbed up and ready to create treats. Frankie got her grandson busy taking the wrapping off Hershey's peppermint Kisses and balancing them on top of mini-pretzels.

As they worked, she kept thinking about the little boy who'd written the letter, and his father. If the man was on his own, maybe finding the right woman was exactly what he needed for Christmas. A man who came complete with a little boy— how perfect would that be for Stef?

So much better than Brock.

The treats were put in a warm oven for a couple of minutes, just long enough for the Kisses to soften. Frankie removed the cookie sheet, and with Warner standing next to her on a stool, she demonstrated how to gently press a Christmas-colored M&M into a melted kiss to spread out the chocolate. It took Warner a few tries to find his finesse, but he did.

"Now we'll put them in the fridge to harden, and soon you'll have treats to take home," Frankie promised as he hopped off the stool.

"Yay!" whooped Warner. He pointed to where the rest of the M&Ms sat. "Can I have some candy, Nana?"

"Of course." Frankie picked up the bag. "Hold out your hands."

The little boy held out two cupped hands and squealed in delight as Frankie emptied a small pile of candies into them. "These aren't as good as what your mommy makes, but they run a close second," she said.

"All that sugar—now we'll never get him to sleep," said Natalie as Warner stuffed the candies in his mouth. But she was smiling.

"'Tis the season," said Frankie.

She smiled down at the little angel with the same green eyes as her daughter's and those darling honey-colored curls. Here she was, surrounded by the people she loved. This was what a perfect day looked like. And days like this were what made life worth living—maybe it wasn't the perfect life she'd once envisioned, but it was darned close.

Yes, it was a good life, she thought later as she settled with a big bowl of popcorn into the corner of Mitch's leather couch that she had long ago claimed as hers.

"Glad you're not mad at me anymore," he said as the show started.

"I don't hold a grudge."

"Good. Anyway, you know I'm right."

Her brows pulled down, and she lowered her handful of popcorn back into her bowl. "Right."

"You ought to get busy and match Brock up with somebody."

"Somebody...younger?"

Mitch was too busy watching the car chase on the TV screen to see her frown. "Maybe Elinor. She's sweet. And isn't she about his age?"

There it was again, that insinuation that Frankie wasn't the right age, that she was past her prime. A fifty-year-old woman was not past her prime.

"What are you all of a sudden, Match.com?" she demanded.

He looked at her in surprise. "Just sayin'."

"You sure have a lot to say lately," she said. She stuffed the popcorn in her mouth and ground her teeth on it. Maybe Brock would like to try the peppermint martinis at Carol's Place.

7

IN ADDITION TO POLISHING UP HER INTERVIEW WITH A local writer who had her first book coming out that week, Stef had more letters for Santa waiting to be sifted through when she went in to work Monday morning. She smiled as she looked at the ones already up on the paper's website. She was happy to see that the page was getting plenty of positive comments from readers. Good for the paper. And for her.

Thanks for the heads-up, Santa...

I hope Jordy gets his drums...

Maybe Santa will bring earplugs for Jordy's parents...

Tell Corcoran I could fit in Santa's sleigh.

Stef read the last comment and frowned. Some women were such predators. The comment was horribly inappropriate and was going to get deleted that very minute. Whatever was happening with the boy's family was serious. Hopefully, both Corcoran and his father would find better things waiting for them in the new year.

She sighed. Life could be so hard when things didn't work out for people. She'd sure found that out. Everyone needed love, and it sucked when those who should have loved you the most treated you the worst.

Griffin Marks had just finished putting in an order for twenty-five more shares of stock that one of his Edward Jones clients wanted to buy when his phone dinged with a text. You are gonna be busy now.

What the heck?

He called his pal Joel, who'd sent the text. "What's this about?"

"You haven't seen the Letters to Santa page on the *Carol Clarion* website?"

"I haven't had a chance to see if yours got printed yet," Griff said.

"Funny. You probably won't be laughing when you read one of them. Mandy just called me and wondered if you'd helped Corky write a letter to Santa."

Corky. Letter to Santa. A premonition that he was about to hear something he didn't want to hear settled in Griff's gut like a giant lump of coal.

"You'd better read it," suggested Joel.

Griff left business behind and went to the paper's website. He pulled up the Letters to Santa page and scanned them, skimming down the page until he saw his son's name. The words jumped out at him.

Can you bring me a mommy for Christmas?

Shit. How had this happened?

He didn't have to read far to figure it out. "Jenn," he muttered in disgust. His meddling, misguided sister was at it again.

"Every single woman within a twenty-five-mile radius of Carol is going to be contacting the paper, wanting to apply for the job of mommy," Joel predicted.

"Don't be a turkey," snapped Griff.

"You think I'm kidding? Do you know how many generations of women have watched *Sleepless in Seattle*? You've just become the new Tom Hanks."

Griff scrubbed his face. The last thing he needed was word of this getting out and women showing up on his doorstep with plates of Christmas cookies. That had happened the first Christmas after Kaitlyn died, and he'd felt like a hunted animal. He had no desire to start that circus again.

And he couldn't have Corky see the page. If his son saw his request there on the paper's website followed by Santa's reply, his hopes would rise quicker than a helium balloon.

"Nobody's gonna replace Kaitlyn, dude. I get that. But maybe Jenn's right."

Griff cut him off. "Don't even say it."

"Okay, okay. Don't shoot the messenger."

He wasn't going to shoot the messenger, but he was going to take aim at the paper. Why don't you ask Daddy to find you a mommy? I'm sure he'd like to help Santa out. Of all the idiotic, ill-considered, thoughtless, stupid replies. There was nothing Griff would have liked better than to hang this Santa from a chimney in nothing but his long underwear and let him freeze.

He said a grumpy goodbye to Joel, then searched the page to find the name of the culprit. There it was: Santa's letters delivered by Stefanie Ludlow. If Corky's letter didn't come down as of yesterday, Stefanie Ludlow would be delivering the paper instead of writing for it.

He found the newspaper's number and punched it into his phone. "Put me through to your editor," he snapped at the operator taking calls. "And don't send me to voicemail. This is urgent."

"Of course," she said, and left him to listen to some tinny Christmas music.

Urgent or not, he wound up getting sent to Camille Carlisle's voicemail. He ground his teeth as he waited for the beep. Then he left his message. "My son's letter to Santa got put on your paper's page without my permission, and the answer to it is completely inappropriate and unappreciated. If you don't take down the letter from Corcoran immediately, you will be hearing from my lawyer today."

He stabbed End on his phone and banged it down on his desk. He didn't have a lawyer, but if somebody didn't get back to him within the hour, he'd find one.

He sat for a moment and fumed, then snatched the phone back up and called his sister. She, too, was hiding behind her voicemail.

"Jenn, what the devil were you thinking letting Corky sucker you into helping him with that letter? The paper will be taking it down, and I'd better not see it pop up again or you're gonna lose your aunt rights."

He stabbed End again and half strangled his phone before slamming it back on the desk. Great. Now he'd cracked it. He swore and glared at his computer screen.

And reread his son's letter and wanted to cry.

I wrot last year abot bringing me a new mommy but daddy fur-got to mal it.

Daddy didn't furgot. Daddy lied about furgotting. It had been easier than trying to explain to his son that the aches piercing his heart had left him emotionally crippled. Corky hadn't been that old when his mom died, but he remembered enough to know he missed her hugs, missed her tucking him in at night. He wanted a mommy like the other kids had, and even though Jenn did a lot to help out, it wasn't the same. As a real estate agent, she was busy, and her hours were all over the map. She couldn't be around all the time. And she shouldn't have to.

"Somebody's got to help fill the gap," she often reminded Griffin when he told her she needed to pay more attention to her own life.

Their parents lived a couple of towns away, so Jenn had been stepping in a lot since Kaitlyn died. Maybe she was tired of wrapping so much of her life around his. She never said, but he was pretty sure it was why things hadn't worked out with her last man. Now she was starting to see someone new. He shouldn't have to stand in line for Jenn's attention behind Griff and Corky, although Griff suspected he already was. She did so much for them. Griff turned down the heat on his anger with his sister.

They were still going to have to have a talk though. Maybe they would even revert back to their childhood and there would be some yelling involved.

His phone rang, showing the number of the *Carol Clarion*. He answered with a curt, "Hello."

"Mr. Marks, this is Camille Carlisle, returning your call. I do apologize for this mix-up. We will, of course, take down your son's letter to Santa immediately."

"Good," he said, and could almost hear his mother scolding, *Not your sweetest voice, dear.* Well, he didn't feel all that sweet.

"I want you to know that the page does state clearly that, by allowing their children to write to Santa care of the *Clarion*, parents are giving the paper permission to print those letters."

Covering her butt. Had she talked to their legal team? "Well, *I* didn't allow it, and it was sent in without my permission," he snapped. Now he was really sounding like a jerk, but he didn't care. "And I didn't appreciate Santa's answer, either. 'Why don't you ask Daddy to find you a mommy? I'm sure he'd like to help Santa out.' Where does your Santa get off dishing out advice?"

"Again, I'm very sorry. It will be taken down immediately," she said. "Is there anything else I can do for you?" Unlike his, her voice was calm and rational.

"No. Thank you."

"All right then. Have a good day," she said, and was gone.

He hadn't had a good day since Kaitlyn died. He rubbed his forehead in an effort to stop the dull throb that was starting. He'd have to have a talk with Corky and explain that mommies weren't that easy to replace. In fact, ones like Kaitlyn were impossible to replace. *She* was impossible to replace. Corky was going to have to learn to be content with his dad and his aunt.

And Griff was going to have to continue working on getting up every morning and setting aside the bitterness that kept him company all through the night, keeping him tossing and turning.

The first year after she died, visions of his wife had lurked around every corner of the house. He'd see her when he first awoke, lying next to him, her hair spread out on her pillow like thick threads of gold. She greeted him when he walked into the kitchen to get cereal for Corky. It felt so real, envisioning her leaning on the counter in that big, ugly T-shirt she loved to sleep in, holding out a mug of coffee and smiling at him. He'd catch sight of her sitting in one corner of the couch, keeping him company as he watched a football game, cheering at all the right moments because she was determined to be a Seahawks fan like him.

He managed to get through the new morning ritual with just him making coffee and pouring cereal into a bowl for Corky. And Corky always cuddled up next to him on the couch when he was watching a game. He'd explain the plays to his son, they'd eat chips and he'd try not to squeeze too tightly when he tucked his kid in bed although he wanted to.

But he'd learned the hard way that when Hades came to take someone, it didn't matter how tightly you held them. They'd be gone anyway.

He could even take a shower now and turn from the image of her in there with him, naked. The steam they'd created in there had had nothing to do with the temperature of the water.

He sighed. He missed being married, missed having his wife to talk to at the end of the day. Missed shared jokes and fighting over the last popcorn in the bowl during movie night. He sure missed getting laid.

But this was his life now. He and Corky were on their own, and that was how it would have to be. They were both going to have to accept that, and so was his meddling sister.

He punched in her number again.

"Hey there," she answered cheerfully. "What's up?"

"You know what's up," he growled. "What were you thinking encouraging Corky to write that letter to Santa?"

"I didn't encourage him. He wanted to," she said in her own defense.

"Well, you didn't have to send it."

"I did, since you conveniently lost last year's."

"I would have lost this year's, too!"

"That's why Corky asked me to help him. What was I supposed to say?"

"That Santa doesn't bring mommies, and Daddy's not looking."

"Maybe it's time Daddy started looking. It's been three years, Griff. Kaitlyn wouldn't want you to wall yourself up for the rest of your life. She'd want Corky to have a mom."

"He's got you," Griff said, forgetting his earlier guilt over taking up so much of his sister's time.

"That's not the same, and you know it."

"Nothing's ever going to be the same again, and you know it."

"Of course, I do, and darn it, I miss her, too. She was my best friend."

"She was my everything," Griff muttered.

"She'd want you to move on and be happy."

"Why do people always say shit like that?" he grumbled.

"Because it's true. You didn't both die. You're still here, and so is your son. It doesn't do either one of you any good for you to wrap yourself up like a mummy."

"We're doing fine just as we are."

"Yeah, right. That's why he's asking Santa for a mom. Dip your toe in the water and at least go on a date once in a while."

So far he hadn't met anyone he wanted to go toe-dipping with. Some of those women stalking him after Kaitlyn died had been downright scary. There was something about their smiles and their condolences that had felt so...fake. Like syrup laid out to attract ants. He could almost feel himself getting crushed under the weight of all that sweetness. Just remembering tugged down the corners of his lips.

"Yeah, well, you bring me the perfect woman, and then we'll talk," he said.

"Maybe *you* need to write Santa," she taunted. "I've got to go. I'm showing a house, and my client just arrived. I'll see you guys tomorrow for cookie baking."

Cookie baking. Kaitlyn had loved to bake, and she'd always gone crazy at Christmas, making everything from frosted sugar cookies to gingerbread boys. Corky was too young to really remember that, but Griff sure did. In addition to gingerbread boys, Jenn had promised to bake Griff's favorite chocolate chip cookies with the mint M&Ms in them. Maybe she could help him talk to Corky. It was the least she could do after the mess she'd made.

On second thought, no. He'd tell her to keep her beak shut. The less said about Santa the better.

Camille summoned Stef to her office. "I had an interesting conversation a moment ago."

She wasn't smiling, which meant it wasn't the good kind of interesting. Stef dropped to the edge of the chair in front of Camille's desk.

Camille was Stef's hero. She was smart and successful and cared about the people she worked with. At forty-eight, she was a tower of strength, a woman who had fired two husbands who had not measured up. She'd finally found her perfect man in a reclusive writer in Seattle, who was now equally reclusive in Carol. He adored her, flattered her and had already turned her into a heroine in his latest bestselling fantasy. Like Camille, the fictitious Ara was a wise elder in her clan, tall and slender with steel-gray hair and matching steely gray eyes.

Camille's eyes weren't usually steely. They were this morning.

Stef swallowed nervously. "What happened?"

Camille turned her screen so Stef could see the Letters to Santa page. "Corcoran happened."

"What?" Stef stared at the page, looking for clues as to what was wrong.

"His father called."

Uh-oh. But still, "Hey, I didn't promise Corcoran a mom."

"No, instead you as much as promised him his father would get him one. Remember when we first started this? I told you to keep everything vague."

"I thought I had," Stef said in a small voice, and Camille's eyebrows dipped into a V. Yes, the eyes were definitely looking steely now.

The same wave of panic she'd gotten when a cop had stopped her for speeding a couple of months back rolled over Stef, going all the way from her face to her stomach. "I'm so sorry." She was afraid to ask, but she had to. "Am I fired?"

"Over one mistake? You know me better than that." Camille sighed. "This is as much on me as it is on you. I should have looked this over more carefully. But really, Stef, I shouldn't have to babysit you on this."

"I'm sorry. I guess I didn't think my answer through very well. I didn't really make any promises, though."

"Nothing concrete, but you put the boy's father in the hot seat, and he didn't appreciate it."

"I was only trying to make his child feel better," Stef said in her own defense.

"That's not your job," Camille said sternly. "This is not an advice column. Your job is to channel Santa and ho, ho, ho and promise the kids Santa will talk to their parents."

"Which I did." Sort of.

"Requests for things like drum sets and...whatever," Camille said with a flick of her hand, "don't matter. But we can't be wandering into sensitive areas like this. It's a good way to lose subscribers, and we can't afford that. So. No more letters asking for intangibles make the cut. I've smoothed ruffled

feathers, and legal assures me we're okay, but we don't need
to put ourselves in this position. Only respond to requests for
toys and goodies from now on and always keep the answers
vague. Like we talked about when we first started this page."

"I'm sorry," Stef managed. She still felt like she was being
blamed unfairly, but it would be pointless to argue any more.

"Be more careful in the future," Camille said.

"I will," Stef promised, and left the office feeling like a kid
who'd just gotten reamed by the principal.

It wasn't right. Here poor Corcoran had poured out his
heart to Santa, and what did his tool of a father do? Call the
paper and make a stink. What a Grinch. What a heartless father. It was a good thing she hadn't talked to the man. She'd
have told him a thing or two.

And probably lost her job.

Sorry, Corcoran. I tried. She plopped down at her desk and
called her sister. "Where are you?"

"I'm shopping with Elinor. What's up?"

"I don't want to be Santa anymore," said Stef.

"Uh-oh. What happened?"

Stef told her.

"Well, it could be worse. Camille could have fired you."

"I wouldn't have deserved that," Stef said. "In fact, I didn't
deserve the lecture. I'm not the problem. The problem is this
poor kid's father. Sheesh, what a jerk."

"It's not easy raising a kid alone. We know that, right?"

Yes, they did. Adele had struggled for the first few years
after Dad died.

"But still. You don't call the paper and yell at them because
your kid wrote a letter to Santa. I need chocolate."

"Want to meet us for lunch at Tillie's? Will that help? We
can split a piece of her Death by Chocolate cake."

Tillie's Tearoom was the town's newest place to eat, and it

catered to women with its lace curtains and tablecloths and mix-and-match fine china. Friends could go there for afternoon tea and enjoy cucumber sandwiches and little cakes and cookies, or they could opt for one of several salads along with freshly baked muffins. The salads were good, and the tea parties were fun, but the sisters went to Tillie's strictly for the cakes—white wedding cake, strawberry cake, carrot cake, lemon pound cake and, of course, chocolate cake.

"I've got too much work to do," Stef said. It was true. Mondays were always busy, and she was buried under Christmas.

"Okay, tomorrow then."

"That sounds good. I'll come by the shop," Stef said just as a call came in from Adele. "Why is Mom calling?"

"Brace yourself. She had a dream," Frankie said.

Sure enough, "I had a dream last night," said Adele as soon as Stef had answered.

"Oh, Mom, not another," Stef protested.

"It was about you."

"Great. Did I just get eaten by a tiger?" If so, there was accurate symbolism in that dream.

"You were sitting on Santa's lap."

"Yeah? Was he hot?"

"I'm being serious," Adele scolded.

"Okay, sorry. Tell me about Santa and me."

"You said you didn't know what you wanted, and he said that he did. Then he reached behind him and pulled out a huge box."

"How did he manage that with me on his lap?"

Adele ignored her. "It was the size of a phone booth. You opened it, and there was a man in there."

"Thank you, Santa. What did he look like?"

"He had short hair, kind of a dark red, and one of those

boyish faces—the kind where the man never looks his age. He was quite cute."

"I haven't met any man who fits that description," said Stef. "Are you sure?"

"I'm sure. And I doubt there is any man who looks like your dream man anywhere in Carol. I'm sure I've dated every single one here in the last six months." And been rejected by the newest one. The last thought made her frown. "Mom, I've gotta go. I'm up to my neck in work here."

"Okay, but keep your eyes peeled. I think this is a sign."

"Thanks, Mom. Love you," Stef said, and ended the call.

It would have been nice if her mother's dreams could be more useful, like warning people not to put certain letters to Santa in the paper.

"Talk about a sexy red dress," said Frankie, holding up a dress for Elinor's inspection. They were hunting in one of the nearby mall's department stores for new outfits for Elinor. It was red with a full skirt and a formfitting bodice that had a scooped neck trimmed with white faux fur. The cuffs on the long sleeves were also trimmed. "How do you like this?"

Elinor gnawed on her lower lip. "I don't know."

"Pair it with some black boots, and you'll look darling in it," Frankie assured her. "Why don't you at least try it on?"

Elinor considered another moment, then nodded decisively. "Okay, I think I will."

That gave them several items for Elinor to try on—a pale pink sweater (Elinor's choice), a red one with a bias-cut V-neck dotted with white snowflakes (Frankie's choice), a black sweater (a compromise between the two of them) to be paired with a red silk scarf and red pants. And black leggings to be paired with anything.

Off to the dressing rooms they went, and Frankie sat in a

nearby chair, offering opinions as Elinor modeled the various outfits. The red dress was by far the best find.

"Wow," Frankie said when Elinor edged out of the changing room.

"Do you think it's too much?" Elinor worried.

"Too much what?"

Elinor shrugged. "Just. Too much."

Frankie suddenly got it. "You're worried that the dress is going to wear you instead of the other way around."

Elinor bit on her lip and nodded. "It seems more like a Frankie dress. Do you want to try it on?"

Actually, Frankie did. The dress fit perfectly, and seeing her reflection in it lifted her spirits. "I'm going to get this," she told Elinor, who was in the next room, trying on the pink sweater.

"You should," Elinor said.

"I'll let you borrow it if you change your mind about wearing it," Frankie promised.

"Thanks," said Elinor.

With that settled, it was back to the task at hand.

The black sweater and pants looked great on Elinor, and the red scarf would dress up the outfit for parties. If Elinor made it to any parties. As Frankie suspected, the pale pink sweater made Elinor look washed out.

"I think you'll definitely need to wear lipstick with that," Frankie said.

She sprang for everything, including the sweater that Elinor was so enamored of. "But now we need to get that lipstick if you're going to wear it," she insisted.

Frankie managed to convince Elinor to buy a dark pink lipstick, and the makeup expert added blush cream, light brown eyeliner, mascara and an eyebrow pencil that proved she had eyebrows. Frankie smiled, pleased with herself, and Elinor regarded her reflection with awe.

"I feel…" Elinor hesitated.

"Pretty?" suggested Frankie.

"Yes, definitely. But also, uh, conspicuous."

"You're just not used to seeing yourself in makeup," Frankie assured her. "You do want to stand out a little. What's the point of getting all these fun clothes if nobody sees you in them? And you do want a certain someone to notice you, right?"

Elinor smiled and nodded.

"Well, he will now," Frankie predicted.

Elinor had yet to confide who that someone was, but it had to be William Sharp, their newest best customer. He would be dazzled, and Frankie could hardly wait to see his reaction to the new and improved Elinor the following day.

8

FRANKIE AND ADELE WERE BOTH RINGING UP SALES ON
Tuesday when Brock entered the shop. Frankie watched him
strolling toward her, smiling, with mixed emotions. This
wasn't going to work, she knew it. She could never feel com-
fortable dating someone younger than her. And yet her pride
wanted her to go out with him again, prove to the world (okay,
one particular person in the world) that she still had what it
took to hold a younger man.

"You free for lunch?" he asked after her customer left.

"I'm afraid not," she said. She could feel her mother's assessing gaze on her. "I'm having lunch with my sister," Frankie
explained, and she wasn't sure if she was relieved or disappointed that she couldn't say yes to lunch.

"How about dinner then?" he suggested.

She hesitated.

Stop this silliness right now, advised her saner self. *You don't really have any interest in this man.*

I could, she insisted.

No, you couldn't. Too old or too young—it doesn't matter which you pick, either one will end up leaving you. Older men die, and the younger ones find greener pastures.

"I get it," Brock was saying. "You'll still be full from lunch. How about we start with drinks at Carol's Place and see where we go from there?"

Frankie rarely went out for drinks—occasionally with Camille or Stef, and in December with Mitch after the Santa Walk, and... There was no other and. Her social life consisted of movie nights, family time and watching cop shows with Mitch. Drinks could be fun.

Adele didn't say anything, but Frankie could feel her watching. "Okay, drinks," she said, and told her saner self to butt out. She had a right to go out for a drink with a nice man if she wanted.

"Great."

"I'll meet you there," she said before he could offer to pick her up.

"I can pick you up, you know," he said. "I promise not to kidnap you."

Or kiss me in your car? The idea was both tempting and scary. The fact that she was nervous about being kissed by a man spoke volumes. She wasn't ready to date.

She was never going to be ready to date.

"So, seven?" Brock suggested.

"Seven," she agreed.

Bad idea, said her saner self.

Probably.

Elinor emerged from the back of the store with a box of

nutcrackers to replenish the diminishing display on a table by the window. Her Holiday Happiness apron hid the full effect of her new pants and black sweater, but there was no hiding the face of the new and improved Elinor.

Brock did a double take. Yep, Mission Makeover had been a success.

"What do you think of Elinor's new look?" Frankie prompted loud enough for Elinor to hear.

"Fire," he said, giving Elinor two thumbs-up.

Elinor blushed and murmured a thank-you.

Hmm. Maybe something could end up happening between this new and improved Elinor and Brock if Frankie stepped out of the way.

The bell over the door jingled, and in walked William Sharp. He made a beeline over to where Elinor stood blushing and arranging nutcrackers and said a soft-spoken hello.

He was in the process of asking if Elinor liked nutcrackers when Mitch made his appearance. Probably shadowing his manager. "I was on my way to get coffee," Mitch said. "I thought I'd see if you ladies wanted something."

"I'm good," said Frankie.

"Caramel latte, please, extra syrup," said Adele from her post at the cash register.

"You got it," said Mitch. He turned his attention to where Elinor stood. "Elinor, would you like something?"

"That's so nice of you," she said.

"How about an eggnog latte?" he suggested.

"That would be great," she said.

"By the way, you look very nice today," he added, deepening the blush on Elinor's face.

"Thank you," she said.

"You certainly do," added William. "But then you always look great."

If Elinor's face got any redder, her head would burst into flame.

Frankie smiled, happy to see her employee getting some male attention. William was bound to ask her out by Christmas. In fact, she and William really would be an even better match than Elinor and Brock. They both enjoyed books, and they would probably never run out of things to talk about.

"Guess I'd better get back to the store," said Brock.

"Good idea," said Mitch, and they both left.

William bought a nutcracker, and he, too, left.

"I think you made quite an impression," Frankie said to Elinor.

Elinor was beaming. "And I owe it all to you."

"You have brought about a change in that girl," Adele said later. She and Frankie were in the supply room, unpacking a delayed shipment of holiday home decor items that had finally arrived.

"I think Brock might be seeing her in a whole new light," said Frankie. "Between him and William, it looks like she's getting plenty of interest."

"I think Brock's too busy looking at you to see anyone else." Adele lifted out a metal Santa candleholder. "This little guy is so cute. You can give him to me for Christmas."

"Done," Frankie said, taking the Santa and setting him aside.

Adele returned to the conversation at hand. "I'm glad to see you getting out and having some fun. It's about time."

Was it? Frankie shrugged.

"So quit poking your nose into everyone else's lives and start enjoying your own."

"I'm not poking my nose into anyone's life," Frankie insisted.

"Oh? What do you call taking your employee on a shopping spree?"

"I call that a good deed."

"And now you need to let her find her own way."

"Sometimes people need an extra nudge," Frankie insisted.

"That makeover wasn't a nudge. It was a push. You'd better be careful. You might end up with some competition."

"I'm not competing for anyone," Frankie said.

"That's because you take the admiration of the men in your life for granted."

"Oh, brother," Frankie said in disgust.

"I'm just dropping a word of warning in your ears, daughter dear. Even the most patient of men won't stick around forever."

"I don't need anyone to stick around since I'm not looking to get serious with anyone," Frankie said.

"Maybe it's time you reconsidered."

"Yeah, well, when you do, I will."

Adele chuckled and kept unpacking.

"It would have been nice if Mom's dream had warned me about Corcoran's angry father instead of telling me about a man in a giant box."

"At least this was a hopeful dream," said Frankie. "It beats the one where our dear departed cat was gnawing on her arm."

"This latest one has as much a chance of happening as that."

"I don't know. When it comes to dreams, you and Mom both seem to have a gift. Remember the ones you had of Daddy?"

Stef shrugged. "I was a kid."

"Who was still open to possibilities." Stef had always been a positive, happy person. Frankie hated seeing her turning so cynical. "You can't give up."

"Because I'm going to meet Mr. Wonderful here in Carol?"

Stef scoffed. "There are no Mr. Wonderfuls left in Carol. Well, other than Mitch. And Brock. Mom told me you guys went out."

Thank you, blabbermouth Adele. "It's not going anywhere," Frankie said, and picked up her menu.

Stef reached across the table and lowered it. "It's okay if it does. Really. You deserve to be happy."

"So do you," said Frankie.

"You're right. Which is why I'm having chocolate cake for dessert, and I'm not sharing. I want the whole big piece for myself."

Frankie laughed. "That's fine with me."

They gave the waitress their orders, then Frankie returned them to the subject of Stef's love life. "Maybe you should try online dating again."

Stef rolled her eyes. "Yeah, I saw how well that worked for Mitch." She pointed a finger at her sister, reminding Frankie of their mom. "And don't go sneaking and putting up my profile somewhere, or I will keep the present I got you for Christmas for myself. But back to you and Brock."

"There is no me and Brock," Frankie said. "I'm just meeting him for a drink."

Stef studied her. "You know, I can't blame him for falling for you. And I can't blame Mitch for hanging around. You've got the biggest heart."

"Oh, brother," said Frankie, dismissing the compliment.

"No, it's true. You're like a peppermint-scented candle. You make a room better just by being in it." Stef bit her lip and looked at her fancy china plate. "You've always done your best to try to make my life better. I'm sorry I was such a brat about the whole Brock thing."

"We already got that taken care of, so stop. Anyway, if

things didn't work out with him, it's because there's someone better for you waiting down the road."

Stef frowned. "The road is too darn long if you ask me. And what if there is nothing down the road? What if all there is ahead of me is a dead end?"

Frankie could see it all in her sister's eyes—the regret over having given so much of herself to the wrong man, the frustration over not finding anyone, the fear that she never would.

She reached across the table and took Stef's hand. "Don't you go there. Don't you dare. You are pretty and fun and smart. And sweet. Well, most of the time," she added, which brought a reluctant smile from Stef. "I know there is someone wonderful in your future. I can feel it in my heart. You hang in there. He will show up. Meanwhile, we have chocolate cake," she said, and that made Stef giggle.

They ate their tea sandwiches and every bit of that chocolate cake for dessert. Frankie picked up the bill for lunch, and Stef left, feeling better.

But Frankie worried that moment of chocolate-induced happiness wouldn't last. If only she knew someone who would be perfect for Stef, if only she could find a way to help her sister get a fresh start on love for the new year.

Their town was not a man desert. There had to be someone, and even if Stef had given up looking, Frankie wasn't going to.

Griff sat in the car line, waiting to pick Corky up from school promptly at five after three. He drummed his fingers on the wheel, trying to figure out the best way to handle the Santa situation. He finally decided there was only one thing to do.

Lie.

Well, sort of lie. A white lie. Okay, maybe it would be more gray than white, but it was the best solution he could think of.

He texted his sister. If Corky asks about Santa tonight, keep your mouth shut.

Yes, sir! came the smart-mouthed reply.

Another letter to Santa was going to get lost this year. Lost and trampled by reindeer. You had to watch those darned reindeer.

When Corky was a little older, they'd have a serious talk about how daddies found mommies...if Griff ever figured that out. Meanwhile, the reindeer would have to take the fall.

The bell rang, and the kids poured out of the school, a swarm of locusts anxious to get home and start devouring every Christmas cookie in sight. And there came Corky, at the end of the swarm, wearing his blue knit earflap hat with the dinosaurs on it, his red parka open and flapping. Griff could already guess what the piece of paper in Corky's hand was.

"I got a A on my spelling test," he announced the minute he was in the car. He handed it over for Griff to see before settling into his car seat.

"You sure did. Good job," said Griff as Corky buckled his seat belt. "Grandma and Grandpa will be proud to hear it." He handed it back, and his son looked at it and smiled.

"Can we FaceTime them and tell them?" asked Corky.

"Sure. As soon as we get home."

"And can we see if Santa got my letter?"

Oh, boy. There it was. "Your letter?"

"My letter I wrote with Aunt Jenn."

"I thought you wanted me to help you write your letter."

"You were too busy," Corky said, already becoming a master of parental guilting.

Griff had always been conveniently too busy when Corky asked. And if he wasn't too busy, it was time for dinner. Or time for Corky to get ready for bed. If he'd known the stunt Jenn was going to pull, he'd never have let her take Corky for the night while he took his staff out for dinner.

"I know he got it 'cause I watched while Aunt Jenn mailed it," Corky continued.

"That doesn't mean he got it. Remember last year? Your letter got lost."

"Aunt Jenn put a extra stamp on it to make sure it wouldn't get lost this year."

Good old Aunt Jenn. "Let's go home and talk to Grandma and Grandpa first. Okay?"

"Okay," Corky said, not quite so excited.

"Since when don't you want to talk to Grandma and Grandpa?"

"I want to talk to Grandma and Grandpa," Corky said. "Aunt Jenn said Santa would have my letter by today."

Santa again. Griff could feel his temper rising.

He tried another tack. "Just because Santa got your letter today, it doesn't mean he's going to answer today."

"Why not?" Corky asked.

"Because he has lots of kids' letters to answer. That takes time. In fact, you might not hear from him. He can't answer everybody."

Corky's face screwed up, and he blinked, a little boy on the verge of tears. "But he brings toys to everybody."

Whoever started this Santa thing should have been forced to eat nothing but dried-out fruitcake for the rest of his life. "Don't worry, I've already talked to Santa and told him what you want."

"You did?"

Out of the corner of his eye, Griff could see the transformation in his son's face. Good. That was taken care of.

"I did," he said.

"A mommy!" crowed Corky, wriggling happily in his seat.

"No, not a mommy," Griff said firmly. "You want a Monster Spotter action game," he reminded Corky. He'd already ordered the thing and had it stored at the office.

Corky's smile tipped upside down, and his lower lip stuck out. Then it began to wobble. "I just want a mommy."

"Son, Santa's not going to bring you a mommy."

"He will if he gets my letter," Corky insisted. "You'll see, Daddy. You want a mommy, too, don't you? Then we can have someone to make dinner for us and bake us cookies."

And smile at us over her morning coffee. Griff felt a catch in his throat. He cleared it. "Santa doesn't bring mommies. He brings toys."

"Aunt Jenn said he might."

Griff could imagine the conversation. Corky looking at Jenn with those big brown eyes, begging her to assure him that Santa, who granted every wish, would hear his request. Softie that she was, she wouldn't have the heart to tell Corky the hard truth. But why the hell did she have to mail his letter? She should have been able to come up with some excuse for why she couldn't.

By the time they got to the house, Griff was in a sour mood. This Santa thing was out of control. What would the saint whose identity got stolen by an old fat guy with a fake beard who everyone practically worshipped think about what modern culture had done to him?

Griff should never have allowed the whole thing to start. He should have told Corky the first time he saw one that Santa was only pretend, that there was no such guy, that those extra presents under the tree were from his hardworking dad who loved him more than anything in the world.

But who couldn't give him what he wanted the most.

Back home, Griff found a snack for his son—the lone apple

left in the fridge, starting to get mushy. Time to go shopping. Maybe he'd do that while Corky and Jenn were baking. Corky took one bite and pronounced it yucky. Griff dug out the last remaining snack bag of nacho-flavored corn chips from the cupboard and handed it over.

Then they set up Griff's laptop and made contact with the grandparents. "I got a A on my spelling test," Corky announced, holding up his test for Grandma and Grandpa to see.

"Smart boy, just like his grandpa," said Griff's dad.

"What words did you learn to spell?" asked his mom, and Corky happily rattled them off.

"Teacher says I'm getting good at spelling."

"I should say so, if you got an A," said Grandma. "And what are you boys going to do tonight to celebrate?"

"We're making cookies!" Corky answered.

"You gonna bake some for Santa?" asked Grandpa, and Griff swore under his breath.

"It's too soon to bake cookies for Santa," he hurried to say.

"I wrote a letter to Santa," Corky announced, and it was all Griff could do not to groan.

"Did you? What did you ask for?" Grandpa wanted to know.

"A mommy."

Griff's dad suddenly looked like he'd encountered a hornets' nest and wasn't sure what to do about it. Griff's mom's pleasant smile faded.

"Well, now," she said, stalling.

"I told him Santa doesn't bring mommies," Griff said.

"True," agreed his father. "Santa specializes in toys. I bet he's going to bring you some good ones."

"I only want a mommy," Corky said, and pouted.

"Well, uh," Grandpa said, and scratched his head. "You've got a grandma, and I know she's got some fun stuff planned for when you visit Christmas Day."

"Oh, yes," chimed in Griff's mom. "We're going to have a birthday cake for Jesus, and you'll get to blow out the candles. And Grandpa has a fun new game to play with you."

"And we've got some special presents under the tree," added Griff's dad.

"I just want a mommy," Corky grumbled.

"Right now you'll have to settle for Grandma and Aunt Jenn," said Griff.

Corky's expression didn't change.

"We'll have a lovely day together," his grandmother promised. "And if we get some more snow, you and Grandpa and your daddy can build a snowman."

"Or have a snowball fight," put in Grandpa.

The way his son was scowling at him, Griff was sure Corky was envisioning taking him down with a snowball.

"Let's say goodbye to Grandma and Grandpa. Aunt Jenn will be here soon," said Griff. "Why don't you go watch for her?"

Corky said a subdued goodbye and then dragged himself off to the living room to perch on the couch and watch out the window for his aunt.

"Guess I shouldn't have said the *S* word. Sorry, son," Griff's dad apologized.

"That's okay. You're not the one who started this. It was Jenn. She helped him with the *l-e-t-t-e-r*," Griff said, spelling out the word so his son wouldn't catch on.

"I know. She told me. I'm sure there was some little boy manipulation going on," said his mother.

Griff frowned. "I'm sure you're right."

"It'll pass," said his dad. "He'll get busy with his toys and treats and forget all about this."

"I hope so," said Griff.

"Otherwise, you'd better leave town when the Easter bunny comes," Dad advised.

"Don't let him make you feel bad. You're doing a great job," said Mom. "Meanwhile, you all have fun baking."

Griff wasn't going to have fun. He had to go grocery shopping.

As soon as he shut his computer, Corky was back at his side. "Can we see if Santa read my letter?"

What was taking Jenn so long to get there? "We need to eat dinner," Griff said. "Are you hungry?"

"No. I want to see if Santa read my letter."

"Let's eat dinner," said Griff. "Aunt Jenn will be here any minute."

Corky's mouth drooped at the corners.

Griff pretended not to see. He sent his sister a quick text begging her to hurry up and come over, then he pulled out the last box of mac and cheese to pair with the hot dogs they had left in the fridge.

Kaitlyn had never given their son boxed macaroni and cheese mix. She was probably turning in her grave.

Griff shook the box. "Look what I found. Your fave."

Still no smile.

Griff pretended not to see. He got out the near-empty carton of milk and got busy.

They sat down to eat at the acacia wood table Kaitlyn had splurged on when she and Griff first bought the house. "Seats four. Room to grow more," she'd said with a grin.

Instead of growing, they'd shrunk to two.

It wasn't long before Corky was down to his last bite. Griff knew there would be yet another request to look for the permanently deleted letter to Santa. He wished it was summer.

The last forkful went into Corky's mouth, and Griff cast a

hopeful look toward the living room window. Yes, that was his sister's car pulling up to the curb. Thank God.

"Aunt Jenn's here. Go let her in."

Corky slid from his seat, put his dish in the sink and then raced to open the door.

"Who's ready to bake cookies?" she asked as she breezed in, carrying two bags full of supplies.

"Me!" Corky began hopping toward the kitchen.

Instant mood change. Good.

Jenn followed him in and started setting things out on the counter. "We've got sugar and flour, molasses and spices and frosting tubes and eggs. Oh, and something for Dad," she said, unloading a six-pack of Griff's favorite IPA.

Trying to bribe her way out of the shithole she was in. He took it with a grunt and put it in the sparsely populated fridge.

"What do you say, Daddy?" prompted Corky.

"I say, 'Nice try,'" Griff said.

"No, you're supposed to say thank you. You know that."

"You're right, I do. Thank you, Aunt Jenn."

"Can we bake cookies for Santa?" Corky asked.

Jenn shot a tentative look Griff's direction.

"Daddy says it's too soon," Corky added, and his tone of voice said exactly what he thought of Daddy's opinion. Pushing boundaries, his son's superpower.

"It is a little early for that. But we can bake cookies for us," said Jenn. "And we've got a lot to make, so you'd better go wash your hands. With soap."

"With soap," Corky repeated, and nodded, then raced off.

"I'm off to get some food," Griff said to his sister. "Can you manage things here? Without bringing Santa into the picture," he added.

"I can handle the cookies, but I don't know how to do mind control."

"Try," Griff commanded. "And if the subject of Santa comes up, it needs to be done with by the time I get back."

"Are you planning on staying away until New Year's?"

"That's funny. Never mind real estate. You should be a comic." Except there wasn't anything funny about this situation.

By the time Griff had his coat, his son was back in the kitchen, ready for cookie duty. He gave Corky a kiss. "If you're good for your aunt, I'll bring back peppermint ice cream."

"I'll be good," Corky promised.

Griff was barely out of the kitchen before he heard his son ask Jenn, "Can we see if Santa answered my letter?"

Maybe he would stay away until New Year's.

But responsible dads didn't get to run away, so an hour later, Griff was back home with fruit and veggies and bread and peanut butter and milk and tuna fish, along with more mac and cheese and a package of frozen burritos, his favorite go-to dinner.

The house smelled like sugar and chocolate when he opened the door. For a moment he stood there, taking in the smells and reliving the memory of the last Christmas Kaitlyn had spent baking. The vision of her in her pink apron, putting cookies onto a cooling rack, was so vivid for a minute he thought it was real and he'd only dreamed she was gone. He could even see the flour on the tip of her nose.

"Got your favorite cookies," she said.

Only it wasn't her, it was his sister. And there was his son, next to her, seated at the kitchen table, decorating a gingerbread boy. He wanted to cry, but he stuffed down the emotion clawing its way up his throat and walked to the kitchen.

"Smells good," he said as he set down his grocery bags.

He shrugged out of his coat, tossed it over a kitchen chair and took a cookie. It was Kaitlyn's recipe Jenn was using—he knew that—but the cookie didn't taste as good as Kaitlyn's had.

"How is it?" Jenn asked.

"Good," he lied.

"Santa didn't read my letter yet," Corky informed him.

Griffin looked to Jenn. "You looked on the site."

"What could I do? He asked."

Griffin ruffled his son's hair. "Don't worry. Santa and I have got it handled."

Corky bit the side of his lip and went back to squirting frosting on a gingerbread boy. "I just want a mommy."

"That's a mighty fine-looking gingerbread boy you're making," Jenn said to distract him, and Corky grinned and took a big bite.

Griffin helped his sister finish cleaning, then she said goodbye to her nephew, who was settled at the table with milk and one final cookie. Griff walked with her to the door and stepped outside with her on the porch.

"If I hear that he wants a mommy one more time, my head's going to come off," he said.

"Remember how persistent you were about getting a dog?" Jenn reminded him.

"Maybe I should get him a dog. That's on par with getting him a mom," Griff said bitterly.

"You know what I mean."

He ran a hand over his hair. It was a good thing it was short. Otherwise, he'd start pulling it out.

"It'll be okay, bro. Hang in there," she said.

What else could he do? At least he had family helping him.

He thought again of how much time his sister was giving up to help with Corky, and a finger of guilt over losing it with her gave him a firm poke. One minute he was lighting into her, the next he was begging her to come to his rescue with cookies.

"Look, I'm sorry I lost it about the letter."

"I know," she said. "What can I say? Corky's hard to say no to."

Yes, he was.

"It'll be okay," Jenn added, and kissed him on the cheek.

He watched her go down the walk, not a care in the world, and half wished he could trade places.

But then he wouldn't have his son. The boy may have been driving him to distraction, but he loved Corky and couldn't imagine life without him.

All the houses on his street were lit up for the holidays. Except his. Maybe he should get something for the yard—a blow-up Frosty the Snowman or a gingerbread boy. Anything but a Santa.

Back inside the house, he pried his son away from the cookies and took him upstairs for a bath. Then it was time for bed and a story, followed by bedtime prayers.

Griff cringed when his son finished with, "And please don't let Santa lose my letter." Corky's "amen" was emphatic, even as Griff was silently praying, *Please let Corky forget about the letter.*

That wasn't going to happen, he knew it. He tucked his son in and amended his prayer. *Help me.*

Frankie and Brock sat in a booth in a dark corner of the town's popular pub, far from the collection of tables by the bandstand where The Grizzly Boys would be playing vintage rock and roll later.

Carol's Place had been around since the seventies. So had its decor. The walls were lined with fake wood paneling, the bar looked like an import from the set of a Western movie, and a couple of the bar stools had rips. But it was well stocked, and the bartenders knew every thirsty customer by name and what they preferred to drink.

The restaurant side of the place served anything and everything fried. The peanuts served gratis in red plastic bowls were responsible for the shells littering the floor. Immediately upon entering, patrons would notice the portrait of "Carol." Carol Clementine, who the town was supposedly named after, had been a buxom woman with neon yellow hair done up in a Gibson Girl bun. According to legend, she ran the first cathouse in the county, which had stood right where the current establishment now was. Come Valentine's Day, people would write messages (*Keep it clean, folks!*) on pink paper hearts, which would get pinned all around the picture. At the moment, a Santa hat hung over the corner of the large frame.

"I'm glad you joined me," Brock said as they worked on their second peppermint martinis.

Was she glad? Frankie wasn't sure. So far they'd shared pictures on their phones and talked about things they enjoyed. Football. They had that in common. He loved to water-ski. She'd never been able to get upright. He assured her he could get her up.

"I don't know," she said. "I think I'm safer on land."

"So do you snow ski?"

"I've been known to," she said modestly. She skied like a demon, loved being up on the slopes.

Correction: had loved being up on the slopes.

"We should go," said Brock.

"I don't ski anymore."

"Why not? Anyone looking at you can tell you're in great condition."

She could feel the prickle of tears and grabbed for her glass. "I haven't skied since my husband died. That was something we used to do together."

Her sister skied. So did Mitch. So did Viola and her husband. Frankie never joined them. The only times she went up in the mountains were when she hiked with Mitch in the summer.

"Oh, man. Did he die on the slopes?"

Their dark corner suddenly seemed darker. She shook her head. "He was hit by a car."

The memory of Viola's husband, Terrill, and his partner standing on her porch, asking if they could come in, rushed over Frankie, fresh as the day it happened. She had to take a deep breath.

"Man, that's awful." Brock fell silent, probably unsure what to say next.

Frankie found herself out of words, too. Her sad memory didn't belong there with them. Yet there it sat. The moment stretched on.

"I'm really sorry," he said at last.

Sorry was in the past. She'd moved on. Theoretically.

He put his big hand over hers. It felt warm and strong. What was there about a man's hand that could make you feel so…comforted?

"Maybe he'd want you to start skiing again," Brock suggested.

Everyone seemed to know what Ike would have wanted for her. She shrugged. "Maybe."

"Maybe he'd want you to be happy."

"Now you sound like my mother," she joked.

"Just don't say I look like your mother," he joked back.

"You definitely don't look like my mother."

He turned her hand over and traced her palm with his thumb, tickling the skin, starting a tingle running up her arm. "You have a long life line."

"Don't tell me you read palms," she said, trying to ignore the little flame he'd lit in her.

"No, I'm just making stuff up. But I bet you do have a lot of life ahead of you. It'd be a shame to live it alone."

"I'm not alone. I've got my family and friends."

"Mmm," he said, drawing a circle on her palm. It felt so good.

Okay, she had to stop this. She freed her hand and took a drink. "Stef skis," she informed him, making one last effort on her sister's behalf.

"Maybe you should again, too. Frankie, you're so full of life, just bursting to really start living it. I could help you with that."

"This really isn't going to work," she protested. Not as firmly as she should have. Those tingles were spreading.

"You won't know if you don't give it a chance." He slid closer to her.

"Oh, I think I have."

"Not really." He slipped a finger under her chin and turned her face toward his. "I'm not done giving you my sales pitch," he murmured.

"I have great sales resistance," she said.

"Yeah?"

He smelled like cologne, and his peppermint-scented breath was warm on her face. And, oh no, she couldn't let this happen.

9

BROCK'S LIPS CAUGHT FRANKIE'S, AND THE TINGLES spread...everywhere. Santa help her! She was in trouble. She was melting faster than whipped cream on hot chocolate.

What was she doing? She pulled away, trying not to look as stupefied as she felt.

He grinned. It was a very cocky grin. "How was that for a sales pitch?"

She had to admit, "Pretty good."

He raised an eyebrow. "Just pretty good?"

"Okay, very good. But, really, Brock. I just don't..."

She didn't get a chance to finish her sentence because he was kissing her again, his fingers threading through her hair. Oh, mercy. It had been so long since she'd been kissed. She'd forgotten how wonderful it felt.

But something was off. She needed time to think. She pushed him away. "Okay, we need to stop."

He looked surprised, then he nodded. "Oh, yeah. Let's go back to your place. Let me finish my sales pitch."

With that second martini and her supercharged hormones conspiring together, she would probably let him. Not a good idea. She was in no frame of mind to think wisely.

She didn't want to think. She wanted to be loved, to feel a man's hands on her, to fall asleep in his arms.

Still. "We'd better quit while we're ahead," she told him.

His smile faded. "You are going to give us a chance, aren't you?"

Take a chance on me.

She shoved the line from the old ABBA song out of her mind. "I need time," she said. "I haven't dated since…" She couldn't finish the sentence. She wanted to cry again. Instead, she sniffed and downed the last of her martini.

He laid a hand on her arm. "I get it. It took me a long time to recover from my last breakup."

He was comparing a breakup with his girlfriend to her husband's death. There was more than an age gap between them. There was an understanding gap. They were planets apart.

"I need to go." She scooted out of the booth, and he followed her. He helped her on with her coat, then walked her out to her car.

"Are you okay to drive?" he asked.

She nodded. "I'm fine."

"Yes, you are," he said with a smile.

The one she returned was weak.

"I'll call you," he said, and gave her another kiss, a quick reminder of the sample he'd given her in the bar.

Don't bother. She kept the words inside her mouth. It would have come across as insulting.

Instead, she nodded and got in her car. He watched while she put on her seat belt and started the engine. Then he stepped back and lifted a hand.

She managed a small wave in return and pulled away. "What am I doing, Ike?"

Back in her house, she turned up the heat, grabbed a blanket and plopped on the couch with her phone. Viola's husband, Terrill, would be patrolling the streets of Carol in the hopes of finding someone misbehaving so he'd have something to do, and Viola would be watching something on HGTV, waiting for Frankie to report in.

Viola answered with, "Why are you calling me so early? You should still be out getting into trouble with Brock."

"I started to," Frankie said.

"Yeah? Tell," Viola commanded eagerly.

"He kissed me."

"Oh, baby. Did he give you a buzz?"

Frankie sighed. "He did. It felt good to be kissed."

"Then why are you home so early and calling me?"

"Because it doesn't feel right."

"What do you mean?"

"We don't think on the same plane."

"What?"

"You know, when I first kissed Ike..."

The memory flooded her, transporting her to that night when they'd parked out at the lake and he'd kissed her. She'd wanted him to go on kissing her and never stop. And he hadn't. They'd only gone out a couple of times, but she'd known he was the one. She'd known from the first hello that they'd be together, and that kiss had been proof.

"I knew we were meant to be together. I felt it."

"Well, you felt something when Brock kissed you, right?"

"Yeah, I felt turned on. But it didn't feel like proof."

"Proof," Viola repeated, mystified.

"That this would work over the long haul."

"You're worrying about the age difference."

"Yeah, but it's more than that. We're not a fit."

"Maybe you could be if you gave it a chance," Viola suggested. "He's a nice guy, right?"

"He is. It's just… He's not…"

"Ike," Viola supplied.

"I know I'm never going to have what I had with Ike."

"You're not. Every relationship is different."

"I understand, but I'm sure this one isn't going to work. I need to stop the sleigh ride. There's someone else he's supposed to be on it with," said Frankie.

"I guess you've got to listen to your heart," Viola said.

"I do," Frankie agreed. Her hormones wouldn't be happy about her decision, but they'd have to deal with it.

Brock texted her the next morning. Want to do lunch?

Sorry, things are crazy right now.

It was no lie. The closer Christmas came, the busier the shop got. There was no time for leisurely lunches with sexy younger men. She was already going to leave everyone at Holiday Happiness to hustle without her since meeting with the Santa Walk committee would take up the morning.

You gonna ghost me? he texted, adding a laughing emoji.

It was hard to ghost someone who worked right next door.

No, she texted, and doubled his laughing emoji. They would have to have a serious talk. As soon as she figured out what it would look like. Meanwhile, it was time to hop on over to the office of the Carol Chamber of Commerce and meet with the Santa Walk movers and shakers.

She entered the meeting room to find the other committee members already there: Hazel Willis, who owned Won-derland Toys; Autumn Silvers, who, along with her husband, owned The Salad Bowl; James Warshaw, who owned Chez James Salon and knew the secrets of almost all the women in town; Theresia Nordlie, who owned Best Bakes Bakery and was the queen of the chocolate croissant; and Barbara Fielding, of course, who had, as chairman of the committee, claimed the seat at the head of the table.

"We were about to give up on you," Barbara greeted Frankie, who was all of five minutes late.

"When would I ever miss a Santa Walk committee meeting?" Frankie said sweetly. "Especially since the Santa Walk is my baby."

Barbara frowned, deepening the marionette lines on both sides of her mouth. Thin and gaunt as she was, someone should have told her not to dress in black. It made her look like the Grim Reaper's wife on a tour of New York City. Frankie always thought someone who specialized in knitting should look soft and pillowy, like everyone's favorite grandma. Like Adele. There was nothing soft and pillowy about Barbara, either in her looks or her personality.

"Your baby belongs to us all. It takes a village," Barbara said lightly, and almost smiled. "Well, now that we're all here, let's get started. How are we coming with our social media, James?"

James looked like he should have owned the yarn store. He was soft and pillowy. He favored jeans and T-shirts when he was working, but in honor of the committee meeting, he'd paired the jeans with a white shirt and a red vest.

"We're good. I just put up a slideshow on Insta of shots from last year's walk."

The one Frankie had been in charge of. If she hadn't gone off on that Christmas cruise right after last year's walk and missed the post-event meeting, she'd still be in charge. Barbara had done a ton of campaigning in her absence, and when the committee met next, she'd already gotten herself nominated as chairman for the following year.

Frankie had had too much class to nominate herself, but she hadn't been above asking Autumn later why the committee had put Barbara in charge. And why Autumn had nominated her. It had felt like a betrayal.

"Barbara told me you were worn out from running the event, and you wanted a break," Autumn had explained.

The only thing Frankie had wanted a break from was Barbara. She still did, but oh well, everyone had someone in their life who was their designated irritant, and Barbara was Frankie's.

"She's jealous of you," Adele liked to say. "You have the cutest shop in town, and everyone likes you."

"Well, someone must like her," Frankie would reply. "She's still in business."

"They like yarn."

There was that.

"I assume the paper is going to start giving us a boost, aren't they, Frankie?" Barbara asked, raising an inquisitive eyebrow.

Somehow it was assumed that because Frankie knew the editor and her sister worked for the paper, Frankie had an in. The paper gave the event lots of space, not because of Frankie or even Stef, but because the Santa Walk was a big deal in Carol.

"Of course," Frankie said.

"Please tell your sister I'm ready for an interview any time she is," said Barbara.

"Will do," said Frankie. She would also suggest Stef look for other stories to cover instead of bothering with an interview with this year's chairman. *Who's passive aggressive? Not* moi.

The discussion continued, with reports regarding arrangements to clear Main Street for the morning's Santa parade, of the vendors and artists lined up for the market in the town square and, of course, Barbara had to pat herself on the back about bringing in the Dickens Carolers. "Always good to keep things fresh," she said.

"Speaking of fresh, I think we should have a baking contest," said Autumn. "Holiday cupcakes. Or gingerbread houses. We could display the entries all over town, and people could vote for their favorite."

"That's a lovely idea," Barbara approved. "But it's too late in the game for this year. You should have suggested it back when we were first brainstorming last spring."

Autumn frowned and muttered, "It wouldn't take that much effort."

Way to encourage people, thought Frankie. "I think it's a great idea, and we should for sure do it next year."

"We can only fit in so many things," Barbara said sternly. "Now, on to Santa and Mrs. Claus," she said, shifting gears and smiling. "As you all know, Mitch Howard has agreed to be Santa again this year."

Frankie smiled, anticipating that she would be announced as Mrs. Claus. She'd told the committee way back in their early planning stages that she'd be happy to continue her role.

"As for Mrs. Claus…"

Frankie tried to look humble.

"I think it would be good to give Frankie a break."

What? Frankie's humble smile got overtaken by a frown. "I said way back last spring I'd be happy to be Mrs. Claus."

"Yes, but you're so busy with the shop and your duties on the committee. We thought you could use a break."

That again. "Who, exactly, thought that?" Frankie challenged.

"Anyway, we should give others an opportunity," Barbara said, skirting her question. "I was talking with James..."

Poor James suddenly looked like he'd cut a finger with his hair shears.

"And we thought it would be fun to have a Mrs. Claus contest, let some of our women here in Carol compete for the honor."

"How will you choose?" Frankie demanded.

"We'll make it like a pageant," Barbara answered.

So, no time for a baking contest, but time to find a replacement for Frankie. "What, you're going to see who's got the whitest hair?" she taunted.

Barbara ignored her. "We'll have it Friday night, before the big day. Our Mrs. Claus contestants can campaign around town, and on the night of the pageant we'll interview them, and everyone will vote."

Autumn snapped her fingers. "Each entrant should have to bake something and display it at the pageant. A gingerbread house! That can be part of the competition."

"There you go," said Barbara graciously. "We can work in some holiday baking after all."

Hazel was looking at Frankie in concern. "What do you think, Frankie?" she asked.

Frankie forced a smile. "I think it's a great idea."

And really, it was. She had no problem campaigning. She'd get Natalie to help her with the gingerbread house, and...

"But committee members should not be eligible to enter," said Barbara, the mind reader. "That way it will be fair and unbiased."

No, that way Barbara would make sure Frankie wouldn't be Mrs. Claus. Frankie forced her clenched jaw to loosen so she could smile as she wished all manner of holiday disasters on her nemesis. *May your Christmas tree fall on you. May you eat raw cookie dough and get sick. May your latest ex start dating a Victoria's Secret model and post it all over social media. May you find a snake in your Christmas stocking.*

Oh, wait. The snake would be the one hanging the stocking. She could almost hear a little elf whispering, *Let it go.*

Okay, fine. She could be magnanimous. She didn't need to be a spotlight hog. Maybe, somewhere in Carol, there was a woman who needed this honor, whose confidence and spirits needed a boost. And who could make gingerbread houses.

"Shall we take a vote?" asked Barbara. "All in favor?"

Everyone raised a hand and said, "Aye," including Frankie. She could be a team player…even if she didn't like the team captain.

"Good. Now, I've already contacted KZAM…"

"Before we even voted on this?" Frankie demanded.

Barbara shrugged. "I knew we'd all be in agreement."

Unbelievable. Barbara wasn't chairing the committee. She was ruling it.

Frankie fumed while the details regarding the newly minted Mrs. Claus pageant were hammered out and Hazel was put in charge of making it happen. Then the meeting was adjourned.

"Are you really okay with not being Mrs. Claus?" James asked Frankie once they stepped back out onto the sidewalk.

Magnanimous. You are magnanimous. She repeated the mantra to herself. "Of course I am," she said. "I have to admit, at first, I was a little shocked. Just between you and me, I feel like the Santa Walk is being taken out of my hands." So she was only semi-magnanimous. It was the best she could do at the moment.

"That's what happens with a good idea. It grows, and soon it's too big for just one person," he said. "But we do all think of you as Mrs. Claus. This whole event was your idea." He looked over his shoulder. "Barbara sort of steamrolled us into going along with this Mrs. Claus thing just now."

"It's okay, James. I'll miss being Mrs. Claus, but if someone else really wants the job, it's fine by me. The whole purpose of the event is to help our local businesses and bring the community together."

And she needed to keep that in mind. Still, she felt grumpy. She needed an eggnog latte. Fast. And a listening ear.

She texted Mitch. Got time for coffee?

Sure, came the response. Meet you there.

Minutes later, Frankie and Mitch were ensconced at a table in The Coffee Stop, sipping on eggnog lattes. Frankie's treat this time.

"It's the least I can do considering the fact that I'm making you my personal shrink," she told him.

"Now what's Barbara done to piss you off?" he asked.

"She's taken away my Mrs. Claus apron, that's what she's done. She convinced the committee that I'm too tired and overworked to be Mrs. Claus. I *am* Mrs. Claus," Frankie finished, and took a big gulp of her latte, burning her tongue in the process. *Punishment for complaining*, she thought as she set down her mug with a scowl.

"You're just mad 'cause you can't spend the day with me," Mitch teased.

Come to think of it, she didn't like the idea of someone else taking her place next to Mitch. They'd been doing this together since she first started the Santa Walk two years earlier. She'd assumed that would continue.

"It's not right," she grumbled.

"Well, cheer up. This way you can come see me and sit on my lap."

"Ha ha."

Sitting on Mitch's lap—why did that kind of sound like a good idea? It shouldn't. They were only buddies, and that was how it had to stay.

"I know I'm being immature about this," she confessed, turning her attention away from thoughts of Mitch's lap, "but darn it all, it hurts being dethroned. And I know Barbara manipulated all of this out of spite. That woman has never liked me."

"She's jealous. Take it as a compliment."

"I would if she wasn't acting on that jealousy."

"It's a done deal for this year. How are you going to cope?"

She held up her mug. "Latte overdose?"

He chuckled. "Christmas will be good for you, no matter who ends up being Mrs. Claus. You've got your family, and you have friends who care about you. It's more than Barbara can say."

True. Barbara was divorced and didn't have any kids. Frankie knew from the dependable town grapevine that Barbara and her sister weren't on speaking terms. All she had was the committee. And her shop with its lame location.

"So, who do you see as Mrs. Claus?" Mitch prompted.

"Nobody," she said, returning to her pity party.

"There's got to be someone."

"I'll have to think about it."

"Here's a chance for you to put on your helper elf hat, and we all know how much you love that."

Hmm.

"I bet you'll think of somebody," he said. He downed the last of his drink. "I've gotta get back to the store."

"And I need to get back to the shop. I'm sure Mom is ready for her lunch break. She has a date with one of her friends."

They said goodbye at the door of Holiday Happiness, and Frankie slipped back inside.

The lights on the trees in her little holiday forest glimmered. The display of nutcrackers saluted her. Customers were milling about, checking out snow globes and ornaments and chatting. She had picked the right name for her shop. It exuded happiness.

In a back corner Adele was giving a hard sell on a hand-crafted wooden Advent calendar that they had marked down 20 percent. Elinor was ringing up a sale for old Mr. Barrows, who always bought his granddaughters ornaments for Christmas, and Natalie was boxing some of her homemade candies for Viola. And there was Stef, taking pictures of it all.

This was Frankie's kingdom, and it was a happy one. She didn't need a committee to dub her Mrs. Claus. She already was.

"What are you doing here?" she greeted Stef.

"I'm going around town taking pictures of all our shops in action. It's for a lead-up piece for the Santa Walk. Like someone suggested a couple weeks back." That someone having been Frankie.

"Someone had a good idea," she said with a wink.

"I've got a picture of you from last year as Mrs. Claus. I'll include that."

"And you can start adding pictures of the candidates for Mrs. Claus this year."

"What do you mean?" Stef asked, and Frankie told her of Barbara's machinations.

"That skunkeroo," Stef said with a shake of her head.

"Oh well. Maybe it is time for someone else to be Mrs. Claus. Maybe someone in town could use the ego boost."

But who? Who would make a cute Mrs. Claus?

Frankie's gaze rested on Elinor, who was smiling at Mr. Barrows as she handed over the red Holiday Happiness gift bag filled with goodies. Elinor was smiling more lately. That makeover had done wonders. Maybe being Mrs. Claus would, too.

"Elinor," Frankie decided. "She's sweet. She'd be perfect."

Stef lowered her voice. "I don't see it. She's so shy."

"But friendly. This would be good for her," Frankie said with a decided nod. "Elinor," she called, and hurried over to the checkout counter, "how would you like to be our town's Mrs. Claus this year?"

"Mrs. Claus?" Elinor repeated. "But aren't you usually Mrs. Claus? That's what Natalie told me."

"Are you giving up your seat in the sleigh, Mom?" Natalie asked.

"For the right person," said Frankie, and explained about the upcoming competition. "And I think Elinor would be the perfect woman for the job," she concluded.

Elinor paled. "Oh, I couldn't."

"Sure you could," said Frankie cheerfully. "You can borrow my new red dress. It will be perfect for the pageant."

"Will I have to answer some sort of question?"

"Probably not," Frankie assured her, conveniently forgetting Barbara's mention of interviewing the candidates.

"But if you do, the answer is always 'I want world peace,'" said Viola, which made Natalie giggle. "Don't laugh. That's how I became Miss West Seattle back in the day."

"There you have it, advice from an expert. You've got Viola to coach you, and we can all help with the gingerbread house."

"Gingerbread house?" Elinor repeated weakly.

"It's going to be part of the pageant," Frankie said, then moved on quickly. "We'll make posters to put up around town, including in our window. It really is fun being Mrs. Claus, and it's not like you don't know Santa. Mitch is great to work with. And all our customers will vote for you," Frankie added.

"Mitch?" Elinor perked up.

"He's always Santa," said Natalie.

"I'll have Terrill get everyone at the station to vote for you," promised Viola.

"There you go. You're a shoo-in," said Stef. "Hey, how about an interview as the first official candidate for the position of Mrs. Claus?"

"What should I say?"

"Whatever comes to mind," said Stef. She pushed Record on her phone. "So, as Carol's Mrs. Claus, what would you like to see happen this year?"

Elinor's eyes got wide. "Umm."

"World peace," whispered Viola, making Natalie smile.

Elinor considered. "You know what, if I was Mrs. Claus, if I could have any Christmas wish come true, it would be to see families able to get together and all getting along and every child smiling on Christmas morning." She smiled at Frankie. "Maybe that's why I like working here at Holiday Happiness. I know that things can't make you happy, but fun holiday decorations can remind you to be happy."

"Wow," said Stef. "That was brilliant."

It was indeed. Frankie smiled on her protégé. It looked like Elinor really would make a good Mrs. Claus.

"Are you looking forward to taking part in our first ever Mrs. Claus pageant?" Stef asked.

"Well, I'm looking forward to meeting more of the people here in Carol. I'm so happy I moved here." Elinor was on a roll, and she obviously didn't need coaching.

A thirtysomething woman had come in and was hovering over by the nutcrackers, watching the proceedings with interest.

Frankie remembered her. She'd been in for their Black Friday sale, looking for a Christmas music box for her mother. She'd also wound up buying some of Natalie's bonbons. "An early Christmas present," she'd said, "for me," which had made Frankie laugh. She'd returned a couple of days later to buy more candy, this time for a friend. She and Frankie had chatted briefly about favorite holiday recipes while Frankie rang up her purchases. A nice woman.

Frankie moved over to her. "Welcome back."

"You remember me?" The woman looked surprised.

"I remember all my customers," Frankie said. "What may I help you find?"

"I'm looking for something Christmassy for a little boy."

"What does he like?"

"The usual—LEGO, video games. I'd like to get him something more traditional for Christmas, though. Maybe a train set if you have something like that. It doesn't have to be fancy."

"We have just the one. It's back here," Frankie said, and led her to where a little engine pulled several cars on a track around a small Christmas tree. She had set up a village for it, complete with lampposts, a church, a store and some houses.

"Oh, that is cute. I think my nephew would love it," said the woman. "It's not on par with getting a mommy for Christmas, but it will have to do."

"No mommy? That's so sad," Frankie said.

The woman's face clouded over, and she shrugged. "She was way too young."

"Cancer?" guessed Frankie.

The woman shook her head. "Aneurysm. It was a shock to all of us."

"I can imagine," Frankie said, remembering the shock of losing Ike so suddenly. "It's hard to keep going after a loss like that."

"I wish my brother would find someone. He's a good man, and he deserves to be happy."

The wheels began to turn. "Maybe he needs to ask Santa to bring him someone fun for Christmas." Like Stef.

"I don't think he and Santa are on speaking terms at the

moment. His son wrote a letter to Santa, and my brother got it taken off the *Clarion*'s page."

The pieces clicked together. This was the angry dad Stef had talked about. "My sister does that page. That's her, at the front of the store. She's interviewing one of my employees."

"I hope my brother didn't get her in trouble," said the woman.

"He might have. He probably feels badly about it. Might want to apologize," Frankie suggested. Like in a cute holiday movie. She could already see the scene playing out.

"He should," said the woman.

"Maybe you and your brother should bring your nephew to see Santa at the Santa Walk. Stef will be there, taking pictures for the paper. Did I mention she's single?"

"Really?" A speculative smile bloomed on the woman's face.

"You never know who you might meet at the Santa Walk," said Frankie.

"You're right. You never know," the woman said, and they shared a conspiratorial smile.

Stef had left for other shops by the time their conversation was done. Maybe it was just as well, Frankie decided as she boxed up the train set for the woman. Stef might balk at meeting Mr. Grinch. And that would be a shame because Frankie had a good feeling about this.

Getting Elinor set up to be Mrs. Claus, possibly finding a man for Stef—all in a day's work for Santa Frankie.

10

BY THE TIME MITCH DROPPED INTO THE SHOP TO PICK UP
the collectible Department 56 Snowbaby he'd ordered for his
mom, Frankie had a Vote for Elinor poster in the shop window.

"Looks like you found a perfect candidate for Mrs. Claus,"
he said to Frankie as she rang up his sale.

Elinor, working the second register, blushed and beamed.

"I'll vote for you, Elinor. You up for spending the day with
me?" he asked.

"Oh, yes," she said, and the blush spread down her neck.

"We're going to stuff the ballot box," said Frankie.

"Thank you for doing this for me," Elinor said to her after
Mitch and their latest wave of customers had left.

Frankie shrugged off her thanks. "Like Mitch said, you'll

be perfect for the job. You're sweet and kind, and you'll make an adorable Mrs. Claus."

She was also shy, as Stef had pointed out, but really, the main focus at the event was Santa. Elinor would be fine.

In a way, getting temporarily bumped from the Mrs. Claus position was a good thing for Frankie. It would give her more time to concentrate on overseeing a meet-cute between Stef and the daddy in need of rescuing. Things did have a way of working out.

Meanwhile, Frankie had Natalie to worry about. Jonathan still didn't know if his job was safe, and more than once in the last couple of days, she'd caught Natalie texting on her phone and gnawing her lower lip.

Natalie would nod bravely in agreement when Frankie assured her that everything would be okay, but when you were in the middle of a storm, it was hard to imagine ever seeing a rainbow.

"That is the last of our Elf on the Shelf dolls," Adele informed her Friday afternoon. Starr March had just left with one to replace the elf the family puppy had discovered and shredded. "I told you those were going to fly off the shelf."

"Well, who knew?" said Frankie.

"Me," said Adele.

"I'll see if I can get in a few more," Frankie promised. Her phone dinged with a text from Brock. She'd deal with him later. At the moment, she had a business to run.

In addition to begging her supplier for more elves, she had a conversation with her business acquaintance Samuel Morgan, who owned the Mountain High Candy Company. "We lost the head of our creative confections team, and I don't know what I'm going to do," he said.

Now, there was an unexpected gift for her daughter straight out of Santa's sack. "What about Natalie? You know her creations have been a huge hit here at the store. We can't keep them in stock. Every time I turn around, she's coming up with a new flavor creation."

"You wouldn't mind me luring her away?"

"I don't have a problem with that," said Frankie. Of course, she'd miss having her daughter around, but the timing of this offer of a full-time job was perfect. It would mean a forty-minute commute from Carol, and they'd have to brainstorm childcare options for Warner, but still, it could be a good thing. If Natalie went to work for Mountain High, she'd earn a higher wage and have better benefits than Frankie was able to give her. "In fact, I think she'll jump at the chance. She's off today. Why don't you give her a call?" Frankie suggested, and shared Natalie's number.

"Thanks. I will," he said.

"I think I've just solved Natalie and Jonathan's money worries," she happily announced to Adele after the call ended.

Adele stopped putting more of the nutcrackers out on their display table. "I didn't know she'd asked you to solve them."

"What's that supposed to mean?" Frankie demanded.

"Just what it sounds like."

"They're worried about his job."

"He hasn't lost it yet. Honestly, daughter dear. If you spent as much time managing your own life as you did everyone else's…" She let the sentence hang.

"What?"

"I'm not sure Natalie wants you running her life."

"I'm not running her life. I'm just helping. And you're a fine one to talk. You're always giving me advice."

"Advice is one thing. Meddling is another." Adele pointed a finger at Frankie. "If you're not careful, one of these days all your helping is really going to backfire."

"That's ridiculous," said Frankie. "Everyone needs help."

A bell over the door jingled, a stranger walked in, and that ended the conversation.

Fortunately, the customer had left by the time Natalie called and a new conversation began.

"What the heck, Mom?"

This didn't bode well. "What's wrong?" Frankie asked, even though she already knew. There could only be one thing wrong.

Adele was watching her with an eyebrow raised. Frankie turned her back.

"Are you trying to get rid of me?" Natalie demanded.

"No, of course not," Frankie protested.

"Then why are you pimping me out to Mountain High?"

Frankie lowered her voice. "I'm not pimping you out. I'm trying to help you. I know Jonathan's been worried about his job."

"Well, he's not now. He just learned this morning that it's safe. And even if it wasn't, I don't want a forty-minute commute to work, and I don't want to work full-time."

"But you love making candy," Frankie protested. This was a great opportunity. Natalie should have been thanking her.

"Only small batches for gifts or for the shop. And I like working part-time. I thought you got that."

"I do. I just thought you might like this better."

"Well, I wouldn't," Natalie snapped. "I've gotta go." And she did.

Frankie could feel her mother's gaze burning into her.

"So much for Frankie Lane's Employment Agency," Adele observed.

Frankie turned and scowled at her. "Not funny, Mom."

Adele instantly lost her snark and came over to give Frankie a one-shouldered hug. "I'm sorry. You mean well, I know. But I really think you should take a break from being so involved in other people's lives. You have your hands full running your own life."

"I was only trying to help," Frankie muttered.

"No, darling. You were interfering. Help is something people ask for. I didn't hear Natalie asking for yours."

"This job would have been perfect for her," Frankie insisted.

"And what was she supposed to do for after-school day care?"

"We could have worked out something."

"What's this *we* stuff? Have you got a mouse in your pocket?"

"Come on, Mom. I would have pitched in and helped, and you know you would have, too."

"If someone asked me. But nobody did. And nobody asked you, either. Get your own life sorted out, and that should keep you plenty busy."

Stef read the text from Natalie. Lunch out? Please?

Oh, boy. What was going on? Had Jonathan's position dried up? OK, she texted back. Salad Bowl at 1?

Yes!!!

"Okay, what's going on?" Stef asked as soon as she and Natalie were seated.

"Mom," Natalie said.

"I thought you were going to tell me that Jonathan lost his job."

Natalie shook her head. "No, we're good. He's not going to be let go."

"That's a relief."

Angie, their regular server, appeared with two glasses of

water and a big smile. "How are you two doing today?" she asked.

Natalie didn't look ready to give a cheery answer, so Stef answered for both of them. "We're good," she said. Any other answer could very well inspire Angie to sit right down at the table with them and offer a shrink session. Angie cared about her Holiday Happiness peeps. Much as Angie cared, Stef was sure Natalie wouldn't want half the town hearing about what was bugging her.

"I assume you both want your usual mint tea with lemon?" Angie asked, and Stef nodded. "And how about some veggie soup?"

"I'll pass and have my usual," said Stef.

"One Hail Caesar," said Angie, not bothering to write down the order. "How about you, Natalie?"

"The same," said Natalie, so Angie nodded and moved on to see if any other customers wanted to share their day with her. "I don't need to eat anything hot. I'm already steamed," Natalie told Stef, once Angie was out of hearing distance.

"Okay, what's your mom done that's so bad?" Stef asked.

"Tried to get me a job," Natalie said, looking none too happy about it.

"Okay." That didn't sound too bad.

"Full time at Mountain High Candy. With a forty-minute commute."

"Working at a candy company doesn't sound too bad," Stef ventured.

"Except I don't want to work full-time right now, and I never said I did. I'm happy making candy when I can and helping out at the shop. And I want time for my family. And... we're going to have a baby," Natalie added.

Stef blinked. "OMG, seriously?"

Natalie seemed to forget she was angry and grinned and

nodded. She pulled a holiday-wrapped package from her purse and slid it across the table. "Don't open it here. I had one made for Mom and Gram Gram, too."

"So you haven't told your mom yet?"

Angie arrived with their drinks and a bowl of herbed biscuits just in time to hear this. "Tell your mom what? Are you okay, Natalie?"

"Natalie's working on a new candy," Stef improvised, ditching the bag. "Don't tell Frankie. It's top secret."

Angie nodded, her eyes alight with the thrill of being in on the secret. "My lips are sealed."

For about two seconds.

"Hey, Ang," called a man two tables down. "We need more bread here."

Angie left, and Natalie continued. "I was going to tell her on Sunday. Am going to," she corrected herself. "I should be over being mad at her by then."

"If she'd known, she probably wouldn't have…"

"Interfered?"

"Helped. She's been worried about you guys."

"I know. I get that. And I love Mom."

"Of course you do. We all do."

"But why does she think she needs to run everybody's life?"

"Habit."

"It's a bad habit. I'm not twelve."

"She knows that. She only wants to help." Natalie's thundercloud expression returned, and Stef felt the need to explain. "Your mom feels things deeply, and she always wants to make things right for people. It started way back when our dad died. Your grandma had a rough time for a while. She sort of… wasn't there."

Natalie looked perplexed. "I've never heard about this."

"It's way in the past and doesn't matter anymore. Your

grandma's a strong woman, and she eventually pulled herself together. But it didn't happen right away."

"I guess I never really stopped to think about Gram Gram's life when she was younger."

"Maybe none of us do. Old people are old people, and that's where we leave them."

Angie was back with their food. Time to take a sip of tea and shut the mouth.

Once she'd moved on, Stef continued. "I was only five—I'd been a surprise baby—and didn't grasp what was going on. My mother was totally shredded, but all I knew was that Daddy was gone, and my mommy wasn't paying attention to me like she used to. Frankie was so much older. She sort of took over as mother for a while. She'd already nominated herself to be a second mother to me because of our age difference, but this really cemented that."

Even after Adele recovered her equilibrium, Frankie had still been there for her little sister, offering fashion advice, encouraging Stef to get involved with her high school newspaper, helping her learn how to drive.

"It's never changed," Stef continued. "And I have to admit, I still kind of look at her as a second mom. I adore your mother."

"I do, too," Natalie said.

"Then you might have to give her a little grace. She's used to trying to smooth out everyone's lives." Including their love lives. Well-meaning as Frankie was, she didn't have the gift for matchmaking. But still. "Everything she does, she does out of love. Which is why I can never stay mad at your mom."

Natalie frowned. "If she wanted me to have a full-time job, she could have offered me one at the shop. At least I wouldn't have a commute."

"Maybe she thought someone else could pay you better."

Natalie shrugged and dug into her salad. "True. They could.

But we're going to be fine now, and really I like working part-time and making candy."

"So, life's good," said Stef. "Let this go."

"Yeah, I guess I need to." Natalie took another bite of salad and chewed thoughtfully. "You know, it's so ironic. Here's Mom, always running everyone's lives—trying to find jobs for me, giving Elinor a makeover."

"And trying to match me up," added Stef. "Don't ask." No way did she want to revisit the super-fail dinner party.

Natalie rolled her eyes. "But she can't figure out her own life."

"She's got most of it figured out," Stef said in fairness to her big sister. "Your mom's done a great job of building her business and picking up and carrying on after your dad died. He was her soulmate. You know that old *love you to the moon and back* saying? Well, she loved him to the moon and way beyond."

Natalie stared down at her salad and blinked, swiping tears from the corners of her eyes. "I still miss him. It's just so wrong that he's not here."

"I know," Stef said, and she, too, wanted to cry.

Ike had been a great man—fun, generous, the kind of man Stef had wanted to marry. The kind of man she'd thought she'd married. Until Richard showed his true colors. Were there any more Ikes out there? Stef sincerely doubted it.

"You know Mom didn't even want to go out with Brock, and I don't think that's going to last." Natalie sighed. "I don't want to see her alone for the rest of her life."

"She's not alone. She's got lots of friends," said Stef, trying to put a positive spin on things.

"She's going to lose them, too, if she's not careful. I still can't believe she put Mitch on a dating site."

That had been one of Frankie's goofier ideas, trying to set up a man who was perfect for her with someone else.

"Maybe we should be interfering in *her* life," suggested Natalie.

Stef laughed at the idea. "No, thanks. I've got my hands full trying to manage my own love life."

Ha! What love life?

Quit ghosting me. I know where to find you.

Frankie read Brock's text and sighed. She was hiding, not wanting to deal with the mess she'd stepped into.

But she needed to step out of it. Sorry. Want to meet up tonight?

Yes. How about Heat?

The restaurant offered interesting food fusions, such as chicken wonton tacos and pad thai quinoa bowls. Their bar specialized in color-changing cocktails, and it was always hard to get reservations.

Made reservations for six.

Well, he'd been confident. She supposed that was hardly surprising considering how she melted when he kissed her at the bar in Carol's Place. He was probably sure that even though she'd been hiding from him, he'd get them past that.

But now she was sure he wouldn't. When something didn't feel right, it wasn't right, and she needed to set the man free to go find someone else.

OK, she texted back, even as she wondered if she should

just take him out for coffee. Or do the ultimate in tacky and say adios via text.

Let me pick you up, he texted.

That would really end up being awkward. Have to run some errands first, she lied. I'll meet you there.

She got a sad-face emoticon in return. He'd probably be a lot sadder after they had their talk. But he was gorgeous and nice and would have no problem replacing her.

That thought was hardly an ego boost. True nonetheless.

Even though she was going to be ending things before they got any further down the love road, her pride demanded she go out looking good, and she still found herself spending more time than necessary deciding what she was going to wear. The red dress with the faux fur trim beckoned, but she told it no. It was too sexy and would say, *Pay no attention to anything I'm saying. I don't mean it.* She settled for jeans and a white blouse, topped with a soft angora sweater, along with her favorite designer-knock-off black boots with the bows on the side. Festive yet casual, pretty but not sending any *melt me for Christmas* messages.

As if she'd have to ask. A huge helping of a man like Brock would melt a woman simply because he was breathing.

He arrived at the restaurant casually dressed in jeans and a plaid shirt, looking ready to model for the cover of a romance novel. Or star in a holiday movie: *The Holiday Hunk.*

He'd have to be someone else's hunk.

He greeted her with a smile. "You look amazing."

She deflected the flattery. "You're easily amazed."

"Our table's not ready yet. Want to sit at the bar?"

Maybe she could end things at the bar, save him some money. She nodded.

He put a hand to her back as they made their way to a tall table. A man's hand on her back felt so good. *No melting*, she commanded herself.

Once seated, he looked at the drink menu and pointed to one. "How about this, the Christmas Chameleon?" he suggested, showing her a picture. The drink sported several colors, *thanks to our exotic butterfly pea flowers*, said the description. Butterfly pea flowers—she was living large.

"Okay," she said with a nod. She could stall the moment of truth by talking about their drinks. And then what? His life? Where he saw himself in ten years? Where he saw her in ten years? Starting to think about social security! She knew how fast ten years would go.

As soon as they ordered their drinks, he jumped right into it. "So, how come you've been avoiding me?"

"I'm sorry. I've been busy," she said.

He cocked his head and studied her.

"I have."

"You don't have to be afraid of this," he said. "Your husband would want you to get out and live."

"I live," she insisted. Okay, so her hormones were nearly in the graveyard, but that was beside the point.

Their server arrived with their drinks. They were so colorful. They said *party*. They were not even remotely a match for the conversation she and Brock were about to have.

He picked his up and held it toward her. "To the rest of our lives."

She could drink to that, even though the rest of their lives wasn't going to look like what he was envisioning.

This was ridiculous. She needed to quit stalling. Pull the bandage off with one rip. She took a fortifying gulp of her drink.

Then she heard it. Two twentysomething women, dressed in holiday finery and looking for fun, had just settled in at the table next to them. "Look, a cougar and her cub," one said to the other in a stage whisper, and her friend giggled.

Frankie's face caught fire. She knew Brock heard it, too, because he frowned.

"They're right, you know," Frankie said to him.

"They're drunk," he said.

They hadn't gotten any drinks yet. They were sober, and they knew exactly what they were doing.

"Drunk or sober, it doesn't change the fact that we have a big age gap." Not to mention an experience gap.

"That's ridiculous," he scoffed. "You look better than some forty-year-olds."

Some, not most. She wondered if he even realized what he'd said. "For now."

Actually, even now wasn't all that good. She was getting creases at the sides of her eyes. And she didn't like to think about the direction her boobs were starting to lean. It happened. Gravity got everyone in the end. Anyway, she was more than what people saw on the outside, right?

"It's just a number, Frankie."

"It's more than that. It's...stages."

Hadn't she already tried to explain this to him? He was determined to be dense. Or he simply couldn't see that far into the future. How farsighted had she been at forty? Stages.

"We will always be at different ones in our lives," she said. "Right now, you don't see it, but down the road, you will. I'll age before you will. I'll get tired at night and want to go to bed with a book..."

"And me."

She ignored him and went on. "You'll start noticing younger women. Thinking maybe you'd like to have kids after all." Notice their breasts riding higher, take in their smoother skin. It would be simple biology in action. "And then you'll want to move on," she continued. "You'll feel guilty. I'll feel heartbroken and humiliated..."

"Why do you think that?" he argued. "I'll be getting old, too, you know."

"But not at the same rate." Why was he making this so hard? She took another big gulp of her drink. "Brock, I'm sorry. I really do like you, but we're just not a fit. I can tell."

"We were fitting pretty good last time we were out," he said, reaching for her hand.

She slid it away before he could catch it. "You really know how to kiss, but I'm not the one you're supposed to be kissing. There is someone out there who you are supposed to be."

"Frankie," said a female voice.

Frankie gave a start and turned to see Barbara Fielding, elegantly gaunt in a black dress and matching heels, topped with a red suit jacket. She looked very corporate and slightly green-eyed.

"Barbara, what are you doing here?" Frankie asked.

Oops. That sounded like Barbara couldn't possibly have a social life. Obviously, she could.

Barbara's eyes narrowed. "I'm meeting some friends. Speaking of, who's yours?" The sour smile turned sweet, and the sour voice picked up honey.

"This is Mitch's new manager, Brock Adams."

"I'm going to have to go to the hardware store more often," said Barbara. "I'm sure I need a new...screwdriver."

Oh brother. *Don't roll*, Frankie commanded her eyeballs.

Brock grinned. "Good to meet you, Barbara. We've got just about anything you'll need at Handy's, and I'll be happy to help you find it."

"Good," Barbara said. An older couple walked in, and she waved to them. "Well, I'll let you two enjoy your drinks. See you soon, Brock."

He nodded. "Sure." Barbara left, and he turned his attention back to Frankie. "Frankie, there's no other woman in this whole town who's as fine and fun as you. I'm never going to change my mind about that."

Oh, the things people said so sincerely, believing every word. "You say that now, but you hardly know anyone in town yet. And really, you hardly know me. You can't know how you'll feel in ten years," she added, circling back to her main argument.

"Nobody can," he protested.

"You're wrong there," she said. Ike had promised to love her till the day he died, and he had. She'd known he was the only man for her, and he had been. "I bet those two women could use some company. Go join them. Tell them you were just keeping me company until my date arrived."

He scowled. "Come on, Frankie, don't do this."

"I have to," she said. "Before things get all tangled and then ugly. This way we can still stay friends."

He shook his head in disgust. "The *F* word."

"Nothing wrong with the *F* word." She stood and smiled down at him. "Thank you for the ego boost, for the kindness and for those kisses."

He didn't smile back. In fact, he was pouting. Being a man, he'd call it brooding. Ah well, he probably wouldn't be brooding for long.

She left the restaurant, got to her car and called Viola. "You got the Hallmark channel on?"

"Of course."

"Good. I'm picking up a pizza, then I'll be right over."

Pizza and Hallmark with her bestie worked wonders. And while she watched the couple have their meet-cute, followed by trouble but ending with smiles and a kiss, she'd remember that she had, once in her lifetime, lived a Hallmark movie.

There would be no sequel.

11

WITH THE EXCEPTION OF THANKSGIVING WEEKEND, NATA-lie had Saturdays off, so Frankie was surprised and wary to see her daughter entering the shop on Saturday. She found herself holding her breath. Was she still Doo-Doo Mom?

No. Natalie smiled at her as she came up to where Frankie stood at the cash register, enjoying a rare lull in business with Adele and Elinor.

Frankie let out the breath she'd been holding. "Am I forgiven?" she asked.

"Yeah. I know you meant well, Mom. But you still should have asked me."

"You're right," Frankie admitted. "I was worried about you guys, and I wanted to help."

"I know. You already help by letting me work here part-time."

"But the shop's my dream, not yours," Frankie protested. "I want to see you spread your wings and fly."

Natalie frowned. "My wings are fine. And who says I can't share your dream? I love the shop and the good vibes here, and I love making candy, but small batches work fine for now."

Frankie nodded slowly. "For now. Down the road you could expand, you know—start selling on the internet. You could become the next Godiva."

Natalie groaned. "Aaaah, not again. Gram Gram, make her stop."

Adele held up a hand in front of Frankie's face and said, "Stop," which made Elinor giggle.

"Et tu, Elinor?" Frankie said in disgust.

Elinor sobered. "No. I really appreciate how much you've been doing for me."

"Mom can be inspiring," said Natalie. "And you know I'm voting for you for Mrs. Claus, Elinor," she added.

Elinor smiled and thanked her, and Frankie felt like saying, *See? Some people appreciate my help.* But she wisely kept her mouth shut. Instead, she asked, "Where's my darling grandson?"

"He and Daddy are working on their LEGO town." Natalie held up two silvery gift bags with red tissue paper peeping out of them. "I just stopped by to deliver a special present to you two." She handed them over to Frankie and Adele.

Frankie reached inside and pulled out a red T-shirt. Under an image of an unopened present, it said Merry Christmas from Next Year's Grandkid.

Frankie gave a gasp of delight and hurried to hug her daughter.

"A great-grandma again," Adele said happily, and held up

her own T-shirt. Its amended message said Great-Grandkid. "Oh, baby."

"'Oh, baby' is right," Natalie said happily. "Another reason I don't want to work full-time and have a long commute. We've waited too long for this one, and I want to enjoy it."

Elinor congratulated her, then moved off to help a customer who'd come in and was inspecting the snow globes.

"I was going to tell you guys tomorrow, but I already told Aunt Stef, so it didn't seem right to make you wait."

"You already told Aunt Stef?" Frankie repeated. Of course, Natalie could tell who she wanted what she wanted when she wanted, but being the second to hear stung a little.

"We were having a shrink session," said Natalie.

Frankie could only imagine what had been said at that shrink session and decided she didn't want to hear any more. "Well, this is the best Christmas present…since Warner," she said, and Natalie beamed. "When does present number two come?"

"August."

"That will be here before you know it. And it gives us lots of time to plan a baby shower," said Adele.

Elinor was back, their customer behind her carrying a huge snow globe with an angel at its center, and that ended the personal sharing.

"I gotta go," Natalie said. "I need to run some errands." She hugged Frankie and Adele, and then was gone.

Frankie was doing the happy dance as her daughter went out the door. "I'm going to be a second-time grandma," she informed the snow-globe purchaser.

The woman, who looked about Natalie's age, smiled. "We just had our first last March. My mom has gone berserk buying presents. I'm not bothering to get a baby's first Christmas ornament because I know she's already been in and gotten one."

"Children and Christmas, they go together like sugar cookies and milk," Frankie said. She turned to Adele. "Oh, Mom, this is the best news ever."

Here it was, her Hallmark sequel. The joy of it all kept her smiling the rest of the day.

"Want to get Chinese and stream a movie?" Frankie asked her mother later. They'd closed the shop and were walking to their cars.

"Sorry, I've got plans."

Adele was usually up for hanging out and watching a movie. "Did one of the bunco babes claim you?" asked Frankie.

"One of my friends. I'd have thought you'd be with Viola. Isn't her husband still working nights?"

"He's home sick, so they've quarantined themselves. I was going to go over there and help her paint her bathroom."

"Are you sure he's really sick? Maybe Viola's hiding from you until she can get her painting project done," Adele teased.

"Funny. Not."

Adele wrapped an arm around Frankie's shoulders. "You have a night free. Call that handsome young man and see if he wants to do something."

"That's over," Frankie said.

Adele studied her and frowned. "That was quick."

Frankie shrugged. "I knew it wasn't right."

"You didn't give it much of a chance."

"I gave it all the chance it needed."

Adele let out a frustrated breath. "Daughter dear, I understand that desire to wall yourself off, but don't give in to it. Hurt will find you no matter how careful you are, and if you spend all your life making sure you won't get hurt, you'll also deprive yourself of a lot of happiness."

"You're a fine one to talk," said Frankie.

"I know. I'm a slow learner. But don't be like me. Don't

wear your widowhood like armor for the rest of your life. You're still young. You have a lot of years ahead of you. There's plenty of time for you to enjoy a second helping of love."

"I'm fine, Mom," Frankie insisted. "And now, with another grandbaby on the way, I couldn't be happier."

Adele chuckled and kissed her cheek. "One can always be happier. Call Mitch and watch a cop movie. See you tomorrow."

Frankie watched as her mother drove away. Adele had lost Dad way too early and always blamed their age difference. "Marry a younger man," she'd advised both her daughters. "They last longer."

But that wasn't true. Anything could snatch away the one you loved.

Instead of going to her car, she did an about-face and walked to Handy's Hardware. Mitch had already strung lights along her roofline for her, but now she decided she needed more. Lights around the windows. Lights on the rhododendrons sitting in front of the house. Lights. Lots of lights.

He was leaving as she walked in. "Here to see Brock?" he asked.

"No." She sounded slightly snotty and wasn't even sure why. Maybe because his question had come out sounding like some sort of taunt. "That's not going to work out." He opened his mouth to speak but she cut him off. "And don't say 'I told you so.'"

He shrugged.

"I'm here to get some more Christmas lights."

"Hoping to start a brownout?" he teased.

"I'm going to put up lights on my windows."

"I can help you with that," he offered. It was so very Mitch. Always ready to help. "We can do it tonight if you want."

She realized that was exactly what she wanted. Back hanging out with Mitch, putting up more Christmas lights—all was right with the world again.

"Okay," she said.

"Pizza afterward?" he suggested.

"Pizza afterward. You get the lights, and I'll get the pizza and beer."

And just like that, she had something to do.

It felt companionable and right as they stood in front of her house, her feeding him the string of lights, him securing them.

The fresh snow that had been promised started to fall just as they finished draping the bushes. She turned on her roof lights as well, then stood on her front walk and took a picture with her phone.

"This might be my next year's Christmas card," she said, showing him the photo.

"Wait and get your family over, then it will be perfect."

"We'll have more family to include next year," she told him as they walked back inside the house. "Natalie and Jonathan are pregnant, and I'll have another grandbaby come August."

He smiled. "Nothing like kids to make life great."

Such a different attitude from Brock, who claimed not to want any. How could she ever have even contemplated being with a man who didn't enjoy children?

She put the take-and-bake pizza she'd bought in the oven, and they got out the beer.

"Here's to the new family member," Mitch said. He held out his beer, and they clinked bottles. "Next year's gonna be a good year."

"Every year's a good year when you have great family and friends," she said. "I'm glad you're mine."

She thought he'd say, *Same here*, but he only smiled and took a slug of beer.

"Right?" she prompted.

"You know how I feel about you."

His tone of voice sent a little shiver running through her while heating her face at the same time. She chose to ignore both. "I know," she said.

Friendship was safe, and friendship was enough.

He took another drink of his beer, then cleared his throat. "I'll always want the best for you, Frankie."

"This is best," she said.

He nodded. "Start the movie."

She did. They ate pizza and watched as the hero dodged bullets, survived car chases and solved a murder. All in a day's work. For a moment, she couldn't help wishing life was as simple as the movies.

"Don't you wish life could be like a good movie, with everything turning out perfect in the end?" she said to Mitch as the ending credits rolled.

"There's no such thing as a perfect life, but you can have perfect moments," he said.

"Very profound."

"I can be."

She smiled at him. "This is one."

He took a final swig of his beer. "It's close." Then before she could ask what he meant by that, he said, "Guess I'd better be going. *Cop Stop* tomorrow?"

"Of course."

She sent him home with the last two pieces of pizza and watched him drive off, his truck headlights spotlighting the gently falling snow.

Close to perfect wasn't half bad.

Frankie got her movie moments the next day after work when everyone gathered at Adele's for lasagna and cookie baking. Of course, they had to make gumdrop cookies for Warner, and sugar cookies, which he was delighted to help decorate, dumping mounds of sprinkles on each one. No one told him that, when it came to decorating cookies, less was more. When you were six, more was more.

Finally, full of lasagna and loaded up with cookies, Natalie and her family left, and Adele and her daughters settled in to enjoy a final eggnog.

"It looks like you found something to do last night," Adele observed as she scraped half the sprinkles off her cookie. "The new lights on your windows look nice."

"Mitch came over and helped me," Frankie said.

"He's the best," said Stef. "I'm surprised Brock didn't come over." Obviously, Adele had said nothing.

Discussing Brock with her sister had felt awkward ever since Frankie's matchmaking dinner-party fail, and she found herself feeling relieved to be able to share that things were not going to work out for them.

"We really are two different people," she said.

Adele shook her head. "I still think you should have given it more of a chance."

"He was too young." In so many ways.

"And Mitch is too old. Too young, too old. What are you, Goldilocks? You're never going to find a man who's just right, trust me," said Adele.

"I'm not looking for one. Honestly, Mom, this is getting old."

"And so are you," Adele retorted, determined to have the last word.

Okay, that was enough family time. Frankie took her share of the cookies and left.

"I worry about your sister," Adele said when it was only her and Stef sitting at the kitchen bar.

"She's fine, Mom. She's tough."

"I worry about you, too, kidlet."

"I'm tough, too," said Stef. Well, she was getting there.

"I want you both to be happy."

"We're not exactly miserable now, Mom."

"No, I mean really happy. Settled, with someone special in your life who cares. You both deserve that."

Stef remembered her miserable years with Richard. "I guess we don't always get what we deserve."

"I think we do eventually. Be on the watch. Your time will come."

Stef thought back to when she was a kid and could hardly get to sleep on Christmas Eve. Even when she was struggling the hardest, Adele had managed to make sure her girls had presents under the tree. Later, Stef learned that Adele had had much-needed help—a grandpa assembling a bicycle on Christmas Eve, a grandma bringing over Christmas cookies and buying treats for the stockings. All Stef had known was that Santa was coming, and waiting for him had felt like a forever task.

"He'll come, but not when you're looking for him," her grandmother had said. "Santa likes to surprise people."

Stef may have been in charge of the Letters to Santa page, but she was long past waiting for Santa to surprise her.

Except Monday morning, she was in The Coffee Stop making a midmorning coffee run when the big-girl equivalent of a perfect gift from Santa walked in.

He was tall and trim and broad-shouldered, with short red hair, wearing a coat over a gray suit and tie. He had a mouth that could probably work devastation on a woman if he smiled, but he wasn't smiling. A person shouldn't look so sober and serious in a coffee shop.

Carol was no longer a small town, but it was hardly the big

city. Why hadn't Stef seen this man before? Had he fallen off Santa's sleigh somewhere on the way to Seattle? Who was he?

The moment of excitement died practically at birth. He was with another man, equally well-dressed and a little older, listening as the redheaded man talked. Were they a couple? It always seemed like the best ones were taken.

The Santa surprise took off his gloves. No ring on either hand. The older guy was checking out a younger woman who'd come into the coffee shop. Maybe they weren't a couple.

She texted Frankie. We know every single man in Carol, right? She was sure she'd dated every one.

No. Why?

Just wondering, Stef texted.
Where are you? Frankie wanted to know.

Coffee Stop.

See someone interesting?

He's with someone. I don't think they're together, though.

Say hi and find out, Frankie suggested, and added a wink.

Richard awoke from his slumbers in Stef's subconscious. *Go ahead and make a fool of yourself.*

Shut up, she commanded him. Maybe I feel like paying it forward, she texted Frankie.

Good idea, her sister approved.

After placing her order and paying, Stef handed over an extra twenty to Suzie the barista. "Whatever they want is on me and keep the change."

She pretended not to listen as Suzie told Mr. Just What Stef

Needs for Christmas that the woman ahead of him had paid for their drinks.

Then, as she was taking hers, she was aware of him beside her. It felt like coming up against some kind of electrical field.

"Hey there."

The timbre of his voice started a buzzing in her veins. She aimed for casual as she turned to him and smiled.

He smiled in return—more of a polite smile than a flirty one. He lifted his to-go cup. "Just wanted to thank you for the pay-it-forward."

"'Tis the season," she quipped, hoping to broaden his smile. She didn't. Polite stayed firmly in place. "So I hear."

"You only hear?" she teased. Her phone dinged from her coat pocket, signaling an incoming text. She ignored it.

He shrugged.

Her phone dinged again.

"Looks like you're popular."

"All the elves want to date me," she joked, and her phone rang.

"Guess I'd better let you get that. Anyway, thanks for the drink. Merry Christmas," he added.

She scowled at her to-go cup as he joined his friend, took his drink and then walked out the door. Pickup fail.

She pulled out her phone, ready to answer with a grumpy hello. It was Camille. She lost the grumpy.

"My computer lost your doc. I need it ASAP."

Of course she did, and since said doc wasn't on Stef's phone, she'd be hustling her hind end back to the office.

"You'll have it in ten," she said as she started out the door.

"Make it five," said Camille, and ended the call.

"Ho, ho, ho," grumped Stef. Too bad she was too old to write a letter to Santa. She'd ask him to spread a little more joy and patience around town. And to help her find the mystery man.

★ ★ ★

"She was hot," said Griff's Edward Jones partner, Jamison.

"Yeah, she was," Griff admitted.

Standing next to her, he'd felt the heat, and it had stirred up that longing for connection deep inside of him. But instead of doing anything about it, he'd stood there like a giant ice sculpture.

Given a few more minutes, maybe her smile could have melted him. She had the kind of smile that said, *Come on, be happy. You can do it.*

He wanted to be happy. He'd gone from mourning to moping to… What was he now? Bitter. Not all the time, not about everything. Just about the way his life had turned out.

Well, that was everything.

Except he had something important that Kaitlyn had left behind with him. He had a great kid. Who wanted Santa to bring him a mom since Dad hadn't come through.

"I bet you didn't get her number," said Jamison.

"She got a phone call. What was I supposed to do, stand there? Wait and chase her down?"

"I would have. You would have, too, if your brain wasn't frozen. Somewhere in there, you've still got it. I know. I remember you chasing Kaitlyn until the poor woman dropped at your feet."

The memory of how hard he'd worked to win Kaitlyn's love brought back happy memories. Him freezing his ass off at that caroling party when they'd first met, wishing he could sing on pitch. Sending her a big bouquet of tiger lilies for Valentine's Day…that she was allergic to. Romantic dinners out and weekends at the Hilton in Seattle that about broke his budget. A summer cruise in the San Juans.

She'd finally had him over to her place on the Fourth of July and set out a picnic for them on her balcony—sub sandwiches, fried chicken, potato salad and bottled iced tea. She told him she'd fallen in love with him the first time she heard him try to croak out "Silent Night," so he could stop with all the crazy stuff. And when was she going to get a ring?

She got one the next day.

Now here was a new woman who'd obviously been interested, and he'd missed his opportunity.

Except, tomorrow she might need a midmorning coffee break.

Maybe he would, too.

Stef had just sent off the needed document when the text from Frankie came in. Call me when you're done having coffee.

Of course, Frankie would be all excited and hopeful, sure that Stef's coffee shop encounter was a matter of serendipity. Serendipity had sure fizzled.

Done, she replied. Camille texted and I had to go and he gave up.

He sure gave up easy.

That could happen when your phone was dinging and ringing like crazy. Oh well.

Maybe he'll be back looking for coffee tomorrow, Frankie suggested.

Maybe he would. Maybe Stef would want to get some coffee at the same time tomorrow. Good idea.

I'm full of good ideas. ☺

That she was, and some of them not so good. It would probably be best if Stef did her own matchmaking without any help from her sister. She'd try the coffee shop again the next day. If the mystery man was there, then she'd know they were meant to meet.

It looked like Stef wasn't meant to be with her coffee shop surprise. She woke up the morning after their brief encounter feeling like an eighteen-wheeler had run over her head, and she was starting to see sparklers go off to the sides of her eyes. Migraine City. There would be no trip to the coffee shop that morning.

She staggered her way to the bathroom, took a pill and called in sick. Then she lay down on her spinning bed, pulled the blankets over her face and hosted her own little pity party.

Griff just happened into The Coffee Stop at ten thirty. An older couple was seated at one of the wooden tables. In front of him, two women stood in line, one of them holding a baby. The other had a toddler hanging on her arm. It didn't look promising.

He ordered an Americano and took a seat at one of the high tables by the windows, thumbing through emails on his phone and keeping an eye on the door. An older guy he always saw when he went into the hardware store came in, along with a nice-looking woman, younger than him. The hair color was different, and she wasn't the same age, but she reminded him of the woman he'd seen the day before. Too bad she wasn't that woman.

This had been a lame idea. He took his coffee and went back to work.

And tried not to think of the pretty woman with the friendly smile and generous spirit.

12

BARBARA OPENED THE FINAL SANTA WALK COMMITTEE meeting by predicting that this year's Santa Walk would be the best one yet. Of course it would because Barbara was in charge. It was all Frankie could do not to stick her finger in her mouth and pretend to gag.

"I think all we need to do now is finalize our Mrs. Claus pageant," Barbara continued.

"What's left to finalize?" Frankie asked. "We've got ballot boxes everywhere, and we're set to use the VFW hall for the pageant."

"Frankie, sometimes you overlook the details. We still haven't got judges for the pageant."

"Do we really need judges? Why can't we just tally the votes?" asked Frankie.

"It would hardly be a pageant if that's all we did. Thanks to the suggestion of the gingerbread houses," Barbara said, her tone of voice showing exactly what she thought of that addition to the pageant, "we now have to have judges."

"People can vote for their favorite gingerbread house at the event," Frankie said. "Then we'll add those to the other votes, which we'll already have tallied. Simple."

"I think we should have judges for those," Barbara insisted. "You can't have a pageant without judges."

"Who are we going to get to judge at this late date?" asked Hazel, frowning. "The Santa Walk is right around the corner."

Everyone looked to Theresia, the queen of the chocolate croissant.

She held up a hand. "Oh no. I don't want that responsibility."

"I'll help you," Frankie offered.

"That's not a good idea," Barbara said sternly, pulling a frown from Frankie. "Your employee is competing. You'll be biased."

"I'll help you," said Autumn.

"I can be on the judges panel as well since none of my employees are competing," said Barbara. Which meant Elinor's gingerbread house wouldn't stand a chance.

"You already have so much to do," said Frankie, throwing Barbara's earlier words to her back at Barbara. "I can see if Mayor Lent would like to judge. As our mayor, she should be involved. And she should be the one to award the winner."

"Excellent idea," approved James.

Barbara stiffened but managed a smile. "All right. I'll contact the mayor." Of course she would. That was too important a job to leave to her underlings.

"That should be enough judges, right? What do you think, everyone?" asked Frankie.

"I think that sounds good," said Autumn, and Frankie smiled sweetly at Barbara, enjoying her petty victory.

"That takes care of that then," Barbara said stiffly.

"We need to make sure we have ballot boxes next to all the gingerbread houses," Frankie insisted. "Even though we have judges, the people's vote should be the most important."

"Agreed," said Hazel.

"Oh, very well, but if you ask me this is turning into a very unusual pageant," Barbara grumbled. "One vote per person," she added, looking at Frankie.

"As if I would stuff the ballot box at the pageant," Frankie said to Elinor when she got back to the shop. There would be too many witnesses.

"I could probably use it," Elinor said. "I have no idea how I'm going to make a gingerbread house."

"No worries," said Frankie. "Team Elinor is here for you. We'll all help. We should do it tonight. That way, if something goes wrong, we'll have time to fix it. Mom," she called to Adele.

Her mother was over by the Disney ornaments, supposedly helping Mr. Bellagamba, their mailman, pick out an ornament for his granddaughter but mostly yakking.

"Can you come help us with gingerbread house construction tonight?" Frankie asked loudly.

Adele said something to Mr. Bellagamba, then called back, "Tomorrow night is better."

Natalie, who was putting out the last of the tree-shaped mint chocolates she'd brought in earlier, called, "Gram Gram, what are you thinking? Tomorrow is Warner's Winter Concert."

"That's right," said Frankie. "Then we'll have to do it on Thursday."

"That's the night before the pageant. What if something goes wrong?" Elinor fretted.

"What could go wrong?" Frankie scoffed. "Anyway, Thursday is better. That will give me time to order a pattern."

Or not. As she searched various sites on her phone, she discovered that gingerbread house patterns were either temporarily out of stock or wouldn't arrive until Friday, the day of the pageant.

"This isn't good," she said in a low voice to Natalie.

"See if Mitch can come up with something. He is a handyman, and he did design that addition he put on his house."

"Good idea," said Frankie, and texted him.

I can come up with something for you, he promised. Will drop it by your place later.

You are the best, she texted back.

And he was. She really should start looking around again for someone for him. Someone who would be willing to share, of course.

William Sharp entered the shop, looking for a new ornament for his tree. More like looking for yet another excuse to see Elinor. These two were definitely a match. When was that man going to get his courage up and ask her out? At the rate he was going, never. Frankie would have to give them a nudge.

"William, are you going to vote for Elinor for Mrs. Claus?" she asked him.

"Of course I am," he said. "I know you'll win," he told Elinor, which—surprise, surprise—made her blush. How cute were they?

"You are coming to the pageant, aren't you?" Frankie pressed. "You can sit with Team Elinor."

He smiled at that and said he'd be happy to. Frankie would make sure they sat together.

True to his word, Mitch stopped by Frankie's house that evening with gingerbread house plans. He found her up to her wrists in cookie dough. She met him at the door, still wiping it off with a damp washcloth.

"I thought I'd make a small batch to see what it tastes like," she said.

"When does construction start?" he asked.

"Thursday night. I know that's cutting it close, but Mom couldn't do tonight. And Wednesday is Warner's school concert. We can't miss that. But we'll have a full crew on Thursday. Hopefully, we can manage this. Your house design isn't too elaborate, is it?"

"Nope. I kept it simple. It's all about the stuff you put on it anyway, isn't it?"

"I hope so," said Frankie. "Anyway, gingerbread houses are only an extra attraction. How many votes Elinor gets on hers shouldn't affect the outcome." Although many elections were won by only a handful of votes. "I hope."

In addition to getting her mother, daughter and sister to help Elinor, Frankie planned to also draft Viola. With so many of them involved, she'd decided to make a party of it. "Everyone's going to bring goodies to decorate the house, and we'll build and party."

"So, a whole construction crew."

"I guess you could say that."

He looked beyond her toward the kitchen. "You need a taste tester?"

"Sure. Want some decaf?"

"Yep," he said, and followed her into the kitchen.

"I sure hope Elinor becomes our Mrs. Claus," Frankie said as she started his coffee. "It would be so good for her."

"The way you've been campaigning for her all over town, I don't see how she can lose."

"I want to do everything I can to help her."

"I'd say you are," he said.

She gave him his coffee, and they chatted about what they were getting for their families for Christmas as he watched her work. It was all so cozy and friendly. Ike would have approved of this arrangement.

"This is good," he said after sampling the first experimental cookies that came out of the oven. "You guys gonna auction off the houses afterward?"

"I never thought of that. Good idea. We could, and then donate the proceeds to the Help Santa fund. I'll have to have Stef get that in the paper. But first, I'll have to suggest it to Barbara in a way that makes her think it was her idea."

Mitch chuckled. "I see you're managing to, er, manage Barbara."

Frankie sighed. "It's not easy to work with someone who basically came in and took over."

"We know who got the Santa Walk ball rolling. Anyway, sharing is caring. That's what my mom always told me when my little brother stole one of my toys," he said, and put the last bite of cookie in his mouth.

"I don't care about Barbara."

"But you care about the Santa Walk, and you care about Carol."

"You're right," she said. She took a big bite of cookie, hoping it would sweeten up her attitude.

She called Barbara after Mitch left and asked if Barbara had any ideas for what to do with the gingerbread houses after the pageant.

"The contestants can take them home."

"I'm just wondering if there's a way we can put them to use," Frankie suggested.

"How?"

"What about some sort of fundraising angle?"

"Selling them?"

"Or auctioning them?"

"Hmm. Auctioning them could be fun."

"So many good causes in town. Animal rescue, the food bank, the Help Santa fund…" Frankie let the last suggestion dangle, a verbal bauble waiting to be grabbed.

Barbara snatched it. "We could auction them off and donate the proceeds to the Help Santa fund. That seems appropriate."

"Yes, it does. Good idea," Frankie added, and almost choked on the words.

"I think we'll do that. I can mention it when I go on the radio tomorrow."

"A very good idea."

"Yes, I'm glad we decided to do the gingerbread houses."

Which you were so not in favor of.

Oh well. Everything they were doing was to benefit the community. As long as the end result was good, who cared how they got to it?

That took care of the pageant. Now, what was going on with Stef? She should have checked in. Frankie picked up her phone and called her sister.

"I'm dying," Stef answered. "Someone drove an ax into my head, and it's splitting open."

"Oh no. When did that hit?"

"This morning."

"So I guess you didn't make it to the coffee shop."

"I don't want to talk about it."

And that encounter had sounded so hopeful. "Don't give up," Frankie said.

Stef just groaned.

"And feel better." Because life was bound to get better for Stef, and Frankie was determined to do her part to make sure it happened.

★ ★ ★

Frankie ground her teeth as she listened to Barbara's interview on her phone the next morning. She was sitting in the back room of Holiday Happiness, doing paperwork.

"The gingerbread houses sound like a fun addition to the pageant," said Carly Rae, radio personality and host of the morning show, *Carol's Life*. "That pageant is something new this year, isn't it? In the past, Frankie Lane from Holiday Happiness has been Mrs. Claus."

"Frankie felt it was time to step down," Barbara said.

"I did not!" Frankie snapped at her phone.

"The whole Santa Walk thing was her idea, wasn't it?" Carly Rae continued.

"Oh, many of us were involved," Barbara lied.

"Not you, until you wormed your way onto the committee," Frankie said.

She could almost hear Mitch saying, *Sharing is caring.*

He was right, of course. Frankie had started the Santa Walk to benefit the town and local businesses. People loved it, so really, what did it matter if she wound up sharing the credit for making it happen? Lots of people had gotten involved, and without their help, she couldn't have pulled it off.

"And Mitch Howard will be Santa again this year, right?"

Without Frankie helping him. But she'd feel a lot less grumpy if Elinor was the one to take her Mrs. Claus cape.

"We're all excited to see who wins the Mrs. Claus pageant," said Carly Rae. "So, everybody come to the VFW hall this Friday and root for your favorite contestant. And bring money so you can bid on those amazing gingerbread houses. It's all for a good cause. Then on Saturday, be sure to visit our downtown shops, which will be offering all kinds of holiday specials. We have added entertainment this year, too, right, Barbara?"

"We do. We'll have strolling carolers to entertain everyone."

"And the Santa pub crawl for the grown-ups on Saturday night," put in Carly Rae. "Is that happening again this year?"

"Yes, put on your best Santa suit or elf hat. Our local restaurants and pubs will be offering discounts on drinks and appetizers."

"Bring your kids to see Santa before he starts hitting the bar," joked Carly Rae. "Right, Barbara?"

"Yes. He'll be at the gazebo in the town square from noon to three."

Hearing all the fun that was planned blew away Frankie's crankiness. She had started this event with pure motives. She didn't need to be undoing that by letting her ego get in the way. And she wouldn't, darn it all. This was for the town and the people she loved, and seeing others catch the vision was a good thing. There. See how good it felt to be noble?

She wrapped her nobility around her like a warm blanket and kept it there when three different customers came in that morning to report that they'd heard Barbara on the radio.

"But it was your idea. She should have given you credit," said Mrs. Whitworth, who always bought Natalie's candy.

"Yes, it was," Frankie said, glad that someone remembered. "But I'm happy to see it growing and getting better every year."

"I think it still sucks that Barbara took over," Natalie said when she brought in more candy to replace their diminishing supply.

"Oh well. I can live with it." *For this year. Don't plan on being in charge next year, Barbara.* Sharing was caring, and it was about time Barbara learned that.

So much for nobility.

The day flew by. Then it was time to grab a quick sandwich at home and head out the door for her grandson's concert. Of course, Warner would be the cutest snowflake of all the little snowflakes on the school's stage.

★ ★ ★

It took Stef longer than she anticipated to recover from her monster headache, and she barely made it to the school in time for Warner's concert on Wednesday evening. The program was about to start when she stumbled to the end of the row where her family was seated. Thankfully, Frankie had saved her a seat on the end.

"I was just about to text you," Frankie said. "How are you feeling?"

"Better. At least I finally pulled the ax out of my head." Stef leaned over to wave at Natalie, who was seated farther down.

That was when she saw him, seated in the same row, on the other side of the aisle. "Oh my gosh, that's him," she said to Frankie.

"Him who?" Frankie asked, following her gaze.

"The man from the coffee shop."

Frankie looked. "Wow, he's cute."

There was an understatement.

"Looks like Santa's delivering him right into your lap," said Frankie. "You can just wander on over that way after the concert and stroll by."

Because he was so interested in you, came the nasty voice of Stef's ex.

Her bubble of excitement burst. "Maybe not."

"Don't chicken out. For all you know, he might have been in The Coffee Stop yesterday looking for you."

Stef nodded. Her sister made a good point.

"What have you got to lose?"

Nothing. You already are a loser.

The ghost of husband past. Stef told him to go find a rock to crawl under. Frankie was right, she had nothing to lose.

"Welcome, family and friends, to our annual winter fest concert," the school principal greeted everyone. "The children have been working very hard this year to give you a wonderful concert. So sit back and enjoy and let the fun begin."

This is one of the good things in life I need to remember to be grateful for, Griff thought as the curtains parted to show several little sugar plum fairies and nutcracker princes dancing to the center of the stage, all students of Mrs. Ballard's after-school dance program.

"Corky's next," Jenn whispered, and got her phone ready as the dancers posed, waiting for the next group of entertainers.

So did Griff. He knew his parents were expecting him to record their grandson's big moment. And there it came. He aimed his phone and recorded as a line of little boy elves marched across the stage, each holding a giant card with a red letter on it. All together, they spelled Merry Christmas.

"To everyone," called Corky as they exited stage right after the dancers. He waved to the crowd, thoroughly enjoying his big part.

"Thank God his tummy got better," Jenn said as everyone clapped.

Corky had complained about his stomach hurting but had managed to wolf down a hot dog and then seemed to feel better. "I think it was nerves."

"That little ham? More like excitement," Jenn said.

Either way, Griff was glad Corky hadn't had to miss out on something he'd been looking forward to.

Meanwhile, the sixth-grade choir had assembled on risers to sing "Jingle Bells," accompanied by the school's music teacher on the piano. Another student, standing next to her, jingled bells with enthusiasm.

Corky would be back on soon with his class to sing about "Rudolph the Red-Nosed Reindeer." He'd been wearing his felt reindeer antlers around the house for the last two days. Of course, the reindeer antlers reminded him of Santa, and he'd bugged Griff each day to check the paper's Letters to Santa page to see if Santa had answered his letter yet.

"Maybe the reindeer ate it," said Griff when their latest attempt got no results, continuing with his blame-the-reindeer plan.

"Reindeer don't eat letters, Daddy," Corky said.

"They might if they get really hungry," Griff replied.

Corky had frowned at that. "We'd better go see Santa."

"We'd better get you ready for bed," Griff said. "You've got a big day tomorrow."

And so the Santa bullet had been dodged again. Temporarily.

Corky's class was about to come out and sing when the teacher's assistant found Griff and motioned him out of his seat. "I'm afraid we have a problem," she said after Griff had stepped on half a dozen sets of toes trying to get to the end of the aisle to her. "Corky's not feeling well."

Jenn had followed right along behind. "What do you mean?" she asked.

"I'm afraid he's been a little sick."

"A little sick," Jenn repeated. "Oh no. You mean, he…?"

The woman nodded.

"He what?" asked Griff.

"He barfed," Jenn translated. "Poor kid. We need to get him out of here."

They did indeed. They found Corky, left behind in the classroom with one of the mom volunteers, weeping as she mopped the front of his white shirt.

"Daddy!" he cried.

Griff hurried to pick him up and hug him. Jenn was right behind, patting the boy's shoulder and saying, "It's okay."

Griff couldn't help wishing Kaitlyn was there to help comfort their son.

"I threw up," Corky sobbed. "Jeremy Jenkins laughed."

"Jeremy Jenkins is a shit," said Griff, making the volunteer mother blink in surprise. "Come on, son, let's get you home."

"I want a cookie," Corky protested.

Cookies had been promised at the end of the show.

"You can't have a cookie. You'll just puke it up," said Griff, which made Corky cry harder.

Okay, he could have been more diplomatic. Kaitlyn would have known what to say.

"I'll get some ginger ale for you while Daddy gets you cleaned up," promised Jenn. "Ginger ale is yummy for the tummy."

Corky sniffled and smiled at her, and Griff mouthed a thank-you and carried his son out of the classroom. They were almost to the car when Corky upchucked again, getting Griff's coat good in the process.

"My tummy hurts," wailed Corky.

"I know," said Griff. "It'll be okay, though. We'll get you in bed, and you'll feel all better."

"Will I feel better in time to go see Santa?" Corky asked.

"Let's not worry about that right now, okay?" Griff said, and his son started crying all over again.

Happy holidays.

"You were my favorite snowflake," Frankie said to her grandson as she hugged him after the concert.

"I want to be a snowflake next year, too," he announced, making the grown-ups gathered around him smile fondly.

Frankie watched as he raced off to shed his costume and get one of the cookies the children had been promised as a reward.

"Just think, this time next year we'll have another little snowflake in the family," said Adele, and Natalie and Jonathan caught hands and smiled at each other.

It was too early to let go of family fun. "Who wants to come over and help me drink eggnog before I consume it all?" Frankie offered.

"We need to get Warner home and in bed," said Natalie.

"Works for me," Stef said. "I've got nothing else going," she added with a small frown.

Frankie turned to Adele. "Mom, you going to join us?"

"I'll have to pass. I've got someone coming over," Adele said.

"Only yesterday you didn't have any plans besides this," Frankie pointed out.

"Life is fluid," Adele replied. Whatever that meant.

"You bunco babes are total party animals," Frankie teased.

"'Tis the season," said Adele, and gave her a kiss on the cheek.

"Is it my imagination, or is she getting too busy for us?" said Stef as they watched Adele move toward the door.

"Starting that bunco group certainly has taken up more of her time. But I don't begrudge her a social life. She's earned it," Frankie said.

She could still remember how hard her mother had struggled to come to terms with her widowhood. Unlike Frankie, she hadn't had a business to consume her. Instead, all she'd had was grief. And that had almost succeeded in eating her alive. It had been a slow crawl out of that dark hole, but Adele had managed.

And when Frankie had fallen in the same dark hole, she'd had her mother to help her out. They'd had many conversations about life and death and life after death.

"I know I'll see your father in heaven someday," Adele had said, "and I know you'll see Ike, too. Meanwhile, you have a family that needs you and a business to run. You still have purpose, and you're still here. I hope it won't take as long for that to sink in for you as it did me. There is always something good in life. Find that and focus on it. There are always good people in life, too. Find them and enjoy them."

Frankie felt she'd done a pretty good job of following her mother's advice. For the most part. The holidays were still the hardest, and she was glad she didn't have to leave her loved ones and return to her house alone.

Back at the house, the sisters settled in with their eggnog for an assessment of Stef's non-love life as Christmas music streamed in the background.

"It stinks that you and your mystery man keep missing each other," Frankie said. "I wonder why he vanished so quickly after the concert. Usually parents hang around for a while."

"Kidnapped by the Grinch?"

"That must be it."

"Between that and my stupid migraine it looks like he goes in the not-meant-to-be column. I guess I made more of it than it was. I'm sure glad I didn't ask Santa for a man this year, 'cause he's not coming through."

With the Santa Walk right around the corner, Frankie couldn't help remembering her conversation with the woman in her shop. A certain lonely man could show up, bringing his son to see Santa.

"Santa hasn't come yet," she said.

Stef studied her eggnog. "You know, it's weird. After I split with Richard, I vowed I would never be with another man again. But here I am, looking."

"Nothing wrong with that. Who wants to be alone?"

"You're managing."

"I am." Although sometimes managing wasn't all it was cracked up to be.

"What if I blow it again?" Stef said in a small voice.

"You're too smart for that," Frankie assured her. "And you're wiser now. You won't blow it."

Stef smiled at her. "You really are my hero, you know."

Embarrassed, Frankie waved away the comment.

"No, I mean it," Stef insisted. "You look out for everyone. But who looks out for you?"

"Oh, I think I've got a guardian angel or two on duty," Frankie said lightly. "I'm doing okay."

"Are you? Really?" Stef asked earnestly.

"Of course I am. Don't worry about me," Frankie said. "My life is good."

Stef gnawed her lip. "Are you sorry you broke it off with Brock?"

"No. It wouldn't have worked. And really, I don't think it would have worked for you, either. He didn't want to have kids. You might want to try again."

"I'd like to, but who knows?" said Stef.

Again, Frankie thought of her conversation in the shop. "Who knows what the future holds?"

Later, after her sister left, Frankie continued to sit by her tree, thinking about her life and the lives of the ones she loved. If she could ask God for one thing, it would be a hopeful beginning to the new year for all of them.

Surely that wasn't too much to ask.

When it came to new beginnings, Elinor was Frankie's pet project. Frankie closed the shop early on Thursday, leaving a sign on the door that read:

CLOSED TO GET READY FOR THE MRS. CLAUS PAGEANT TOMORROW. VOTE FOR ELINOR!

Then she raced home to bake more gingerbread, cutting it into pieces according to the pattern Mitch had made for her.

She was just finishing up her royal icing when Natalie arrived with edible metallic beads, coconut for snow, peppermint discs and decorating tips and parchment paper and gumdrops. The gumdrops package had already been opened.

"Warner wanted to come. The only way I could get him to not throw a fit was to leave some gumdrops with him," she explained. She held up a small LEGO man. "He wants us to be sure and put his person in front of the house."

Elinor arrived, bringing M&Ms and mini candy canes. Right after her came Adele with a plate of brownies. "For sustenance," she said.

Stef and Viola arrived together, bearing wine and cheese and crackers. "We figured you guys would have the candy supply all taken care of," explained Stef. "And it looks like we were right." She eyed the pile on the kitchen counter.

"I think we're good to go. I've got the gingerbread and the frosting ready," said Frankie.

"But first, the important stuff," joked Stef, holding up two bottles of Gewürztraminer.

"Good idea. We can toast to our success," said Frankie.

"We haven't succeeded yet," pointed out Elinor.

"We will," Frankie assured her, and started pulling glasses down from the cupboard. Once the wine was poured, she held hers up. "To Elinor, this year's Mrs. Claus."

"To Elinor," echoed the others, and they all clinked glasses.

Then they got to work. Adele put herself in charge of sketching where the various treats would go on the house while Stef unwrapped candies and Viola covered a piece of heavy cardboard with tinfoil to make the base.

That left Frankie and Elinor to put together the walls and

put on the roof under Natalie's supervision, sealing every-thing with royal icing.

"That stuff is so gross," said Viola. "It's like cement."

"Which is what we need to hold our house together," said Natalie as Elinor held two walls in place, waiting for them to seal.

"It's taking forever," Elinor fretted.

"Rome wasn't built in a day," said Adele.

"But we need to build a house in a night," Elinor said.

"Don't worry, we'll get there," said Frankie. "Okay," she said, once their walls looked sturdy. "Now the roof."

The two sides of the roof were set on the house and glued together along the top with more icing. Construction was looking good.

Until the workers began to tile the roof with candy, and the house started to sag.

"Oh no, what's happening?" asked Stef.

"Hold it together," commanded Frankie, pressing on her side of the roof.

That was all it took. The roof caved in and broke in half. Two walls followed suit and their demise was accompanied by a chorus of groans.

At the sight of the collapsed gingerbread house, Elinor burst into tears. "This is a sign. I shouldn't be doing this. I'm not meant to be Mrs. Claus."

"The only thing this is a sign of is that we need to go back to the drawing board," Adele said firmly.

"This has nothing to do with you being Mrs. Claus," Frankie said.

Stef refilled Elinor's wineglass and handed it to her. "Here, drink this."

"People make these all the time. We just have to figure out what we're doing wrong," put in Viola.

Natalie was already on her phone, doing research. "I think I know what we did wrong. Our dough has to be thicker. And…" She stopped and groaned.

"And what?" prompted Frankie.

"It needs to be chilled for three hours."

"Three hours?" Adele made a face and shook her head. "We won't even be able to start baking until ten thirty."

"We can do this," Frankie said firmly. "It'll be like being back in college, pulling an all-nighter studying for finals."

"I'm too old for all-nighters," grumbled Adele. Then, on seeing Elinor's crestfallen face, she added, "But I'm not dead yet. I'm in. Just don't expect me in the shop tomorrow before eleven. I need my beauty sleep."

"I probably can't stay that late," said Natalie.

"It's okay. The rest of us can handle this. Right, Team Elinor?"

The others nodded, and Elinor looked at them all with tears in her eyes.

"You're all so kind," she said. "Thank you."

"It's all part of the adventure. This is the kind of thing we always look back on later and laugh about," Frankie said.

Stef grabbed her wineglass and raised it in a new toast. "Memorial service for House Number One. You tried," she said, looking down at the collapsed mess. "You gave your all for Elinor. Rest in peace. In my stomach," she added, making the others laugh. Then she broke off a piece and ate it. "It tastes good anyway."

"Find me a recipe, and I'll make another batch of dough," Frankie said to her daughter, and Natalie obliged.

Ten minutes later the dough was chilling in the fridge, Natalie was on her way home to her family, and the rest of Team Elinor was chilling in the living room, watching a Christmas movie. The heroine happened to be a shy baker in need of love. She also just happened to specialize in making gingerbread houses. How handy for her that the man who had come into her shop looking to buy one for his grandma was single.

"Now, there's a sign," Frankie told Elinor. "I can already see a certain someone bidding on your house."

Elinor smiled and took a sip of her wine.

Try Number Two held together. It was almost one in the morning when the crew finished, but they all concluded it was a work of art. Frankie created a royal icing hat for their LEGO man and topped it with a tiny cinnamon candy decoration from the jar in her cupboard.

"There," she said, setting him down with a flourish. "Now we are ready."

Yes, they were.

It was a slow day at the shop the next day, which was hardly surprising. Residents were waiting for the big day of fun on Saturday and the sale prices of twenty-five percent off on all holiday merchandise. In addition to the sale, they would be putting out free samples of some of Natalie's candy creations— tiny bites of eggnog-and-mint-chocolate fudge. Normally Frankie would have been in her Mrs. Claus outfit. This year she'd promised to loan it to Elinor if she won, which Frankie was sure would be the case.

They closed the shop early again, leaving a sign on the door that said:

GETTING READY TO CHOOSE THIS YEAR'S MRS. CLAUS—COME VOTE FOR ELINOR. WE'LL BE HERE TOMORROW!

Then Frankie went back to her house and got out the red dress she'd promised Elinor, along with the Mrs. Claus outfit and wig. After those were loaded, she carefully settled their gingerbread creation into a small cardboard box. The sides weren't very high, but they were high enough, and it would offer extra stability. She then settled the whole thing in her trunk and headed for Elinor's apartment on Huckleberry Street by way of The Salad Bowl.

Let the fun begin!

Corky had recovered from his upset stomach and made it to school, and now Griff was regretting that he hadn't kept his son home for the rest of the week.

"Tommy's mommy is taking him to see Santa tomorrow," Corky informed Griff when he picked him up from school.

Good for Tommy's mommy, thought Griff, and tried not to frown. After the letter to Santa mess, the last thing he wanted to do was to fight the crowds downtown on Saturday just so he could take his son to see a fraud in a red suit. The whole Santa thing was such a lie. People shouldn't lead their kids on. Especially when their kids thought that Santa moonlighted as Cupid.

"You can't not take your kid to see Santa," Jenn had insisted when she checked in to see how Corky was doing.

Sure, he could.

"It will be fun for Corky, and who knows? You might actually have fun yourself. It would be good for you to get out, meet new people."

"What new people?" he'd demanded. He had enough people in his life.

The pretty woman he'd met in the coffee shop came to mind. What were the odds he'd ever see her again? Maybe he needed to go back to the coffee shop and find out. He sure preferred meeting new people there to fighting the crowds at the Santa Walk.

"I don't know, just people," Jenn had said. "Get out there and pretend you're a human being."

Being a human being was exhausting.

So was coping with his son.

"I want to go see Santa," Corky said at dinner. He stuffed a chicken nugget in his mouth and watched his father, waiting for an answer.

"Come on, bud, you don't really want to do that. The guy didn't even answer your letter." Yep, no lying happening here.

Corky frowned. "Tommy said his mommy saw my letter, and Santa answered it."

It was all Griff could do not to swear. "I bet he didn't promise you a mommy."

Corky's lower lip jutted out. "I want to see Santa," he muttered, and kicked the table leg.

"We have other things to do tomorrow," Griff said. He'd think of something.

Corky scowled and pushed away his dinner plate, which held two more chicken nuggets, some reheated french fries and carrot sticks. Carrot sticks always made up for french fries, right?

"You need to eat your dinner," Griff said sternly.

"I want to see Santa."

"We're not going to see Santa!"

Corky let out a wail, and tears began to trickle down his cheek. "I just want to see Santa," he sobbed.

Sobs and tears and a heartbroken little boy. Griff felt like a monster. "Okay, we'll go see Santa," he said.

Corky took a jagged breath and smiled.

"But only if you ask him for toys. He's not going to bring you a mommy. Got it?"

Corky's lower lip trembled. He pressed down on it, stared at the dinner plate. Finally, he nodded.

"Okay, then," said Griff as if he'd actually gotten a promise. And if he saw that Stefanie Ludlow, who'd started this mess, he was going to let her have it.

Elinor was renting a cozy little one-bedroom place. Frankie noticed the hand-crocheted afghan on Elinor's couch when she walked in and suspected it was a gift from a relative.

"Your afghan's lovely," she said.

Sure enough, "My grandma sent it to me as an early Christmas present."

Elinor was ready for Christmas. She'd decorated a small tree with pink LED lights she'd purchased at the shop and silver balls as well as some collectible ornaments probably saved over from childhood. She'd put an Advent wreath on her kitchen table, and an elegantly sculpted Santa-face teapot sat on her little kitchen counter.

Frankie recognized the maker of the teapot immediately. "Fitz and Floyd, right?" she said as she set the takeout bag on the counter.

"Yes, it was my mom's. She gave it to me when I moved out here."

"You're a long way from home, aren't you?" said Frankie. "I think you said your family is back in Michigan?"

Elinor nodded, biting down on her lower lip. "I'd hoped to get home for Christmas this year, but that didn't work out. Hopefully, next year."

Elinor would be getting a raise in the new year. That should help. If not, Santa would bring her a plane ticket. Meanwhile, "Well, you're welcome to come to my Christmas Eve open house," Frankie offered.

"Thank you. In fact, thank you for everything you've been doing for me. At first, I thought I'd made a big mistake moving so far from home, but working with you and your family at the shop and meeting so many nice people has convinced me I made the right decision."

"Why did you move so far away?" Frankie asked. "That was pretty adventurous of you." And a little out of character.

"My life was...stalled out. I had a friend who'd moved to Marysville. She kept telling me how nice it is out here." Elinor sighed. "I barely got here when she met someone and moved to Canada. I was ready to go back home and admit I'd made a mistake when I happened to see your ad. Working in a Christmas shop sounded so charming. I thought I may as well give it a try before giving up."

"I'm glad you did. You're a wonderful addition to our staff," Frankie told her, and Elinor smiled. "Now, how about something to eat before we start getting you all gorgeous? I picked up salad on the way here."

"I couldn't eat. I'm too nervous."

"No need to be nervous. All you have to do is be yourself and you'll have this in the Santa bag," Frankie said, and set to work.

A hot iron, a makeup session and Frankie's cute red dress was all it took to transform Elinor into the adorable candidate for the position of Mrs. Claus that Frankie had known she would be. That and the red heels Frankie insisted she buy for the event. If seeing her like this didn't motivate William to ask her out, nothing would.

"There, look at yourself," Frankie said as they stood in Elinor's bedroom, taking in the sight of the finished product in the dresser mirror.

"I hardly recognize myself," Elinor said.

"You're still you."

"I've never done anything like this before," Elinor said. "I'm not used to being in front of people. I even got nervous in high school when I had to give book reports in front of my English class."

"This is different," Frankie assured her. "This is for fun, and you'll be the cutest future Mrs. Claus there. Plus, you'll have the cutest house."

Elinor was still too nervous to eat, but Frankie gobbled a few bites of salad and drank some of the peppermint tea Elinor had brewed to settle her tummy. Then they were out the door, in the car and on the way to the VFW hall.

The parking lot was already nearly full. "What a great turnout," Frankie said.

"Oh," said Elinor weakly.

Frankie recognized Stef's baby blue Toyota Corolla, and the van for KZAM was also there. The press was out in full force.

She decided it would be best not to point that out to Elinor. Instead, she said, "You'll be fine. Everyone loves you. Remember that."

"I wish we'd had some sort of rehearsal," Elinor fretted.

They should have. Frankie should have thought of that. Or Barbara. Someone. But it was too late now. It wouldn't be much of a show anyway. Simply introducing the candidates after allowing everyone to chat and vote for their favorite gingerbread house.

They had just parked when Natalie and her family pulled into the parking lot, Adele riding shotgun.

"All right, Team Elinor is here," Frankie said, hoping to drive away some of Elinor's nerves. "Let's get our creation and get you in."

Elinor nodded, looking like a prisoner about to stand in front of the firing squad.

"Come on now, how about a smile?" coaxed Frankie. "Ho, ho, ho."

Elinor repeated a sickly, "Ho, ho, ho," as they got out of the car.

"You're going to be fine. Remember, everyone loves you," Frankie told her.

Elinor nodded and managed a weak smile.

Frankie took the box with the gingerbread house from the trunk and was starting across the lot when her excited grandson barreled into her with a hug, knocking her off balance. She lost her grip on the box, and it started to tip.

"No!" cried Natalie, rushing to grab it.

Elinor echoed it in a squeak and stood frozen.

Frankie tried to regain her hold but failed. The box tipped sideways just out of Natalie's reach and flew to the ground, spilling out the gingerbread house and raining coconut snow.

There it lay, their lovely creation, now looking like pieces of a hobbit mobile home waiting to be delivered. With a disconnected roof.

Elinor burst into tears.

"Snotballs," muttered Frankie.

"Oh no," moaned Natalie.

"Crap," said Adele.

"I'm sorry, Grandma!" cried Warner.

The gingerbread house said nothing.

13

NATALIE AND FRANKIE RETURNED THE BROKEN HOUSE TO its box while the others stood around it. Doctors examining the patient.

"I may as well not go in," Elinor wailed. "I have to have a gingerbread house."

It didn't look good.

"Superglue," suggested Adele.

"Mom, someone's going to eat that. You want to poison them?" Frankie scolded.

"No one's going to want to eat that. It's been on the ground," said Adele.

"No one's going to want to eat it because no one's going to bid on it," Elinor corrected her, and a little sob escaped.

"You go on in," Frankie said to her. "We'll figure this out. And no more crying. You'll ruin your makeup."

Adele took Elinor by the arm. "Come on, hon. We'll think of something. Come on, Warner."

"What are we going to do?" asked Natalie when it was just mother and daughter and a box of mess. "It looks like it got hit by a hurricane."

"Or stomped on by Godzilla," said Frankie. Then inspiration hit. "Nat, I need you to race home and get Warner's toy T. rex."

Natalie stared for a minute, then laughed. "And then the dinosaurs came." It was the family joke whenever a room didn't get picked up or when a soufflé fell. Always a good way to laugh off disaster.

"That's right. I'll run to the shop and make up a sign. Meet you back here in fifteen minutes."

It was closer to twenty by the time they entered the hall, but since they'd been fifteen minutes early to begin with, it didn't make them too late getting to the spot on one of the long tables that had been reserved for Elinor's house. It was at the far corner of the room. Thank you, Barbara.

Frankie could see that the competition was stiff as she threaded her way through the crowd, greeting people and encouraging them to vote for Elinor's collapsed house...which, she assured everyone, was intentionally destroyed. Mrs. Myrtle, a kindergarten teacher at Carol Elementary, had created a little gingerbread school, complete with tiny toy children enjoying a playground that included a slide made from cookies. Sandra Jackson, who was retired, had obviously spent hours building a gingerbread castle complete with turrets. How the heck had she done that? Another contestant had created a log cabin, and Pastor Gorton's wife, Becky, had made a gingerbread church.

"Just so you know, this wasn't my idea," Becky said to Frankie as Natalie set up their disaster next to Becky's creation. "Edna Darling bribed me to enter at the last minute. She's making a big contribution to help repair the church roof. I don't expect to win, and that will be fine with me." She eyed the sad, broken house. "Uh-oh."

"Prayers would be appreciated," said Frankie as she set out the toy dino and the little sign she'd made.

"Dinosaurs, huh?" Becky said, reading it, and chortled.

"We had a little mishap in the parking lot," Frankie explained.

Viola was next to arrive, making a beeline to the table where Team Elinor's house was displayed. "Good Lord above, what happened?" she asked, staring at it.

"The dinosaurs came," said Natalie.

Elinor looked down at her sad house. "A dinosaur?"

"You have to watch out for them," said Frankie.

Elinor sighed.

"It's cute. And unique," Becky assured her. "People will love it."

"No one better try to eat it," said Elinor.

Two little boys ran up to the table. "A dinosaur, Mommy!" cried one.

"Oh, that is fun," said the mother. "Clever idea."

"That's our Elinor, always thinking outside the box," Frankie said, and brushed a piece of gravel off the roof. "I hope you'll vote for her house as the best."

"I want to vote," said one of the little boys, and Frankie handed him a ballot slip.

"There's your first vote," she said to Elinor as the boy's mother helped him check the correct box.

"Probably my only vote," Elinor replied.

A loud squeal interrupted their conversation, making almost everyone in the room jump, except Mrs. Graham, who was deaf. This was followed by tapping on a microphone and, "Is this thing on?" which signaled that the party was about to start.

There stood Barbara, in a black dress accented with a red scarf and black high heel boots. She smiled from a tiny make-shift stage at the front of the room right next to where the flag was on display. "Can you all hear me?" she asked.

"Loud and clear," called someone.

"Good. Welcome everyone to our first annual Mrs. Claus pageant."

First annual? This was going to become a tradition? Frankie frowned. Of course, Barbara would take full credit as she basked in the spotlight. Ugh. *Sharing is caring*, Frankie scolded herself.

"We want you all to enjoy looking at our contestants' gingerbread houses and chatting with them. Cast your vote for your favorite. We'll be gathering votes in half an hour and tallying them up along with the other votes that have come in earlier. Then we'll chat with our candidates and announce a winner. As you can see, we have some wonderful entries, and I expect some bidding wars when it comes time to auction off those gingerbread houses. I know you'll want to be sure to purchase hot chocolate or apple cider from the Boy Scouts booth. And do check out the cookies being sold by the Friends of the Library. And finally, a big thank you to Carly Rae from KZAM for bringing her crew to join us tonight. She'll be giving our Mrs. Claus candidates airtime so those who couldn't be here with us won't have to miss out on anything. Now, let the fun begin."

A couple of men gave a whoop, and people went back to milling about and visiting. Many were already lining up to visit with the various candidates, and Frankie caught sight of Stef interviewing Mrs. Myrtle.

"Airtime?" whimpered Elinor.

"Just say how happy you are to be in Carol," Frankie coached her. She caught sight of Mitch at the far end of the second display table, chatting with one of the contestants, and hurried over to him. "Can you come give Elinor some encouragement?"

He looked to where Elinor stood, watching the main door as if considering bolting through it. "Cold feet?"

"Frozen. She'd have been okay if our house hadn't gotten wrecked in the parking lot."

"Not good," he said.

"She's ready to withdraw, I'm sure," said Frankie.

"If she's stressed, maybe she should."

Frankie frowned at him. "I know she's going to win. This would be so good for her. Come on, help her out."

He shrugged. "Okay."

Once she had Mitch pointed in the right direction, she hurried off to fetch Adele away from the hot drinks stand. Of all the times to be thinking about her stomach.

"Mom," she said, catching Adele just as she was about to order. "What are you doing?"

"I should think that would be obvious. Did you get the house fixed?"

"Yes, but Elinor is in panic mode. I'm sure she's ready to bolt."

"Well, then let her. This is supposed to be fun. If it's not, quit pushing the poor girl."

"I'm not pushing. I'm helping."

Adele rolled her eyes. "That again."

"Come on, please go over and give her some moral support." Elinor loved Adele. Having Adele nearby along with Mitch would surely be a calming influence.

"I'll be over as soon as I get my hot cider."

"Honestly, Mom, where are your priorities?"

"Right now? Here. She's fine. Quit fretting."

Frankie frowned at her mother, then started back to where Elinor stood. Oh no! Carly Rae was making a beeline for Elinor and her destroyed house.

Frankie hurried over, threading her way through the crowd and narrowly missing getting hot cider spilled on her by one excited reveler.

She got to the table just after Carly Rae and in time to hear Mitch say, "This makes me think of when I was a kid. I loved dinosaurs, and I'd have loved a gingerbread house like this."

Elinor looked up at him with adoration, and Carly Rae stepped in with her microphone. "That's pretty high praise. What inspired this?" she asked Elinor.

Elinor's cheeks succeeded in matching her loaner red dress. "We had an accident in the parking lot. But you have to make the best of things, right?"

Great fast thinking. Frankie smiled at Elinor. Her smile grew into a self-satisfied grin when she saw William Sharp making his way toward Elinor and the little crowd around her. She would be fine now.

Sure enough, Elinor's confidence appeared to increase as the minutes ticked past. Finally, it was time to collect the gingerbread ballot boxes, and Frankie took Elinor's to the far corner of the room where James was in charge of tallying votes.

"Looks good for your candidate so far," he whispered.

"Good," she whispered back. Hopefully, Elinor had a big enough lead that no matter what happened with the houses she'd still be sitting in Santa's sleigh the next morning during the Santa Walk parade.

More time passed, and then the microphone squealed again. Once more Barbara asked if it was on.

"You're on," James called.

"All right, everyone, let's bring up our candidates," Barbara said.

Tony Errico, the high school music teacher, had been strolling around the room, serenading people on his accordion. As the contestants made their way to Barbara, he played "Here Comes Santa Claus" accompanied by hoots and applause from the attendees.

The hall was packed, and it took a while for the women to get to Barbara, but they finally made it. Frankie followed in Elinor's wake and squeezed in right in front of Barbara there on the stand. Barbara looked over her head, pretending not to see her.

Viola joined Frankie. "She looks terrified," she whispered, looking to where Elinor stood.

"She'll find her groove," Frankie whispered back, sounding more confident than she felt. Elinor did indeed look terrified.

"Ladies, we know each of you would make an excellent Mrs. Claus," Barbara said to the women, who stood lined up next to her. "Can you each tell us why you'd like to be our Mrs. Claus this year?"

Elinor's face turned as white as Santa's beard, and she looked at Frankie in terror. *What have you done to me?*

Frankie nodded and smiled at her. *You'll be fine.*

"I think I definitely have the girth for it," said Mrs. Myrtle as Barbara held the mic in front of her. There were a few unsure laughs, and she continued, "And you all know how much I love children."

"Maybe she should be Mrs. Claus," Viola whispered, and Frankie frowned at her.

Barbara was on to the next contestant.

"My husband talked me into it," said Sandra Jackson.

Becky and two more women explained that they also had friends or family members who thought they would make a good Mrs. Claus.

Then it was time to interview Elinor.

"I don't know if anyone can really fill Frankie Lane's shoes, but I'm honored that she nominated me," Elinor said.

Nailed it! It was the perfect thing to say, both humble and kind enough to acknowledge the town's first Mrs. Claus.

"Go Elinor!" called Adele, and one of the men punctuated it with a loud whistle.

Barbara barely smiled. "Thank you, Elinor." She turned her attention back to the audience. "There you have it," she said. "The votes have been tallied, and I'm sure you all want to know who will be this year's Mrs. Claus."

"So, tell us already," yelled a man at the far end of the room.

Barbara looked disapprovingly at the impatient heckler. "But first we want to thank our veterans for the use of the hall."

"You're welcome. Now get on with it," called the man.

Barbara ignored him. "Let's thank our judges for offering their expertise," she began. "I'm sure it wasn't easy coming to a decision." She announced the judges' names, and the crowd applauded politely. "And we are fortunate to have our mayor here with us tonight." She smiled at Mayor Lent, who was standing next to her, looking festive in a black skirt and a glittery red sweater. "Thank you, Mayor, for joining us."

The mayor barely had a chance to say, "My pleasure," before Barbara turned her back on her.

"So. This year's Mrs. Claus is..." Barbara paused dramatically.

"Tell us, or we're gonna start throwing cookies at you," hollered the heckler.

Barbara's face turned Christmas-stocking red, and she handed the paper with the results to the mayor, along with the microphone.

"This year's Mrs. Claus is Elinor Ingles," Mayor Lent announced, and the room exploded in applause.

"You did it," Stef said to Frankie, and Frankie beamed, proud of her success in transforming Elinor. Elinor would wear the title, but Frankie couldn't help feeling like she was still Mrs. Claus. It was a very satisfying feeling.

Barbara picked up a Mrs. Claus cap from the table behind her and snatched the microphone back from the mayor. "Let's see how our new Mrs. Claus looks in her cap. Come on over, Elinor."

A blushing Elinor walked over to Barbara to applause and whoops.

"Elinor, we know you'll make a wonderful Mrs. Claus," Barbara said to her when Elinor reached her and the mayor, who was standing to the side, ignored. Next, Barbara would be inviting herself to grand openings and ribbon cuttings. "Would you like to say a few words?" Barbara asked after she'd settled the ruffled cap on Elinor's head.

She held the microphone in front of Elinor's face, and Elinor did a deer-in-the-headlights blink.

But then she gathered her poise. "I would just like to say thank you, everyone. I'm honored to be able to be part of this wonderful community and this lovely celebration that my employer, Frankie Lane, started."

"That was sweet," Adele whispered to Frankie as Barbara's determined smile faltered.

More kudos to Frankie. Elinor was definitely getting a raise in the new year.

"I'm looking forward to helping Santa spread plenty of joy tomorrow," Elinor finished, then stepped away.

"There you have it," said Barbara. "And now, while our contestants are rejoining their fans, let's get ready to auction off the wonderful gingerbread houses they made. As you all know, the money we raise from auctioning them off will go to our Help Santa fund and do lots of good in the community, so I hope you came with fat wallets. Mayor, will you be our auctioneer?" she said, and gave the microphone to Mayor Lent.

It looked like the mayor was going to get to do something after all.

"Congratulations. We knew you could do it," Frankie said to Elinor when she joined the team, which Frankie made sure included William.

"It was probably a vote for you and Holiday Happiness more than it was for me," Elinor said humbly.

"You're part of Holiday Happiness, and everyone loves you," Frankie said, then hurried to fetch Elinor's house.

Meanwhile, the mayor had the microphone and was saying all the proper mayoral things required on such an occasion, praising the stores, the committee and their Mrs. Claus contestants while committee members gathered the houses and brought them up to a table set up onstage.

The bidding began, starting with Mrs. Myrtle's gingerbread school. The bidding among her former students was fast and furious, and she was delighted when it went for a hundred dollars. Becky Gorton's church also raised a hundred dollars for the Santa fund, and Sandra Jackson's castle went for two hundred.

A gingerbread log cabin came next, and that also did well. So did the others.

But the star of the show was Elinor's dinosaur disaster house, with William Sharp, Mitch and the mother of the two little boys bidding like crazy, the boys bouncing up and down in excitement. The mom dropped out after fifty dollars, shaking her head sadly. Mitch and William stayed locked in a battle until finally, Mitch called out, "Five hundred dollars." William gave up.

Everyone applauded after Mitch called out instructions to give it to the mother of the two boys, and Frankie could see Natalie hurrying over to warn the woman that their prize was not edible.

"I wanted to buy your house," William told Elinor as her supporters gathered around her once the bidding was over.

"It was awfully nice of you to try," she told him.

He cleared his throat. "It was for a good cause."

Oh, good grief, what kind of romantic response was that? "And anything for Elinor, right?" Frankie prompted him.

"Of course," he said.

The admiration in his eyes was certainly plain to see, although Elinor didn't. She was looking worshipfully at Mitch, the big spender. "That was such a generous bid," she said to him.

"I appreciate creativity, and how you saved your house was very creative," he said to her.

Frankie expected Elinor to inform him that the dinosaur theme had been Frankie's idea, but Elinor kept quiet.

Which was odd considering how much she'd just praised her employer onstage.

Oh, well, Frankie thought, and kept her mouth shut. No way did she want to spoil Elinor's moment of triumph. And she also didn't want to take away from the hero worship that Mitch was enjoying.

But something shifted in her when Elinor said, "I can hardly wait to spend the day with you tomorrow, Santa."

It was the polite thing to say, but the delivery... Was Elinor flirting with Mitch? The thought pulled down the corners of Frankie's mouth. Somehow, Elinor flirting with Mitch felt like friendship trespassing. She was imagining things, of course. Elinor and William were a match. Elinor belonged with William. She didn't have any interest in Mitch.

So there was no reason for the little Grinch poke to Frankie's heart when Mitch smiled at Elinor and said, "You're gonna be a great Mrs. Claus."

Elinor would be a lovely Mrs. Claus, for sure, and Frankie wanted her to enjoy the experience. Really. But Frankie was Mrs. Claus. Elinor was understudy Mrs. Claus. She would be fine, but she wouldn't be great.

Stop this right now, her better self scolded.

Elinor turned to Frankie. "I couldn't have done this without you. Thank you for how supportive and wonderful you've been to me."

"You're welcome," Frankie said. Elinor was so happy, and Frankie knew the fun of getting to play Mrs. Claus would be a huge confidence builder. How could she begrudge her employee that thrill?

People were leaving, and the committee was starting to take down tables and put away chairs. Time to get to work.

"I'll be ready to take you home in a few minutes," Frankie told Elinor. She got to work collapsing folding chairs and stowing them away.

She half expected to see Mitch helping with cleanup, but instead, only a few minutes later, he and Elinor were leaving the hall together. Her phone dinged with a text from Mitch.

Running Elinor home.

William should have been running Elinor home, but there he stood, watching them go. William definitely needed some serious coaching on how to win over a woman. Frankie was just about to abandon her chore, hurry over and give him some pointers when Mrs. White, one of her regulars, stopped to talk.

"This was a great event," the woman said. "Frankie, you are so clever at coming up with fun ideas. And we all benefit."

If she couldn't be Mrs. Claus, getting thanked for coming up with fun ideas was a nice consolation prize. It was good to be appreciated. It would have been even better to be appreciated by Mitch, who was now off with the new Mrs. Claus.

"Thanks," Frankie said. "I'm glad everyone enjoyed it."

"And Elinor is going to be a darling Mrs. Claus. That girl has certainly blossomed over the last few weeks."

"Yes, she has," Frankie agreed, inwardly taking credit for Elinor's transformation.

"She's such a sweet young woman."

"Yes, she is," Frankie agreed again, and knew she couldn't take credit for that. Elinor was indeed a sweet woman. Hopefully, Santa and Cupid would get together and bring her a lifetime supply of love this year. One of them needed to give William a textbook on winning over a woman.

Adele stopped, said hi to Mrs. White and then informed her daughter that she and Natalie were headed home. "I'll see you bright and early at the store tomorrow to get the hot cider going."

"Thanks, Mom," Frankie said, and kissed her mother's cheek.

Natalie kissed Frankie goodbye. Warner gave her an enthusiastic hug and asked when he was going to get his dinosaur back.

Oh yes, the dinosaur. "He might have run away, but don't worry, he has cousins coming to stay with you soon." As soon as Frankie could find a replacement.

Stef was next to leave, about to go out for drinks with a couple of friends from the paper.

Frankie was ready to leave, also. Most of the cleanup was done. Anyway, Barbara was the committee chair. Let her stay for the final sweep-up.

"How about you?" Frankie said to Viola. "Feel like going out for a hot buttered rum?"

"I need to get home and finish the cookies I started baking. I promised I'd have some for Terrill when he gets done with his shift."

"Can't ignore your man," Frankie said like the understanding friend and good sport that she was.

"I'll catch up with you tomorrow," Viola promised, and gave her a hug, then hurried off.

There went the team, scattered to the winter wind. Even though she was pooped from her busy day, Frankie felt too keyed up to go straight home. She wanted to go over the event with someone, maybe enjoy some hot chocolate or a drink at Heat or Carol's Place.

Mitch probably had Elinor safely delivered home. He'd be free. She texted him. Up for a drink?

Sorry. Can't. Going over stuff for tomorrow with Elinor.

Frankie frowned. What was there to go over? Elinor would put on the Mrs. Claus costume and join Mitch outside of town at the wooden sleigh made especially for Santa by Mitch's crew from the hardware store back when Frankie had first conceived of the idea. The sleigh would be pulled by horses on loan from a nearby farmer. Two committee members had already decked it out in greenery and red plastic ribbons. All Elinor had to do was climb aboard, put a blanket over her lap and sit and wave. Once Santa was set up in the town square on his Santa throne, she'd welcome the children, give them each a candy cane and escort them up to see him. This was not rocket science.

Where are you guys?

Her place.

How long are you going to be? She looked at what she'd typed and then wiped it out. What was she, a stalker? OK, she texted instead.

It looked like she was going to be alone. She said good-night to the few remaining committee members, giving Barbara a wave from a distance. Barbara probably didn't want any holiday hugs from Frankie anyway. Then off she went to her car.

No gingerbread house to haul, no nothing but her purse and a slightly dampened spirit. Going home alone felt so anti-climactic.

She was almost to her car when her fellow committee member Autumn came running after her, calling her name. She was holding out a cell phone in a pink sparkly case. Frankie recognized that case.

"I think your mom left this behind when she was helping us with our booth cleanup. It had fallen on the floor, and I picked it up. I almost forgot I had it."

"I'm surprised she hasn't noticed it's missing," said Frankie as she took it. "Thanks."

Now she had something to do. Her mother was probably in her jammies and getting ready to relax. They could sit on the couch and talk about the evening's adventure.

She drove to Adele's house. The same SUV Frankie had seen several times before was parked outside on the curb, a little way down from the house. Somebody had company.

Not Adele. Her living room was dark, and the tree lights

were off. So much for a cozy chat over a glass of wine or hot chocolate.

But if Adele was in bed this early, she needed her rest. Frankie used her key and slipped inside. She'd leave the phone on the hall table. She didn't bother to turn on the hall light. No need. The table was only a few steps away and...

Whoa! She tripped over something and went crashing into the table with a yelp, knocking off the pewter bowl where Adele kept her keys. It landed with a metallic *boing*.

What the heck? She felt around on the floor for it and found...a shoe? Since when did her mother leave shoes in the hallway? She stumbled over another on her way to the light switch. Flipping on the switch, she saw two very big shoes lying on the floor.

Wait a minute. What was going on here?

14

THE UPSTAIRS LIGHT SWITCHED ON, AND THERE STOOD Adele in her fuzzy pink bathrobe, smoothing down her hair and frowning. "What on earth are you doing?" she called down to Frankie.

"Bringing you your phone, which you left behind," Frankie replied. She grabbed a shoe and held it up. "And what are *you* doing?"

Adele's chin lifted. "None of your business."

"I come in here and trip over a shoe twice as big as yours, and it's none of my business?" Frankie demanded. "What's going on, Mom?"

"I have company," Adele replied stiffly.

Mr. Bellagamba appeared behind Adele looking red-faced. His sparse dark hair was mussed, and his hefty stomach was hanging over red reindeer-dotted pajama bottoms like a giant mushroom cap.

Frankie dropped the shoe. "Mr. Bellagamba, um, Merry Christmas?" she tried. It was the best she could come up with.

"Oh, go home," Adele said irritably.

"I want to marry your mother," Mr. Bellagamba assured Frankie, and put an arm around Adele's shoulders. His expression begged Frankie for absolution.

Adele was right. Frankie needed to go home. She managed a nod, then left.

This was… She couldn't even find the right word. Weird? Unexpected? Naughty? Nice? Where did Adele's behavior fall on Santa's list?

Naughty. Adele should have told her family she was seeing someone—a lot of someone in this case, more than Frankie had wanted to see, for sure—instead of sneaking around like a misbehaving teenager. Or at least hung a Do Not Disturb sign on the front door.

Once home, Frankie called Stef. Stef needed to know what their mother was up to.

She could hear voices and music in the background as Stef answered, "Heyyyy." She was obviously enjoying her night out with the girls. Everyone except Frankie was enjoying the night with someone. The thought didn't improve her mood.

Stef was in no condition to digest this news, so instead of sharing it, Frankie demanded, "Do you have a designated driver?"

"Calling Uber," Stef assured her, clearly buzzed. "Why don't you come join us? I can crash at your house afterward."

"I have too much to do tomorrow. And you do, too. Don't stay out all night," Frankie snapped, and then ended the call.

Okay, that had been bossy. But somebody needed to watch over Stef, and obviously their own mother was too busy to.

Sheesh. Frankie wandered into the kitchen, found some left-over scraps of gingerbread from her earlier baking and wolfed them down. Then she went upstairs to take a long, hot bath.

The woman staring back at her from the bathroom mirror looked downright cranky.

"Shame on you," she scolded her reflection. "You have no reason to be cranky."

It took her a long while to settle down for sleep. Concern for her mother eclipsed self-pity, and she began to worry that Adele had rushed into this relationship and would wind up getting hurt. Mr. Bellagamba was a widower, had been for several years, and he seemed nice enough. But would this last? Would *he* last? In spite of all that walking around the neighborhood, delivering letters, he wasn't in the best of shape. What was Adele thinking?

Every time Frankie closed her eyes she either saw that big shoe or Mr. Bellagamba's reindeer pajama bottoms.

If Mitch had been around, she'd have discussed her feelings with him. The thought of Mitch not being around had her punching her pillow.

"Oh, stop," she told herself. "Go to sleep."

She and Mitch would catch up the next day after all the festivities. As for her mother…mother knew best, right?

True to her word, Adele was already at the shop the next morning and making cider for their Santa Walk customers in the electric hot pot in the back room when Frankie arrived. She didn't turn around when Frankie walked in.

Frankie suddenly found herself at a loss for how to start this conversation. *Did you sleep well?* Uh, no. *How long has this been going on?* Too accusatory. This was more awkward than she'd thought it would be.

She didn't have to say anything. Adele launched them into

it. "I love him," she said softly, still not looking Frankie's way. "And he loves me."

That said it all. Frankie put an arm around her shoulder. Just like Mr. Bellagamba had done the night before. "I'm glad, Mom."

Adele finally looked at her, her brows pulled together. "Are you really?"

"Of course. You deserve to be happy. But why didn't you tell me?"

Adele let out a sigh. "I worried that maybe you'd think I was being disloyal to your father."

"This from the woman who's been telling me that Ike would want me to move on?"

"Doesn't make sense, does it? Do as I say, not as I do."

"So, you thought I'd be mad."

"I wasn't sure. I was waiting for the right time to tell you girls."

Frankie frowned. "When you first started seeing him would have been the right time."

Adele nodded. "I know. I thought we were going to be friends at first. But then, things changed. He's such a lovely man. And I am going to marry him. We're not just fooling around. I want to spend the rest of my life with him. I have a lot of good years left in me, and I don't want to spend them alone."

"And you shouldn't," Frankie said, and kissed her mother's cheek. "I want you to be happy, Mom."

"I am. Can you say the same thing?"

"Of course I can," Frankie said, blocking out the memory of her sour attitude from the night before.

"Don't wait as long as I did to let your heart be happy, daughter dear. The joy far outweighs the risk."

Did it? Did she really want to risk starting a life with a new man only to lose him?

"I'm glad to see you joyful," Frankie said, "but make sure Mr. Bellagamba knows that his kids have to share you two on the holidays."

Adele smiled. "They've all scattered to the wind, and none of them are making it back for Christmas. He's looking forward to your open house."

"Good. I'm looking forward to getting to know him better."

Adele hesitated, then asked, "Have you told Stef?"

"Did I tattle?" Frankie translated. "No. I'll let you tell her."

"Thank you. Mario and I will tell her on Christmas Eve."

"Mario? Like the game?"

Adele shrugged. "He saves the princess, right? Well, this Mario saved me."

So sweet, so romantic! That comment deserved a hug.

Then it was time to put the mini candy canes and chocolate Santas in the big bowl they used for downtown trick-or-treating and open the shop. It would be just the two of them in charge as Elinor would be busy being Mrs. Claus, and Natalie had the day off to be with her family.

"I can handle things here on my own for a while if you want to go on over and see how Elinor and Mitch are doing later," Adele said, and Frankie decided that would be a good idea. They'd get some shoppers after the parade, but many would be standing in line with their children to see Santa or checking out the artisan vendors and food booths in the town square, so Adele should be able to handle things.

The parade wouldn't start until eleven, but by ten in the morning, when the shop officially opened, people were already setting up camp chairs along the parade route and dropping into shops to take advantage of bargains and enjoy the various treats shop owners were offering. Snow was predicted for later, but for the moment it was holding off, hiding in a gray sky and merely breathing down cold drafts to keep everyone stamping feet and clapping mittened hands to stay warm.

"Hot cider, just what we need," said one shopper as she and a friend entered the shop.

"And bargains," added her friend.

"We've got both," Frankie assured them as a young couple wandered in, both ready for the cold in their parkas, jeans and boots. He wore a Santa hat, and she had on a plush brown reindeer one.

Chatting with them, Frankie learned they were newly engaged and wanted to buy something special to commemorate their first official Christmas. Frankie had the perfect ornament for them, a rustic wood circle with Our First Christmas carved into it, along with two connected hearts.

"Perfect," said the woman, and smiled at her man.

Watching them brought back the memory of Frankie and Ike decorating their first tree. Adele, who was into the Precious Moments brand, had bought them a first Christmas ornament that they'd proudly hung on the tree, right next to the personalized one his mother had sent them with their wedding picture on it. After they'd decorated the tree, they'd started Christmas music playing and made love under it. They'd also made Natalie that night.

Other customers were coming in, and there was no time left to hang out on Memory Lane. Frankie rang up the couple's purchase, wished them a Merry Christmas and then got busy helping the next person in line.

The hour before the parade went faster than a reindeer on speed, and before Frankie knew it, Viola was at the store, informing her she was going to miss seeing Santa if she didn't get outside.

Frankie could hear the Carol High School marching band playing "Santa Claus Is Coming to Town" as she and Viola squeezed into the crowd.

There they marched, in all their red uniformed glory, almost in tune. Behind them came the drill team, in black leggings and boots and red sweaters, Santa hats perched on their heads. They were followed by the local dance school, which had a gaggle of sugar plum fairies and little lords a'leaping.

Grandma's Tree Farm had a truck decked out for the holidays with a giant decorated tree in the truck bed, surrounded by elves tossing out candy for the kids.

The nearby equestrian riding school followed, the pooper scoopers walking behind with their shovels. Actors from the community theater, who had been performing *A Christmas Carol*, were walking behind them, with Bob Cratchit holding Tiny Tim's hand as the boy limped along beside him. They were followed by a scowling Scrooge and other Dickensian characters.

The police and fire department were out in force, the firefighters waving and throwing candy—more sugar overload for every child in town—while the police looked properly serious. Except on seeing Viola, Terrill grinned and waved as his wife jumped up and down and blew him kisses.

Two floats from neighboring towns lumbered by with their local princesses waving white gloved hands at everyone, then came the main attraction—Santa and Mrs. Claus in their sleigh.

Even that scraggly white beard and the padding couldn't hide the fact that Mitch was a handsome man, and Frankie's heart gave an appreciative flutter as he waved in her direction. Elinor made a cute Mrs. Claus in her red cape worn over her Mrs. Santa outfit that Frankie had loaned her. She, too, should have been waving, but instead she was snuggled up against Mitch with her arms threaded through one of his.

"Wave," Frankie called to her.

Elinor probably hadn't heard because she stayed glued to Santa.

Frankie's mouth dipped down at the corners. What was Elinor doing, for crying out loud? And why was Mitch letting her do it?

"They're sure cozy," Viola observed as Mitch smiled at Elinor.

Frankie's frown embedded itself more deeply.

"I thought you said she was into William Sharp," Viola continued.

"She should be," said Frankie. All those times he'd been coming into the store, all those cozy conversations. What had that been about?

"It doesn't look like it."

It sure didn't.

"You did want Mitch to find someone," Viola reminded her, and Frankie forced her lips into a smile.

"I did," she said. "But…"

"But what?"

"Elinor's not right for Mitch." That was the problem. There was no jealousy here. Frankie could feel Viola's assessing gaze on her. "What?"

Viola pointed a finger at her. "You're jealous."

"Of Elinor? I certainly am not."

"You certainly are. All that talk about finding someone for Mitch," Viola mocked.

"I did want to find someone for Mitch. Do," Frankie corrected herself.

"Looks like you succeeded," said Viola.

"Don't be ridiculous. He's just giving her confidence a boost."

"That's some boost."

"They are Mr. and Mrs. Santa Claus. They have to look the part." Although Elinor was playing her part a little too well, if you asked Frankie.

"I guess. I've gotta go meet Terrill at the station," said Viola. "He's off tonight. See you at the Santa pub crawl later?"

"Probably," Frankie said. She and Mitch had done the pub crawl for the last two years. It was a tradition. They could crawl and drink and talk, and she'd find out exactly what he was thinking encouraging Elinor. And if need be, she'd explain that Elinor wasn't right for him. Elinor was too quiet, too shy.

Except she hadn't exactly looked shy in that sleigh.

The sleigh trundled on, and the crowd closed in after it, moving like a human wave in its wake. Frankie left Adele in charge of the store and joined them, making her way to the gazebo in the town center where Santa would be seeing children. Just to make sure Elinor was doing her job properly.

There was a crowd of parents and hyped-up children waiting to see Santa. Mitch was already on his Santa throne, listening intently as a little girl shared her holiday wish list, gesturing excitedly with mittened hands while Elinor stood nearby, beaming, looking like she was born to be Santa's missus.

Well, good, Frankie told herself. This was good for Elinor, and Frankie had done a good deed by helping her get bold and get out there. That was all Elinor was doing, just getting into her part. Frankie had been imagining things.

In the background, she caught sight of Stef and the paper's photographer. He was taking pictures while she interviewed parents, recording the event for local history. Elinor was doing a good job. Everyone was happy. Yes, all was well. Frankie couldn't help but feel proud as she watched Elinor bend down and talk to a little girl who was next in line.

Behind the little girl and her mother stood a red-haired little boy, bouncing up and down with excitement as he waited his turn. With the boy stood a tallish man with short rust-red hair, wearing a parka and a frown. Next to him stood... Frankie's coconspirator, the woman she had talked to about Stef in the shop. She hurried over to where they stood to say a casual hello.

"Hello there," Frankie said to the woman. "Merry Christmas."

The woman smiled in recognition. "Merry Christmas to you, too. I hope you have some good sales going on at Holiday Happiness. I want to get over there later today."

"We do," Frankie assured her.

"I never introduced myself. I'm Jenn, and this is my brother, Griff."

The man looked vaguely familiar. Where had Frankie seen him before?

Frankie introduced herself, and he said a polite hello and shook hands with her. He was a fine-looking specimen, for sure—not much of a smiler, though. Of course, from what his sister had told Frankie, that was understandable. Stef was just the person to help this man find his smile again.

"And this is Corky," continued Jenn.

"Hi, Corky," Frankie said, smiling down at the boy.

"I'm going to see Santa," he informed her. "Daddy says I can't ask for a mommy." He brightened. "But I think he'll bring me one if I ask."

"He won't, so don't," said the father sternly, losing his forced smile.

Stef might be what this man needed, but Frankie wasn't so sure he was what Stef needed.

"Is your sister here?" Jenn asked Elinor.

"Sister?" the man repeated, looking suspiciously at her.

"Just someone I thought you'd like to meet," she said.

Here came the someone, right on cue, all rosy-cheeked and smiling. Stef looked properly adorable in black leggings and boots under a Christmas-red coat, and she wore a red stocking cap.

"Well, hello again," she said to Griff.

"Hello again to you, too," he replied, mirroring her smile, proving that he knew how.

Hello again? Frankie took a closer look and realized why this man looked familiar. Her sister had pointed him out only a few days earlier at Warner's concert. This was the coffee shop mystery man. Well, well.

"Griff, do you two know each other?" Jenn asked her brother.

"Not really," he said, still smiling at Stef. "I'm Griffin Marks. This is my sister, Jenn."

Griffin Marks, what a great name. It sounded like a name out of the novels their mom loved to read.

"I'm Stefanie Ludlow," said Stef, "and I think you might owe me a latte."

"Stef works for the *Clarion*," Frankie bragged.

As they were speaking, Griff's eyes got big, then narrowed to… Whoa, eyes really could narrow to slits. "Stefanie Ludlow?"

15

ELINOR ARRIVED ON THE SCENE. "HELLO, EVERYONE, Merry Christmas," she chirped. "Are you ready to see Santa?" she asked the little boy.

"No," said his father even as the boy hooted, "Yes!"

"Let's follow Mrs. Claus, Corky," said Jenn, and they led the boy away.

"You," Griffin Marks snarled, pointing a finger at Stef even as his sister looked back over her shoulder at him in concern.

Frankie stepped in front of her and delivered a haughty, "Excuse me? What do you mean by that tone of voice?"

Stef stepped out from behind Frankie. She could fight her own battles. "Do we have a problem?" she demanded.

"You bet we do. You're the one behind the letters to Santa. You're the one who printed my son's letter."

It wasn't said thankfully, and suddenly Stef knew why. She pointed a finger back at him. "You're the Scrooge who had a fit because we printed your son's letter, aren't you?"

"I am not a Scrooge, and you shouldn't have printed that letter. What were you thinking? Oh, that's right. You weren't."

"You can't talk to my sister like that," Frankie said, taking a step toward him.

Stef held an arm in front of her. "I can handle this." She turned her attention back to Griff. "It was sent to us. What was I supposed to do with it? All your little boy wanted was to talk to Santa and you... Grinched him. What is wrong with you anyway?"

"What is wrong with *me*?" he demanded, his voice doubling in volume. "A kid writes asking for a mother, and you print the letter and raise his hopes? Are you dead from the neck up?"

People were starting to stare, and Stef could feel a sizzle on her cheeks. What was with this jerk? Who had dubbed him Krampus the Second? Who cared? She didn't have to take this kind of abuse.

"Santa did not promise your son a mother, and if you could read, you'd have seen that," she snapped. It was all she could do not to kick him in the shins. But that kind of misbehavior at the Santa Walk would not be cool, especially from the reporter who was covering it, especially with the paper's photographer standing right there, aiming his camera. Anyway, she was better than that. "I don't know who invited you here, but you need to go back to your Krampus cage and write a letter to Santa yourself, apologizing for being such a jerk," she finished.

His cheeks turned russet, and he clenched his jaw, standing there like an ice statue. Then he shook his head and growled, "You are something else, lady."

"Yeah, well, nothing like you—something I sure don't want to ever be," Stef retorted, determined to have the last word.

She got it. He marched off to the other side of the gazebo to wait for his little boy, who was sitting on Santa Mitch's lap, speed-talking his Christmas list.

"Good Lord, what was that?" Frankie said.

Stef gave a disgusted snort. "My dream man."

"That poor little boy. He's probably asking for a mommy right now," said Frankie.

"Good luck with that. No woman in her right mind is going to want anything to do with his dad," Stef said.

As Stef glared at the back of her coffee shop disappointment and Frankie tried to console her by calling the man every insulting name she could think of, Jenn returned to where they stood. "I just want to say I'm sorry about my brother."

"I'd be sorry, too, if I had a brother like him," Stef said. Then she reminded herself she was representing the paper and managed a smile. "Never mind. It's all right. This can be a stressful time of year." That was still no excuse for being rude to a stranger, someone who was only doing her job. The man deserved a lump of coal up his ass.

"It's been hard for him since his wife died." Jenn looked ready to cry herself. "Hard for all of us. She was my best friend. And his."

"No wonder he's so angry," Frankie said.

Her words pulled Stef away from her own anger. She remembered how horrible it had been for Frankie after Ike died. She'd been the walking wounded. She also had a vague memory of her mother, who'd turned into a zombie after Stef's father died. Stef had felt sorry for little Corcoran when she'd read his letter. Maybe his father needed a serving of sympathy, too.

Still, he'd just taken his anger out on her and publicly humiliated her. She looked to where the little boy was hopping down the stairs, holding the candy cane Mrs. Claus had given him and smiling. At least someone was happy.

"Don't let Griff's behavior discourage you from what you're doing," Jenn said to her. "Everyone loves your Letters to Santa page. *I* love your Letters to Santa page." She bit her lower lip, then confessed, "I'm the one who sent the letter in for my nephew. It seemed like a good idea at the time, especially since the year before his dad conveniently lost his letter." She shook her head. "Griff really is a great guy."

"I'm afraid he didn't show off very well just now," said Frankie.

"I know. But that's not the real him. He's trying hard to be a good dad. I guess I can see why he doesn't want Corky asking Santa for a mommy. It would only set him up for disappointment. But he wants one so badly, wants to be like the other kids. He doesn't remember much about his mother. All he knows is that he used to have one who loved him, and he wants one again."

"He's a cute little boy," Stef said. His father was good-looking, too.

Richard had been good-looking. In the end he'd proved to be a super tool. Looks counted for nothing.

"Anyway, I really am sorry. Please don't hold Griff's moment of anger against him."

"It's Christmas. Peace on earth, goodwill toward men," Stef said. She still didn't care if she ever saw this particular man again, though. Hurting or not, he was a jerk.

"Thanks," said Jenn. Then, with a final apologetic smile, she hurried off to catch up with her brother, who was already leading his son away.

Stef frowned as she watched them go. "Boy, can first impressions be misleading. He seemed nice when I met him in The Coffee Stop. If I ever see him there again, I won't be buying him a drink. I'll be dumping it over his head. I get that he misses his wife, but that's no excuse for yelling at people. I mean, who acts like that?"

"So much for that idea," muttered Frankie as she watched her not-so-perfect candidate for her sister march away through the crowd, towing his son along.

"What idea?" asked Stef.

This would not be a good time to mention how she'd talked Stef up to Griff's sister the last time she'd been in the shop. "Nothing. I'd better get back to the shop, and you need to get back to work. I'll see you later."

Stef was studying her suspiciously. Time to go.

"Don't. Say. A. Word," Griff growled as Jenn caught up with him and Corky. The effort of trying to hold himself together had him grinding his molars so hard he probably wouldn't have teeth by the end of the day. Meanwhile, his son was skipping along beside him, holding his hand, clueless to the charged current in the air between his aunt and his father.

"Okay, I'll say four. Way to go, Scrooge."

"Don't you put what just happened on me," he snapped.

"Why not? That's where it needs to be. Talk about rude. You had a chance to start something with someone nice, and you blew it."

"And you know she's nice because?" The question was barely out of his mouth before he knew the answer. "The sister. You talked to her sister."

Jenn said nothing. She didn't need to. Her red face said it all.

"You were talking to a complete stranger about me."

"Not a stranger. I've been shopping at her shop."

"A stranger. You didn't even know her name."

"I was buying a *t-r-a-i-n* last time I was in and happened to mention that someone had a dad who was single and a nice guy. Thanks for making a liar out of me."

"Don't you dare turn this back on me, not after what you did." He glared at his interfering, mess-making sister. "Talking to a total stranger about me!"

Corky had caught the tension in the air and wasn't skipping anymore. He looked up at his father in concern. "Is Aunt Jenn in trouble?"

Big-time.

"Aunt Jenn shouldn't be," Jenn said, frowning at Griff.

"But Aunt Jenn's a grown-up," Corky pointed out.

"Even grown-ups get in trouble," Griff said, trying to keep his voice calm. It was taking a supreme effort since inside he was an erupting volcano.

"It's okay, Corky. Your daddy's just having a bad day."

More like a bad life.

"But he'll get over it because he knows he's loved. Now, I have to go. You be good for your daddy," she said, and ruffled Corky's hair. "Bye, Scrooge," she said to Griff, her tone of voice not as pleasant as it had been when she was talking to his son.

"Hate to see you go," he said.

"Why is Aunt Jenn in trouble?" Corky asked as they continued toward the car.

Because she's making me crazy. "Never mind. It's just boring grown-up stuff. Let's go home and have some hot dogs."

"I don't want Aunt Jenn to be in trouble," Corky said, no longer happy.

"Okay, she's not," Griff lied. "Everything's okay."

Nothing was okay. He could hardly wait until Christmas was over.

The crowd was growing as more people came to town to check out the wares of the various vendors and artisans, which made Frankie's walk back to the shop slow going. She was halfway there when a man in a lumberjack jacket and a stocking cap who was laughing with some buddies stepped backward into her, knocking her sideways.

"Sorry. Are you okay?" he asked, catching her arms. The pub crawl wouldn't start until six, but his breath smelled like he'd already been crawling. His eyes brightened at the sight of her. "Well, hello there."

One of the men with him was Brock. He lifted a hand and gave her a frosty smile. "Hi, Frankie."

"Frankie, huh? Cute name," said the man, looking her up and down like she was a giant piece of beef jerky. "You know this lady, Brock?"

"We've met," Brock said stiffly. So, still mad at her for ending things with him.

"Brock, it's always nice to see you," she said, determined to be polite.

"I wouldn't mind seeing you," the stranger said to Frankie.

"Don't waste your time," Brock told him.

Oh, for heaven's sake. His behavior couldn't have been any smaller if he'd been an ant. She forced a smile. The male ego was a fragile thing, but she was sure it wouldn't be long before Brock found someone to patch his up.

"You all enjoy yourselves," she said, addressing the group in general, and then moved on.

She returned to the shop to find it empty except for Adele and Mr. Bellagamba, who was keeping her company. At the sight of Frankie, red crept up his neck and onto his cheeks. He gave her a sheepish hello.

"I see we have a lookie-loo," Frankie teased, trying to lighten an awkward moment.

"I'm going to buy something," he rushed to assure her.

"Mr. B, I'm only teasing," she said.

"Oh." He nodded, taking that in. "Frankie, I hope you're okay with me seeing your mom. I should have asked your permission."

"No, you shouldn't have," Adele said.

"That's sweet of you, but Mom's right. You certainly don't need to. You're both adults. I'm happy she's found someone wonderful to hang out with."

"I meant what I said last night," he went on. Then he smiled at Adele. "If you don't mind me stealing your mother for a while, we're going over to Treasured Jewels to look at rings."

"Santa Walk sale," Adele added.

"I think that sounds wonderful," Frankie said, and hugged him. "Take her and don't come back. And welcome to the family. Now you'll have something to show off Christmas Eve," she said to her mother.

"And someone," Adele added, and smiled at Mr. Bellagamba.

Happily ever after, thought Frankie as they left the shop hand in hand.

It was a joy to see her mother so happy. If only things could have worked out as well for Stef.

What a horrible coincidence that her coffee shop dream man had turned out to be the angry father who'd caused trouble for her at the paper. The meeting that could have been so cute had been nothing but ugly. So disappointing.

For Frankie. Stef was too angry to be disappointed.

Frankie understood that hurting people often hurt others, and it was obvious this man was hurting. It was too bad it had spilled over onto Stef. That romantic candidate was out of the race. Stef didn't need to take any more emotional hits than she already had.

Customers began to drift back into the shop. Soon it was full, and Frankie was swamped and wondering what she'd been thinking to let her mother off the hook for the rest of the day.

"Sorry for the wait," she told the line of people ready to purchase holiday goodies on sale. "My best employee just got engaged, and she's off ring shopping."

"That pretty young girl who works here?" asked one woman.

"Elinor? No, she's busy being Mrs. Claus. My mom's getting married."

One of their regulars piped up. "Adele?"

Frankie nodded.

"Good for her. And what a great way to celebrate Christmas."

Indeed, it was.

Finally, closing time arrived. The hot cider had long run out, and there wasn't a candy cane anywhere in sight. Holiday Happiness had done a brisk business. Now Frankie was ready to relax.

She turned the sign on the door to Closed, locked up and texted Mitch. Ready to pub crawl?

Maybe Stef would like to join them. It would probably be good for her to end the day on a happy note.

Starting right now with Elinor.

Elinor! Elinor? Frankie texted.

Mrs. Claus. She was expecting it.

Well, Frankie wasn't. She frowned. Where are you? I'll catch up with you.

Sips, came the reply.

Sips was another new hot spot in town, a wine bar that specialized in high-end wines and charcuterie boards. Frankie could go for something to eat. She wished she'd gotten back her red dress from Elinor, but oh well. She hurried home and changed into jeans and a red sweater and her favorite boots, then grabbed her winter jacket and her Santa hat and went out the door, looking forward to enjoying a glass of white wine and recapping the day with her Mrs. Claus and Mitch.

Holiday lights were on all over town, and the predicted snow was lazily making its way to the ground. Let it snow. Frankie had all-wheel drive.

Everyone in Carol had decided to party. The sidewalks were packed, and there wasn't a parking place to be had on any of the town's main streets or in its paid lot. She parked in the special parking in back of the shop, but it was still a bit of a walk to Sips. She was glad for her sturdy boots and her warm coat and gloves.

The wine bar was housed in one of the town's older buildings, but inside it was modern all the way—chairs of black leather and wood around tall wooden tables. A couple of artsy paintings of wine bottles and glasses on white walls. Hanging cylinder lights. A tree strung simply with white lights stood in one corner, and that was it as far as Christmas decor went.

The people inside made up for it. Ugly sweaters abounded, and Santas of all shapes and sizes were sipping wine and laughing. Some of the women wore fancy red dresses with their snow boots, and a couple of women had donned white wigs and fake spectacles and red skirts with aprons to look like Mrs. Claus.

But the day's official Mrs. Claus was nowhere to be seen. Neither was the Santa. What the heck?

I don't see you, Frankie texted Mitch.

Sorry. Elinor wanted to go to La Bella Vita.

OK, Frankie texted back, and hurried out the door and down the street. Her hurrying wasn't quite as fast as she intended as several people stopped her to compliment her on the success of the day's activities. But she finally made it. Now, where were they?

A text came in from Mitch. On our way to Carol's Place.

What? Already? Frankie felt like she was playing a grown-up version of tag as she started for the new destination. This was a pub crawl, not a pub race. What was Elinor's hurry?

"We wish you a Merry Christmas," warbled the Dickens Carolers as she rushed past them.

She was beginning to think she could use all the wishes she could get.

Carol's Place was packed with more Santas and Mrs. Clauses, as well as elves, Grinches and ugly sweater fans. "Grandma Got Run Over by a Reindeer" was playing at top volume, and people were on the wooden dance floor line dancing to it.

At a far corner table, she caught sight of…Barbara and Brock? Frankie blinked to make sure she wasn't seeing things. She wasn't. There they sat, holding hands across the table, Barbara looking emaciated but elegant in her black sweater and leggings and red scarf, Brock in a matching black sweater and jeans. It looked like he'd found a woman who wasn't bothered by age differences. But of all the women to latch on to. She'd feed his ego well, though, so good luck and Merry Christmas.

Frankie continued to search the room and finally caught sight of Mitch and Elinor at a table on the other side of the place, their server setting down what looked like peppermint martinis in front of them. The same drink Frankie and Mitch had enjoyed together the year before. Elinor had changed from her Mrs. Claus outfit into the hot red dress she'd worn the night before. Frankie's dress. A holly leaf of jealousy poked at Frankie.

No need to be jealous. This was Elinor's big day. Mrs. Claus had a right to enjoy a peppermint martini with Santa.

But not in Frankie's dress.

They were seated at a table for four. Perfect. Frankie texted Stef to come join them, then donned a smile and went to their table.

"Hi, guys," she said as she slid into a seat.

"Hey there. Glad you found us," Mitch greeted her.

Elinor didn't say anything. In fact, Elinor didn't look at all pleased to see Frankie.

That was when Frankie knew that the suspicions she'd been denying all along were not simply suspicions. Viola was right. There was a reason Elinor was turning the pub crawl into a pub chase.

And Frankie didn't like it one little bit.

16

ELINOR OBVIOUSLY WAS ENVISIONING HERSELF WITH
Mitch beyond this day. She needed to get her vision checked.
She did not belong with Mitch. Frankie belonged with Mitch.

And there it was, reality staring her right in the face. She'd
been perfectly happy to keep him at arm's length, figuring
that was so much safer than taking their friendship to a deeper
level. She'd even tried to match him up with other women.
But now, seeing him looking so cozy and at ease with Elinor,
she knew that she didn't want to see Mitch with someone after
all...unless that someone was her.

Selfish, really.

"I hope you don't mind me wearing your dress one more
time," Elinor said. "You were right. I should have bought it."

Sharing is caring, Frankie reminded herself. She liked Elinor, wanted her to have a good life, but she was done sharing her dress. And Mitch. So what had all her earlier matchmaking been about anyway?

Fear. She'd been afraid to risk her heart, so she'd kept pushing away the one man she could really share that life with. Dopey her! Now what was she going to do?

Sit there and be jealous, it would appear.

Or get proactive.

"You can give it back to me tomorrow," she said to Elinor. "Good job today, by the way. You must be pooped. You don't have to keep up with the Mrs. Claus thing." *Go home.*

"Oh, I'm fine," Elinor said breezily. "I'm having so much fun." She smiled, not at Frankie, the one who'd been behind her success, but at Mitch. "It's been a wonderful day. Mitch is the best."

Mitch, the big fathead, smiled like a golden retriever who'd just been patted on the head and told he was a good dog. "You did a great job," he said to Elinor. He caught Frankie's frown and added, "Of course, you were following in some impressive footsteps."

That was better. Frankie rewarded him with a smile. "I'm glad the event was a success."

"Never doubted it would be," he said.

At that moment Stef arrived and plopped onto the last vacant seat at the table. "I need a peppermint martini," she announced. "What a day."

"It was a good day," said Elinor.

"For you, maybe," Stef said. "I had to deal with Scrooge the Second. Plus, a kid barfed all over me when I was doing an interview."

"Should have gotten a picture of that for the paper," Mitch teased.

Stef was not amused. "Ha ha," she said with a frown. She

stuck out her arm to summon a passing waiter. "Peppermint martini, Cam, ASAP. I'm dyin' here."

"You don't look bad for a dying woman," he joked, and gave her a wink.

"Future husband?" suggested Mitch as the server headed for the bar to put in her order.

"He still lives with his mom. Yeah, he's at the top of my list," Stef replied. "I swear, there's not a decent single man left in this whole town."

"Oh, I don't know," said Elinor. "Mitch is pretty amazing."

Frankie frowned. *Gag.* Although she'd been about to say the same thing. Elinor had beaten her to the punch. Since when did Elinor throw flattery around like confetti?

Mitch grinned. Frankie wanted to kick him.

"That goes without saying," said Stef. "Mitch, how come you've never asked me out on a date?"

"He's holding out for Mrs. Claus," Frankie answered, and smiled at Mitch, sure he would remember his comment in the coffee shop earlier in the month.

"Might be," he said, and Elinor preened.

Frankie sent her a psychic message. *Not you!*

Elinor laid a hand on Mitch's arm. "Mitch, do you think we should make a couple more stops? I'm sure there are more people wanting to talk to Santa."

"We're not lacking for Santas tonight, in case you didn't notice," Frankie informed her. She sounded irritable. Hardly surprising, since she was feeling irritable.

Mitch looked apologetically at her, then said to Elinor, "Sure." He pulled out enough money to pay for all their drinks, then stood. "I guess we'd better get over to Lulu's."

"We'll catch up with you," said Frankie.

"No worries if you don't," Elinor said airily. "You're probably tired," she added, using Frankie's earlier tactic.

Tired of watching you try to take over my life. "I'm not that tired," Frankie said, but Elinor was already leading the way out of the restaurant.

"I'll see you tomorrow," Mitch told Frankie, then followed her.

"Unbelievable," Frankie said, frowning.

"That was kind of weird," said Stef. "What's going on?"

"Elinor's after Mitch."

"Elinor?" Stef looked disbelieving.

"You didn't see the way she was looking at him?" Frankie demanded. "Putting her hands on him? She's been playing keep-away-from-Frankie with him all night."

"Well, you did want him to find someone," Stef pointed out, echoing what Viola had said earlier.

"Not Elinor."

"Why not Elinor?"

"She's not right for him." She needed to play with someone her own age.

Stef cocked her head and studied Frankie. "Who is, sissy?"

Frankie squirmed. It was one thing to pry into Stef's love life—quite another to expose her feelings. "Nobody, and Elinor should be with William Sharp. They're a perfect match."

"Looks to me like she's settled on her perfect match," said Stef. Cam arrived with her drink, and she thanked him, took a sip and sighed. "That's better. I wish I'd had this when I met that poor little boy's beast of a father."

"He's certainly not what you need," Frankie said.

"I feel sorry for his kid."

"I feel sorry for the dad, too," Frankie said. "It's hard to make a normal life for yourself after losing someone you love, especially when you've got a young child. Still, that's no excuse for the way he behaved."

"You've got that right." Stef raised her glass. "To lucky escapes." Then she frowned and took a very long draw on her drink.

"Hey there," boomed a voice, and the sisters turned to see they had company. It was the same man who had almost knocked Frankie over earlier. He'd added a Santa hat and a sloppy leer to his outfit.

"Oh, please," said Stef. "Go away."

He bent down and leaned his arms on the tabletop. "You don't mean that," he said, and hiccuped.

"I do," Stef told him. "We're waiting for our boyfriends. They're cops."

Their visitor blinked. "Cops."

"Got any outstanding tickets?" Stef asked.

His brows dropped and met at the center. "Well, I guess I…need another drink."

"Yeah, that's what you need," Stef said as he swayed off. She downed the rest of her martini. "You know, I think I'm gonna go home before I get all sloppy and maudlin. I'll go stream *Sleepless in Seattle*."

The last thing Stef needed to watch. Frankie looked at her in horror.

"Just kidding, sissy," she said, and managed a smile. "I'm going to find something with murder and mayhem. That fits my mood better."

Frankie sighed. The night hadn't exactly gone as planned so far. She strongly suspected it wasn't going to get better. "I think I'll go home, too."

Stef gave Frankie a kiss on the cheek, then left. Several Santas watched her go, but she didn't notice. Somewhere the right man for her was waiting in the wings. Frankie wished he'd hurry up and make his appearance.

She, too, started for the door. Burl Ives was singing, wishing her a holly jolly Christmas. It had been holly jolly until she'd seen what was going on with Elinor and Mitch.

"Bah, humbug," Frankie grumbled.

She was going out just as Viola and Terrill were coming in. "You're leaving already?" Viola asked.

"The party's over," Frankie said.

"Since when is the party ever over for you?" Viola teased.

"Since now. You two have fun." Somebody needed to. Frankie sure wasn't.

The snow was really starting to come down, and it looked like they'd get a lot more than predicted. Which meant there wouldn't be a lot of shoppers the following day. Maybe that would be just as well. She wasn't sure she'd be in the mood to greet people with a smile and spread the Christmas cheer.

Elinor had better bring back her dress.

"And God bless Santa," Corky said, then finished his bedtime prayer with an enthusiastic "amen."

"Amen," Griff echoed, not quite so enthusiastically. Corky scrambled into bed, and Griff pulled the covers up to his chin. "Remember, Santa only brings toys."

Corky nodded. "I know. But I told him I wanted a mommy anyway."

Griff groaned inwardly. How many times were they going to go over this?

"What did Santa say?" he asked. If that fake Santa had promised to deliver a mom for Corky, Griff was going to hunt him down and knock his bearded face off.

"He said, 'Merry Christmas.'"

Good. No false promises. Santa could live to ho, ho, ho another day.

"All I want for Christmas is a mommy," Corky said.

Griff sighed. "I know. And I'm sorry you don't have one,

but meanwhile, we're gonna be happy with Aunt Jenn and Grandma and Grandpa, right? And you've got me." He kissed the top of his son's head.

"And you," Corky said with a nod, smiling up at Griff.

That trusting smile, it squeezed his heart like a vise. If only Griff could give his son what he wanted. But he couldn't. There was no one who could take Kaitlyn's place.

He wandered back out into the living room. Looked at the artificial tree his sister had helped Corky and him decorate. He smiled at the memory of his son standing on tiptoe, trying to help them string the garlands around it.

The smile faded as he remembered decorating that tree with his wife their last Christmas together. She'd been wearing red leggings and a short black T-shirt. She'd bent over to pull an ornament out of one of the too many boxes they had and caught him admiring her butt.

She'd winked at him and said, "If you're a good boy, you might get lucky tonight."

He'd come over, pulled her to him and teased, "What if I'm a bad boy?"

"Then for sure you'll get lucky," she'd said, and he'd laughed.

She'd laughed, too, as they fell on the couch.

"I'll love you forever, Griffin Marks," she'd said right before he kissed her.

I'll love you forever, Griffin Marks.

He felt ill, like he'd been sucker punched. Every time he thought he was doing better, the memories came at him like ninjas, jumping on him out of nowhere. He went to his fridge and pulled out a beer, plopped on the couch and wished he could wash them away.

No, that wasn't right. He wanted to keep the memories.

He just didn't want the pain anymore. He wanted to get out from under the crushing weight of it, wished he could find that mother that Corky so desperately wanted. Wished he could start again.

For a moment, in the coffee shop, he'd had a glimpse of possibility. What a joke. The hottie from the coffee shop had turned out to be the pill from the paper. Ugh.

He took a swig from his bottle, shut his eyes and relived their afternoon encounter. He could clearly see the flash of anger in those pretty hazel eyes of hers, could almost hear again the scorn in her voice.

He could definitely remember the scorn in his sister's voice when she'd said, "Way to go, Scrooge."

Just because he'd let Stefanie Ludlow know how wrong she was, that made him a Scrooge?

A text came in from his sister. **You know, Scrooge changed.**
He ignored it.

His phone rang. It was his mother's ringtone. He could ignore his sister, but he knew better than to ignore his mom.

"Hi, Mom," he answered, schooling his voice to sound pleasant. *Nothing wrong here in Scrooge Land.*

"How was Corky's visit with Santa?" Mom asked.

Griff wished he hadn't told her they were going to the Santa Walk. The last thing he wanted was to relive the day. "We got it done," he said.

"I'm glad you went ahead and took him."

"I'm not. He's still convinced he's going to get a mom. It doesn't matter what I say or do. He's going to be disappointed."

"For a minute. Until he gets distracted playing with his toys."

"Yeah, every kid will take toys over a mom."

"We'll get him through," Mom promised.

His son's disappointment would be short-lived, and yes, they'd all keep him busy and distracted. But the longing would return. Griff knew. You could move away from those longings, but in the end they always caught up with you. How did you outrun them?

He said goodbye to his mother, and misery came crashing down on him. An unmanly sob escaped before he could catch it. Was this what the rest of his life was going to feel like?

He wanted to move on with the memories but without the pain. That probably wasn't possible, but was it possible to at least bring the pain down to a more manageable level so he wouldn't feel so bitter and frustrated? So he wouldn't lash out at people who really didn't deserve it?

His behavior earlier had been over the top. What would Kaitlyn have had to say about that? Moot point. If she was still with him, he wouldn't have behaved like that. He'd have been happy.

Stefanie Ludlow had told him to go back to his Krampus cage. He was living in a cage. How had she known?

How could he break out?

He texted his sister. How did Scrooge change?

The answer came back. He got up the next morning and did something different.

Hmm.

Frankie was still feeling grumpy when she opened the shop on Sunday. Neither church nor a good helping of Christmas cookies during the social hour after the service had helped. Neither did entering her little Christmas kingdom.

Natalie was off, spending the day with her in-laws, which was fine. Frankie didn't expect many customers and probably didn't need both her mother and Elinor. She wished she'd given Elinor the day off as well, as Frankie wasn't in a proper frame of mind to deal with her employee.

"No one's going to come out today," she grumbled as she came in from spreading ice-melting compound on the sidewalk.

"Okay, spill. What is wrong with you?" Adele demanded.

"Nothing," she said.

"I always know when there's something. Don't make me drag it out of you."

"Okay, if you must know, it's Elinor."

"Elinor? What did she do wrong?"

"She's late."

"All of ten minutes. After the snow we got last night, she's probably taking her time on the road. Or she's dragging from her big day."

"That's no excuse. It was only a couple of inches. And you made it in fine."

Adele frowned at Frankie. "All right, what's really bugging you?"

Frankie ignored the question. "Do you think Elinor and Mitch are a match?"

Adele blinked in surprise. "Elinor and Mitch? Does Mitch know?"

"Funny, Mom."

"What happened yesterday?"

"Elinor latched on to him like a little Christmas leech and wouldn't let go. That's what happened."

"You were wanting Mitch to find someone," pointed out Adele. "You should be all puffed up like a toad over this."

If one more person told her what she'd wanted for Mitch, Frankie's head was going to blow off. "I wanted William to find Elinor, not Mitch."

"I guess she didn't get the memo."

Frankie ignored the crack. "Everything I did for her—helping her with a makeover, campaigning for her for Mrs. Claus. Now she thinks she *is* Mrs. Claus. She thinks she's me!" Frankie fumed.

"So, you've spent all this time helping Elinor come out of

her shell and look her best, and now that she's out, you're dis-
satisfied with her and want to put her back. Good luck with
that. Looks like you've created a monster, Frankiestein."

That she had. "It's not that I don't want her to be happy."

"You just don't want her to be happy with Mitch," Adele
suggested.

"She's living my life!"

"No, she's living hers. Maybe not the way you want her to,
but we don't get to decide how other people live their lives.
The only life you have any control at all over is your own."

"I don't like the way my own is going," Frankie grumbled.

"Then what are you going to do?"

Good question.

Adele put an arm around Frankie's shoulders. "I had a
dream last night."

Frankie rolled her eyes. "Oh no. Here we go."

"This is serious. It was about you."

"Me? What did you dream?"

"You were at some kind of fair, standing next to a merry-
go-round. It was slowing down, and people were calling to
you to get on, but you wouldn't. In fact, you were backing
away. They gave up, and it started going faster. Everyone was
laughing and having fun. You finally tried to get on, but it
was going too fast and it bucked you off and sent you flying."

"Yikes. What kind of dream is that?" Frankie protested.

"You tell me," said Adele.

The bell over the door jingled, and in rushed Elinor, her
cheeks rosy from the cold. She was smiling, wearing the lipstick Frankie had bought for her. Frankie had felt like a fairy
godmother when she'd helped Elinor with her makeup. This
morning she felt more like Maleficent.

"I'm sorry I'm late," Elinor said breathlessly. "I had two
cars almost skid into me."

"See? Told you," Adele said to Frankie.

"It's all right," Frankie said, determined not to sound like Scrooge. "We probably won't get a lot of customers in today after how busy we were yesterday."

"You were busy. How did you like being Mrs. Claus?" Adele asked Elinor.

Elinor beamed. "It was wonderful. Mitch is wonderful."

Okay, enough already. Elinor needed to be reminded of who she was supposed to be with. "Now, how would William Sharp feel if he heard you raving about Mitch?" Frankie said, keeping her voice light.

Elinor looked at her, puzzled. "I don't know. Why would that matter?"

"Elinor, we've talked about that special someone you were interested in," Frankie reminded her.

Elinor's rosy cheeks turned scarlet. "Yes. And I hope he's interested, too. Mitch is the sweetest man in Carol."

"But what about William?" Frankie pressed. *William's your man.*

"He's nice," Elinor said with a shrug, "but I was never into him. I'd better get my apron on and get to work." She hurried to the back room to shed her coat.

Shocked, Frankie looked to her mother.

Adele merely shrugged. "Looks like you've succeeded in finding a match for Mitch."

A match for Mitch—it sounded like a bad book title. Frankie had to force the scowl from her face when a customer walked through the door.

She spent the whole day fighting off that scowl and was glad when the day was over and she could finally turn the sign on the door to Closed. Spending time with her family for their usual Sunday get-together would, hopefully, improve her mood.

"I'm off to heat up the lasagna. See you in an hour," Adele said to Frankie. "What are you up to, Elinor?"

"I'm going to go home and bake. I have my grandmother's brownie recipe."

"Sounds good. I hope you'll share some," Adele said.

"I'll make another batch and bring it in on Tuesday," Elinor promised, then hurried out the door.

"At least you know she's not with Mitch if she's home baking brownies," Adele said to Frankie. "See you at the house."

And then she was gone.

Frankie locked the door and slowly made her way to her car. The temperature was dropping, and the streets were turning icy. If it kept up, she'd have to throw out a ton of rock salt when she came back in on Tuesday.

She drove home, avoiding the occasional parked car stranded at an angle on the street. Even though snow was becoming more common, people in the Pacific Northwest still hadn't figured out how to drive in it.

She changed into her favorite leggings and comfy red sweatshirt. She took the garlic bread she'd bought to take to her mother's from the pantry, along with the bag of her daughter's chocolates, then she pulled on her coat and her snow boots and made her way down the street.

Surprise, surprise, Mr. Bellagamba's car was parked out front right along with Stef's, and Frankie entered to find everyone already celebrating with eggnog. A nice bit of bling was glinting from Adele's finger, proof that she'd decided not to wait until Christmas Eve to make her big announcement.

"Did you know about this?" Stef greeted Frankie.

Adele's warning look informed Frankie that she was not to blab how she'd learned about the new man in their mother's life. "Wow, really?" she said, doing an excellent job of faking surprise. "Congratulations, you two." She set down her

SHEILA ROBERTS

goodies and went to take hold of her mother's hand for a closer look. "That's gorgeous. And what a great Christmas surprise." She hugged her mom and future stepfather.

"Natalie's going to be mad that she missed out on this," Stef predicted.

"She'll learn soon enough," said Adele.

"When's the wedding, Mr. B?" Frankie asked.

"Call me Mario," he said before adding, "Soon, I hope."

"Fourth of July," Adele decided. "That way, no matter how senile we get, we'll never forget our anniversary. Plus, we'll always have fireworks."

"Good idea," he said approvingly, and grinned.

"I hope one of you girls is next," Adele said to her daughters.

"Don't hold your breath for me," Stef said, opening the silverware drawer. "I really think I'm through with men. Let's get the table set and eat."

"I'll help you," said Mario, and opened the dish cupboard.

"He sure knows his way around your kitchen," Frankie said to her mom as the other two went to the dining room table. "Good thing he had honorable intentions."

"Don't get smart," Adele scolded. "And speaking of intentions, what do you intend to do about your future? Did you figure out the symbolism of my dream?"

"Mom, even Freud couldn't figure out the symbolism of your dreams."

"I think this one is pretty easy," Adele said softly, and gave Frankie's arm an encouraging rub. "It's time to quit stalling and get on the ride. If Ike were here, he'd say, 'What are you waiting for?'"

"A guarantee?" Frankie ventured. Although, look where that had gotten her. Mitch was now pub crawling with someone else.

"You know there's no such thing. Stop worrying about what might happen down the road and let something good happen right now. When a certain someone comes over tonight to watch that cop show, get out some handcuffs and go for it."

"Mom! As if I have any."

Adele shrugged. "I don't have any, either. I guess you'll have to improvise. Seriously, daughter dear, you two are natural together. The man's crazy about you. Don't wait around. He might get sane and go looking somewhere else."

Frankie got the message. It was her turn to host *Cop Stop*, so after they ate, she hurried home, then got busy lighting candles, turning on her tree lights and setting out Mitch's favorite Chex Mix munchies. And redoing her makeup and hair and spritzing on that perfume she hadn't worn in a long time.

At ten to eight, she was perched on the couch, trying not to watch out the window for his truck. At five till, she was looking out the door to see if she could spot it coming down the street. No sign of him. Where was he?

She grabbed her phone and texted. Almost Cop Time. Where are you?

There came the dancing bubbles. Hopefully, he was letting her know he was on his way.

Words appeared. Sorry. Something came up.

Nothing ever came up on *Cop Stop* night. What??? she texted.

Got drop-in company.

Company! On *Cop Stop* night? Who trumped *Cop Stop* night?

Anybody I know?

Elinor.

Elinor and her brownies!

Catch you tomorrow? he texted.

Not even an invitation to come over and join them.

Clobber you tomorrow. But Frankie deleted her reply before she sent it. She threw her phone onto the sofa with a growl, then marched to the kitchen and dumped the Chex Mix in the garbage.

Then she returned to the sofa, grabbed the phone and called her mother. "Elinor's over at his place."

"Well, Frankiestein, what are you going to do about it?"

What, indeed?

17

SINCE THE SHOP WAS CLOSED ON MONDAY, IT WAS THE perfect time to invite Mitch out to lunch and get to the bottom of what was going on with Elinor. She'd better have tied him to the couch and held him captive. It was the only excuse Frankie would accept for standing her up.

Don't be bitchy, she lectured herself as she toasted her English muffin. She'd brought this on herself by remaking Elinor and then pushing her into being Mrs. Claus.

She and Mitch often met for lunch on Mondays, so inviting him out wouldn't look suspicious. She'd find a way to extend lunch into spending the afternoon together and use that time to explain to him why Elinor wasn't right for him. Brock could manage the hardware store just fine in his absence.

Lunch? she texted.

No reply.

Hellooo.

It was eight in the morning. He practically lived at the store. He should be up and at work. Why wasn't he replying?

Okay, maybe he was meeting with his staff. She'd give him some time to answer. She gave him an hour. More than enough time. She abandoned texting and called.

It took several rings before he answered with a sleepy, "Hello."

"Were you still asleep?" Frankie asked in surprise.

"Yeah, I'm in bed. I feel like shit. I think I picked up some kind of stomach bug. Was up half the night."

Probably the result of eating Elinor's brownies, Frankie decided. Served him right.

"Can I bring you anything? Chicken soup?"

"No food," he said firmly. "I'll sleep this off and be fine. Did you need something?"

Other than to have a serious talk with him. "No, no, that's okay. I'll catch you when you're better."

"Okay," he said, and ended the call before she could even say goodbye.

At least he hadn't been ignoring her texts because he was with a certain someone. Tomorrow Frankie would get this all sorted out.

Meanwhile, she had a post-event meeting with the Santa Walk committee. She made sure she got an eggnog latte on her way to the chamber of commerce office. She knew she'd need a stiff shot of caffeine to face a gloating Barbara. The woman would, of course, be basking in the glow of success, hogging all the credit in spite of having a hardworking committee doing all the heavy lifting.

Frankie entered along with Theresia, who was happy with the volume of business the bakery had done on Saturday. "We sold out of everything," she told Frankie. "There wasn't so much as a crumb left behind. And, of course, our gingerbread Mrs. Clauses were the first to go. That was such a great suggestion. Thank you."

"I'm glad, and you're welcome," Frankie said.

"You come up with so many cool ideas. I swear, you're a regular idea factory."

"Always thinking of ways to make the Santa Walk better," Frankie said.

Theresia stopped before they entered the meeting room. "So, what did you think of the pageant? Really? Are you okay with someone else being Mrs. Claus?"

"It was hard to give up," Frankie admitted. But it looked like a new tradition had begun and she suspected her reign as Mrs. Claus was over. "But that's okay. It was someone else's turn."

Theresia lowered her voice. "I feel like Barbara sort of took over. How would you feel about chairing the committee again?"

Like I'd be back where I'm supposed to be. "I'd love to take on that responsibility," Frankie said.

Theresia nodded decisively. "I'm going to nominate you. I just wanted to make sure you weren't burned out."

"I was never burned out," Frankie said, and Theresia gave a knowing nod.

The others were already in the meeting room, and just as Frankie had predicted, Barbara was all smiles and pontificating on how well the event had gone. "I've heard lots of good feedback on our Dickens Carolers," she said, "and I think the pageant was a huge success."

"The gingerbread houses made a great fundraiser. We should definitely do that again," said Autumn.

Barbara doled out a triumphant smile to Frankie as she seated herself. "Frankie, I hope you're happy with how well your Mrs. Claus replacement did."

Replacement. Nice word choice. Frankie took a big gulp of her drink. "I'm happy with how everything went. You did a good job of filling in this year," she added, and offered Barbara her sweetest smile.

It wasn't returned. "Well, we should get right down to it," Barbara said.

The next forty minutes were spent analyzing all aspects of the event, from how the new location for the vendors had worked to the entertainment.

"The principal at the high school told me that she'd like the school glee club to be allowed an entertainment slot after Santa's done with the kids next year," said Hazel.

"That sounds good. James, will you make a note of that?" Barbara said.

"Will do. But I can't be secretary next year," James said.

Barbara looked at him in shock.

"Sorry," he said. "I've got too much on my plate."

"James. We all have things on our plates. We all have to make sacrifices," Barbara said sternly.

"I'll help with setup and takedown at the pageant again next year, but I can't do all the other stuff."

"All right, fine," Barbara said in a clipped tone. "I accept your resignation. Now, we all do want to do the pageant again next year, don't we?"

Everyone looked to Frankie. If she said no, they'd back her.

But maybe there were other women who wanted to have the fun of greeting the children who came to see Santa. She'd started the Santa Walk with pure motives, had played Mrs. Claus because it seemed like a great addition to the fun. She'd achieved what she started out to do. She'd created a successful party for the whole town. She didn't need to hog the spotlight. In fact, she realized she'd rather be running the show than in it.

"I think the pageant is a fun idea, and we should do it as long as we have women who'd like to play Mrs. Claus," she said.

Barbara smirked. She obviously thought Frankie was surrendering her role because she'd been beaten. Let the woman think what she wanted. Frankie knew she was surrendering her role because adding the pageant made the Santa Walk that much more fun for everyone.

One thing Frankie wasn't ready to surrender, though, and that was being in charge of the whole shebang. This was her baby, and she wasn't ready to adopt it out.

"I agree," said Hazel. "Let's keep the pageant going."

Barbara nodded and made a note on one of the many papers in front of her. "So, we're all in agreement then?"

Everyone was.

"And other than James…" here Barbara looked at him like he was a defector "…everyone else is still good with their responsibilities?"

The others nodded.

"All right," Barbara said. "I hope one of you will consider filling the secretary position for next year. I'll give you all time to think about it. Now, if that's all, I think we can adjourn."

"Wait. One more order of business," said Theresia. "I'm thinking we should see if Frankie would like to come back as our chairperson."

Barbara's smile froze, then cracked and fell away. "Well," she said.

"Good idea," said James. "You up for chairing next year, Frankie?"

"Yes, I am," she said firmly.

"We know you've had so much to deal with ever since, er, your loss," Barbara said.

"It never stopped me from serving my community," Frankie said. "And if you remember, I started this after my loss." It had helped keep her sane.

"We thought you were burned out," Barbara continued.

Only gaslit. "I'm not. And I'm sure you could use a break," Frankie said.

"Then I motion we elect Frankie to chair the committee," said Theresia.

Barbara cleared her throat. "Well. We have a motion to elect Frankie as our chairperson for next year's Santa Walk. Do we have a second?"

"I'll second that," said James, Autumn and Hazel simultaneously.

"All right," Barbara said stiffly. "Shall we vote? All those in favor?"

It was almost unanimous. Barbara abstained from voting. Afterward everyone was smiling.

Barbara even managed half a smile. "I'm probably going to be busy this year now that I have someone new in my life," she announced.

"How nice," said Hazel.

Nice for Barbara. Poor Brock.

"I think Barbara did an excellent job of keeping things going," Hazel said to Frankie as she followed the others out. "But it's nice to have you back at the helm. I just wish you'd still be our Mrs. Claus."

"Oh well. I can share." The job, not the man.

"Maybe we need to have a Santa competition next year as well as a Mrs. Claus pageant," Hazel said thoughtfully.

"Maybe," Frankie agreed. She rather liked the idea of someone other than Mitch doing the pub crawl with Mrs. Claus.

Mitch. Hopefully, he'd be feeling better soon. She was anxious to talk with him.

★ ★ ★

Stef was coming out of a meeting at the paper when Harlan the receptionist found her and told her someone was waiting in the lobby to see her. An intriguing mystery. Friends and family simply texted if they wanted to get together. No one came to the paper. Who could be looking for her?

She froze on reaching the lobby and seeing who it was. *Oh no. Not him*, she thought as he left his seat and started toward her. She could feel her pulse picking up speed.

"What do you want?" she demanded.

"To make up for being a jerk," he replied.

How did you make up for being a jerk when you were one? She kept the thought to herself and waited for him to continue.

He took a deep breath. "I've been going through a rough time, but I shouldn't have taken it out on you."

"You're right. You shouldn't have," she said.

"I'm sorry."

A man saying he was sorry. Now, there was a refreshing change.

"I'm not a total jerk. Give me a chance to prove it. Could I buy you a cup of coffee or a latte? I think I owe you one," he added.

"Along with a big serving of sorry," she said.

"As big as it takes."

It was tempting. He was tempting. "So, you're really not a jerk? I mean, you could have fooled me."

He dropped his gaze and nodded. "I know. I've been fooling a lot of people." His gaze returned to her. "How about it? Give me a chance to make peace?"

She considered. This man was broken. His out-of-proportion anger was evidence of that. But everyone got broken at some point in life. Hadn't she herself been broken by her disastrous marriage? But she'd healed. Maybe he could, too. Maybe she should give this man a chance. Anyway, it was only coffee.

"All right," she said. "I can make time for an eggnog latte in an hour."

"An hour. Meet you at The Coffee Stop, then?"

She nodded. "The Coffee Stop."

He smiled. It was tentative, the kind of smile that looked like it had been kept in storage for a long time. But it was enough to flush away the scowling Scrooge mask. What a difference from the angry man who'd come at her at the Santa Walk. He was the holiday version of Dr. Jekyll and Mr. Hyde.

Maybe he needed someone to help him find his lost hope again. Maybe, like most people, like her, he simply needed a second chance to get his life on track.

And maybe she'd better not expect anything to come of a shared moment in a coffee shop.

All the way there, she told herself that this was no big deal, certainly not the beginning of a romance novel come to life. Until she walked in the shop and saw him waiting at a table, looking like he should be in a TikTok video in that gray suit, his coat over the chair next to him.

He stood when she approached the table, and there was that smile again. Just big enough to hint at how, if turned on full force, it could keep a woman warm on a cold winter night.

"Thanks for coming," he said. She started to shrug out of her coat, and he was quick to help her.

"Every Scrooge deserves a second chance," she said lightly.

"So, what are you, the Ghost of Christmas Future?"

Did she detect some cynicism in that teasing? She frowned.

He held up a hand. "Just joking."

"Were you now?"

He cleared his throat. "I'll get you that eggnog latte," he said, and strode to the counter to order.

She studied him as he walked. He didn't slouch like some men. Instead, he walked with his shoulders back. He looked like a man who could face any storm.

She wasn't so sure he was succeeding. She suspected he was having trouble trying to raise a child alone after the loss of his wife. Was he mourning her out of guilt because they'd had trouble in their marriage, or was he, like Frankie after losing Ike, mourning the loss of a part of himself that had been cut away? What had his wife been like?

Griffin returned with large drinks for each of them. "I came back here looking for you," he said as he settled on his seat.

"No."

"I did. I was in here the next day, sitting at this very table."

"I was home all day with a monster migraine. I saw you at the school concert, though."

"You were there?"

She nodded. "My nephew was a snowflake."

"My son was an *S* in Merry Christmas. His big speaking part was, 'To everyone.'"

"A future star." Stef took a sip of her latte. "I looked for you afterward. I was going to come say hi, but you vanished. Did you get sick?" she teased.

He made a face. "My son did. You wouldn't have wanted to see either of us."

"You have a sweet little boy."

"He takes after his mother."

It seemed like the perfect time to ask about his wife. "Tell me about her." Pain shot across his face, and Stef instantly regretted asking. "You don't have to."

"No, I want to. I think I should have been talking about her a lot more than I have."

He pulled his wallet from his back pants pocket and took out a picture. His wife had been pretty. Not gorgeous but pretty. She had a longish face framed by long blond hair, a delicate nose and full lips and nice green eyes. And a big smile.

"She's lovely. What was she like? Tell me."

He looked at the picture and blinked hard. Got busy returning the picture to his wallet, then putting it back in his pants pocket. "She was amazing."

"What was amazing about her?"

"I don't even know where to start."

"Sure you do," Stef coached.

"She laughed a lot. She was always happy. And patient. She never got mad."

"Seriously?" Who never got mad?

"Not really. She'd get irritated sometimes, like when I'd forget to pick up something at the store on my way home from work. But she'd make a joke out of it, kiss me and say, 'You'll do better next time, Mr. Wonderful.'"

"Mr. Wonderful," Stef repeated.

"Hard to believe, huh? It was her way of always forgiving me. Always urging me to be better. We both knew I wasn't wonderful. Unlike her, I wasn't patient. And I'd get mad easy. I, uh, guess you noticed that."

"I guess so."

"Mostly I'd get mad over unimportant stuff—a flat tire, messing up trying to fix a leaky kitchen sink." He gave a grunt. "What did any of that matter, really? What does any of that little stuff matter? It's the people in our life…" He shook his head. "Okay, this wasn't supposed to be a shrink session. Sorry."

"Don't be. I asked."

"You can stop asking now," he said, but not meanly. More like he was embarrassed to have shed his manly shell and revealed his vulnerability.

"I can't help myself. I'm a reporter. Remember? So, one more question. What's her name?"

"Kaitlyn. Her name was Kaitlyn."

"It still is. She may not be here with you anymore, but her memory is."

He nodded slowly but said nothing.

Stef raised her cup. "So, here's to Kaitlyn and the great memories she gave you and the great kid."

There was the smile again, small, almost balancing out the sadness in his eyes. "To Kaitlyn," he repeated, and took a sip. He set down his cup and said, "Okay, that's enough about me. How about you? How did you end up being Santa's helper?"

"It was my sister's idea, actually. She suggested it to my editor, and I got to do it. I love doing the page. And most people really like it," she added.

He held up a hand. "I know, except for us Scrooges."

"Scrooge changed," she pointed out.

He gave a grunt. "Now you're channeling my sister. But never mind Scrooge and me. Tell me more about you. What do you do besides fill in for Santa?"

"I like to read, watch movies. I ski occasionally. Badly," she added. "I do a lot with my family."

"No real Santa in your life? No Mr. Wonderful?"

She shook her head. "Only an ex-Grinch. Every time I find myself wishing I had a child, I think of Dick and am glad we didn't have children together. They might have turned out like him."

"Dick, huh? That's his name?"

She grinned. It gave her such wicked pleasure to shorten her ex's name. "He preferred to be called Richard, but Dick fit him better."

"You do have a way with words," he said.

"He didn't appreciate it."

"I bet not. That tongue of yours is probably a lethal weapon."

"Not always. It has many uses," she said, then felt herself blushing. *Behave yourself, Stef.*

He chuckled. "Are you always this funny?"

"Oh no. Sometimes I'm funnier."

He sobered. "I really am sorry I lit into you like that."

"I'm over it." She cocked her head and studied him. "You're kind of like the proverbial bear with a sore paw. Only in your case, you got your paw completely cut off."

"More like my heart cut out," he said. "My sister keeps telling me I need to move on for Corky's sake."

"Corky, that's such a cute name."

"He's a cute kid. He deserves better."

"He's already got better than a lot of kids. He's got a good dad and an aunt who cares."

"And two sets of grandparents," he added. "Hard to keep in touch with the in-laws. They're in Arizona, and the last time we visited, it felt..." He shrugged.

"Uncomfortable?"

"Yeah. Hard to keep a conversation going, you know."

"I don't know, but I can imagine."

"They want to talk about Kaitlyn, and every time they bring out the old pictures it nearly kills me." He swore. "There I go again, spilling my guts to someone I just met. Maybe I need to see a shrink."

"Or maybe you just need to get out more," Stef suggested. "What do you like to do?"

"Besides feel sorry for myself? I don't know."

"Oh, come on, you must like to do something."

"I used to ski. Before I got married. I like watching the Mariners. Kaitlyn and I played in a Jack-and-Jill softball league when we were first married. It was a lot of fun. You like sports?"

"I was never any good at softball, but I intend to go to every one of Warner's Little League games. I don't like football."

"Who doesn't like football?"

"Me. But I do like a good Super Bowl party. Does that count?"

He smiled. "Sure. What else?"

"Board games. My ex would never play them with me. He said they were childish."

"Not into Monopoly, huh?"

She grinned. "Not into anything. He hated losing, and he lost a lot. Especially at Sequence. Nobody beats me at that."

He cocked an eyebrow and smiled. "Yeah?"

"Oh yeah."

"We might have to see about that," he said, and his words coupled with that smile he was getting more accustomed to using made her heart do a little skip.

"Might we?" she said playfully.

He hesitated a moment, then asked, "Did we survive having coffee together?"

"I'd say we did," she said. There was so much to this man. She'd never have seen it if they'd stopped with their skirmish at the Santa Walk.

"Then how about dinner tonight? Corky's baking cookies with my sister, and I've got nothing to do."

"Poor you."

"So, what do you think?"

"I think you'd better tell me you like Chinese."

"I do. Can I pick you up?"

"Are you strong enough?"

He pointed a finger at her. "You enjoy being irritating, don't you?"

"Only sometimes," she replied. "Yes, you may, and here's my address."

She gave him both her address and her phone number, and he put them in his phone.

And just like that, she had a date with Jekyll and Hyde. And maybe, just maybe, Hyde was on his way out, and the good man who was starting to emerge would be able to break free.

"By the way, Griffin is a cool name. Do you know what it symbolizes?"

"Don't tell me you do."

"I looked it up before I came. It symbolizes power and prestige. And courage."

"Courage, huh?"

"Just thought you'd like to know."

"Thanks. It is good to know. See you tonight. Six?"

She nodded. "It'll be you, me and the general."

His lips cocked up in a half smile. "Tso?"

"That's the one."

"All right," he said. He gave her a little salute and then left the coffee shop.

She stayed put and texted her sister. Can't come over tonight. Having dinner with the Grinch.

????

He came to the paper to apologize. We had coffee. I think there's a good guy hidden in there somewhere.

Keep me posted, Frankie texted, and added a smiley face emoticon.

Will do, Stef assured her.

Of course she would. Stef adored her mother, but Frankie was her confidant and adviser, had been since Stef was little. Frankie had been rooting for her little sister to find true love and erase the bitter taste of what Richard had dished out.

Eating Chinese with Griffin Marks would be a good place to begin. Maybe nothing would come of seeing this new man, but they could at least help each other look for the road to happily ever after.

18

STEF STAYED CASUAL FOR THEIR DATE—JEANS AND A RED
sweater—but she did her hair and makeup and used her favorite peppermint-vanilla-scented cologne. It was Christmastime, after all.

Christmastime. She had to laugh when they were seated at
the table in a near empty restaurant and the waiter laid out their
sweet-and-sour pork, General Tso's chicken, egg rolls and rice.

"You know what movie this makes me think of?" she asked
him.

He didn't smile. This time he gave her a great big grin. "*A
Christmas Story*, where the family all ends up at the Chinese restaurant. We watched that every year when I was growing up."

"You dogs of Bumpus!" she ranted, pulling out her lowest
voice, and he laughed.

Then he looked surprised. "I haven't laughed in a long time."

"Then I guess it's time you did," she said, and dipped her egg roll in the sweet chili sauce.

"I guess it is," he agreed.

Inspired, they spent the rest of the dinner throwing out famous lines from movies.

"May the odds be ever in your favor," Stef quoted.

He gave a cynical snort. "And may the Force be with you."

"Everyone knows that one. Come on, guess mine."

He shrugged. "I dunno."

"*The Hunger Games*. You never saw those movies?"

"Nope."

"Your life has been deprived. Okay," she said, and tried another. "Don't judge me."

"Just what I was about to say," he said.

"What's it from?"

"Beats me."

"Is that a movie, or are you giving up?"

"I'm giving up," he said.

"*Trainwreck*."

His smile shrank. "No wonder I never saw that movie. It sounds like my life."

No, no. They weren't going to get all depressed one day before Christmas Eve. "Okay, how about this?" She cleared her throat and sang, "The sun will come out tomorrow."

He looked puzzled.

"Oh, come on, everyone knows *Annie*—the kid with all the red hair?"

He nodded slowly.

"Well, okay, it's not exactly a new musical. I know all this stuff because my grandma was into it. Anyway, it's cute. Lots of positivity. She made me watch it after I left my husband."

He nodded. Was silent a moment. Then he asked, "Do you believe that?"

"What?"

"That the sun will come out tomorrow."

"I do," she said. "I'll admit it hasn't always been easy, but I try to." She popped the last bit of her egg roll in her mouth.

"Trying is good," he said.

She put on her Yoda voice. "Do or do not. There is no try." She sobered. "I'd say snarfing down Chinese food in a nice restaurant counts as doing, wouldn't you?"

He nodded. "I'd say it does. Thanks for coming out with me tonight."

"I'm glad I did," she said.

His smile got bigger, and she reflected it back. Yes, maybe, just maybe this man could be mended. Maybe they both could be.

"Okay, here's one for you," he said. "I'll be back."

She snickered. "That is a cheesy accent, Mr. Terminator."

He shrugged. "But take it to heart, because I will be."

"Good," she said.

Jenn was finishing up a game of Sorry! with Corky when Griff came back home. "I'm winning, Daddy," Corky announced.

I'm winning, too, thought Griff as he helped himself to one of the peanut butter blossoms sitting on the cooling rack on the counter. At least, so far. Too soon to tell, though. *Don't rush*, he advised himself, then wondered if he'd listen.

Corky got his last piece safely home and whooped, "I won!"

"Yes, you did, you little stinker," said Jenn. "But now, we know what your dad's going to say, right?"

"Time for bed," Corky said, much less enthusiastically, and put the game back in the box.

"How was dinner?" Jenn asked. Corky was all ears, so she added, "With your friend?"

"Good." Griff took the game box. "Okay, little dude, get on your pj's and brush your teeth, and I'll be right up."

"I don't want to go to bed," Corky grumbled.

"Yeah, I never wanted to go to bed at your age, either," Griff said. "Kiss your aunt good-night and scram. I'll be up in a few."

Corky gave Jenn a hug and kiss, then dragged himself up the stairs to his bedroom and little-boy solitary confinement.

"So, what do you think?" Jenn asked once Corky was gone.

"I think you better not make a habit of babysitting for me or your man's gonna start getting pissed."

Jenn waved that away. "Tonight was poker night. No problem. Anyway, you need a break."

Yes, he did. The weight of being both Mom and Dad to his son pushed down on him constantly. The night out had done wonders for lifting his spirits. Or maybe it had been the woman he'd been with.

Jenn downed the rest of her pop and put the glass in the dishwasher. "Quit stalling and tell me how it went."

"Good," he said again, and leaned against the counter. "I like her."

"Ha! You can thank me now for helping Santa put her in your life."

"I'll just stick with thanking you for watching Corky," he said. "And don't gloat."

"You going to go out again?"

"I think so," he said.

No, he knew so.

★ ★ ★

Frankie was settled in with a bowl of popcorn and a Christmas movie when her sister called. "I think this man is not what I thought he was."

She could hear the smile in Stef's voice. "In a good way, I take it."

"Yes, for sure."

"Are you going to see him again?"

"Absolutely. I really like him. He's…real."

After the narcissistic hypocrite she'd been married to, that had to be refreshing.

"And vulnerable. I finally get why he was so mad about the letter to Santa. Camille was right. I shouldn't have put it up. Talk about making light of something so big. Ugh."

"You didn't know."

"I should have figured it out."

"Do you think he's ready for a relationship?" Memories could circle a heart like chains, keeping it pinned down. Frankie understood how hard it would be for this man to move on with anyone else.

"I'm going to find out. Ready or not, I think he needs one. It's easy to get so caught in the past that you forget you're living in the present and you have a future to face."

Stef was only musing, but it felt like her words had dropped down from heaven in big red letters and dangled in front of Frankie. It was time to break her chains. She only hoped it wasn't too late.

"That was very profound," Frankie said.

"I don't know about that, but I do know I don't want to be dragging my past around. I'm sure not going to let what happened with Richard ruin the rest of my life. I want to try again, and I think I want to try with Griff."

"His sister did tell me he's a really nice man," said Frankie.

But then she'd seen how that really nice man had behaved to her sister. "Still, are you sure you want to take that gamble with him?"

"I am. Sometimes you gamble, and you win big."

"Yes, you do," Frankie agreed.

Rarely, but it did happen. She remembered the old saying, *You can't win if you don't play.* She wanted to see her sister win, that was for sure.

"Follow your instincts," she advised.

"I am, and I have a good feeling about this man. Even though he behaved like a jerk, I don't think he is one. He's… honest. And I think he's got a good heart."

What more did a woman need? "Go for it, then," Frankie said. "But take your time. And you'd better plan to bring him to dinner at Mom's in the new year. No more getting involved with men who don't get the family seal of approval."

"Got it," said Stef.

"I hope this works out. I want so much for you to be happy," Frankie said.

"Thanks, sissy. I love you."

"I love you, too. And I'm excited to see where this leads."

Hopefully, Stef's love life was now on track. That left only Elinor to sort out. Once that was done, Frankie and Mitch would have a serious talk about who the best Mrs. Claus was for him.

Frankie opened up the shop on Christmas Eve day with fixing Elinor's love life at the top of her to-do list. She didn't expect a heavy volume of business. Her customer base tended to shop early, and their final big day had been the Santa Walk. There should be plenty of time in between customers to talk with Elinor.

Frankie was tying on her apron when Elinor breezed in, all smiles and Christmas cheer.

"Merry Christmas," Frankie greeted her.

"It is!" Elinor replied, and hustled to the back room to shed her coat and stow her lunch.

Adele and Natalie came in right on her heels, each also in a happy Christmas spirit. "I'm glad we're closing early," Natalie said. "Santa still has a lot to do between now and tomorrow. Don't worry, I'm still bringing cherry coffee cake to Christmas brunch," she said to Adele.

Adele grinned. "Good, because I'm too busy to bake."

"Yes, and we know who you're busy with," Frankie teased. "You are bringing Mario to my open house tonight, right?"

"Of course," said Adele, and followed Natalie to the back room to dispose of her coat and gloves.

Elinor passed them on her way back to the counter. This was the perfect time to have a little chat.

"You're looking happy," Frankie began.

"I am," Elinor said. "I can't thank you enough for helping me…find myself."

There were a couple parts Frankie preferred to see get lost, like the one that was glomming on to Mitch.

Their conversation was interrupted by William Sharp walking in, bearing a blended drink. "I know you love peppermint," he said as he offered it to Elinor, who blushed and thanked him.

Frankie got busy somewhere else, giving him time to impress Elinor while she was under the influence of peppermint. There was still no one in the store, so she drifted toward the back to inspect the train display she'd set up to replace the one that Griff's sister had bought.

"Don't go up front," she whispered to Adele and Natalie, who were ready for duty.

"Why not? And why are we whispering?" Adele asked.

"William's with Elinor," Frankie explained.

Her daughter nodded her understanding.

Adele looked skeptical. "I think that Christmas ship has sailed. She doesn't want him."

"Why not?" Natalie wanted to know.

"Because she's fallen for Mitch," Adele explained, which made Frankie frown.

"You know he's not right for her," Frankie insisted.

Adele said nothing, just wandered off to another corner of the shop. The bell over the door rang, and Natalie went to see if their new customer needed help. Frankie edged closer to the cash register to eavesdrop.

There was nothing to hear. William had already left. This was not good.

She returned to stand next to Elinor as if ready to work the twin cash register. "William is such a nice man," she said, gesturing to the blended drink sitting on the counter.

"He is," Elinor agreed. Pleasantly but not enthusiastically.

"Whoever ends up with him is going to be one lucky woman," Frankie added.

"I hope he finds someone," said Elinor. "I want everyone to be as happy as I am. Mitch is so wonderful, and I'm the luckiest woman in the world, and I owe it all to you," she gushed. "I'd never have...done anything if you hadn't encouraged me."

No way had Frankie encouraged Elinor to glue herself to Mitch.

"He's the sweetest, most handsome man in all of Carol," Elinor continued. "We had such a good time at the Santa pub crawl."

Where you monopolized him. Frankie could feel the anger swelling inside her. She was turning into the Incredible Hulk.

"And things have been getting better ever since. I took Mitch brownies on Sunday, and we watched TV."

"TV," Frankie repeated. *Better not say...*

"*Cop Stop.* It's one of his favorite shows."

"I know. He usually watches it with me," Frankie said, her eyes narrowing.

Elinor didn't see. She was too busy reliving her happy weekend. "I don't usually like police shows. Well, not made-up ones with all that violence. But this was interesting. I hope we can do it again."

Not in my lifetime, Frankie thought. "I'll be back," she said to Elinor. Then she marched out the door, headed for Handy's Hardware Store.

19

THERE WAS PROBABLY ENOUGH STEAM COMING OUT OF Frankie's ears as she marched into the hardware store that she could have scalded half the customers in there. Brock was at the help center in the middle of the store, chatting with—oh good grief—Barbara.

She greeted Frankie with a smirk and an insincere "Merry Christmas."

After Frankie reclaiming her leadership role for the Santa Walk, it was a wonder Barbara didn't wish her a spanking from Krampus. But appearances had to be maintained.

Frankie repeated the wish, then turned her attention to Brock. "Where's Mitch?"

"Home sick."

"Still?" Mitch was never sick.

"Anything I can help you with?" Brock offered. In such a friendly way. Oh, how quickly the cold had melted and how quickly his wounded pride had healed.

"No," Frankie said irritably. Then added a less irritable "Merry Christmas" in parting to show there were no hard feelings that he'd moved on so quickly from her dumping him.

He smiled at Barbara. "Planning on it."

Great. Everyone was having a Merry Christmas. Good for all of them. Ho, ho, ho.

She returned to the shop feeling cranky, and Elinor's cheerful mood exacerbated it. It was a good thing she was closing the shop early because by closing time at four, Frankie had had enough of Elinor and her beaming face.

"Have you got plans for tonight?" Natalie asked Elinor once they'd all donned their coats and were starting out the door.

"I thought maybe I'd go see Mitch. I didn't hear anything from him yesterday," Elinor said.

"That's because he's sick," Frankie informed her. "Anyway, you're coming to my Christmas Eve open house, remember?" It would be much better to have Elinor at her house under her watchful eye than at Mitch's, banging on his door.

"That's right," Elinor said happily. "I almost forgot."

"Great. We'll see you there," said Natalie.

"I am happy to have someplace to go tonight," Elinor said to Frankie. "Thank you so much for including me."

"Yes, so very kind," said Adele. As Natalie rushed off and Elinor skidded her way through the snow to her car, Adele cocked an eyebrow at Frankie. "Keep your friends close and your enemies closer?"

"We're not enemies," Frankie said.

"Oh. Frenemies."

"Not even that. I like Elinor. I just don't like her thinking she owns Mitch."

"I hope, for your sake, she doesn't," Adele said. "See you later, daughter dear."

Back at her house, Frankie got busy putting together her various food offerings—the mini quiches she bought at Costco every year, the bacon-wrapped dates and the meatballs in cranberry sauce, her brie cheese in puff pastry that Mitch liked so much…and wouldn't be there to eat since he was still home sick. She took one of the frosted cookies she'd just set on a plate, a Santa-shaped one, and bit his head off.

"What are you so grumpy about?" she scolded herself. "If Mitch wants to watch TV with someone else, he can."

No, he couldn't, darn it. They always watched *Cop Stop* together. That was their thing. And she baked him cookies for Christmas. And he always came to her open house and went home with a tinful. It wasn't going to be the same without him. She grabbed her phone from the counter and called him.

"You reached Mitch. I'll get back to you," his recorded voice promised.

"I hear you're still sick," she said. "Feeling any better? I'll save you some goodies from my open house."

She half hoped he'd call back.

He didn't.

Guests came and went—the various members of her Santa Walk committee and their families, her mom and Mario. Natalie and her family. Stef, Stef's editor, Camille, and her husband. Viola and Terrill. And Elinor, who came and appeared ready to stay until New Year's.

"She's sure looking good these days," James said to Frankie as they stood by the punch bowl, watching Elinor flirt with old Mr. Winchell from down the street.

"Yes, she is," Frankie agreed. "And she's certainly gained confidence."

A little too much. Elinor hadn't climbed out of her shell. She'd burst out of it. There was no putting her back now.

By seven, the party was winding down. People were getting ready for their own Christmases. "Great as always," said Hazel, and gave Frankie a hug before parting.

Elinor was the last to leave. "Thanks for inviting me," she said. "You've been so good to me. You're the best boss ever."

Her praise made Frankie squirm. She intended to cancel Elinor's Christmas and ruin her new year by reclaiming Mitch, which probably qualified her to join the pantheon of holiday villains. Frankie Lane, Candy Cane Love Crusher.

But Elinor didn't love Mitch. She couldn't. They wouldn't be happy together. There was only one woman in Carol he would be happy with, and that was Frankie, and they were going to fix this.

She called him again later, after getting home from attending Christmas Eve service with Natalie and her family. Still only his voicemail. He couldn't be *that* sick.

She tried him again on Christmas morning. No answer. "You'd better be dead," she said after the beep.

He didn't call back. She gave up on Mitch with a sigh, grabbed her shopping bag full of presents and walked down the street to Adele's house for Christmas brunch.

Natalie and her family were there, and Warner was racing around the house with a toy airplane. Natalie looked like all mothers on Christmas morning—tired. But happy. She sat on the couch next to her husband, drinking decaf coffee with an arm draped over her baby bump.

"Hi, Mom!" she called.

"Merry Christmas," Frankie said, kissing first her daughter and then her son-in-law.

Stef was setting dishes out on the dining table and called a cheery hello as Warner circled the table with his toy airplane.

Frankie suspected that her sister's good cheer had as much to do with her new man as it did with being with her family on Christmas Day. She hoped whatever was starting with Griffin Marks would blossom into something beautiful and lasting.

Warner stopped circling the table and ran over to give Frankie a big hug. "Nana, look what Santa brought me," he said, holding up his toy.

"Lucky you," said Frankie.

"It really flies, but I can't do that unless Daddy's with me, helping," Warner explained.

"Good idea," Frankie said.

That was the extent of Warner's contribution to the conversation. He zoomed off and began racing around the table again, and Frankie hurried to add her presents to the collection under the tree.

"Is my daughter finally here?" Adele called from the kitchen.

"I'm here," Frankie called back. She set out the last present, then went to join her mother.

Who already had kitchen help. If there was a prize for the woman with the most Christmas cheer, Adele would have won it, Frankie decided, seeing Adele and Mario working together on their breakfast. She couldn't remember when she'd seen her mother smile so big. Adele had managed *happy* over the years, but since Mario had arrived on the scene, she'd gone from happy to ecstatic.

There they stood, him adding canned pineapple to a fruit salad, her standing next to him, oven mitts on her hands. She was giggling over something he'd said. Giggling. Adele had never been a giggler, but she was now.

"What's so funny?" Frankie asked, and kissed her mother's cheek.

Adele blushed, and so did Mario. "Nothing," she said. "Merry Christmas, daughter dear."

"I'd say Merry Christmas to you, too, but it looks like you're already there."

"I am," Adele said with a grin. She looked to Mario. "Mario spoils me."

"I would do anything for your mother," he said.

Adele smiled at him, then got busy taking their breakfast casserole from the oven. "We are ready," she announced as she took it to the table. "Let's eat this while it's hot. Bring the salad, Mario. And Frankie, grab the coffee cake."

Frankie and her family had always celebrated the holidays together, even during the dark times when they didn't feel like it. But this year there was no sadness overshadowing them, no forced smiles, no determined counting of blessings. This year they were awash in gratitude and joy.

And laughter over some of the silly presents. Warner received a hoodie blanket made to look like a shark from Frankie, which he happily modeled, rolling around the floor. In addition to socks and a book, Adele also gifted him with a whoopee cushion, and he was delighted when she and his father demonstrated how to use it.

"Thanks, Gram Gram," said Natalie with a frown.

"I could have gotten him a drum set," Adele retorted.

Mario opened his present from Adele and turned as red as the boxers she'd given him. They sported sweater-wearing reindeer.

No embarrassment for Frankie. Adele gave her a cookbook she'd been wanting.

Adele loved the adult coloring book from her daughters and granddaughter, which had a variety of gift cards tucked between the pages.

Stef was thrilled with the game Adele had given her that

involved throwing squishy toy burritos at each other. "I think this might come in handy in the future," she said, and Frankie was sure she was thinking of a certain reformed Scrooge and his son.

"Never mind the future, let's play it now," suggested Jonathan.

Later, after much squealing and chaos, Natalie and company left to go to the next set of parents and eat another meal, and Adele, Stef and Frankie settled in with eggnog while Mario built a fire in the fireplace.

"I used to love having a fire in the fireplace when I was a kid," said Stef. "I loved watching the flames."

"And toasting marshmallows," Frankie added. "I remember doing that with Dad."

"I wish we'd had him longer," Stef said wistfully. "I barely got any time with him."

"There's never enough time," Frankie mused, thinking of both her father and her husband.

Adele fell silent. For a moment it felt to Frankie as if something dark had floated out from those flames and was reaching for them, ready to pull them into sorrow with invisible fingers.

Adele banished it. "Of course, we wish we had the people we loved for longer. But I'm betting that those who have gone on before us would be glad to see us making the most of our lives and making the most of being together."

"Dad would be happy that you've found Mario and to see you doing so well," Frankie said.

"We are all doing well, aren't we?" Adele asked.

"I think I am, finally," said Stef.

Adele looked pointedly at Frankie.

"I'm doing fine," Frankie said. As long as she didn't dwell on the past.

Or stew over the future.

By the time she got home she realized she'd somehow missed a call from Mitch. "Not dead," he said on her voicemail. "I'm in Seattle, visiting my aunt. See you tomorrow."

"You bet you will," she said after the message finished.

Griff called Stef later that evening. She hadn't expected to hear from him again so quickly. It was Christmas, after all, and they both had families.

A little thrill of excitement raced across her chest as she answered.

"Are you still with your family?" he asked.

"No, just got home. How about you?"

"We've done it all," Griff said. "Dinner at Grandma's, presents." He hesitated a moment. "Santa came."

Stef was half afraid to ask, but she did anyway. "How was that?"

"Corky liked his toys, but he was mad that Santa hadn't come through with a mom. I'm not blaming you anymore, honest," he added. "He'll get over it eventually. Kids have a hard time taking no for an answer."

She didn't know what to say, other than "I'm sorry."

There was a moment of silence, followed by, "Oh, well. It's over for another year."

How sad to be glad that Christmas was over. "Maybe next year will be better."

"I'm hoping," he said. "So, look, I might be rushing things, but I'm wondering if you want to meet for lunch tomorrow. I've got a light day at work, and I'm hoping you do, too."

"I think I can manage lunch," said Stef.

"Good. How about one at The Salad Bowl?"

"One," she agreed.

She smiled as they ended the call. Last Christmas had sucked big-time, and the new year had held no promise. What a difference a year made!

★ ★ ★

December 26, Elinor was late to work. "I'm sorry I'm late," she said to Frankie. "I just stopped by Handy's to see how Mitch is doing. He's all better now. I'm going to surprise him and take dinner over to him tonight."

"I'm glad he's back." *And I'm going to surprise him first*, thought Frankie. If he was well enough to come to work, he was well enough for a long overdue talk.

Adele came in as Frankie was leaving. "Where are you going?" she asked.

"I need something at the hardware store," Frankie said.

"Yes, you do. It's about time you did something about it," said Adele.

Brock was at the help center, conferring with a man in worn jeans, a parka and a ball cap that said Hammer Man Inc.

"Where's Mitch?" she asked.

"Every babe in town wants to see Mitch today," observed Hammer Man. "What kind of cologne is he wearing?"

Just then Mitch showed up. He smiled at Frankie. "Hey there, I was about to call you."

She frowned at him, grabbed his arm and moved him an aisle away. "Before or after seeing Elinor?"

"What?"

"We need to have a talk," she said, and dragged him farther down the aisle. "What is going on with you and her?"

"What are you talking about?"

"I'm talking about you crawling all over town with Elinor on the pub crawl. And probably crawling all over her afterward."

He blinked in surprise.

"And you watched *Cop Stop* with her!" Frankie accused, her voice rising.

A man in paint-spattered coveralls had walked into the aisle and started looking through the myriad bins of nuts and bolts. "Man, I love that show," he said.

Frankie frowned at him and towed Mitch to the end of the aisle. "*We* watch *Cop Stop*."

"What could I do?" he protested. "She came over with brownies. Then she asked me what I do on Sunday night, and I started to tell her."

"But you didn't get as far as telling her you watch *Cop Stop* with me?"

The man in the coveralls was still listening in. "Dude, you're in deep shit."

Frankie glared at him. "Do you mind?"

"Sorry," he said, sounding mildly offended, and went back to searching the bins of nuts and bolts.

She turned back to Mitch. "That was no time for you to work on good manners."

He held up both hands. "Okay, my bad. I didn't think you'd get so mad."

"Well, I am!"

He stared at her, then shook his head slowly. "If I didn't know better, I'd swear you were jealous."

"I am," she said, not quite as loudly, not quite as insistently.

"That doesn't make sense. The woman who's been telling me for years that I should find someone, the woman who only earlier this month was trying to sic Wilhelmina What's-Her-Name on me is now chewing me out for spending time with a woman who she—you—made Mrs. Claus."

"She wasn't Mrs. Claus when she brought you brownies!"

"Oh, for crying out loud," he said in disgust. "What was I supposed to do, kick her out?"

"How about telling her you had a long-standing commitment? She's the wrong woman for you," Frankie insisted. "You can't be interested in Elinor."

SHEILA ROBERTS

He studied her. "Why shouldn't I be? Tell me, Frankie."

"Because I don't want to share," she blurted. "I don't care if sharing is caring. Darn it all, Mitch."

He leaned against a shelf and crossed his arms over his chest. "What are you trying to say here?"

Words started tumbling out randomly. "I didn't realize... I just didn't think..." She started tearing up. "I felt like I was being disloyal to Ike. And darn it all, Mitch. You're eight years older."

He raised an eyebrow. "Thanks for reminding me."

"The idea of losing another man I love... Oh, what am I thinking? I can't do this." She turned to leave.

He caught her arm. "Yes, you can. Come on, Frankie. You know how I feel about you. And you've just made it pretty clear how you feel about me. Are you going to deprive us of a great life we can have now and keep us hanging in limbo all because you can't see into the future? None of us knows what the future holds."

He was right. Her mother was right. Everyone was right! She didn't want to be a bystander watching everyone else on the merry-go-round. If she kept playing it safe, someone would come along and steal Mitch's heart, and then she'd be playing alone. She didn't want to be alone. She wanted to be with Mitch.

"Quit being a chickenshit," he continued, "and—"

That was as far as he got. She grabbed him by his Handy's Hardware polo shirt and yanked him to her and kissed him. At first, he stood there in shock, stiff as a totem pole, but then he caught fire and wrapped his arms around her. And that was when the kiss exploded like gunpowder, both the physical sensation and emotional thrill, packing enough of a wallop to leave her weak-kneed.

"Score!" whooped the man in the coveralls.

"I'd say," said Mitch, smiling down at Frankie. "And you're right. We need to have a talk."

He led her to his back office, plopped onto his desk chair and pulled her onto his lap. "Now, where were we?"

"With me, coming to my senses. I guess it took seeing you really enjoying being with another woman to make me realize what I was about to lose."

"You weren't about to lose anything. I like Elinor, and I was being nice, but there's only one Mrs. Claus I want to be with."

"Oh, Mitch," she said, feeling suddenly all teary.

"We are going to have a great life together," he assured her. "I can promise you that. I'll make sure of it."

She studied his face—that strong chin, the easy smile, the eyes with the deep laugh lines at the corners, and that lopsided grin. This man had been a friend to her for years, and it had been a good friendship. Now it was more, and suddenly her life was more because of it.

"Kiss me again," she murmured.

He smiled and did, cradling her face in his big hands. It was a tender kiss, filled with promise and warmth. She could have gone on kissing him forever.

She pulled away and blinked.

"What?" he asked, puzzled. "You can't have changed your mind already."

"No. Kissing you… I felt the same way the first time I kissed Ike." She smiled. "And that's how I know this is right. It's like…a sign."

His grin took over his whole face. "Well, Happy New Year."

She could almost hear her husband, whispering approvingly, *And Merry Christmas, Frankie.*

Stef and Griff sat side by side in a booth at The Salad Bowl, dodging the ferny fingers of one of the plants behind the booth. "Feed me, Seymour," she quoted from *Little Shop of Horrors.*

"Feed it. I'm gonna croak it," he said, and gave the thing a shove.

"Ow," she said in a tiny voice, and he laughed.

"My wife would have loved you," he said.

Maybe Stef should have felt jealous but instead she felt complimented. "I bet I'd have loved her, too."

"My sister's ready to adopt you."

"And how about you?"

"I don't want to adopt you. That'd be pervy," he said, and she snickered. "I gotta say, I was really mad at Jenn for constantly nagging me to get out there and meet someone. Did you know that she had a talk with your sister in that shop of hers before the Santa Walk?"

"No," Stef said in surprise. "I didn't."

"Yeah. She kept getting on me about taking Corky to see Santa. Of course, Corky was on me to take him, too, so I just thought she was backing him up."

"Maybe she was."

"In a way. But she had a hidden agenda. She was hoping we'd meet like in some sappy holiday movie."

"I love sappy holiday movies," said Stef.

"So does my sister. She thinks life should be like those movies." He took a sip of his coffee. "It's hard when your life's gone to shit to see anything good coming out of it."

Stef nodded. "I get that. My marriage was a mess and so was my self-esteem for a while there. And dating? Don't even get me started. But you know what my mom says? Shit happens, but you need fertilizer to make good things grow."

"Your mom sounds like a pretty smart woman," he said.

"She is. She'd get what you've been going through. My dad

died when I was young, and she had to do the single parent thing. It can't be easy."

"It has its challenges."

"But at least you've got your son." Okay, what kind of thing was that to say? Feeling foolish and at a loss, Stef focused on breaking off a piece of her roll. "That was probably a stupid thing to say. It makes your boy sound like a consolation prize in some sick game."

"Kind of up there with people telling me Kaitlyn is in a better place," he said, and she could hear the frustration in his voice.

"Or people telling me to be glad that at least Richard and I didn't have kids." She sighed. "I mean, it is a good thing we didn't. I still wish I had a couple, though." She dropped the roll and turned to him, putting on a determinedly bright smile. "But here's another mom-ism. Don't waste time on what you don't have. Either get it or get on with your life without it. So I am. And maybe someday my life can be like those movies."

"Maybe it can. You never know," he said.

"You never know," she agreed. "I'm ready to be pleasantly surprised."

"I already am," he said. "And I've gotta say, I'm not mad at my sister anymore for interfering in my life. In fact, I'm glad she did."

Stef didn't need any more soup to warm her up. The way Griff was looking at her did that.

His phone buzzed with a text, and he checked it. "Looks like my lunch break is over."

"I need to get back to work, too," she said.

He paid the bill, and she insisted on paying the tip. They left the warm, spice-scented restaurant and emerged into frosty air and a gray sky.

Stef sniffed. "Smells like more snow is on the way."

"You can tell just by sniffing?"

"I can," she said.

"How does snow air smell?"

"Fresh. And…snowy. There, how's that for a great description?"

He laughed. "Oh yeah. I can tell you're a writer. You have a way with words." He sobered. "You also have a way of making a guy smile."

"You have a nice smile," she said, and tapped his lips. That was a mistake. Now she wanted to do more with those lips than give them a friendly tap.

His eyes told her he wanted more, too. He took a step closer. "You are going to go out with me again, right?"

"I am," she said.

"Promise?"

"I promise."

"You do know how you seal a promise, right?"

He didn't wait for an answer. He leaned down and kissed her.

It wasn't a long enough kiss to make a scene right there in downtown Carol—although she wouldn't have cared if they had—but it was enough to send a jolt to her chest.

"We need to make a lot more promises," she said, and he grinned.

"Yes, we do," he said. "I'll call you."

She watched him walk away down the sidewalk in his business attire and overcoat. There was something sexy about a man in an overcoat.

Correction, there was something sexy about *that* man in his overcoat—tall and lean and broad-shouldered. And now that he had relearned how to smile…wow! This man, taking tentative steps into a better life, this man, who hated Santa but loved his kid, this man was worth investing more time in.

Unlike Richard, who had been slick and polished and thought he was so perfect, Griffin Marks was perfectly imperfect.

Oh yes, she wanted to spend more time with him.

A very long "talk" in Mitch's office was followed by a very long lunch at La Bella Vita and a slow stroll back to their workplaces that included a stop by Treasured Jewels to look at the diamonds winking at them from the other side of the window.

"Too soon to be looking at those," she said.

"Yeah, we should remain friends for another ten years, at least," he mocked, and she stuck her tongue out at him.

"I still want to get you something. Come on," he said, and led her inside. "What about this?" he asked, pointing to a delicate diamond infinity necklace with white gold.

It was lovely, but she balked. "It looks expensive."

"You saying you're not worth it?" he teased. "How much?" he asked Sam, the shop owner.

"It's actually on sale," said Sam.

"On sale," Mitch said to Frankie. "Can't resist a sale, right? I'll take it," he told Sam.

"Oh no," Frankie said. "All I have for you is cookies."

"Your cookies are priceless," Mitch assured her.

Next thing she knew she was wearing a new necklace out of the shop. "I love it," she said, hugging Mitch's arm.

"Don't forget what it stands for," he said, and smiled down at her.

He dropped her off at Holiday Happiness, giving her a quick kiss before confirming he'd be over that night to pick up the cookies that she'd made for him. And to pick up where they'd left off.

"You were gone a long time," Adele observed from her post at the register as Frankie drifted into the shop.

"I was with Mitch," Frankie said, and joined her.

"Ah," Adele said knowingly.

"Ah is right," Frankie said, beaming. She held out the necklace so her mother could see. "We are now officially a couple."

"About time," said Adele, and hugged her. "That is lovely. When can I start telling all my friends?"

"Anytime. It's not going to be a secret for long."

Adele nodded to the back of the shop where Elinor was busy marking the ornaments with the year's date on them down to half price. "I'll wait until you've told her."

Frankie felt some of her elation turning to lead and settling in the direction of her stomach. It had to be done. She took a deep breath, then went to join Elinor.

Elinor smiled in greeting. "Almost done," she said.

She was a nice woman and a good employee. Maybe, after Frankie had delivered her news, she'd be neither.

"Elinor, I have some news to share."

Elinor regarded her with an expectant smile.

"About Mitch."

"Oh?"

Elinor looked so eager, so ready for her own happy ending, one Frankie had unwittingly helped her believe in. Frankie felt bad for her. And more than a little guilty.

But not bad or guilty enough to give up Mitch.

"About Mitch and me." If only she could find some way to coat the words with emotional anesthetic. There was no way. *Make the cut and make it quickly.* "We're together."

Elinor's eyebrows took a dip, and two worry lines formed between them. "Together?" she repeated as if trying out a foreign language.

"We're a couple."

"I...don't understand. When?"

"Elinor, he and I have always been close," Frankie said gently.

"But he and I... I mean, I thought..." Tears began to rise to high tide.

Frankie put a hand to Elinor's arm. "I think you might have misread some of his actions."

Two tears spilled, and Elinor's lips did a wobbly frown. "No," she protested.

"We were just out together."

Elinor began shaking her head in disbelief.

"I know he'd never lead you on intentionally," Frankie hurried to add.

Elinor said nothing. Instead, she pressed her lips firmly together, and her eyes narrowed.

Frankie now officially qualified for the role of new Disney villain. "You know, when things don't work out with a person, maybe it means someone better is waiting in the wings. You can love more than one person in a lifetime."

If looks were daggers, Frankie would have been dead from multiple stab wounds. "That's easy for you to say," Elinor said.

Frankie thought of how hard her life had been for the last few years, thought of how many times she'd cried herself to sleep in those early days after losing Ike. She bagged the consoling smile. "Actually, it is. Now. But it took me a long time to get here."

Elinor knew she was a widow. It didn't take her long to understand what Frankie was saying, and she immediately backpedaled. "I'm sorry," she said. "That was unkind. It's just that, well, I thought you two were only friends," she finished, her tone accusing. A tear trickled down one cheek.

"We were, but there's always been something there. I was simply too afraid to acknowledge it. I had my stumbles," she added, thinking of Brock, "but really, my heart's belonged to Mitch for a long time. I just had to have my eyes opened."

"Who opened them?"

You. No way was Frankie going to complicate things by

saying that. She shrugged. "I had an aha moment. You'll have one, too."

Elinor fiddled with an ornament. "I doubt it."

"Don't. It will come. You know, at Christmas there are a lot of presents under the tree, and there's always one for each of us. Keep your eyes peeled, Elinor. You'll have your aha moment and find your perfect man."

Elinor nodded glumly, swiped away fresh tears and stared at the little ornament.

"You will. I promise," Frankie said, giving her arm a comforting rub.

Elinor gave another nod, then turned her back on Frankie and returned to pricing the ornaments.

Frankie left her to deal with her emotions, dealing with a few of her own as she went to join her mother. The shop was empty. No customers to talk and drown out their voices.

Adele lowered hers and asked, "How did it go?"

"She's miserable," Frankie whispered. "I don't know what to do."

"Hopefully, you won't think of something. You need to take a break from helping everyone," Adele informed her.

Frankie sighed. But Elinor needed help. If only she could get Elinor to see that the perfect man for her was right under her nose. Frankie herself was walking proof that those good things under your nose tended to be invisible.

William Sharp was the Invisible Man.

Frankie was going to find a way to make him visible by New Year's Eve.

If only she had some idea how to do that.

20

FRANKIE'S FAMILY ALL KNEW THE GOOD NEWS WITHIN AN hour. It was time to tell Mitch's. He came over to her house after they were done with work and they FaceTimed with his, announcing to one and all that they were officially a couple.

"About time," said one of his sons.

Yes, it was, but Frankie knew she wouldn't have been ready for a lasting love relationship any sooner. "It's also the right time," she said to Mitch after they ended the visit.

He hesitated a moment, rubbed the side of his nose, a sure sign he was working up to saying something.

"What?" she prompted.

"It's stupid," he said, brushing away whatever he'd been about to say.

"Tell me."

He shrugged, embarrassed. "I made a promise to Ike."

"What? When?"

"Not when he was alive. After. I mentally vowed I'd watch out for you, always have your back. Not that you needed it. You've done fine."

"I needed the emotional support," she said, "and you gave it. You've always been there for me."

"I liked Ike. A lot." He smiled. "And I liked you. More and more as I watched how strong you were after he died, how determined to keep moving on."

"Only in some areas," she said.

"I know there were times you were hurting, but seeing how you could set that aside to focus on the people you care about, the things you care about—your shop, this town—how could I not fall completely for you? You are an amazing woman."

"Amazing, huh?" That was a little over the top, but she liked how the compliment felt anyway.

"Yeah, amazing," he said, and kissed her.

One kiss wasn't enough, so of course, she came back for seconds. And thirds. It felt so good to be wrapped in strong arms, to feel sensations she never thought she'd feel again and, even more, to feel a connection so strong she knew nothing would break it. To be loved was truly the greatest gift of all.

"We are definitely getting a ring come Valentine's Day," he informed her. "And don't make me wait forever while you plan a wedding."

"I don't need a big wedding," she said. "Been there, done that."

"Then what are we waiting for?" he asked.

"Good question. I don't know."

"Okay, ring for New Year's, and we go to Vegas for Valentine's Day." He saw her frown. "No, forget that. We get married here and invite our families."

She beamed. "Yes! Chocolate and champagne for all."

Adele was on board with the idea when she took Frankie and Stef and Natalie out to lunch to celebrate the next day. She insisted on hosting the wedding.

"Red and white roses everywhere," Natalie said dreamily.

"And a heart-shaped cake," Stef said, smiling. "I'll take care of the cake. I am going to be maid of honor, right? Or is it matron? Divorced matron? Whatever."

"You and Natalie both," Frankie said, smiling at her daughter. "We're not having a big wedding, so you two won't have many duties."

"Other than throwing a big shower and inviting all of Carol," said Natalie.

"I don't think either of our places are big enough to hold everyone who'll want to come to that," Stef said. "We might have to see about renting a room at Sips. Or the VFW hall."

"Maybe that will be big enough," Natalie joked.

"I'm so happy this is happening for you," Adele said to Frankie.

"Same here. After all my balking and stumbling around... Well, I know it's right." Frankie turned to her sister. "I bet you won't be far behind."

"It's still too soon to tell, but we do have a date tonight. Hamburgers with his son."

"I'm surprised he's introducing you to his son already," said Frankie.

"Only as a friend of Santa's."

"That should be interesting," said Adele. "By the way, I had a dream last night."

"Oh no," groaned the other three in unison.

"It was a good one," Adele said. "We were all on a cruise ship, and our men were with us. It was someplace tropical, but we were all wearing Santa hats. Then suddenly, we were jumping overboard and swimming to some island, and Santa was there, waiting for us and waving. What do you think it means?"

"That we all go on a cruise," said Stef. "Christmas in July!"

"I like the sound of that," said Frankie.

"Me, too," said Natalie. "We'll start saving now. Except it will have to be Alaska since I won't be able to fly come July."

"We can pretend we're at the North Pole," quipped Stef.

"So, that confirms it. We're supposed to take a family cruise," said Adele. "For Mario's and my honeymoon."

Frankie laughed.

"Oh yeah, he'll be all over that," said Stef.

"He'll do whatever I want," Adele said.

"Poor man," said Stef.

"I don't know about the cruise, but I do think Mom's dream means that we're all going to be happy in the new year," Frankie said.

Stef didn't have to wait for the new year. She was already happy.

"We're going to Frank's Good and Fast," Corky informed her after Griff introduced them. Corky took her hand as they walked her from her door to Griff's car.

"That sounds great," she said, smiling down at him. "Thanks for letting me join you."

"They have Grinch milkshakes," Corky informed her.

"Green chocolate chip mint," Griff explained.

"I love Grinch milkshakes," Stef said to the boy. "And candy canes." She produced one from her coat pocket for Corky, who happily snatched it.

"Not until after dinner, little dude," Griff said to him, and Corky's lower lip jutted out.

Griff held out a hand. "I'll keep it for you until then."

Way to go, Stef chided herself. "I should have asked," she said to Griff.

"It's fine," he assured her. "That was nice of you. What do you say?" he prompted his son.

Corky started jumping his way to the car. "Thank you!"

"He's so cute," Stef said to Griff. Just the kind of little boy she'd loved to have had. First she'd fallen for the man, and now she was falling for the son. What if this didn't work out? She already knew. She'd be crushed.

Where had that come from? She had no reason to be thinking so negatively.

"Did Santa bring you?" Corky asked her once they were in the car.

Her heart rate went from a walk to a trot. "Umm."

"We talked about this," Griff said sternly. "Santa doesn't bring mommies. You know that. You got toys instead."

"But I really wanted a mommy," Corky grumbled.

"How about friends?" Stef suggested. "You don't even have to ask Santa for that. They just come. May I be your friend?"

"Okay," Corky said. "I like friends."

Frank's Good and Fast was packed with teens, young families and a few seniors sharing Franktastic meals, which consisted of two very basic hamburgers, two small drinks and two small orders of fries, all for a senior friendly price.

"Everything looks so good," Stef said to Corky as they waited in line to order. "What should I have?"

"A Grinch milkshake," Corky said with a decisive nod of his head.

"All right. I guess I'd better have a Grinch milkshake," she said to Griff.

"What else would you like?" he asked.

"I think I need a Franktastic burger," she decided. "You can't have a burger without the good stuff, like lettuce, tomatoes, pickles. And onions, of course." That would make her breath smell good. "Maybe not the onions."

"I'm having onions," said Griff. "Don't make me be the only one stinking up the car later."

She laughed. "Onions it is."

"I want chicken nuggets!" Corky announced, jumping up and down like he'd grown springs on his feet.

"Okay," said Griff. "There's an empty booth. You two go and grab it."

"Come on, Stef," said Corky, taking her hand and hauling her through the crowd.

She laughed. This little boy was adorable. She wanted him. And she wanted his dad.

Come on, Santa, forget what Griff said and come through for me.

Maybe he would. They ate their meal in between having straw wars, shooting the wrappers at each other. After dinner, they drove around town to look at all the houses still decked out in their Christmas lights.

"I'm glad people don't take their lights down right after Christmas," Stef said. "They're so pretty. I always hate to see them go."

"If they stayed, you'd take them for granted," Griff said.

"Maybe."

"Look at Frosty," cried Corky, who was getting nice and sticky enjoying his candy cane. He pointed to a giant inflatable snowman.

"He for sure doesn't stay around very long, does he, Corky?" Stef said.

"No. He had to go. But he'll be back again someday," Corky said. Then, a moment later, he added, "I wish my mommy would come back."

And just like that, the happy atmosphere in the car started

to evaporate. Griff's easy smile faded, and Stef felt like a movie extra who'd been told she wasn't needed.

They drove around more, but no matter how pretty the lights, her oohs and ahs and comments felt forced, and it was impossible to recapture the magic they'd been feeling.

"You know, I've got some things I need to do early tomorrow," she lied. "Maybe we should call it a night."

Griff nodded and turned the car back out of the housing development they'd been in and onto the main street.

The ride back to her place was silent. Corky had run out of steam and was asleep. So was Stef's brain because she couldn't think of a thing to say.

They pulled up in front of her place, and Griff parked the car and cleared his throat. "I'm sorry I clammed up. Sometimes…"

She laid a hand on his arm. "I understand. I really do." This man wasn't ready for a relationship. She managed a smile for him, then kissed his cheek. "Thanks for the burger." Then she left the car and ran up the walk. She slipped inside her condo without looking back and shut the door behind her.

Frankie and Mitch spent the evening cuddling on her couch, watching *Die Hard*—you had to over the holidays. It was the perfect way to end the day. Later, as he was leaving, he suggested she start thinking about what kind of honeymoon she wanted.

"Maybe someplace tropical," she said.

"Just me and you and a bikini. Bikini optional," he added with a grin.

Enjoying a tropical paradise with Mitch sounded wonderful.

Frankie was turning into her mother, because that night she, too, had a dream. This one wasn't a pleasant dream of cruise ships and Santa hats. Or even tropical islands. And Elinor had inserted herself into the dream.

They were at sea, all right, but they weren't on a big ship. Instead, the three of them were in a tiny life raft, floating in the middle of nowhere in shark-infested waters somewhere in the tropics. The sun was blazing, and they were sunburned and scraggly-looking with cracked lips. And Elinor was hysterical.

"Go ahead, feed me to the sharks," she screeched. "You don't care about me. All you care about is yourself! And Mitch. You didn't even want him until I had him."

"That's not true," Frankie protested. "I do care about you."

"No, you don't!" Elinor stood up, and their raft began to wobble like a floating bouncy house. "I'm going to jump. Nobody will care if I get eaten by sharks."

"Mitch, do something," Frankie cried.

He shrugged. "I can't. Only you can save her."

"It's too late," Elinor wailed, and jumped into the water with a great splash.

Frankie woke up just as a shark was swimming toward poor Elinor.

Okay, she really had to do something before Elinor got eaten by sharks.

Natalie was enjoying her usual Saturday home with her family, so it was Frankie, Elinor and Adele minding the shop. If Elinor's attitude was any indication, the sharks had already been nibbling on her. Frankie was glad to have her mother with them as a buffer. Not only was Elinor's expression glum, but any sympathy she might have felt for her widowed employer had vanished, and she kept looking at Frankie with judgy eyes. As if Frankie had deliberately set out to ruin her life.

"I didn't," she said to her mother after sending Elinor upstairs to start setting out Valentine decorations in their changing seasons section. "I mean, I knew I would, but... Darn it all, if she'd only given William a chance, we wouldn't be in this mess."

"William is a dear," said Adele, "but you put him next to Mitch, and he fades. Mitch is the kind of man who makes women salivate. Add to that the fact that he's just plain nice, and it's no wonder she preferred him to William."

"But William is also nice. And can't you see him and Elinor curled up side by side in front of a roaring fire, reading books? If she'd wound up with Mitch, she'd have been hiking the Cascades. Does Elinor strike you as a hiker?"

"No, but neither do you."

"Very funny. I've hiked with Mitch."

"Hmm. I thought I heard you complaining about your feet hurting the whole time the last time you two went hiking."

"My boots were pinching. Anyway, that's not the point. Elinor needs her eyes opened. I don't want her going into the new year miserable."

"Frankiestein rides again," Adele said with a shake of her head.

"Not this time. I had a dream, Mom," Frankie said, and recapped the dream for her mother. "I know it meant I have to save her."

"Or tell her not to go near the water."

"Funny."

"You can't force her to fall in love with someone she's not interested in," said Adele.

True. And so far William had not managed to make himself interesting. But then, how hard had he tried?

"He needs to get proactive. And make himself interesting. He just comes in here and…buys things."

"Good for business," said Adele.

"But he can't be so timid." Frankie was sure William could be interesting. All he needed was a little coaching.

Elinor came back down. "I have all the Valentine merchandise arranged," she said to Frankie. No smile. She was like a black cloud roving all over the store.

"Thank you," said Frankie.

"What else do you want me to do?" Elinor asked, and her tone of voice added, *You bitch.*

Cheer up? Frankie decided to buy a little love. "I think it's time for a morning pick-me-up. Would you mind going to The Coffee Stop and getting some lattes?" She fished a twenty from the petty cash drawer. "I'll take eggnog if they have any left. And Mom will want a caramel. Extra—"

Elinor cut her off with a snapped, "Caramel. I know."

"Okay," Frankie said, handing the bill to Elinor. "And get whatever you want for yourself."

"I don't want anything," Elinor said curtly.

"So much for buying her affection," Adele said after Elinor left. "You'll be lucky if she doesn't slip poison in yours."

"I don't care about buying her affection." Although that would have been nice. Frankie hated having people mad at her. "I want her to be happy."

"She'll get there eventually," Adele said.

Sooner than eventually would be good. How was Frankie going to get Elinor and William together?

New Year's Eve was right around the corner. Did William have plans? Maybe he would like some suggestions.

The shop was quiet save for one of their regular customers browsing the merchandise upstairs. Adele could handle the cash register. It was the perfect time to slip over to Carol Reads and give love a helping hand. Frankie needed something to read anyway.

She took off her apron and went to the back room to fetch her coat and charge card.

"Where are you going?" Adele demanded when she came back out.

"I have a quick errand to run," Frankie replied.

"Where?" Adele was looking at her suspiciously.

"I need a book."

"Since when? You haven't read a book in ages."

"So, it's time."

"You are up to something," Adele accused. "Are you about to start meddling in people's lives again?"

"I just want something to read. Sheesh. Keep an eye on things here while I'm gone."

"I'll keep an eye on things here, but who's going to keep an eye on you?" said Adele.

Frankie ignored the remark.

It was starting to snow, the sloppy, wet kind that would be just dry enough to stick and then turn icy and slippery as temperatures dropped and people and cars compressed it. So, Frankie was hardly surprised to see there weren't many people in the bookstore when she entered.

An older man stood in the history section, perusing a book. A woman and her little girl were hustling toward the door with their purchase. William was still at the register, frowning at the flurry outside the window.

He smiled at the sight of Frankie. "Frankie, this is a nice surprise."

"I'm looking for something to read," she said. Well, duh.

"Anything in particular?"

It had been so long since she'd read a book. After Ike died, she'd found it hard to concentrate. Words blurred and swam on the page.

"Bedtime reading," she decided, "so nothing scary."

"Do you like to read the same kind of books as your mother?" he asked.

"Maybe more general fiction."

"I have something you might like. It's by a new author, Karissa Newcomb." He left his post and picked a book off the sale table. The cover art showed a fountain in a Mediterranean courtyard. The publisher had added some shimmer and sparkle to the water, and Frankie could vaguely make out a hidden image of a woman's face.

She took it and read, *"The Woman in the Fountain."*

"It's quite lovely for a first book. I think you'll like it," he said.

"Then I'll take it," she said, and followed him back to the register.

"Are you all ready for the new year?" she asked as he rang up her sale.

"I think so," he replied.

She handed over her charge card. "Have you got any plans for New Year's Eve? I bet you're going to some fancy literary soiree."

"That sounds like fun, but no."

"You could do something here at the bookstore. An afternoon wine and cheese party to kick off the evening," Frankie suggested. "That would be fun."

He considered. "I never thought of doing something like that."

"I bet a lot of your regulars would come."

"Would you come?"

"Of course. I'd even close my shop early so my staff could as well."

"They probably all have plans by now," he said.

"Not so far as I know. Elinor's been a little down lately. I think she could use some cheering up," Frankie added.

"Oh?"

"Think about it," Frankie said. Should she say more? Yes.

Smart as he was, when it came to love William was a slow learner. "You know, William, I think Elinor needs a hero in her life."

William looked more scared than encouraged.

"Not like a superhero, just a take-charge kind of man who's not afraid to say how he feels. Someone who would do anything for the woman he loves, who's not afraid to really pursue her. I don't think that kind of man exists only in books. Do you? I mean, I found one like that."

He nodded thoughtfully.

"Anyway, I'd sure like to see her find someone in the new year."

He gave Frankie back her charge card and put the receipt in the bag along with the book. Said nothing. Who knew whether she'd gotten through to him or not?

"I guess I'd better brave the cold and get back to the store," she said. "Do think about hosting something here. I think it could be a lot of fun."

"I will," he said.

"Good." And maybe, just maybe Elinor would come, and they'd start talking about books and drinking wine, and magic would happen.

Adele had her latte by the time Frankie returned and was perched behind the register, reading her latest novel. "Looks like the stuff's starting to stick," she greeted Frankie as she walked in. "Snowmageddon again."

"I didn't think we had any predicted for today," said Frankie as she slipped off her coat.

"Surprise."

"And not a good one. Shoppers are going to run for home and stay there."

"Maybe you should close early," Adele suggested.

"I'll stay open a little longer," Frankie said, and went to stow her coat and her book.

Adele handed Frankie her latte when she came back to put on her apron. "I'll stay long enough to make sure you haven't been poisoned," she joked.

"Not funny."

"How are things at the bookstore?" Adele asked.

Frankie smiled. "Good," she said. "I think I managed to motivate William."

Adele shook her head. "We shall see."

The snow kept falling, and by two in the afternoon Adele had had enough. "I'm leaving. I hate driving in this stuff, and I don't trust my snow tires."

Frankie didn't trust Adele's driving. "I think you should definitely go home," she said.

"You should, too."

"I'll stay a little longer. I can always get a ride home with Mitch."

"You should let Elinor leave."

"Where is she now?"

"I put her to work dusting the Christmas villages."

Which were at the back of the shop. Which meant Elinor hadn't seen the snow piling up yet. But once she did, she'd probably want to go, and Frankie wouldn't blame her.

Although Elinor was used to snow. They'd stay open a while longer.

"Whatever you were concocting, it looks like it didn't work. Don't make that poor girl stay here all day when business is dead."

"I won't," Frankie said.

Business wasn't the only thing that was dead. So was Frankie's hope that the seeds she'd sown in the bookstore would grow into action and William would come over with a party invitation. William's brain was not fertile.

Maybe he hadn't gotten the message. Maybe he needed a stronger one.

As soon as Adele left, Frankie grabbed her phone and brought up the number for Carol Reads, then called it.

William answered right away in his usual quiet, friendly voice.

Frankie plunged right in. "William, it's Frankie. Have you thought any more about my suggestion?"

"Well, yes, actually, I have been thinking about it."

"Good. Then I think you should close up for a few minutes and hustle on over here while my staff is still around." What was left of it. "You have to give people some notice when you're planning a party."

"I was going to put a sign in the window," William said.

Frankie opted for blunt. "Elinor might not see the sign. And that's so impersonal. This is the perfect opportunity for you to show her more of who you are."

There was a long silence.

"Oh, honestly, William, I can tell you like her. Anyone with eyes can. Get over here and do something about it," Frankie commanded, exasperated.

"I don't know if she's interested in me," he said, sounding panicked.

"No, you don't, because you've never actually invited her to something. William, opportunity will knock, but it won't stand at your door forever. I think Elinor is a really sweet woman, don't you?"

"I do," he said, finally with some muscle behind his words.

"Well, then, I suggest you not delay. We're going to be closing very soon."

"All right. Thanks for the heads-up," he said. "I'll see you in a bit."

A bit? Forty-five minutes later, Frankie gave up. She couldn't risk Elinor's neck trying to save her heart. She texted Mitch that she was leaving.

Frankie and Elinor were on their way out the door when William finally hurried up to them. With his skinny frame inside a dark peacoat and a red scarf wrapped around his neck, he could have passed for one of the red-ribboned streetlights along Main Street. He was carrying a book-shaped package wrapped in red foil. That package was probably the reason he'd taken so long coming over.

"Elinor, I'm glad I caught you," he said, holding it out to her. "I meant to give this to you before Christmas."

If he had, he obviously hadn't worked up the nerve. It made a great excuse to talk to her though. *Good job, William.*

Elinor took it, looking surprised. "Thank you, William."

"It's a special issue of *The Greatest Gift.* That's the story the movie *It's a Wonderful Life* was based on."

"I'm afraid I don't have anything for you," she said.

"I didn't expect anything. I just wanted you to have it."

Good, good, now ask her out.

"Well, I'll be sure to read it," Elinor said. "I do like to read."

So do you. Tell her!

"Frankie," called Mitch.

Frankie turned to see him coming their way.

Elinor saw him, too. Frankie could tell by how deep the pink in her cheeks had suddenly gotten. "I have to go," she told William.

Of course, her humiliation was still too raw. The last thing she'd want would be to stand on a snowy sidewalk and make small talk with the man she'd made a fool of herself over.

Elinor didn't go the extra few feet to the crosswalk, which would have put her in Mitch's path. Instead, she rushed out into the street, not looking. Not seeing the car sliding toward her.

21

"ELINOR! LOOK OUT!" SHRIEKED FRANKIE.

Elinor turned in time to see the car, an older midsize model, and froze.

Happily for Elinor, William didn't. Neither did Mitch, but William, with his longer legs, beat him to the rescue, grabbing her and hauling her back onto the sidewalk where they both tumbled to the ground just as Mitch got to them.

The car slid to a stop, narrowly missing one of the remaining few parked at an angle in front of the stores. A middle-aged woman jumped out and slid over to them.

"Are you all right?" she asked Elinor.

Elinor looked at her, dazed.

"She came right out in front of me. I almost didn't see her," the distraught woman said to Frankie.

"I know," Frankie said. "You weren't at fault."

Which would have been small consolation if the woman had taken Elinor down. Thank God she hadn't.

William got to his feet. "Can you stand, Elinor?" He reached down and held out his hand.

"I think so," she whimpered, and took it.

Mitch got on her other side, and the two men helped her up.

The woman began wringing her gloved hands. "I'm so sorry."

"No, it's my fault," Elinor stammered. "I wasn't paying attention."

"Are you all right?" the woman asked again.

Elinor bit her lip and nodded.

"No harm done," said Mitch.

"If you're sure you're okay…" the woman began, and Elinor nodded again. The woman let out a huge sigh. "Thank God. I think this took ten years off my life. I'm on my way home right now. I hate being out in this stuff."

Elinor wasn't aware of her leaving. She was too busy looking adoringly up at William. "You saved my life," she told him.

Mitch backed away and positioned himself next to Frankie, who was busy eavesdropping.

"I told him she needed a hero," she whispered to Mitch.

"Nice of you to provide the car," he teased, and she stuck her tongue out at him.

"Are you sure you're all right?" William asked Elinor. "Maybe we should go over to Sips and get you some brandy."

She nodded, and the shy-bookseller-suddenly-turned-hero put an arm around her and led her to the crosswalk.

As they walked away, Frankie could hear William saying to Elinor, "Maybe you'd better let me drive you home."

It was a proud moment, and Frankie beamed as Elinor

smiled up at him and nodded. Frankie had done all she could. The rest was up to William.

"Now that you've got them squared away, how about I leave Brock to close up and we grab something to eat?" Mitch suggested.

"At home. Out of the snow," she said.

"I'll follow you to your place."

That sounded perfect, and an hour later they were standing at her counter, chopping vegetables for soup. After that it would be gin rummy and sidecars. They had a fire going in her fireplace, and her tree was still up, its lights softly glowing. Mannheim Steamroller was playing in the background. Outside, the snow had stopped, and the street wore a white blanket.

"This is a perfect way to end the day," she said.

"Oh, I think we're gonna get a lot more perfect before the night is over," he said, slipping an arm around her. Then he kissed her.

"You know, I think you're right," she said.

Stef was surprised to see Griff's name come up on the screen when her phone rang. She said a cautious, "Hello."

He didn't say hello back. Instead, he said, "Awkward moments suck."

It made her sad all over again, remembering. "Yes, they do. Last night was a little more than awkward, though, wouldn't you say?"

"It was hard. Are you going to give up on me?"

She didn't want to. "Should I?"

"Yeah, you probably should. But I'm hoping you won't."

"If you're not ready, I understand," she said. It had taken her long enough after her disastrous marriage to decide she was ready to try again.

"I am ready. I miss what I had with Kaitlyn."

Wrong thing to say. "I'm not Kaitlyn, and I can't be her duplicate."

"I wouldn't want you to be. Stef, I'm so tired of being alone. I want to be with someone I can laugh with, someone who's kind and smart and who likes kids. I think that someone is you. I'm sorry about last night, I really am. I just have these moments… It's hard to put into words. They're like phantom pains. You know, like when you lose a limb? Only…"

"You lost a person," she supplied. "How about your heart? Did you lose that, too?"

"It's still beating."

That wasn't enough. She took a deep breath. "Look, I'm not out to erase your wife from your mind. Or even your heart. I just want to be sure there's room for me, too."

"There is. In fact, I could almost believe she sent you. I want to get back to happy. It's going to take me a while is all. Can you help me get there, Stef? Will you?"

She felt like she was standing at the edge of a cliff, poised to jump, but she couldn't see what was below.

"Please," he added.

Her pulse was climbing. Jump? Back up? Run away? She needed a sign.

"I'll even write Santa. Maybe if I'm lucky, he's putting in overtime."

There it was. She smiled. "You know, I'm feeling like Chinese food," she said.

She could hear the smile in his voice. "Funny, so am I. I've got snow tires and all-wheel drive. Corky and I will be right over to pick you up. We have plans."

An hour later, Stef was at Griff's house, eating takeout Chinese along with his sister, Jenn, and her boyfriend. Corky sat between his father and his aunt, beaming across the table at Stef as if she was the sugar plum fairy come to life. She gave her arm a surreptitious pinch to make sure she wasn't dreaming.

She wasn't. She was with a good man with a good heart and a darling kid. She had a feeling she and Griff's sister could easily become besties. Now, if his mother turned out to be as nice, she'd know she'd won the love lottery.

The grown-ups entertained Corky by playing Wii games, and after he was in bed, they switched to a trivia game. Stef came close to winning but decided coming in second after Griff's sister wasn't a bad thing.

"She's too smart," joked Jenn's boyfriend.

"I'd say you're pretty smart," Jenn told him. "After all, you're with me."

Ah, the confidence. Stef was finally getting hers back. Lucky Jenn wouldn't have to face such a challenge. The man she was with was secure enough in who he was not to be threatened by her.

"We've got a couple of smart ones here," said Griff.

Stef swallowed those words whole and was instantly warmed.

Later he drove her home while Jenn and her man watched over Corky.

"Did you have fun?" he asked.

"I did. I like your sister."

"She's okay. I owe her big-time for keeping on me. I want to keep this going."

Stef smiled. "Me, too."

"Have you got plans for New Year's Eve?"

She cocked her head to the side. "Let me see. Chris Hemsworth was asking. I haven't said yes yet."

Griff chuckled. "Good. Then how about spending it with me? I'll get my parents to take Corky for the weekend. You can come with when I drop him off if you want. My mom's itching to meet you. Jenn's already told her all about you."

"Good things, I hope?"

"Of course. So, how about dinner at La Bella Vita, then dancing at Carol's Place?"

"And he dances, too," she cracked. Total love lottery win.

"I can manage a couple of steps," he said. "So, what do you say?"

"I say yes." To anything he wanted.

"It looks like William finally figured out how to win over Elinor. Does she even remember who Mitch is?" Adele joked when the family gathered around her table for their Sunday evening dinner.

"I don't know. Right now, William is pretty high on her hero list," said Frankie.

"That's so romantic," Natalie said with a sigh.

"Hey, I'd pull you out of the way if a car was coming at you," her husband said to her.

She put a hand to Jonathan's cheek. "I know you would."

"Warner, you want to grow up to be just like your daddy," Adele informed her great-grandson.

"Daddy's the best burper," Warner said, and tried a big burp of his own.

"You don't need to become a great burper," his mother informed him, and frowned at her husband, who smirked.

"It looks like it's going to be a great new year for us all," Adele said.

Yes, it did, thought Frankie as she smiled at Mitch.

Stef's phone rang, and she stepped away from the table to answer, cooing a hello.

"Gee, I wonder who that might be," Adele teased.

"Oh," Stef said, sounding disappointed.

All three women at the table exchanged worried glances.

Until Stef said cheerfully, "No, that's not a problem. In fact, I think that will be fun."

"What was that all about?" Adele asked when she rejoined them.

"It was Griff. His parents can't babysit for New Year's Eve. They're sick."

"That and Valentine's Day, the two hardest days of the year to get a sitter," Adele observed.

"But it's okay. I'm going to his place, and he and Corky and I are going to party together."

"Perfect," Frankie approved. "But before any of us do our own thing, we have to make sure we all go over to Carol Reads for William's happy hour."

The snow had finally moved on to bother other regions, the snowplows had done their job, and both the air and the streets were clear. And the residents of Carol were all ready to party in the new year. Several of them were starting out at Carol Reads.

William looked properly literary in his suit and tie, and Elinor was wearing an elegant black dress and red cardigan that she'd picked out...with no help from Frankie. Viola and her husband were present, and she was showing off pictures of her refinished bathroom on her phone.

"And to think you did it all without my help," Frankie joked.

"You've had your hands full helping everyone else," said Viola. "Good job, sista."

Several of William's other customers had shown up, and everyone stood around with plastic glasses filled with white wine or sparkling cider. Elinor had picked up appetizers at the store and was happily circulating, offering people mini quiches.

"You can stop looking so puffed up," Mitch teased Frankie as she looked on proudly.

"I can't help it. I feel like I had a hand in their happiness."

"Your instincts were good. For once," he added.

"My instincts turned out to be pretty good where you're concerned," she said.

"Finally," he said, and she kissed him.

He checked his watch. "We should probably take off. There's a quiet corner at La Bella Vita waiting for us."

And after that, a celebration for two at his place. Happy New Year!

Stef followed Griff and Corky home from the bookstore party. Griff had bought Corky a book and insisted on buying one for her as well—a romance novel that Elinor had recommended entitled *Happy Ending*.

"I think it's appropriate," he said when she thanked him. "I feel like I'm well on my way to one thanks to you."

"And thanks to our sisters," she added. "Sometimes we all need a little help."

"We do," he agreed. "But I think we can take it from here." He squeezed her hand.

Later, after Corky was in bed, they had their own party for two. They turned on the TV in time for the countdown to the new year, and as the crowds in New York City went crazy and Griff's neighbors shot off their fireworks, he said, "This is the happiest new year I've had in a long time thanks to you."

"I could say the same about you," she said.

"It's going to be a good year."

"Promise?"

"I do."

"Well, you know how we seal promises."

He grinned. "I do," he said, and kissed her.

★ ★ ★

"Happy New Year," Mitch whispered in Frankie's ear as they sat cuddled on her couch, then kissed her.

It was, indeed.

That night she had a dream. She and Mitch were standing in her mother's living room, surrounded by family and friends. She wore a simple cream-colored cocktail dress, he was in a black tux, and they were toasting each other with champagne. Elinor and William stood arm in arm, each raising a glass. So did Adele and Mario and Stef and Griff. Natalie and her family were present, and so was Mitch's.

"I know you two are going to have a great life together," the minister told them.

And come Valentine's Day, just like they'd planned, the dream came true.

One Year Later

Dear Santa,
Thank you for bringing me a new mommy. I luv Mommy
Stef. I have another gramma now and another aunt and uncle
and cusin named Warner. We got to be ring berers at Daddy
and Mommy Stefs wedding yesturday. They went away and I
am here with Aunt Frankie. She says she helped you find my
mommy. I like her. Tomorrow gramma is piking me up I get to
stay at her hose. We are gong to bake cookies for you. But don't
worry. You dont have to bring me any toys or stuff this yer cuz
I am good with what I got and you have a lot of other kids to
take care of. I wish you a Merry Christmas.
Sincerely, Corky

★ ★ ★ ★ ★

Acknowledgments

As always, I need to start by thanking my brilliant editor, April Osborn, who continues to bring out the best in my stories, and my amazing agent, Paige Wheeler, who is just the best and is always working on my behalf. I'm so lucky to have both of you in my corner, along with publicist Nancy Berland and the whole incredible team at MIRA. You all work so hard bringing stories to life and don't get nearly as much praise as you deserve. A big thank-you, also, to my husband, Gerhardt, my first reader, live-in copy editor and best friend. Love you! A big shout-out to my street team, who have been sharing this journey now for several years. And finally, to readers. You have no idea how important you are to us writers and how much we value you. Thank you for sharing some of your valuable time with me!

Frankie's Favorite Recipes

Pasties
Makes six

....

Ingredients for crust:
3 cups flour

2 tsp salt

1 ½ cups shortening

8 tbsp water

Ingredients for filling:
1 large russet potato,
peeled and cut into bite-size pieces

¼ medium onion, chopped

1 ½ cups round steak,
thawed and cut into bite-size pieces
with fat trimmed off

Salt and pepper to taste

Extra flour for rolling out crust

Directions:
Combine the flour and salt. Cut in shortening until the mixture is crumbly. Add water and mix together until pie-dough consistency. Set aside.

(If preferred, you can use premade pie crust. You'll need crust enough to make two and a half pies.)

Mix together all the ingredients for your filling in a separate bowl. Divide the pie dough into six equal-size balls. Roll each one out on a floured surface into a slightly elongated circle (also known in Frankie terms as a fat oval).

Spoon the filling on one half of the pie, leaving enough room at the sides for crimping over the crust. Then flip the other half of the circle over the filling, making a turnover. Turn up the crust and crimp.

Set each pie on a large cookie sheet very lightly sprayed with cooking spray. Vent the pies by making a small slit on top with a sharp knife. To help them cook, Frankie slips a teaspoon of water into that vent on the crust. She also will often freeze the meat before making, then semi-thaw it as it's easier to cut and trim off the fat. If the meat is a little frozen that's okay—just don't add that dab of water.

Bake pasties for half an hour at 350°F or until golden brown and the potatoes are tender. Test by slipping a small fork or the end of a steak knife inside the pie's vent. Great served warm, but they're also tasty when cold.

(Frankie always gets carried away and makes double the amount of filling, winds up with enough left to make hash for a later meal.)

Peppermint Pie

Ingredients:

1 prepared pie shell, shortbread or chocolate

1 small package (3.4 oz)
instant white chocolate pudding mix

½ cup hot fudge sauce (not heated)

2 medium-size candy canes, crushed

Sweetened whipped cream for topping

Directions:

Gently spread hot fudge sauce on pie crust, covering entire crust. Sprinkle with crushed candy cane. Mix pudding according to package directions, let set for two minutes, then spread over hot fudge.

Set in refrigerator for thirty minutes to set up. Top with whipped cream before serving.

Frankie's Easy Candy Treats

Ingredients:

Hershey's Candy Cane Kisses

Snyder's of Hanover Snaps (square pretzels)

Red and green M&Ms

Directions:

Place as many pretzel squares as you want on an ungreased cookie sheet. Unwrap the Kisses and place them in the center of the squares. Put in a 250°F oven for five minutes or until the chocolate is soft but not melted. It only needs to be soft enough to be able to press candy down into the chocolate.

Once chocolate is soft, remove from oven and gently press an M&M in the center of each. Transfer to a large plate and put in the refrigerator for about thirty minutes to harden. Store leftovers (if you have any) in an airtight container.

(Make sure your Kisses aren't stale. If they are, they won't melt well. Even the best candy doesn't last forever!)

Merry Christmas and Happy Eating!